Sparkles
of
Blue

SLEEPER CHRONICLES

Ray Zdan

I was as tired and starving as a stray dog. Another day was ending between piles of folders, documents and letters. The computer monitor was too bright, hurting my eyes, and I had to blink more often, wiping away the excess moisture with my fingers. I aimlessly shuffled through the stack of printouts in a silly pretence of studying them. In fact, I secretly glanced at the clock and waited with growing impatience for an acceptable time to switch off the machine and leave.

Several figures in dark raincoats rushed down the corridor, ending their day at work already. I counted the last seconds and put those printouts aside. It was time.

I sneaked into the corridor where people were marching in only one direction – outside, and joined the flow. Nobody looked at me. The silent faces around were as tired as mine, barely able to lift their eyes from the floor.

The crowd oozed through the front door like a ruptured boil

and dispersed into the dying day. I wrapped myself more tightly in my raincoat and fished out the brolly as the first drops of cold rain started to hit the pavement.

I turned right, making my way downhill to the train station. Endless traffic followed me, but it was soon halted, as the loudly wailing ambulance rushed by, its lights flashing blue.

People were gathering at the train station when I briefly stopped in front of the ticket machine. It was wrapped in yellow plastic ribbons with a large "Out of Order" sticker soaking in the pouring rain. I had no other options but to rush on to my platform, where the train was already approaching.

My usual seat next to the window was empty, and I slumped into it, placing my folded wet brolly on the floor next to my feet. The doors closed hissing, and we started to move.

The gloomy darkening scenery outside of the window was in complete unison with my mood – I felt drained and as low as the pieces of mud at my feet. We passed several stations, and I absentmindedly looked at the depleting crowd in the carriage.

"Tickets, please…" The voice brought me back to my senses.

"In fact, I need one," I said to the ticket collector standing next to my seat. "The ticket machine was broken."

"No problem," said the man. "Where are you going?"

He performed his magic on the portable device and produced a yellow-orange slip of paper for me. I paid with my card.

The collector went on, waking a few more sleeping passengers on his way. Several stations later, the carriage was almost empty. I was looking at the landscape outside, nearly invisible in the darkness now, when I felt a strange feeling building up at my left temple. It was one of those weird tingling sensations when you instantly know you are being watched. I didn't pay attention at first, but the feeling was persistent. I looked up, and my gaze met the black eyes of an elderly gentleman who was shamelessly staring at me. He was dark, probably Indian, with a silver snowstorm straying through his glistening black hair. I was sure I hadn't seen the man before and tried to hide my embarrassment behind a smile, but he kept on staring, with a strange expression. That was unsettling, and I turned my eyes back to the window, hoping that he would just pick up the newspaper, leaving my humble self alone, but that feeling of being watched didn't go away, and I felt a sense of rising panic. The train went into a brightly lit station and stopped there. I helplessly watched passengers rushing out, and soon I was left alone with just that strange man in front of me, his eyes still burning my left temple. I gathered all my courage and turned to face him again. The man stared calmly back, and a barely perceptible smile crooked his lips.

"What do you want?" I braved to ask.

He didn't answer. The train moved on into the night, leaving the brightly lit oasis behind.

The strange, intense minutes that followed seemed like hours. I was unable to move; I felt pinned by his gaze like a dead butterfly in a museum display.

The train began to slow down as it approached the next station. That strange man stood up, still keeping his gaze fixed on me. His lips were quickly moving, but I couldn't make out a word.

I helplessly looked around as the train slowed to a standstill and the man moved forward, nearing my seat. He stopped just for a moment and dropped his hand on my right shoulder as if accidentally. As he did, his long skinny fingers sunk into my deltoid with incredible force. I screamed as sudden pain drilled into my bones, flashing through my brain like a thunderbolt. The man mumbled something under his nose and quickly slipped through the hissing doors outside.

For a few insanely long seconds, I felt like paralysed as the sharp pain ripped through my neural tissues. The next instant, it was gone.

What the hell had he done to me?

I must find out! I sprang from the seat, rushing after the retreating backside of that strange man, but my feet tripped on my brolly, and I landed painfully on the floor. The door closed in front of me, and the train started to move.

I got up just in time to get a glimpse of that man slowly walking on the platform, as the train gained speed and we moved off back into the night.

I silently cursed, rubbing my still numb shoulder, then collected my brolly and sat down back. My heart was fluttering like a frightened bird, but there was nothing more I could do.

The man was obviously insane. I had no other explanation.

I closed my eyes and took a few deep breaths, trying to calm down. The menace was over. Still, I felt uneasy.

A group of children boarded the carriage at the next station, filling it with giggles and jokes. I opened my eyes just in time to get a glimpse of the distant skyline of Canary Wharf emerging from around the bend. The train started to slow down, and I stood up – this was my station.

Gusts of cold wind met me on the platform. Luckily, the rain had stopped.

I rushed downstairs to street level.

That strange encounter had drained me of self-confidence – my nerves were on edge, and I just wanted to get back into my bed as soon as possible, to cover my head with a blanket and forget everything.

I grabbed my dinner from a Chinese takeaway on my way.

A new bout of rain started the moment I stopped in front of my door trying to fish the keys out of my pocket. The narrow squeaky stairs to my flat were dark – the bulb had burned out when it was most needed. Several minutes passed until I succeeded in placing my key in the lock, and then I was in at last. I closed the door and left the whole world behind.

For a few seconds, I only stood there, holding my breath in the darkness, before I turned on the lights.

The flat I was renting was small, with a tiny kitchen and a sitting room facing the busy street and bedroom at the quieter side of the garden.

I hung my raincoat and brolly in the corridor and then had a quick dinner. Strength was slowly leaving my limbs. I stripped, preparing for the shower, and as I did so gasped – the right sleeve of my shirt was stained with blood! What was happening?

With a trembling heart, I rushed to the bathroom and froze in front of the mirror – my right shoulder was stained with blood too. It felt fine; I had no pain there, but it was blood-red!

Carefully, I washed it with soap and plenty of running water and then inspected again. The skin was pale and, at first glance, looked unbroken. I felt it with my fingers and located two tender spots where that man's fingers had squeezed my deltoid. *Was it the needles? Was I now dying?*

That crazy man had jabbed me! And I had no idea what it was.

I sat down on the floor as my legs refused to hold me any

longer. I had no friends or enemies; I was the most insignificant rat in the office – it must have been a random attack by a madman. But why me? What would happen next?

It wasn't poison – if it had been, I would be dead by now. But could it be some kind of virus? An infection? I rushed into my bedroom and found the thermometer. For several minutes, I paced the room while I waited for the thermometer reading, my swollen brain painting dreadful images of me as Patient Zero in a zombie apocalypse. But there was nothing abnormal in the reading.

I nervously picked up the phone several times, then put it back. Whom would I call? Police? The madman was gone long ago. Ambulance? What would I show them? Nearly invisible pricks on my skin? I guessed they had more important things to do.

For a good hour, I walked around my tiny flat in desperation until I had calmed down. I was still unable to decide on anything.

It was well past midnight when I finally took a shower and then managed to get into bed. Sleep didn't come easy. I restlessly turned from side to side until my consciousness slowly drifted into darkness, lulled by the soft tapping of the rain on my window.

It was only a sound at the beginning. A sound of a falling drop which a second later splashed somewhere on a hard surface. Another followed it, then a series of two. They pulled my consciousness drifting in the blessed darkness with the persistence of ants collectively struggling with a large caterpillar. I tried to resist.

Then the sound of running water surfaced. I was trying to drift back to sleep, lulled by the white noise, but a chilly thought promptly anchored me on the shore of reality – how could water be splashing in the middle of the night when I was alone asleep in my tiny London flat? That could mean only trouble.

I opened my eyes. It wasn't dark as I expected. When I had fully focused, at last, my gaze was met by damp moss and ferns. I sat and looked around.

I was still dreaming.

A small creek was rippling on my right, at arm's length, its crystal waters flowing over a rocky bed.

I got up, noticing my strange robes. I was wearing black trousers, made of coarse woven fabric and fitted with a wide, dark brown leather belt. A light dagger with an intricate golden metal handle was attached to the right side of the belt within a neat sheath, decorated with several blue sparkles. On the sleeves of the carefully buttoned dark blue shirt was an intricate embroidered pattern. A black leather waistcoat was on top of it. The boots were light, made of soft brown leather. Everything felt comfortable, well-fitting and in the right places, but looked unfamiliar and alien.

The forest around me was dark and thick, mostly firs, framing a small piece of clear blue sky above me.

I touched the swift current of the creek and washed my face. The water was icy cold.

I was puzzled by the complexity of my dream. The forest looked real, and I was keen to explore it further.

I followed the creek downstream through thick shrubs along a barely visible path, which was abruptly blocked several yards later by a massive black cliff in the form of an arch. The creek just went on, while the path I was following joined a decent-looking dust road. I touched the cliff. The rock surface seemed real. I took a risk and punched it and immediately cursed; it hurt.

I turned left, where a narrow ribbon of the road was slowly climbing uphill, hoping that it would lead out of the woods to some hill or clearing, where I would be able to catch a glimpse of the surroundings.

I went on between two walls of dark green firs. Occasional black boulders were randomly scattered on either side of the road – some flat as a dish, some tall like a pillar. The forest was silent around me, disturbed only by the soft sound of a splashing creek. Half a mile later, the sound distanced to the right and died in silence.

It was a bizarre dream, indeed, with a convoluted sense of reality, but not too much was happening. I marched a few miles on the road, eagerly looking around, but all I could see was firs, strange shrubs with silver leaves, ferns, black rocks and a narrow strip of clear blue sky above me.

I stopped to catch my breath and was leaning on a tall rock resembling an ancient Egyptian obelisk when a sudden wave of low-pitched growling fell on me from the other side of the road. I pressed my back to the stone, clutching the handle of the dagger, but whoever had made that sound was obscured by the shrubs.

Another wave of growling reached me at about the same moment when I finally was able to spot a massive black shadow behind the shrubs. Cold sweat cascaded down my back, and I desperately grasped the dagger. The beast moved a little, breaking a few branches, and I noticed two greenish glowing eyes peeking at me.

The third wave of growling was more high-pitched, as an enormous black dog parted the shrubs and leapt onto the road in front of me. His fur was standing up on end, making him appear even bigger. The exposed massive fangs were dripping with saliva, and I realised that my chances of defeating the beast were non-existent.

The dog lowered his head, sniffing, and I saw his huge muscles growing tense under his skin. Luckily, I remembered that it was only a dream (a nightmare, to be precise), and I hoped I'd wake up before that animal begins to tear me into pieces.

The dog moved a few paces closer, still sniffing the air in front of me, and then slowly, his tail started to wag. He yelped a few times before jumping onto his hind legs and starting to lick my face. He acted as if he knew me.

Finally, he calmed down. But it took much longer for my hands to stop shaking. I even managed to tap his back and scratch behind his ears. We were friends now.

I resumed my journey, and the dog happily kept me company, only occasionally leaving my side to chase some squirrels or rabbits.

The road led uphill. We crossed several shallow creeks as we went before a new sound sneaked into my dream. It was low, like distant continuous thunder, but got louder with each step. The dog didn't seem alarmed, and I tried to suppress my sense of agitation, which was increasing again. Finally, the road took a few sharp turns before the impenetrable green walls of the forest stepped aside, and a broad perspective opened out.

A high snow-covered peak emerged to my left, crowned with a flock of fluffy clouds. It was a part of a majestic mountain range, stretching far away to the north and disappearing beyond view below the misty horizon.

The source of the disturbing noise was a little in front of us – a huge waterfall making a rumbling sound like a thousand trains, the water falling into the abyss on the right and smashing onto the sharp rocks somewhere below. The earth trembled slightly under the pressure of the mighty stream, and strands of white mist spread around like a slowly moving milky lava, painting skies with rainbows. A seemingly endless beautiful valley stretched far off to the right, full of dark forests and colourful meadows. I could see a series of green hills beyond.

I took a few more steps forward, then froze, paralysed by the breath-taking beauty of the scenery. The canine, however, didn't seem that impressed.

The dog marched straight to the edge of the waterfall, briefly stopping a few times and looking back as if urging me to follow him. He seemed quite confident and familiar with the territory, waiting just enough for me to join him.

I was hesitant at first, frightened by the vast unknown landscape unfolding before me. But if it was a dream, what could go wrong?

I carefully approached the stream. The river here was perhaps a few hundred feet wide, falling into the abyss between two massive cliffs, which towered high above the riverbed. The other bank was almost entirely hidden behind a veil of white mist, while the dark cliff on my side of the river resembled a tall pillar of frozen flame.

Just at that moment, I noticed stairs carved in the rock between the falling stream and the cliff, and we started to descend. The rocks were damp and slippery, and I carefully probed them with my feet before stepping down. The dog stayed close behind me. Several yards later the stairs moved to the right, away from the falling water, where someone had planted a wooden bannister on solid rock, making the descent much easier. The light breeze from the valley blew clouds of mist away to the left, keeping the stairs dry. I watched my steps, but it was quite challenging, as new beautiful sights and wonders met my eyes as soon as I lifted my gaze from the ground, and the end of the stairs was too far below, still invisible.

We passed a small platform, and then one more before the stairs reached the foot of the mountain, next to a narrow stone bridge. The waterfall was far to our left, and could now be seen in its full glorious beauty. High walls of black stone surrounded the city on the other bank of the river, with spiky towers at each corner where the walls met. Red rooftops spread far to the east, slowly descending downhill beyond my visibility, with occasional poplars, lime and chestnut trees obscuring the display. A green wall of the seemingly endless dark forest was on the right, south of the town. The northern side of the city was framed by maze-like terraced gardens, alternating with white balustrade stairs, which climbed the foot of the mountain up to the distant redbrick Gothic-style arched building shaped in the form of a flat pyramid, which was sinking into the greenery of those gardens.

I hesitantly stopped in front of the bridge and shaded my eyes to get a better view. The massive wooden gate blocked my way on the other side, closed. The dark castle was raising its tall, proud pillars just behind the wall, but I couldn't make out any movement. I stood there, listening, but any sounds were carried away by the swift currents in front of me. Tiny threads of smoke rose through the high chimneys behind the wall but instantly dissipated in the light wind as the day slowly moved into a lazy afternoon.

I had a feeling of being watched, but I couldn't make out whose eyes were on me. Nobody was on the wall.

My canine companion rushed past me through the bridge

above the swirling rapids and before I had the chance to stop him, started to scratch on the gate, barking loudly.

A few moments later, the gate opened, and a tall, muscular young man in light armour peeked outside.

"Bysh!" he said to the dog, tapping his back.

At this point, I suddenly panicked. I had stupidly followed the dog, and the beast had brought me here. Behind the walls was a strange city full of strangers, and I had no idea how hostile they might be. It was stupid to come here, even in a dream.

But it was too late for regrets either. I had been spotted, and now I couldn't just turn away and hide. I hadn't been challenged yet, but my imagination was already vividly painting horrific images of torture and death, of me being fed to tigers or drowned in boiling oil. I was nearly hysterical as I hesitantly forced my feet onto that bridge.

The young guard straightened his back and turned to face me.

"You are back, my Lord," he said with a smile.

The tension eased a little – it was my dream, and that meant my rules. But this society of strangers still looked frightening. Even the smiling face of the young guard was unknown to me.

I smiled back hesitantly but chose to remain silent. His statement required no answer.

The guard stepped aside when I came nearer, letting me

through the gate into a short dark tunnel behind. Metal hinges squeaked, closing my only retreat. I had no choice but to follow Bysh, the dog.

The inner yard was full of armoured men. They stepped aside, letting us through and paying their respects as we passed. They smiled at us, but all the unfamiliar faces peeking at me triggered a sense of panic, which slowly rose behind my poker face. I had a sickening feeling; it was like I was an ant drowning in sticky resin, watching the yellow walls of the trap hardening into amber. The feeling was a mixture of helplessness and curiosity. I slipped my hands into my pockets, trying to hide their trembling and forced a silly smile on my lips as I walked through the yard, all eyes fixed on me, all heads in respectful bows. I followed the dog.

Bysh knew the place. We crossed the yard and took the stairs on the right, which led to a large black brick building with narrow windows and a smoking chimney on the roof. The long and dimly lit corridor ended in the arched terrace where Bysh stopped, hesitantly looking at me.

I nearly heard the trap closing. My hand was trembling as I stroked Bysh's head. The dog wagged his tail and licked my hand. We were friends.

"Good boy," I whispered. "Let's go. Let's go somewhere. Go!"

limits of that importance. Was I just another noble in the palace of the king? Or was I the ruler? What was my name here? I couldn't even introduce myself! Could I use my *own* name here? Would they regard me as a usurper if the name would sound unfamiliar? I felt that this might be deadly dangerous.

Desperately, I glanced around, searching for any clues, but found none. I paced around the bedroom, touching the walls, lifting small things, inspecting, looking, feeling... Everything looked real enough, and I panicked again – would I be able to return to my previous grey life, where everything was clearly labelled, sorted and well-known? *Would I wake up in my tiny London flat?*

Panic came in waves, dumping me ashore in those strange chambers. I sat on the bed motionless, gathering pieces of my courage together and pushing those waves aside. The silence felt encouraging, and I waited until my heart stopped fluttering. Later, I felt brave enough to peek into the empty hall. I ran my eyes across the large wooden table and the chairs around it. The hearth gave the impression of importance but offered no clues to my situation. I tried several books, but they all were hand-written in strange Gothic letters and were almost impossible to read.

Just briefly, I stopped in front of the map, which was topped by a red-green-blue banner with the word "Rehen" embroidered in gold on it. The land below the banner was vast, framed by several ranges of mountains to the north and west, and a sea or ocean to the south and east. It was unevenly divided by the large river, which swelled in the middle into a vast lake, like a blue eye of God with two islands resembling two halves of an apple close to each other in place of the iris. I counted eleven smaller divisions of the realm, painted in different colours on the map. The capital city Wagorn (there was a crown atop the name) was depicted far to the south, in the mouth of the great river where it made its way to the ocean. In the land named Patna at the northern corner of the realm, there was a smoking volcano. In the west, there was a waterfall, and a city called Chadrack was next to it, same as the land around it. Was I in Chadrack? South of the waterfall was land named Porlok, but the capital of Porlok was too far away from the waterfall, at the foot of the mountain range. *This country must be Chadrack then.*

I briefly ran my eyes over the lands to the east and south, struggling to memorise the names – it seemed useless. Then I took a slow tour along the walls of the hall, looking at the flags, antlers, trophies and guns, mainly swords, shields, spears and crossbows, hanging there as decorations. There were no rifles or pistols.

Still, the most crucial piece of information was missing. The chambers apparently belonged to a very important person, someone who gives orders and makes decisions, but I couldn't found the name or rank of that person.

I hated this dream. I was desperate to find a way to stop it. How had I got here? I was just a mere grey office rat, flinching every time someone's eyes landed on me. I felt trapped inside this outlandish body and unfamiliar life. I felt an urge to run away and hide somewhere, but I was too afraid to go back to the corridor.

I need to find the door out – this thought kept on buzzing around my head until it took root and became a firm conviction. How had I got there? I didn't remember any doors in the forest next to the creek, but I hadn't been paying attention. Had I overlooked something? An "Exit" sign, an "off" button?

I needed to find out, but the next moment, I remembered the yard full of people staring at me, and I felt paralysed. I had no idea how to slip outside without attracting attention. The corridors of the castle were unfamiliar and frightening. How could I explain my aimless wandering around if anybody asked me what I was doing?

I sat on the floor in the corner next to the hearth and closed my eyes, hoping the alarm clock would wake me up in London. But when I opened them several minutes later, I was still in the same place, sitting on the floor.

Nobody troubled me for the rest of the day. I did a few more rounds sneaking like a thief around the chambers in search for any clues for the owner's identity – found none. The evening dusk was slowly spreading its wings over the world when I finally got enough courage to peek into the balcony.

Men in the yard were building a fire and preparing for the night. A gentle breeze from the distant waterfall carried their words away, and all I could hear was indistinct murmur only. A nightingale started singing in the dark shrubs just outside the castle walls. The sun was setting, and the first bright stars lighted up in unknown constellations as the night started its slow approach.

I looked at the changing of the guard, at the people sitting around the fire and quietly talking when a hint of silvery light hit the periphery of my vision. I lifted my eyes to the moon, but it wasn't there. I began to feel weak at my knees, then grasped the bannister in disbelief when the contour of the enormous silver globe appeared, surrounded by several graceful sets of rings. Nobody else paid any attention to it.

I kept on staring at the magnificent view in the darkening sky until the chill of the night finally got to me. Hunching quietly, I returned to my bedroom.

Night demons were already crawling from every corner and pressing down on my lead-heavy eyelids. I couldn't resist them any longer. I stretched out on the bed and slowly drifted into the darkness.

My consciousness returned slowly, as the alarm clock kept on screaming with all its might. I blinked as the morning sun touched my cheek, while sounds from the noisy street outside my window filled my ears. I sat up and glanced around my London flat with a great sense of relief – that strange dream was over! It seemed too complex and real, too frightening; I had even started to believe that I was stuck in that peculiar world forever!

I brushed my teeth smiling, then hastily combed, dressed and ran out to catch the train. The morning was fresh after the night of heavy showers. Two bright red double-deckers passed down the street, gently humming like overgrown ladybirds. My head felt a little dizzy – was it due to wine I drank in my dream?

At the train station, I joined the queue at the ticket machine. An old gentleman was struggling to top up his Oyster card. The young girl behind him stared at him indifferently while listening to some music on her earphones. I was standing behind her, enjoying the morning sunshine when I felt a chill on my neck – that eerie sensation of being watched. I carefully glanced back. It took several attempts until I spotted an elderly woman leaning on her umbrella. She was standing on the other side of the street, beyond the heavy traffic; her face expressionless, like most other faces you may see on any busy street, but her pale blue eyes stared at me, unblinking. Several red double-decker buses slowly passed down the road, obscuring the woman for a few moments, but her eyes still were drilling me when she came back into view. I felt uneasy and impatiently looked at the front of the queue.

The gentleman with an Oyster card left without any success. The girl with the earphones quickly checked her card and left as well. I bought my tickets and rushed to the platform, still feeling that unsettling look on my back.

I hoped the train would not be late, and it wasn't. The rest of the journey to the office was uneventful.

I was sitting in my room and shuffled through piles of documents, searching for one particular letter, when Julie, our secretary, popped in.

"Are you going, Kyle?"

"Where?" I asked, not looking at her, still busy with the papers.

"Nobody told you?" She sounded surprised.

I shrugged, not raising my eyes.

Julie glanced back to the corridor as if checking for any spying ears.

"Care for some coffee?" she asked me in an undertone.

Inside this offer was hiding a secret office code. I knew it and instantly glanced at Julie. She winked and indicated the direction to the canteen with her right eyebrow.

"That would be nice. Thank you," I responded. "Just give me a few minutes to find that damned letter."

She smiled and glanced again over her shoulder. I noticed Big Bertha passing down the corridor.

Julie left, but I couldn't focus on those damned papers again. That hugger-mugger meant a secret plot in the office, but I was not aware of what it was. It might be about something serious, or it might just be about something silly. Julie never differentiated well between the two, but she was good at keeping secrets.

Big Bertha passed again through the corridor, now accompanied by Tom. She stopped in the aisle, chatting with him and completely blocked my door with her impressive physique. Chuckling at some joke of Tom's, she ignored my polite nod, and I had to stare at her mighty back, waiting for my chance to get through. She had a few more chuckles until she moved her frame away from my door, then turned right and continued down the corridor while Tom followed, a few steps behind. I slipped outside and went after Julie.

When I reached the cafeteria, I spotted her at the far table. She waved to me.

"Where have you been for so long? I got you a latte," she smiled guiltily. "Do you want anything else?"

I sat down.

"What is it?" I asked, skipping the preliminaries.

She took a sip of her espresso before answering.

"You know Fiona?" she asked.

I nodded. Everybody knew the lovely elderly lady with an honest smile and shiny blue-grey eyes.

"This is her last week in the office," Julie whispered, placing her cup on the table.

So, this time, it was something silly rather than serious.

"That's what this is all about? Why is it a secret?"

Julie glanced around.

"We don't want Bertha to find out. You know how she dislikes Fiona," she said, so quietly it was barely audible. "The farewell party is tonight. Are you going?"

I shrugged. It was so unexpected.

"Bertha dislikes everybody. It is her typical view of the world," I took a sip of my coffee. "Why make it a secret?"

"Are you going?" demanded Julie.

"You know I am not a social animal," I shrugged.

"Why not? Fiona is such a lovely lady..."

"There's nothing wrong with Fiona," I assured her. "I just need more time to think. This is too sudden and unexpected."

In fact, I needed some mental preparation before socialising, and this party dropped down on my head like snow from the last winter, unplanned. It was true: I wasn't sociable...

"You need to ask Mrs Kyle?" winked Julie, smiling.

"There is no Mrs Kyle," I admitted. "I'm just not prepared for the party."

"C'mon, what kind of preparation do you need?" She touched my hand, still smiling.

I took my time to take another sip of coffee before I answered.

"It's hard to explain," I sighed and honestly added, "I think I'm somewhere on the Asperger's spectrum, but I've never had a proper consultation to prove my self-diagnosis."

Julie gasped, placing a hand over her mouth. She seemed more frightened than concerned.

"Don't worry," I said in a clumsy attempt to calm her. "It is not a big deal. I only need proper mental preparation before I step out of my comfort zone. This party is too soon for me to do that."

"I see..." Julie turned the cup in her hands before taking a sip. "How long have you had this – Asp... whatever?"

"I think, since childhood. Socialising has never been easy for me..."

"Are your parents aware of this? Why didn't they seek any help for you?"

"I never knew my parents," I said, after a short pause. "My aunt raised me, and she is dead now."

"So sad... You must have a few friends to help you cope with this…"

"I have no friends." It was a simple statement.

"I am sorry..." said Julie.

"No need to be sorry," I said. "My life is just like this, and I am used to it."

We grew silent for a few nervous moments.

"I am sorry, Kyle, for forcing you into this revelation," said Julie. "You have always been too distant..."

"I know," I sighed. "You are all very kind people. The problem is with me, not you or anybody else."

"It is not a problem, Kyle." She cautiously took my hand again. "You only need to be in the right mood. Think about that. It will be fun to have you there."

"I will try," I promised. "But I cannot guarantee it at such short notice..."

"Great!" she said, smiling excitedly.

I took back my hand. Then fear squeezed my brain with a sudden realisation.

"Julie," I whispered. "You must promise me – don't ever tell anybody about my Asperger's, okay?"

She quickly nodded, her absentminded gaze already fixed on Fiona's party. She finished her espresso with a quick gulp and stood up.

"Don't worry, Kyle," she said, trying her best to sound comforting. "You'll be all right. Just try to get into the right mood. I will check on you later."

She left without looking back. I sat at the table, suppressing my fear and anger, but it was too late to regret my slip of the tongue. I could only hope that Julie would keep her promise and wouldn't make big news out of it.

I gulped my latte, looking at the gloomy scenery outside the cafeteria window, as dark clouds started to pour down streams of rain.

I returned to my desk. Nobody bothered me; however, the usual traffic down the corridor seemed more intense. The rest of my day was uneventful. Only once, while chewing my tasteless lunch, I caught myself smiling, remembering that majestic view from my dream: the ringed silver globe in the velvet sky.

Later that afternoon, Julie poked her head in again.

"How are you, Kyle?" she asked, with a hopeful expression.

As I started to shake my head, Big Bertha somehow squeezed through the doorway, gently pushing Julie away.

"Are you travelling home by train?" she asked me entirely

ignoring Julie. "Aren't you?"

Julie blushed red.

"Nobody seems to be able to give me a lift today," stated Bertha firmly, fixing her gaze on me. "And I have forgotten my brolly."

"I only have a small one..." I began protesting, but it was not easy to slip out of Big Bertha's grip.

"We will fit," she said with firm confidence. "That's no problem. I will fetch you on my way out."

"But..." My last word was left hanging in mid-air as Big Bertha turned around and squeezed back into the corridor.

I only shrugged to red-faced Julie and started collecting my things.

"I will pass your best wishes to Fiona," Julie mumbled, attempting a nervous smile, and left.

I looked through the window at the dark landscape again. The weather was nasty. Showers were pouring down, and the earth was sweating strands of white fog. I almost wished that I had joined Fiona's party, but quick heavy footsteps in the corridor brought me down to earth.

"Are you ready?" Big Bertha poked her head in, not attempting to risk pushing her raincoat-wrapped body inside.

"Just give me a moment," I told her, putting on my jacket and searching for my brolly.

was a full moon glancing through my window.

A gentle tap on the door dragged me out of the darkness. I sat up, and for several long moments, only blankly stared at the wall, shaking my head. Someone tapped again, and I glanced around. It was the same bedroom from my nightmare on the previous night. My heart was struck by bouts of panic. I was having the same dream again!

"Come in!"

An elderly man appeared, bringing a large bowl. Another followed with the jar and a towel.

"We are sorry to wake you up so early, my Lord. You wished to hunt at down..."

"Did I?"

They stopped midway.

"I must have had too much wine yesterday," I mumbled.

Another man came in, bringing a fresh set of clothes.

"Leave everything here..." I waved my hand.

"Don't you want us to assist you?" the elder butler raised his brows.

"No, thanks," I said. "I can handle this myself."

The older man with the bowl whispered a few short orders to the other two. They placed everything on the table next to the only window in my bedroom and left.

"And I would like to have my breakfast here," I added. I didn't want to wander around this unknown place.

"Yes, my lord, I will tell Abinaer to bring your meal here."

They left, closing the door behind them, but the tension and uncertainty they had brought in remained. This strange dream was aggressively pushing my boundaries, and again, I felt a wave of panic rising in my soul like a giant tsunami. *I can't do that! I won't do that! I need to find a way out.*

I poured some water into the bowl with shaking hands and washed my face, then splashed some on my chest and rubbed my body dry with a towel.

The problem didn't go away. I knew nothing about hunting. I was unable to stalk or read tracks of wild animals. *Would it be enough for me just to walk around the woods? Do I need to bring a game for my dinner?* I froze with my heart pounding loudly – had they grown suspicious for my ignorance? Were they testing me? I carefully folded the towel before placing it on my bed. I couldn't let them find out that I was a stranger. I must find a way out of this situation – a safe way. Hunting was a slippery slope for me, and without proper knowledge of the situation, I could easily make mistakes. I wasn't prepared for this.

I put on the dark trousers and a fresh shirt, and I found my belt with the dagger and boots just next to my bed.

Fears and concerns were piling on me with increasing weight. I kept on shaking my head, but they didn't go away and continued to tease me from every corner. Hunting? It wasn't my idea.

Several moments later another, slightly louder tap on the door broke into my muddled thinking and made me jump. The door opened just enough to let in a glimpse of Ahinaer – the skinny teen with curling hair who served me dinner in the kitchen yesterday.

"Carwyn told me you wished to have your breakfast here, my Lord."

"Come in!" I waved my hand absentmindedly. "Place that somewhere…"

Abinaer came in, bringing a basket of food. On my table, he placed a piece of juicy ham; some bread and cheese; a few apples; and a bottle of red wine. *No coffee?* He bowed and left without dropping a word.

The smelled and looked appetising, and I circled the table a few times before sitting down and starting to chew, still unsure of how to solve my hunting problem. The food was delicious, and the wine was excellent – not too strong. I took my time, carefully chewing every single bit of the meal in a foolish attempt to postpone the approaching decision. Half an hour later, I was full, still feeling sleepy and without any plan.

I got up and began pacing the room, unable to contain my restlessness inside. I was stopped by a gentle tap on the door. Carwyn, the old butler, came in, paying his respects. He brought in a light crossbow with a full set of arrows.

"You horse is saddled, my Lord," he announced.

That was too much for my nerves. I collapsed on the bed. *Crossbow? Horse?* I had never ridden a horse before! The other hunters would immediately suspect that something was wrong, I was sure. My lack of knowledge wasn't the only bad thing. I had no skills! No skills to ride a horse, no skills to fire a crossbow, no skills to kill. I must avoid that hunt somehow!

"My Lord!" Carwyn rushed to support me. "What happened?"

"I can't go hunting," I told him in a weak voice. "I don't feel well enough..."

"Is anything wrong with you, my Lord? Are you ill?" The old man seemed frightened.

"I just don't feel well enough. I don't think it's anything

serious. Most likely it's only simple indigestion or food poisoning."

"Poisoning, my Lord?" His eyes widened. "Do you need a healer?"

"No, I don't think it is bad enough. I only need some rest. Perhaps later, I will take a walk around, to see how things are going and to breathe some fresh air," I tried to sound encouraging, but my voice was still trembling from anxiety. "I will be all right, just let me have some rest. Please…"

"Yes, my Lord. I will leave Dahryl outside your door in case you need anything."

He left, casting a few worried glances at leftovers of my food.

My little lie looked like it might offer me salvation. I only needed to lay low for some time, and then I would be able to sneak out of the castle without raising anyone's suspicion and try to find some exit from this crazy dream. I only needed to gather sufficient courage to cross the yard. I was sure I could do that with proper preparation.

A few minutes later, a frightened woman appeared through my door. She curtsied too much, and then quickly collected what was left from my breakfast and carried away.

It was quiet outside, and I was boiling with impatience to start moving, but still, I had to pretend of being sick and spend more time in bed, or I risked blowing my brilliant story. I almost smiled half an hour later when I heard a gentle tap on my door. I adjusted my pillow.

"What is it?" I did my best to sound impatient.

"I am so sorry to disturb you, my lord," Carwyn poked his head through the barely open door. "But Kyaal, the priest is kindly asking for an audience with you."

"What does he want?" I wasn't very excited to see the priest; I wasn't dying.

"He didn't say... he insisted."

"Let him in..." I caught myself pulling the blanket closer to my chin as if trying to hide.

The man who rolled in was enormously fat, dressed like a drag queen in a long, flamboyant red gown embroidered with blue and green sparkles. His pink wig was slightly messy, carelessly sliding to the left. He was followed by two youngsters with big feathery fans, pushing his sticky bittersweet perfume ahead of him.

"Pardon my looks, my Lord," he started almost immediately. "I rushed over as soon as I heard the news... It's unthinkable! It's unimaginable!"

With a quick gesture of his left palm, he stopped his entourage by the door and approached my bed.

"How do you feel, my Lord?" He gasped half covering the face with his sweaty palms. "It's such a horrible thing!"

"There is no need to panic," I responded, pulling my blanket even higher as his small pale grey eyes drilled into my face. "I am almost fine; it's nothing serious. I only need some rest..."

"How dreadful, how terrible it is, my Lord." He clasped his hands. "You can't be safe even in your own castle. You can't even eat your food safely! By almighty Qu'mun, I swear, this is the worst thing I have ever heard."

The man was irritating me. His small eyes were hiding behind his fat smile, but I still caught them secretly darting around as if searching for something. I fought with an urge to jump out of bed and rush him out, but my period of pretended sickness wasn't over yet.

"I'll be fine..." I said in a calm and confident voice, but the priest didn't seem convinced.

Kyaal adjusted his wig with a quick and gracious gesture of his fat palm, stumbling towards my bed.

"I beg your pardon, my Lord," he said, looking at me. "I am so worried about that dreadful attempt to harm you. Could I hold your honourable hand?"

"Is this some trick?" I asked, disturbed by the thought of this sweaty priest touching me.

"Dear Lord." He clasped his hands, and his messy wig began its slow journey to the left again. "I only want to be sure that you are fine."

I hated to do it, but I realised it might be a local custom to hold sick people's hands – that might be something I didn't know about. I could only guess how influential this man was here. My rank was higher than his; this was evident. I didn't know my friends here, and I didn't want to make any enemies, especially when I was still covered by that thick veil of ignorance.

Hesitantly, I extended my hand, and Kyaal grabbed it, a pained expression on his face. He pressed it to his lips and then to his forehead, mumbling something under his breath.

"Oh, sweet tits of Maralyn," he moaned, with his eyes closed. "You are burning with heat!"

He released my hand and stepped back a few paces.

"My Lord, it's terrible!" he exclaimed. "What are you going to do with that animal?"

"Which animal?" I asked, feeling lost entirely.

"The one who did this to you!"

Was he hinting that someone must be punished for such a triviality? That was ridiculous!

"I don't feel that terrible... I am not certain if there is any need to do anything," I said, still unsure of how to get out of this interrogation with the least damage.

A few moments of silence followed. Too long...

"You are sick, my Lord. Your mind is clouded," said the priest, stating it as a fact. "This matter needs to be solved urgently.

I would like to handle this on your behalf, with your permission, of course."

I had no idea what he was talking about but nodded. Was it another local custom?

"Don't worry, my lord. You will be satisfied with the result. And we certainly need to do something about your fever..." he mumbled, carefully adjusting his wig. "I will send you my best ice wine from the temple cellar."

I was losing my patience with Kyaal.

"I need some rest, please," I said weakly. "And I'll feel better in no time."

"Of course, my lord," Kyaal's clumsy attempt to bow looked like a parody. "May the Gods send you good health and long years of prosperity!"

He waited a few moments with his eyes down, but I failed to answer.

"I will pray day and night for your health, my Lord!" he announced, straightening.

I thanked the priest for his efforts, and half closed my eyes, dismissing him. Kyaal backed from my bed, keeping his piggy eyes fixed on me. He didn't say another word, only gestured to his entourage and left, leaving his sticky smell behind.

Half an hour later, a frightened young boy brought in clay jug containing the promised wine. He only cast a few frightened glances at my side and quickly left, leaving the wine on the table. I stared at the ceiling until my eyes began to hurt. *Stupid hunt!* I cursed and sat up. *Was I a captive here?* I listened for a few long minutes. All that reached my ears was dead silence only, interrupted by occasional bird cries outside of the castle. Nobody troubled me. I got up and started to pace my room, pouring some of the priest's wine into a crystal goblet on my way. It was sweet – and indeed, it did taste great, but I didn't want to get drunk and left the half-finished goblet on the table. Still, it was too soon to heal my sudden "illness", and I spent some time studying the map again.

My confidence and courage grew slowly. I sneaked around the hall like a thief, looking at the glistening sparkles decorating hilts of swords which were hanging on the wall around the hearth, at the antlers of strange animals I never knew they exist, at long spears and lances, carved with odd symbols. I circled the display several times until I braved enough to sneak into the balcony.

Instantly, countless eyes were on me, and I stopped hesitantly. The inner yard was full of armed men. They were holding back the silent crowd, which was oozing from the street on the left. The faces were grim and very concerned, nobody was talking or laughing. They spotted me instantly, and a low murmur passed over the people with a visible agitation.

I leant at the door but didn't step back. The eyes looked at me with hope, and I couldn't just slip away. I took a few deep breaths before taking another step forward and left the safety of the hall behind.

"He is alive!" It was a whisper at first, but it grew into cheer when countless lips began repeating it. They seemed relieved and smiling, but my heart sank. I felt an immense urge to run away and hide somewhere in a dark corner, but I couldn't kill hope in their faces. I lifted my hand and waved them. They waved back, cheering. Then I turned around and retreated to the hall.

I managed a few steps only. I collapsed on the floor as soon as the crowd hid behind the balustrade of the balcony since my shaking legs weren't holding me anymore. I breathed heavily, waiting for the waves of panic wash over me. Cheering outside of the balcony subsided, but it took nearly half an hour for me to calm down.

I got up and carefully peeked outside again. The yard was empty, only two guards stood at the gate. It was an opportunity I couldn't miss. I had to find a way out of this dream world.

Hastily, I crossed the hall and opened the door. Dahryl was sitting on a small bench just outside. He was a tired-looking, dark-haired young man in full armour.

"Do you need something, my lord?" he asked, springing up as soon as I appeared in the doorway.

"No, I am alright. I feel much better now. I'd like to take a walk around," I told him. "You may go. There is no need to guard the door any longer."

Dahryl bowed before picking up his bench and turned right down the corridor. I wasted only a few moments watching his back, and then put on my mask of carelessness and started down the hallway in the opposite direction. My urge to run was immense, but I had to hold it or risk ruining my story with poisoning. I went slowly, peeking through every door which I found on my way.

The next room to my chambers must be a dining room, I decided – there was a big table in the middle with several rather comfortable looking chairs. Embroidered dark blue curtains framed two windows. A big hearth was on the right with traces of tar and ashes in the fireplace; most likely, it was used frequently.

The next three rooms down the corridor were bedrooms, much smaller than my own and probably rarely occupied by guests.

The corridor ended with a wide staircase which was heading down. I went on quietly like a shadow, meeting no one on my way. Not a soul was in the chamber downstairs as well.

I stopped, listening. The hall in front of me was as large as a cathedral, and it had a feeling of grandeur. Two gracious colonnades held the ceiling on both sides of the aisle. The high windows on the right were glazed with blue stained glass and framed with heavy dark purple curtains. The filtered light played tricks of shadows with polished marble floors – blue streaks in the stone kept on vanishing and reappearing as I went, creating a fascinating impression of the rippling surface of a lake on a windy day.

I went on enchanted by the view, and then stopped in the middle when I noticed a dais in the far end of the hall. A massive throne was on the dais, carved out of black basalt stone. The backrest was decorated with a carving of a strange winged beast with the body of a lion and the head of an eagle – a gryphon, its eyes glistened with the blue sparkles. The seat was covered with the white-furred skin of an unknown animal.

I took a few steps closer. *Was it appropriate for me to be here?* The placed seemed sacred, and I felt like an intruder. I backed a few paces and then turned around and went down the aisle, where a massive door was at the right side of the grand staircase.

The door opened without a single sound, and I found myself outside, in the inner yard, facing the walls of the city. Bysh stretched out in the sunlight just outside of the door. He raised his head and lazily wagged his tail, recognising me. I glanced around, feeling instant relief. The yard still was empty with only two armoured men standing on guard at the gate.

The weather was beautiful: the sky cloudless, the sunshine

bright, the light breeze just enough to keep me cool – it was perfect for a little walk. I only needed some company.

I whistled to Bysh, and, when he approached me, I scratched behind his ears. We were still friends, and he gladly joined me without any hesitation. We unhurriedly paraded through the yard.

The guards at the gate stepped aside as soon as we approached them. I waved my hand, pretending impatience, afraid that the guards might refuse my attempt to escape, but they opened the gate without a single question. Bysh ran a few paces forward and then turned back, waiting for me to catch up.

I crossed the stone bridge across the river and started to climb the stairs carved into the rock, slowly getting nearer to the waterfall. I was sure I would be able to find that arched cliff by the creek where I had first woken up in this world. I was sure I must start my search there.

Bysh followed me closely. The sight of massive streams of water falling from steep cliffs was mesmerising, despite the deafening sound. It was a long climb, and I was a bit short of breath when I reached the top of the stairs. Bysh didn't seem too exhausted. He ran a few paces ahead and disappeared into the thick green shrubs. The next moment, his barking reached me from the woods on the left.

I sat down to catch my breath, but the increasing pitch of

Bysh's barking annoyingly interfered with my appreciation of the peaceful view in front of me: a beautiful valley behind the curtain of thousand rainbows.

I cursed. *What was happening?* Another squirrel was sitting in the tree, and that stupid dog couldn't get enough of chasing it?

A deep roar suddenly interrupted Bysh's barking, and at that very instant, I knew that it was something far more dangerous than a squirrel.

I grabbed my dagger and started to approach cautiously, more driven by an overwhelming sense of fear rather than curiosity. I couldn't just leave the dog behind and flee back to the safety of the castle. The sound of breaking branches signalled an intense fight, and behind the shrubs, silhouettes were moving so fast I could barely follow them.

Bysh was howling and barking, and I flinched with every wave of that horrible roar. I reached the woods and peeked at the scene of the fight from behind a thick fir, doing my best to remain unnoticed. It was a big, grizzly-sized black bear rolling on the ground and gripping Bysh in the middle of a life-or-death battle.

I watched from a distance, afraid to take a breath.

Blood was already gushing from a large wound in the bear's side, exposing a piece of gut, while Bysh seemed unharmed, as far as I could judge from where I was. He was gracefully jumping on his feet, as though dancing, avoiding the lashes of the fearsome claws, but continually biting, barking and growling.

The bear was roaring and failing to catch the swiftly moving dog as that deep wound was slowing him down. His life was leaking from the torn side, along with streams of bright red blood. The bear shook his head as Bysh circled him, growling and barking without a break and tried to keep up with the pace, fighting Bysh's teeth with his claws, but failing each attempt.

The fight seemed hopeless for Bysh at first – the bear was at least twice his size, but now I wouldn't have bet on him losing it.

The green leaves of the broken shrubs were painted red already. A few more circles, a few more broken branches...

Suddenly the bear stopped as if trying to catch his breath. Bysh didn't wait a second. He leapt on the animal's back and sank his teeth deeply into its neck. It was over. Even from my distance, I could clearly hear the sound of breaking bones, and the black-furred body slumped heavily to the ground, followed by a victorious howl from Bysh.

"Bysh?" I was still hiding behind that tree, afraid to approach.

He glanced at me briefly, wagging his tail. Still, Bysh had unfinished business with the bear, and I was afraid to come any closer. He circled the limp, lifeless body, growling and biting it randomly. I watched helplessly with no idea how to calm him down and was afraid to interfere.

The hairy body was limp and didn't move, but the dog kept

on with his attacks, sinking his teeth deep into the dead bear and shaking it with all his might. Bysh shook its skin like a bunch of rags, raising clouds of dust. Suddenly, he jumped back and howled as a strange, faint, barely visible strand of mist separated from the dead body. It rose to eye level, glistening like distant starlight, and then was blown away by a light wind.

Bysh barked a few more times and approached me, breathing heavily, with his tongue out and his eyes full of pride. Hesitantly, I touched his head. The dog was covered with blood, but I was sure it wasn't his blood.

We returned to the track. The forest was silent again. I cautiously looked around, ready to jump and run at any moment – who knew what other dangers were hiding behind the dark firs? Bysh was at ease, exhaustedly strolling by my side, and I gratefully patted his back – that bear could have ripped me apart in a few blows. Bysh licked my hand, and we moved on.

We reached one of the creeks which ran down the slope of the mountain, and Bysh splashed into it. The clean waters turned red, and I had to walk a few paces upstream to wash my hands. Then I waited until Bysh drank his full and we were ready to go.

The road wound between large black boulders, precisely as I remembered it. Soon we passed the spot with the tall pillar of black rock where I first met Bysh, and the forest grew taller and darker as we strolled down the dirt road.

I wasn't sure if the dream hadn't changed as we went on – the trees and rocks seemed alike, and I had to admit that I wasn't attentive the last time. I was immensely relieved when I finally recognised the place – the same arched rock and the same curve of the creek. I took the barely visible path to the right between the leafy shrubs and stopped at the exact spot where my bizarre dream began. It was the same damp moss and ferns, but I wasn't sure where to start my search nor what I was looking for. There was no switch, no exit door and no clues – nothing.

I dropped down to my knees and began searching around, parting every bunch of ferns, lifting every dead leaf. Bysh stood by the stream and looked at me, apparently trying to understand what I was doing. Then he started to sniff around – not looking for anything in particular, but just keeping me company.

A blue spark caught my eye while I was shuffling through the dead leaves. I carefully parted the moss, and there it was – an intricate golden ring with two gryphons holding a large sapphire. Would it stop this dream? I rubbed the sapphire with my sleeve until it shone like a morning star. Nothing happened, no genies appeared, no doors opened, no exit signs lighted up.

Probably, I lost the ring yesterday unaware of its existence. I slipped it into my vest pocket and returned to my search, hoping to find some clues how I got there if not the way out. I looked through the area twice without any results – I only crushed a few mushrooms and found several acorns. If there was any way to stop this dream, I wasn't going to find it there.

Bysh sat next to the stream and without any interest watched me.

A chilly wind reminded me of the fading day. It was time to go back. I whistled to the dog and began retracing my way back. My moods were as dark as the fading day.

I was deadly tired when I reached the castle and went upstairs directly to my chambers. Bysh preferred to stay in the throne hall.

Carwyn popped in, and I asked him to bring my supper to my chambers. When the food arrived, I quietly ate and then slipped into bed.

I was asleep before my head reached the pillow.

My alarm clock returned me to London. For two minutes, I only laid flat on my back, my muscles aching as if I was running a marathon, and pushed away all remnants of the vivid dream. Then I remembered that the train wouldn't wait for me.

I hastily brushed my teeth, dressed and dashed out, grabbing a cup of coffee at the petrol station on my way. I hurried downhill and ran into the train station just in time to see my train arriving.

I boarded the train and dropped on the nearest empty seat, still sipping my cappuccino. The carriage filled with people, but I looked through the window and silently watched trees and houses passing by as the train began to accelerate. We arrived on time, and I didn't have to deliver any degrading apologies.

All day at work, I kept recalling that bloody fight between the dog and the bear. The strange dream started to frighten me, and I wondered how many more nights I would be forced to spend in that strange dream world.

It was late in the afternoon when Julie poked her head in. Her face was split in a wide smile.

"How was the party?" I asked politely but without any particular interest.

"Great!" her eyes sparkled. "Gorgeous party! Lots of fun! I even had a chance to dance with Tom!"

She looked behind her shoulder.

"Such a pity you were unable to go," she sighed sincerely. "But big thanks for saving us from Bertha!"

"She knew..." I said.

Julie paled instantly, raising a hand to her mouth.

"How?"

"It doesn't matter now," I said. "Strange, but she thanked me for saving her from the party..."

Julie grabbed the chair and lowered herself on it, her face still colourless.

"We are bloody stupid idiots," she said, finally exhaling. "Now I must apologise to her."

"I don't think that is necessary," I said and shuffled through my papers. "She seemed more relieved rather than upset."

"I don't know. I must consult others..."

I shrugged. It was not my business anyway.

"Thanks, Kyle," she smiled nervously. "Could I bring you a

cup of coffee?"

"That would be nice, thanks," I turned back to my computer.

A large mug of coffee appeared on my table several minutes later, but Julie didn't say a word. She was still uneasy with the situation.

Several hours passed, undisturbed. When the working day ended, I collected my things and headed downhill to the train station.

The journey home was uneventful, and I ate my dinner watching TV. Then I brushed my teeth before slipping into bed.

Tomorrow is a Saturday, I remembered that with a smile. It was my last thought before I drifted into the darkness of sleep.

A hushed murmur of a crowd was annoyingly dragging my consciousness out of the blessed nothingness. I couldn't make it out if it were part of the dream or part of reality at first. Then I opened my eyes and sat up. The murmur grew a little louder. I looked around, realising that I was back in Chadrack again. My shirts and trousers were hung neatly on a nearby chair, and there were my boots at the foot of my bed.

I had just finished dressing when a gentle tap on the door drew my attention.

"Come in!"

Carwyn appeared, carrying the bowl. He was followed by two other men with water and towels.

"Would you like me to bring your breakfast here, my lord?" Carwyn asked when the other men left.

"Well... yes," I didn't feel very familiar with the castle yet.

Something heavy dropped on the ground outside, and the murmur grew even louder. I heard a few women crying.

"What is that noise?" I asked frowning.

"It's nothing important, my lord. You don't need to worry – it's only a simple execution." He spoke casually.

I was shocked. "Who is being executed?"

"Cook Abinaer."

"What?! Why?"

"He confessed to trying to poison you, my Lord."

Sudden guilt pressed down on my shoulders as heavy as a mountain.

"How did he confess?" I asked in disbelief. "Did you torture him?"

"Of course, my Lord, everything was done in the usual way. You don't need to worry."

I didn't wait for him to finish his speech and hastily stormed out, onto the balcony. Carwyn followed me, a few paces behind.

The weather was jolly, and I was blinded by the sun as I stepped through the door, but when my eyes adapted to the brightness, I felt weak at the grim sight in front of me.

I saw a headless body in a pool of blood in the middle of the yard, surrounded by a crowd of horrified onlookers. A thin spike was high above them, with something on top of it, what, at first, looked like a bunch of rags.

My hand was trembling as I shaded my eyes, trying to get a better look. Another wave of weakness hit my legs, and I had to grab the rail – the head of the poor cook was on the spike still dripping blood, with his curly hair swinging in the light wind. His eyes were wide open and lifeless, fixed on nothing.

I gasped, looking away. My empty stomach turned into knots, and I started to vomit. Carwyn helped me in my convulsions, as my shaking legs failed to support me.

When the moment of sickness slowly passed, and I lifted my eyes to look at the yard again, I spotted Kyaal, the fat priest, in front of the crowd in an important posture, apparently orchestrating the event. His pink wig was sitting firmly in place this time, and his long gown sparkled in the light of the morning sun. Kyaal held a strange staff, with a neatly carved white snake in his right hand and sometimes raised it high above, pointing at the head on the spike. I couldn't hear what he was saying; he was facing the headless body and the crowd behind it, and his massive backside was turned to the balcony.

"Why did he must die?" I whispered, knowing the answer already.

It was entirely my fault, the grave consequence of my innocent lie.

Kyaal finished his preaching and began to sing in a high-pitched falsetto, adding weird taste to that farce. The crowd was silent.

I heard the cawing of a few ravens, circling in the sky above already, and another wave of sickness dragged my stomach back into convulsions.

Carwyn gently supported me, a very concerned look on his face.

"You are very sick, my lord," he said. "Do you need a healer? Damned Abinaer! How could he dare..."

"No," I said, unable to lift my gaze to the severed head on the spike.

Kyaal, the priest, was still shrieking his psalms in that terrible falsetto, but I couldn't take any more of it. Carwyn helped me back to my room. I washed my face before speaking again.

"Do you believe he was guilty?" I asked.

"Kyaal announced that Abinaer had confessed and that he deserved the punishment," said Carwyn. "He ordered an immediate execution to scare everybody who dares to threaten your well-being, my Lord."

I bit my tongue as the enormous mountain of guilt crushed me again. The poor guy had lost his head because of my stupid lies. Why couldn't I think of a better excuse for that hunt? It was too late for regrets.

Carwyn helped me into my bed and left without a single word.

I kept on blankly staring at the ceiling, boiling inside but afraid to show my rage. I couldn't believe that my innocent lie could have had such consequences!

I didn't notice when Carwyn brought my food, nor I had any desire to eat.

A few hours later, the old butler returned.

"Are you still feeling unwell, my lord?" he asked cautiously.

I sighed, shaking my head. I wasn't ill, only genuinely shocked. Then I realised that my shock would be neither understood nor helpful in these circumstances. Their lord was supposed to be as hard as a rock. I couldn't let another disaster happen.

"I feel much better now," I told him, getting up from my bed.

Carwyn rushed to help me, but I stopped him with a simple gesture. I knew I must be strong.

"We have tested your food, my Lord," Carwyn assured me, gesturing at my untouched breakfast. "Three people ate from the same pot, and all are well. We have a new cook."

I had no appetite.

"I am not hungry. I just need some rest," I said firmly, and added after a short hesitation, "take Abinaer's head off that spike. I want him to be put at rest, and a proper funeral arranged. He has been punished too harshly. Make sure there are no more executions without my prior knowledge."

"Yes, my Lord," Carwyn quickly nodded. "It will be as you wish, my Lord. I will place Dahryl outside of your door, in case if you need anything."

He left hastily. I paced three or four times around the hall but still was afraid to step into the balcony and face that severed head again. I cursed, punching the walls along my way, but nothing helped. The guilt followed me like a lost dog, backing away at the moments of rage and returning the next instant.

It was too late for any regrets. I was too slow to realise how cruel this world was. I must be more careful about those innocent lies. They might be deadly.

I pressed my back against the wall next to the hearth and gazed through the door open to the balcony. The spike was out of my view, but I saw a large black raven sitting on the railing and watching the scene unfolding in the yard below. The bird looked at me twice but made no sound.

I stood there, observing the raven, and the band of sunshine slowly travelling through the hall. Only later, when the bird flew away, I realised that the body had been removed. I had no idea about the customs of a proper funeral in this world, but I hoped Carwyn would make it right.

I squeezed my fist and punched the wall again. *Fool!* I was in the shoes of the ruler of this land, and it was my duty to make sure that no innocent people would ever suffer. It was my duty!

Damn…

The sunshine band moved a little more across the floor of the hall. It was quiet outside, and I finally returned to my bedroom. Later, when Carwyn popped in, I was ready.

"How are you feeling, my Lord?" he asked with a genuine concern in his voice.

"Not as well as I would like to be yet… It must be the effects of that poison," I told him with my best sad expression, only short of tears in my eyes.

"Almighty Gods," moaned Carwyn, looking frightened. "May I humbly suggest you seeing a healer?"

"No, that isn't necessary. I will be fine, I am sure, but the poison took some of my strength, and my memories became very vague," I lied to him. "You must keep my illness a secret; it is vital. I will recover in time, I hope, but you must be patient with me. And I will need a man for some training to help me to regain my strength which I have lost. He must keep my illness a secret too."

"Yes, my Lord. Do you have any particular man in mind?"

"No, you choose. He must be reliable, patient and good at keeping secrets. And, please, cancel all my hunting. I have no taste for it until I feel better."

"Yes, my Lord."

He bowed more times than usual and left. I sat alone in

silence.

The bloody sun slowly sank behind the dark line of the forest, with a single stray of black smoke visible on its face like a scar. It must be the pyre for the dead cook, I guessed, and sadness squeezed my heart again.

I stretched out on my bed and closed my eyes, wishing to end the dream, wishing it had never happened.

That Saturday morning was rainy in London. I stayed in bed with my eyes closed, listening to the soft sound of drizzle. The nightmare world visions were distant, but the overwhelming sense of guilt still kept me company.

I got up and made myself a cup of strong coffee. The TV told me about another crisis in the Middle East, the lazy life of some unknown starlet on a Caribbean beach and rising optimism in the stock market.

I sipped my coffee, but my thoughts were far away. I still saw Abinaer's severed head on the spike, dripping blood. Chadrack and its strange customs wouldn't let me go.

I hated blood, horror movies and nightmares, and now my dreams were nightly presenting me with a full set of everything I hated. Maybe I needed to visit a psychiatrist?

I frowned as the thought about stacks of pills crossed my

mind and flinched with disgust, rejecting the idea immediately. Certainly not!

The day stretched lazily. I watched TV and listened to the endless rain outside my window. Even the nearby street was less noisy than usual; the inclement weather kept everybody at home.

It was early evening when I inspected the contents of my fridge and decided to order pizza from the nearest pizzeria. I became increasingly nervous while I waited for the delivery. The night-time was approaching, bringing the nightmare on its dark wings. I wasn't prepared for Chadrack with its cruel customs and blood. Maybe I could somehow avoid slipping back to that damned dream world again. Maybe I could try to stay awake. One sleepless night wouldn't kill anybody. The idea seemed tempting – then maybe Chadrack would be gone from my mind forever?

I was happily drinking my second large mug of coffee and getting ready to implement the plan when my pizza arrived. I only needed an exciting film and a few more cups of strong coffee and the morning would come in no time. I hoped this would break the cycle.

A few hours later, the talking heads on TV bored me into sleep despite caffeine in my circulation. I had to find something else. Loud music wasn't an option since my neighbours were sound asleep long ago. I couldn't go outside either: it was raining, and I didn't feel safe enough, wandering around at night.

Instead, I opened the window, letting in cold, damp air, and I started to search through the TV programme. I found a criminal drama, then watched some news. It wasn't exciting, but in combination with the coffee, it kept me awake. I scrolled through the channels full of talking heads and then finally arrived at some old movie about zombies. I hated zombies, but they were far better than talking heads.

It was a few hours past midnight already when suddenly that creepy feeling of being watched overtook me again. I knew I was alone in the flat and that there was nobody outside my window – I had checked. But I had a terrible feeling of an invisible ghost touching my hands.

I carefully inspected the skin, but still couldn't see anything. Suddenly, a sharp pain drilled into my brain, and in front of my eyes, the skin on my left wrist was somehow pierced, although I could see no one doing it. Dark blood instantly oozed out of the wound, staining my clothes. I could hardly hold myself back from screaming out. *What was happening?!*

I didn't have too much time to wonder or to think – I reached the toilet in a few leaps, grabbed the towel and wrapped it around my bleeding wrist, then watched with growing horror as it slowly turned red from inside. I had to press harder!

I sat on the floor, close to tears. It was painful, unexpected and meaningless. I had no idea what was going on and what to expect next.

I found a fresh towel and tossed the one soaked with blood away, then pressed as hard as I could on the wound. Blood still was pouring out, but less intensely now. I waited with a trembling heart until the bleeding stopped. Only then did the tension finally ease, and I began to sob helplessly. I was crying with pain and fear, then from desperation... What had happened? *Why?* Would it happen again?

It was hard to calm down. My heart was trembling, and a few more times, I felt a ghostly touch on my palms, but no other wounds appeared. I spent nearly an hour sitting on the floor clutching my wrist, flinching at every sound in my empty flat.

Then I carefully unwrapped the towel. The wound was small and neat – gaping only a little. I found my box of bandages, sprayed on some antiseptic and dressed it. Still, I had no idea what had happened. I couldn't understand how a bleeding wound could just appear out of thin air on my wrist as if pierced by an invisible knife.

Still wondering, I began to clean off the blood. I put the bloodied towels and bed dressings into the washing machine and started to scrub red pools on the floor. It seemed that the zombies on TV watched me with increasing curiosity.

By six in the morning, everything was over. I made myself another cup of coffee.

Sunday morning was breaking over London. The rain had stopped, but dark clouds still were covering the sky, disturbed only by occasional passing planes.

I fished some meat, some cheese and two boiled eggs out of my fridge and ate it all. Only then I noticed that my hands were shaking – blood loss? Stress? A sleepless night? Or maybe just too much coffee?

I made myself a cup of tea to wash down my breakfast.

I was too tired to go anywhere and crawled back into bed. The day was worse than the previous – I was tired and frightened and flinched on every louder sound from outside. Later in the afternoon, I ordered one more pizza and watched more movies. Then tiredness got to me. The last thing I remembered was the weather forecast on TV before I drifted away into my dream to find out if my plan had succeeded.

I felt a presence. I was awake but didn't make any attempt to move or open my eyes yet. The squeak of a chair under someone's weight immediately confirmed my suspicions. I slowly turned my head as if sleeping. There was another squeak. Then I opened my eyes, preparing to fight if necessary.

Carwyn was looking at me, an expression on his face in which joy and concern were mixed.

"Thanks to the mighty Gods, you are well again, my Lord!" he said, smiling genuinely.

"What happened?" was my obvious question.

"We were unable to wake you up yesterday, my Lord. The poison was too deep in your blood. Please, forgive me, my Lord, but I disobeyed your order. I invited a healer. Your heart was very sick and trembling as you slept. He let some blood, and now you are better! He said he would repeat the procedure today, to let all that poison out..."

It was a white clean cloth bandage on my left wrist. I couldn't believe my eyes – the cut in my dream was in the same place as it had been in real life. What if my real body and the body I had in that dream were somehow connected? What if everything that was happening to my body in my dream was instantly reflected in reality? The thought was sickeningly crazy, but I couldn't get rid of it, as it circled my mind with the continuous nagging determination of a hungry fly.

"Carwyn!"

My voice sounded rude, and he jumped to his feet immediately. "Never let anybody to perform bloodletting on me again! Never! I do not wish to see that healer."

His face grew deep crimson.

"Yes, my lord. Will you command us to be executed for such an impertinence?" Carwyn's voice was slightly trembling

"No, of course, not! That's ridiculous!"

I felt guilty since it was my own bright idea to spend the night without sleep! He had just done his best and tried to save my life. I felt so stupidly confused.

"I am much better now, thanks to you," I added, more calmly, "but I don't require any further treatment."

He smiled faintly, slowly regaining his colour.

"Would you like breakfast, my Lord?" he asked, with some

hesitation.

"Yes, bring it here. I still need some rest."

He left.

I probed my bandaged wrist with a finger. It was hard to feel through the cloth, but the wound appeared to be in the same place and the same size. Maybe I only had been dreaming about the same injury?

Carwyn returned with a basket full of food and a bottle of red wine. I tried to get up, but suddenly felt dizzy – a sleepless night or blood loss? Carwyn helped me to dress.

I felt a sudden burst of hunger and waited rather impatiently while he arranged the contents of the food basket on my table and poured some wine into my goblet.

Then he left, leaving me alone to kill my hunger.

The food was generous and excellent. The pieces of ham on fresh bread were delightful, as was the cheese and chicken. I washed everything down with a few gulps of wine, then rested, enjoying the pleasant sense of fullness, before eating some fruit.

I decided to test my strength and stood up. The dizziness returned, but it didn't seem as bad this time. I waited a few minutes letting my body to adjust and then took several steps towards the balcony. It wasn't difficult, and soon I was breathing full lungs of cool and fresh morning air.

The yard was full of people, and at the sight of me on the

balcony, a murmur ran through the crowd. I raised my hand and waved. They cheered as I waved again and returned to my bed, feeling much stronger.

Nobody bothered me until noon when Carwyn popped in with an even more generous lunch. This time, he was accompanied by Bysh who whined and wagged his tail insanely. I shared some of my food with him, and the dog gratefully licked my face.

I asked Carwyn to find a soft rug for Bysh. Carwyn didn't question why I wanted my dog to sleep in my chambers. And I didn't bother to explain why his presence would make me feel so much more secure either.

My order was fulfilled in no time. They placed a bed for Bysh in the big hall, next to my bedroom door. He cautiously sniffed it first and then got on it without hesitancy.

I felt stronger after my breakfast, but still not ready for any lengthy trips, either within the castle or outside. All I did was a few circles around my chambers. It was around noon when Carwyn came in and began to apologise for some urgent affair of the state which required my decision.

"What is that?" I asked, sitting down next to Bysh.

"Our party of jaegers caught two hunters from Porlok in our forests near the castle, my Lord. Do you wish to torture or just to kill them? They might be spies..."

"Remind me, are we involved in any war with Porlok?"

"No, my Lord."

"Do we have any reasons to hate Porlok?" I was whispering.

Carwyn shrugged. "No, my Lord. You have always been on good terms with your sister!"

"Then why would you want to torture or kill those people? Let them go! Arrange an escort for them to the border to make sure that they don't get lost again."

"It will be as you command, my Lord!"

He left hastily, and for some time, I could hear him shouting orders down the corridor. Then everything returned to silence.

He came back in the evening with another food basket for me, followed by a young boy with a food basket for Bysh. The day was nearing its end.

I ate in silence. Then I spent some time on the balcony admiring the majestic view of that silvery ringed giant floating in the purple sky. I still had no idea what name they called it.

I plotted to carry out a small experiment to find out whether the cut to my wrist by some mad healer in Chadrack had caused bleeding back in London. Was the wound in my dream only an imagination? Or was it a part of reality? I needed to make another small cut.

It was easy.

I undressed unhurriedly, preparing for the night. Bysh got on his bed.

Then I took out my dagger and made a quick cut on my left little finger. I cursed silently – it was more painful than I expected. A few drops of blood stained my skin, but the wound wasn't deep, and the bleeding stopped almost instantly.

Then I slipped into my bed and closed my eyes.

The usual sounds of morning traffic woke me up well before my alarm clock went off. A short glimpse at my left hand confirmed all my weirdest suspicions. Now my hand had two cuts – one on the wrist, carefully bandaged and clean, and another – on my little finger, exactly as I had remembered it: a clean cut from a dagger, with a few drops of dried blood.

I stared at the wound, suddenly petrified with fear. The meaning of that small cut was terrifying – I wasn't an observer of my dreams any longer; I was living in them. It had been a disturbing and confusing suspicion before, but now I had solid proof on my little finger.

The wave of self-pity was interrupted by the alarm clock, shrieking at the side table with all its might. *Damn! I must hurry. I will have time to think more about this later…*

I washed my face, brushed my teeth, dressed and hastily left.

Thick clouds were covering the gloomy sky, but, at least, it wasn't raining.

I clutched my brolly and rushed downhill to the same train station and the same platform, keeping on my usual tracks. All this time, I couldn't help but think about the increasingly dangerous situation which was squeezing my heart with fear. *Whatever happens to my body in that dream has a direct reflection in the real world,* – the thought was frightening. I wasn't a cat with a stack of nine lives behind me; I must be very cautious.

The train arrived on time, and I followed to my usual seat.

I had to find a way to end that dream as fast as possible. The idea of visiting a psychiatrist didn't seem that repulsive any longer. Was I crazy? Was I *really* crazy?

Several stations later, I suddenly noticed that same eerie dark man who had pricked my shoulder a few days ago. He was standing on a crowded platform and preparing to board the same train when his eyes met mine. He instantly froze in recognition. I jumped to my feet, desperation overcoming my fears and prejudices. I knew I had to find out more about him. Maybe he held the key to my dreams? But the man turned away and melted into the crowd.

I stormed out of the train and hastily rushed through the platform. I aimlessly rushed about, and several minutes later, I realised that I had lost him. It was the morning rush hour, and the station was full of people, but the man was nowhere in sight.

I turned back just in time to see my train leaving. *Shit!* I would be late.

Silently cursing, I kept on pacing up and down the platform, waiting for the next train and hoping to catch a glimpse of that dark man again. Half an hour later, the train arrived; the man hadn't shown up.

Of course, I was late, but nobody paid any attention when I finally sneaked into the office. The workday went, as usual. So was the journey home.

I ate a tasteless dinner, and then I watched TV in my bed, falling asleep while it was still on.

The morning was rainy in Chadrack. I scrubbed, dressed and ate my breakfast unhurriedly. Then I reminded Carwyn about my training.

"Yes, my Lord, at once!" He left and, after a short while, returned with a tall, muscular young man.

"Rhys will help you with the training, my Lord," Carwyn said seriously. "He is your best jaeger and as silent as the dead fish in keeping secrets."

"When would you like to start, my Lord?" asked Rhys. His eyes looked at me calmly, but I caught a hint of concern in them; his face remained expressionless.

"What about now?"

"Could I advise you to wait until the rain stops, my Lord?" the young man shrugged. "It would be better to start somewhere outside of the castle if you want to keep it secret."

"Good idea," I hadn't thought about the dangers of making a public display of my clumsiness.

They both waited for my decision.

"If it clears, we will go training this afternoon," I said, making up my mind. "If not, let's hope we will be luckier tomorrow."

Rhys nodded, his serious expression remained unchanged. They both paid their respects and departed, leaving me with my doubts.

I wasn't sure if I was ready for that training. My body didn't feel weak, but I never was a keen sportsman. I had no idea what strength was required for acquiring resemblance to their true ruler but was determined to give it a try.

I waited until their footsteps had faded in the corridor and then made a few sit-ups, push-ups, testing the limits of my slightly weakened body. It felt stronger than I had expected after all that stress and bloodletting.

I opened the door to the balcony and peeked around. Soft drizzle covered all Chadrack in impenetrable mist. Grey clouds were stuck to the foot of the mount, hiding the high peaks from view. Then my gaze stopped on the gracious red brick temple slightly below the imaginary line where heavens touched the mountain. A wave of guilt and black anger began to build up in my guts as I remembered Kyaal orchestrating the brutal death of Abinaer. Suddenly, I wanted to look into those porky eyes and ask why that poor lad had to die.

I was sure I would be able to find my way – the temple was high above the town, standing just below the line of clouds and, I supposed, clearly visible from everywhere. And it wasn't raining too much. The journey might get strenuous, but I had to test my physical capabilities before I started training with Rhys.

I peeked into the corridor, stopped a boy passing by and asked him to find Carwyn. The old man appeared in a few minutes.

"I would like a warm cloak to protect me from the rain," I told him in a firm voice, leaving no room for discussion. "I would like to have a walk in the city."

Carwyn nodded.

"Would you like somebody to accompany you?" he asked.

"No," I said, hoping my exchange with the priest wouldn't get too heated.

I only hoped that the castle was as visible as the temple and that I would be able to find my way back easily.

I did my best to build up enough courage and determination to ask the priest a few uncomfortable questions. There would be no more executions in Chadrack as long as my dream was landing me here. I was adamant about that.

Carwyn returned a few minutes later, bringing the dark cloak and high boots.

"I thought you might need these as well, my Lord," he said, apologetically.

I thanked him and started to dress.

The cloak was comfortable, made of soft leather with fur lining and a large hood. The boots were less comfortable, with thick solid soles, but they were supposed to keep my feet dry.

I sneaked into the empty corridor and with a slight hesitance found my way outside. The yard was empty when I got there, except for guards at the gate. All traces of Abinaer's execution were gone.

I turned left and followed the narrow and curved cobblestone-paved street running uphill, glancing up a few times to check the direction – still, the temple was clearly visible. I got into problems later when the road turned right, heading down, away from the mountain foot. My head boiled with anger, and I went on without paying too much attention – I was building plans on how to question Kyaal. Suddenly, I was in doubts – I wasn't sure if my authority was enough to scare the priest. *Would he dare to oppose me? Or would he just laugh at my face?* A few times, I considered returning, but my own sense of guilt pushed me forward. I could save Abinaer if I knew what was waiting for him. If only that priest weren't pressing with the execution, I could have an opportunity to stop that insanity. Now that innocent blood was on my hands as well, and I wanted to have a look at those piggy eyes of the priest and ask – why? Those thoughts swarming in my head were grim, and I was too occupied to noticed my surroundings. When I lift eyes to check my position, at last, the temple wasn't there. I was facing the dark green woods behind the city wall.

I stopped and glanced around. The buildings were tall – three or four stories high – and looked like fortifications. Drizzling clouds were swirling above them, and I couldn't have a single glimpse of the mountain I needed. The street was empty, and there was no one I could ask. *Was it appropriate to ask for directions?* The shame would be immense – the ruler was lost in his own city!

I cursed and turned back. Several hundred yards later, the view of the temple emerged from behind the corner, but it was too early for a victorious grin. I had to embrace the city and get off the road, which – I knew – would bring me back to the castle.

I dived into the first side street to the right. No one crossed my way, as I hurried forward, losing the sight of the temple again. Half a mile later, the street ended in the cul-de-sac. I had to return and try a different way. I wasted more than an hour trying to get through the tangle of streets – more elaborate than the labyrinth of Minos. Streets, squares and gardens blended into one in my head. I knew I will have a hard time on my way back, but I built my determination as I went as well.

I passed a few small squares before getting onto a wide stone-paved staircase, several blocks away at the foot of the mountain. The rain was stronger here, with nasty gusts of wind. No one saw me, a lonely figure behind the white balustrade. I only wrapped myself more tightly in my cloak and rushed forward.

At the top, I paused for a few moments to catch my breath and entered the building through the arched door, leaving the rain behind. I walked along a short corridor and found myself in a large hall. It was warm and pleasant inside, with a faint scent of musk hanging in the air. Intricate sounds of a harp, flute, and cymbals created a strange soft rhythmic music, which seemed omnipresent, although I couldn't spot where it was coming from. The dim light from the outside was filtering through the stained-glass windows and playing shadow games with statues of gods and goddesses. A massive statue of the Serpent carved out of white marble was in the centre of the hall, raised up on a high pedestal. The snake was in an attack pose and about to strike, looking at the believer with its black basalt eyes.

I stopped glancing around. Someone was approaching me from the right. The shape was human, but I couldn't work out if it were a man or a woman. A pair of blue eyes looked calm, slightly tense, in the pretty, ageless face, lips pressed tightly together above the gracefully curved chin.

"Qu'mun is the greatest," the lips barely moved as they mouthed the ritual phrase. "I am Obie. Welcome to the Great

Temple. Would you like a male or female as a medium for prayer? We have all looks, ages and sizes."

"I need to speak with Kyaal," I said.

"Kyaal?" Obie raised the right brow. "It is costly to use the priest as a medium for prayer..."

"I am not in a mood to pray," I cut the tirade and took off the hood, exposing my face. "Find me the priest."

"Very well, my Lord," said Obie, expressionless. "Please follow me..."

We passed through the hall and entered the long, dimly lit corridor with pink canopies randomly placed along the walls and many closed doors on both sides. The music was slightly louder here, but it couldn't mute the rhythmic moans, screams and occasional laughter.

"What is this?" I asked.

"People are praying," Obie answered without looking back.

The doors were tightly shut, and I could only imagine what was going inside. We entered another hall, turned left and took the narrow spiral stairs, leading to one of the towers. Then we passed a small, roofed terrace with its sides open to elements and stopped in front of a tightly shut wooden door.

Muffled moans and cries were audible here as well, but that didn't seem to bother Obie.

"Please wait here, my Lord." A faint smile crossed the ageless face. "I will inform the priest about your request."

Obie slipped through the door without knocking. The low moaning and high-pitched screams stopped immediately. Minutes later, a half-naked boy escaped through the door, dashed past me and ran away down the corridor. A few more moments passed before Obie showed up again.

"The priest is waiting for you, my Lord," announced Obie, stepping aside and letting me in.

Kyaal appeared tired and was profusely sweating. He was in a dark green gown (naturally, as he wouldn't have fit into anything tighter than that). His pink wig rested on a stand in the corner, and, as I entered, he was drying his bald head with a napkin.

The room had no windows, and all the light came from candles in several chandeliers hanging randomly on all walls, except the one with the entrance. The air was thick with the heavy odour of sweat and perfume, which hit my nostrils as soon as I passed the doorstep.

"I am so glad you are feeling better, my Lord," he said, smiling his fake saccharine smile. "I was praying day and night for it! Qu'mun almighty, master of the dead, granted you health and a speedy recovery. Let us see his silver kingdom of dusk with our unseeing eyes..."

"What was that?" I asked, ignoring his rambling.

"What do you have in your mind, my Lord?" he looked around as if thinking he would be able to spot the object of my questioning glowing in a dim light somewhere.

I decided to refresh his memory. "I just saw a half-naked boy running out of this room."

"Oh!" The sweet smile returned to his face. "He is a medium in training, a hopeless one, I guess. That boy is so stupid. He can't even memorise a few verses of the psalm and deliver it at the right pace and the right time! You know, my lord, my duties are to watch over this temple and all the lost souls around it and make their prayers more efficient to the temple and pleasant to almighty Qu'mun. Mediums need to be well trained. They must chant their psalms correctly as the one who is praying reaches divine ecstasy."

I couldn't believe my ears; this looked like a brothel, rather than a temple.

"And you preach this to the people?" I asked, realising that it sounded more like a rhetorical question.

"You can't imagine how successful the idea to use mediums was." The priest dried his forehead with a napkin. "Incomes have never been higher. Of course, it's hard to find the right mediums, but, to be honest, hopeless mediums can still be used as the Silent. And they are quite expensive..." He winked.

"Silent?"

"You are certainly very far from the religion, my Lord," he carefully folded his napkin. "If the medium is stupid and unable to memorise psalms, still we can carve those psalms on their fresh bodies for the use of those who prefer to pray in silence..."

"Bodies?" I couldn't believe my ears.

"Yes," the priest nodded. "Still, silent bodies... that's why they are called the Silent."

I nearly choked – a spasm in my throat.

"And whose bright idea was this entire establishment?" I was boiling inside, but glancing at the size of Kyaal's neck, I instantly suppressed the urge to strangle him.

"I know, I know..." he sighed. "Two-thirds goes to the treasury, as agreed. I had some unexpected expenses, but I will pay everything back, only give me two more weeks. I have one stubborn here, and a particular merchant, who prefers to pray in silence, is coming next week. Everything will be solved."

He was clearly implying that I was supposed to be aware of this atrocity, and even that I was benefiting from it! That was outrageous even for a dream! I could never have even thought of anything like this. Never, even in my worst nightmares! Someone else had trapped me into this, I was sure, but this realisation came with a sense of guilt. I started to hate the sick person who had occupied my Rehen body before me. And I began to hate that mountain of fat which stood in front of me. The priest was a powerful man, thanks to this brutal and disgusting idea of my predecessor. I had to find a way to put an end on this.

"Sweet tits of Maralyn!" the priest exclaimed suddenly. "How ignorant I am! Please forgive me, my Lord. If you wish to thank Qu'mun almighty, we could provide you with the best medium – the best girl or woman you choose. Or would you like to pray with a man? We have all types and sizes. Just name it, my Lord."

Had my predecessor used to *pray* here? That felt like a trap. Would Kyaal dare to oust me or even kill me? The situation was a swamp, and I felt that I couldn't confront him directly without exposing my weakness.

"I don't feel well enough for this..." I told him vaguely, feeling less heroic with every passing minute.

The priest was three times, at least, bigger than me; he was still polite, but I felt a distant menace behind his cunning smile. I had to dig deeper before taking any action.

"You have never been particularly religious, my Lord," admitted Kyaal. "But maybe this time, when death has been so close to you, you will find some strength to thank Qu'mun for the second chance in life."

I suppressed my disgust, as the priest took my elbow and led me to a soft couch alongside the wall to my left. A sense of danger slowly crawled into my heart, nearly paralysing my will. He fished out two goblets and a bottle from the nearby drawer.

"I did not come here to pray," I told him.

"Of course, my Lord," he nodded, pouring wine into the goblets. "But I hope you will not refuse me the honour of sharing a few drops of wine with you?"

I accepted the goblet and carefully sniffed the wine. The bouquet was fruity, with a touch of pepper.

"You must not fear, my lord," chuckled the priest, taking a good gulp. "It is not poisoned. You have a friend here."

Such a flat declaration of friendliness made me even more cautious.

"To those countless lost souls down there." He gestured towards the wall to his left as he made the toast, grinning.

He looked at me with unblinking eyes, like a snake would look at the approaching rabbit. I forced myself to raise the goblet, pressed it to my lips, but refrained from swallowing a single drop. I didn't trust him and now regretted my hasty decision to come here alone.

"Any news from the Order, my lord?" asked Kyaal, filling his goblet with another portion of wine and landing his massive body on the edge of the couch, next to me. "Maybe we should play differently?"

I shook my head, having no idea of what he was talking about.

"Then may I ask you what concerns brought you here?" The

priest took a long look directly into my eyes, and the smile vanished from his face.

"Abinaer," I said, returning the gaze.

He chuckled, making a quick gesture like scaring away a fly.

"You don't need to worry," he said with his smile crawling back on his lips. "I have solved everything as you wished – quickly, efficiently, not too harshly."

"Why was his death necessary?"

"I see your point," he said, smiling again and even attempting to wink. "He could make a decent medium after proper training. Waste of material, of course. But under the circumstances, that public death had a strong educational value for other lost souls down there. It was an easy decision. He confessed after the lightest of tortures; we barely touched him."

The talk was a waste of time. I felt sick of him. The man sincerely believed that he did the right thing! Then I remembered that poor medium, sentenced to be one of the Silents. The vision of Kyaal carving someone's skin with a sharp knife was scary, and this instantly made up my mind.

"I want to see that your stubborn useless medium," I told him.

"Honestly, my Lord, it's a waste of time. I have never seen anybody less useless." He smiled bitterly. "May I suggest someone else, more experienced?"

"No, I want to see this one," I said firmly. "And I am not in the mood to argue with you..."

Kyaal looked into my eyes as if expecting to read the answer to his puzzle there.

"Very well," he said at last. "Let it be as you wish. You had been warned about his skills. And keep in mind that I may need five weeks instead of two to fill your treasury."

"I don't care about skills, priest," I said calmly. "I won't let that medium die."

I knew this sounded too harsh. Kyaal jumped to his feet, suddenly gasping for air and casting his goblet aside.

"Your people are *my* lost souls, my Lord, and a very good source of income for both – the temple and the castle," he wheezed through his teeth. "The Order will not approve this..."

"It's my problem, not yours," I told him, still sitting. "Will you dare to disobey your Lord?"

I felt myself on a slippery ground and in complete darkness. I had no idea what I was challenging, but I couldn't let another innocent person die.

"Very well, *my Lord*," Kyaal was still short of breath. "I hope you have another plan for how to keep the Order amused."

"We will see..." my voice was sufficiently low that it hid the crippling fear and anxiety.

Kyaal crossed the room and barked a short command to

someone in the corridor. Then he returned, fished out another goblet from his drawer, filled it with wine and gulped it all down in a single shot. When he looked back at me, his eyes were calm again, and his tight lips even managed to squeeze out a nervous smile.

"Forgive me the roughness, my Lord," he said. "I am only a humble servant, while you are the player of a higher level. I have no knowledge of your ways."

He sat down on the couch next to me again, and we waited in silence. A few minutes later, Obie came in, followed by somebody wrapped in a dark cloak.

"As you requested, your holiness," Obie said, addressing Kyaal and completely ignoring me.

"Thank you, dear friend," said the priest. "You may go now."

Obie slipped a damning glance at me but didn't say a word.

"He is all yours," the priest said to me when Obie left. "Care to unwrap?"

The silhouette under the dark cloak visibly shrank and shuddered. Kyaal chuckled, pouring himself more wine.

"No," I said. "It's cold outside. We are leaving now."

"As you wish, my Lord." He raised his gobbled and grinned widely before gulping down the wine.

"Let's go," I told the wrapped silhouette and headed to the door.

We left without saying goodbye. The door closed with a bang when we were several paces down the corridor, and I stopped.

"Do you know the shortest way out?" I asked.

"Yes, my Lord," the breaking voice of the teen boy answered.

"Then lead us out," I hated the place and didn't like the aimless wandering around.

The boy obeyed without a word. We swiftly paced up several staircases, then through terraces, halls, and corridors. Cries, moans, and chants marked our way through omnipresent music. *Faster! Faster!* I felt sick of the place.

It was raining outside. I wrapped myself tightly in my cloak and lowered the hood, and we started down the long way to the foot of the mountain, where the city soaked in the misty rain.

"Will you kill me, my Lord?" asked the boy quietly as we went.

"No." I was firm and sure. "You are safe with me. What is your name?"

"Milo."

"No one will harm you, Milo," I assured him. "Do you know the shortest way to the castle?"

"I do, my Lord," said Milo. "But that route is not a very pleasant one."

"I don't care. I want the fastest route."

"Then follow me, my Lord..." Several paces later, Milo turned sharply to the right, off the main road, and we slipped into a narrow track through the thick shrubs. It was barely visible, but Milo seemed to know the way. We crossed a tiny creek and entered the green wall of the woods, which engulfed us like a hungry mouth.

Several paces later, the track turned steeply uphill, winding between occasional black boulders. That was strange, since the castle was at the foot of the mountain, not on top of it.

"Are you sure you know the way?" I did my best not to sound frightened – *why had I trusted that strange youngster when I hadn't even seen his face?*

"Yes, my Lord, don't worry. It is the fastest route." He sounded certain. "We only need to bend over the city."

"I can only see the woods around." I stopped walking. "Where is the city?"

"I can show you if you want..." Milo stopped too. Only now did I get a partial glimpse of his face – deep, dark eyes, thin brows and a flock of thick black hair sticking out from under the hood of his cloak.

"Yes," I said. "Let's have a look..."

Milo went off the track and turned left behind a large hanging rock. I followed closely. The path was narrow, winding between thick shrubs. Several hundred yards later, we got out of the woods and into the rounded rocky plain, not larger than two hundred paces wide. The other side of the plain ended abruptly with a massive hanging cliff rising over the abyss, edged by crooked stone pillars at the far side. It resembled a giant's palm lifted to the sky.

I frowned when a sudden stink of rotten flesh hit my nostrils. "What is this place?" I asked.

"The Grave of the Silent, my Lord," said Milo quietly. "The city is below."

I climbed a few stairs carved into the wrist of the giant palm and froze in disbelief. Bones were scattered everywhere across the place, unmistakably human, judging by several skulls, as well as a few piles of rotting flesh and bare carcasses in their midst.

Beyond this horror were the countless red roofs of Chadrack's capital, laid out below, with the black castle visible in the distance, all covered with a mist of light rain.

I turned back to Milo, who was waiting for me at the foot of the cliff.

"They never build pyres for the Silent. Their bodies are just dumped here," said the youngster quietly. "The Silent never get up to the Wyrna through the Road of Gods, and their souls are lost forever."

"How do you know this?"

"Everyone in the temple knows," Milo's voice was slow and sad. "I don't want to die like this..."

"That is ridiculous! No one will touch you, Milo. You have my word," I said, taking one more glance at the bones, and then stepping back from the cliff. "I didn't know anything about that horror. This needs to be fixed. Let's go!"

"Yes, my Lord!" Milo led us back to the track.

I stepped after the boy silently, barely paying attention to the surroundings. The Grave shocked me deeply. It was wrong in so many ways! Everything about the temple was wrong, but the most disturbing thing was the implication of my part in all those atrocities. *But how to end this?* The question slashed me like a whip, and fears began a battle in my head – a difficult battle against the rage and sadness, and I felt the latter winning.

Milo stepped silently, and I could only imagine what thoughts of horror were swirling in his head.

The path went down, and later, when the crooked trees stepped aside and were left behind, the black walls of the castle appeared drowning in the verdancy of gardens.

"We have arrived, my Lord," announced Milo, before stopping and stepping out of my way. "I have brought you to the castle."

The task was still too complicated for me.

"I am not familiar enough with this part of the castle," I gave up without even trying. "Please, take me closer to my chambers."

"I am not that familiar with the castle either, I am afraid, my

Lord," said Milo, shaking his head. "I have never been closer than that..."

He looked at me, his dark eyes full of fear, like a lamb would look at its slaughterer.

"Do you know the way to the gate near the river?" I wasn't sure how to explain that. "The one next to the Throne Hall?"

As I finished my question, he visibly shrank but nodded quickly.

"We had to attend the latest execution... The priest told us..."

"It doesn't matter what he said!" I exploded, and Milo jumped back, covering his face. "Don't be afraid; only show me the way."

The rain started pouring down again.

"Let's go, or we'll get cold." I took his elbow. "Which way?"

"I thought you would release me now, my Lord," he whispered. "I have brought you to the castle, as you wished."

"I am not holding you," I told him, taking my emotions under control and letting go of his elbow. "Only show me the way, and you will be free to go."

He nodded quickly, and we started to move left, along the tall wall of black stones. The path was narrow, circling the garden from the south. We passed the gate to the inner yard, and then entered the long gallery paved with hewn black basalt. We stopped there, waiting for the rain to ease.

"Do you have a family here?" I asked Milo.

"No, my Lord, I am alone."

"Where will you go then?"

Milo shrugged before answering, "To the caves..."

I knew nothing about the caves, of course, but it didn't sound like the right place for the frightened teen to be. I felt guilty for this lad and those other youths whose bones I saw scattered across the Grave of the Silent today. I felt a bitter desire to crush the temple, but I knew I had to act wisely – Kyaal could easily break my back if I attacked without proper preparation. I had no idea how strong religious feelings were here, but it was the temple, not the castle that dominated the skyline in Chadrack.

We resumed our way and were instantly soaked by a sudden burst of rain. The air began to cool, and when we reached the yard in front of my balcony, the day was slowly sinking into dusk already. Milo was visibly shivering.

"Would you like a cup of hot tea, or maybe some dinner?" I asked.

Milo glanced at me with his sad eyes but said nothing.

"Don't be afraid, be my guest. You are still free to go and may leave whenever you like," I assured him. "When you have eaten something last time?"

"Almost a week ago, my Lord," Milo's voice was barely audible. "Silents are supposed to fast before the final ceremony.

103

They must be clean for the final prayer."

That bloody priest! I clenched my fists under my cloak, but Milo noticed.

"Please, my Lord," he nearly begged. "Don't tell anybody, or they will kill me!"

"You are under my protection, remember?" I took his elbow and gently led him to the door. "Let's go. You need dry clothes and some warm food."

He followed me without objection, but I noticed some stiffness in his steps.

We crossed the corridor and met Carwyn on our way. The old butler bowed when I asked to dress Milo decently and get us some hot meal. He took the kid somewhere, and I traced the way to my chambers. My room was filled with dusk and the soft sound of the rain outside.

I quickly stripped and placed my wet clothes on a chair and then rubbed myself dry with a towel. I found the fresh set of garments and began to dress, but was interrupted by a gentle tap on my door.

"Come in!"

Carwyn came to ask where I would like to dine.

"Any room with a hot burning hearth around?" I asked, still feeling chilled by the damp weather.

Carwyn nodded.

"Follow me, my Lord."

We got back into the corridor and turned left. Carwyn led me to the room next to my chambers, opened the door and then politely stepped aside.

The room was spacious with a dark wooden table placed in the middle. Flames were happily crackling in the fireplace, and it was pleasantly warm.

"Nice." I smiled. "I will have my dinner here. And bring that boy as well, please."

Carwyn bowed and left without saying a word. I placed my chair closer to the hearth and sat down, enjoying the warmth.

Carwyn returned a few minutes later with Milo. The boy was dressed in dark brown trousers and a clean white shirt. They were shortly followed by several kitchen boys who brought in food baskets, placed our dinner on the table and left.

"Be my guest," I gestured Milo, pouring myself a glass of wine.

He hesitantly approached the table and took an apple, looking like a frightened bird.

"Calm down, Milo," I smiled to him. "You are my guest, and nobody will hurt you. You may eat as much as you like, so help yourself."

He took a small bite of his apple, fear still in his eyes.

"Why are you afraid?" I demanded.

"I don't want to be ungrateful, my Lord," Milo muttered. "But everything was the same with the priest in the beginning..."

"I am not that bloody priest!" I wasn't quick enough to hold my temper. Milo flinched at the outburst. "And I keep my word," I added in a quieter voice. "No one will harm you. You may leave whenever you want. Just fill your stomach before you go, please. Take a seat and eat as much as you want."

"I will do as you wish, my Lord," Milo took a seat.

"That's better," I nodded, encouraging him and put a piece of ham on my plate.

Milo filled his plate with salad and put a small piece of ham on top as well.

"How did you get into the temple?" I asked him while chewing my ham.

Milo blushed and put the food aside.

"They caught me stealing, my Lord," he murmured. "I took a loaf of bread from the baker's store, and they caught me. I know I did wrong, my lord, but I was starving."

I repeated my question. "But how did you got into that temple?"

"They brought me to the temple for a trial," Milo shrugged as if I was asking something trivial and well-known. "And the priest sentenced me to serve as a medium."

"Did he rape you?"

"He taught me to be a medium if that is what you mean. He made me memorise the psalm, but when he forced his... thing into me, I couldn't chant any psalm – I could only scream. I was a bad medium. That's why he condemned me to be the Silent."

I was shocked and speechless.

"He will never lay his hands on you," I promised. "Do you believe me?"

"I do, my Lord," whispered Milo, lowering his head.

"Don't be afraid, please," I said. "You are safe here. Please eat whatever you want. You are hungry."

Milo attempted a shy smile and then added some chicken to his plate. I kept my calm expression on the outside but was raging inside. How could that bloody priest be so heartless and selfish? Who gave him power? Then I remembered that, sadly, it was the ruler of Chadrack. I must correct these errors somehow. But I must do it wisely.

"There is only one thing I would like to ask you to do before you go to the caves," I said, sipping my wine and looking at Milo chewing the chicken.

He stopped.

"I am not sure, that my men will be able to find the way to the Grave of Silent," I said. "Would you be able to show the way? We need a proper funeral for all those bodies up there."

Milo nodded.

"Of course, my Lord," he said. "I will gladly show the way. But the priest will be furious..."

"I don't care." I was firm. "Do you?"

Milo shrugged and returned to his chicken. I ate some cheese and a piece of ham, washing everything down with perfect red wine.

Later, when Carwyn checked on us, I instructed him to organise a funeral for the human remnants we had seen today and to give Milo a suitable chamber to stay until the issue was resolved.

"Yes, my Lord," said Carwyn. After a short pause, he added: "what kind of pervert could do that?"

"First, we have a duty to put those people at rest. We will avenge them later," I said, choosing not to disclose my confrontation with the temple at this moment. "Milo will show the way tomorrow..."

Carwyn nodded and led Milo to his room. I was left alone to enjoy the warmth of burning logs in the hearth and the pleasant warmth of wine in my stomach.

It was getting late. I filled my goblet and retraced the way to my room. The bed was cold but inviting. I slipped under the covers, and the soft sound of falling rain lulled me into nothingness.

Soft tapping of raindrops on my window carried me out of the darkness. For a few heartbeats, I thought I was back in Rehen, but then an ambulance siren screamed down the street. I sat up and grabbed my phone. Three missed alarms, and two missed calls – both, of course, from the office. I had missed my train as well, and I was terribly late!

I jumped out of bed, erratically dressing, brushing teeth and combing on my way. Then I called Julie.

"Are you okay?" she asked.

"Yes, I am fine. Did I miss anything serious?" I asked, grabbing my brolly and running downstairs.

"Mrs Patel was asking for you," she said, after a short pause. "Is that serious enough?"

Mrs Adrika Patel was an elderly Indian lady. She was our boss. Her quiet voice with its perfect, Queen's-English pronunciation was seldom heard around the office, but when it was, this usually meant trouble. I felt weak at the knees but forced myself to run downhill to the railway station.

"What did she want?" I asked, hoping for some trivial and innocent answer.

"She wasn't that specific," said Julie. "I said that your train was late due to flooding. And it actually was cancelled – I checked on the web."

"Thanks Julie!" I was overwhelmed with a sudden wave of gratitude. "I owe you a coffee!"

"You'd better hurry..."

The train was on the platform already. I squeezed in through the closing door and then dropped down onto a random seat.

Trees and houses were moving past my window, rinsed by generous pouring rain, but I only closed my eyes, unable to look at anything, still trembling inside. Mrs Patel had never laid her dark eyes on me before. *Why had she asked for me now? I was just another grey rat in the office...* I hid behind my closed eyelids, letting only sounds to penetrate my consciousness.

I paid no attention to the stations where the train stopped, or to the people getting on or off. The endless green hills of Kent were in front of me when I opened my eyes again. The rain was behind us, still soaking London. The clouds were low and thick, but the roads here were dry.

When I finally rushed into the office, my wet brolly under my arm, Julie was chatting with Tom. She noticed me and nodded lightly, but turned all her attention back to Tom. I sneaked into my room and turned on my computer, my hands shaking. Nearly half an hour passed before Julie appeared on the doorstep, carrying the pile of papers.

"What about Mrs Patel?" I asked.

She smiled, teasing me.

"She left more than an hour ago – something urgent in London," she winked. "She asked me to give you this."

"What is this?"

"Some old files," she said, placing the pile on my desk. "But I think you should look at them more urgently. Mrs Patel doesn't like to wait for too long "

"Then I need a large cup of coffee," I told her. "I didn't have any time for this in the morning. And I still owe you a cup – will you join me?"

"That is nice, but not necessary." Julie blushed slightly. "But if you insist…"

I insisted.

The cafeteria was sleepy and nearly empty. The rush, when everybody tried to grab some stimulus in the form of tea or coffee before the working day began, was over.

"What would you like?" I asked.

She asked for a medium latte and a toffee muffin. I placed an order, adding my large cappuccino to what Julie had requested, while she navigated to the side table at the far end of the canteen.

"I forgot to ask – is that your... Asper... whatever, contagious?" she asked cautiously trying her coffee, which I had placed in front of her.

"No... it is congenital," I explained patiently. "I am not sure if I have it. I just feel better by alienating myself from society. I prefer to be alone, and any socialising is hard for me, not for society."

"Then I need to cancel that daily disinfection of your room," she murmured.

"What? That's silly."

"I am sorry," she blushed. "I had no idea what you were talking about, so I asked the cleaners. Just to be on the safe side..."

Damn! How far that my silly innocent confession went in the office?

"I'd better go," Julie said, standing up and taking her coffee and muffin. "I have a lot of work."

She left me gaping, sitting at the table and clutching my cappuccino. *Fool! Why did I have to say that?* I was doomed – now everyone in the office would make jokes about this and laugh behind my back.

I picked up my coffee and returned to my room, passing Julie's desk on my way. She pretended to study her computer, holding the muffin in her right hand, and paid no attention to my glances.

Back in my room, I sat at my desk and drank my cappuccino for a couple of minutes before I was able to organise my thoughts at last and dive into Mrs Patel's files.

I spent the rest of the day shuffling through those old folders. Mrs Patel didn't show up. Later on the train, I kept on rolling over that silly talk with Julie in my mind when my damned tongue had slipped on Asperger's. I knew I had to be more cautious.

On my way home, I quickly bought some groceries from a nearby shop and ate my lonely dinner before slipping into bed.

The night pressed down firmly on my eyelids, as my mind drifted away.

The morning in Chadrack was sweet and merry. I opened eyes as the sun warmly touched my cheek. The room was empty, but I noticed a bowl of water and towels on my table – Carwyn had checked on me already.

I washed my face and got dressed, and before I could get bored, the old butler appeared in the doorway, carrying my breakfast.

"Lovely morning, my Lord," greeted me Carwyn, placing the food basket on my table. "Do you wish me to find Rhys for you?"

I told him that I did want him to, indeed. Then I filled my stomach with juicy ham and fresh bread. I reminded him to summon Milo and several men to the Grave of the Silent.

"They are on their way as we speak, my Lord," said Carwyn. "You must not worry. Those people will be placed on their pyres with dignity, as you wished."

"Thank you, Carwyn," I said, washing my food down with a gulp of wine.

He bowed and left. An hour later, he returned with Rhys, who was carrying two wooden sticks. I whistled for Bysh. Rhys raised a brow but kept his remarks to himself. I felt much more confident with my dog!

We silently passed through several corridors and a few staircases before we got outside. Rhys took a different route, one I hadn't seen before. We emerged to a narrow backstreet framed by tall windowless walls. Rhys went first, leading the way. Bysh was close to his heels, and I stepped after them. The road was winding and dark, only with a narrow strip of the blue sky above us. It ended no more than a hundred yards later, and we turned left to the broader street with red-roofed buildings, which stretched up to the foot of the mountains to the north. A few blocks we went uphill, then Rhys turned right to another backstreet which was winding between the dark houses, and several turns later we reached the outer wall. Two men were guarding the small but heavy door. Rhys dropped a few words, and they let us through.

There was no roads or paths outside, only tall and dark forest.

We went on, silently as before. Rhys marched ahead, apparently knowing the way. I tried my best to keep up with him, while Bysh ran alongside us, sometimes disappearing into nearby shrubs to check for rabbits. We passed a few small creeks but didn't stop at any of them.

The barely visible path wound uphill. We passed between spiky shrubs and large boulders covered with moss. Rhys followed the track for some time until we reached an ample grassy clearance, and stopped.

"This place is big enough and far from any peeping eyes, my Lord," he told me, glancing around.

I shrugged, slightly gasping air from the long run. It was no big difference to me.

"You are known to be a famous swordsman, far better than me. What kind of training do you expect, my Lord?" asked Rhys. "I am don't know if I could show you any tricks which you haven't mastered yet."

I was prepared for the question like this. "I don't know either." I sighed. "I think I don't remember anything. Let's start with the most trivial things, and we will find out if and where we can make any shortcuts."

Rhys shrugged and gave me one of the wooden sticks, quickly explaining how to hold it correctly. Then we stood *en garde*. His first attack was a slow *en sixte* – I easily blocked it. He smiled.

"Just let your body free, and it will remember, my Lord!" Rhys smiled and raised his stick.

His next attack was *en quarte*, which I quickly blocked as well before attacking myself and, surprisingly, reaching his shoulder through his defence.

I was amazed when my body swung into automation, waking up reflexes which were buried somewhere deep in my subconscious. Rhys was right – I did things I had no idea I knew! Soon we were running around the clearance, attacking and blocking, attacking again and blocking again.

Bysh stretched out on the soft grass, lazily watching us as we sweated in that strange dance with wooden sticks. We chased each other across the field like two kids – attacking and blocking, seeking out weak spots, then attacking again, until we were both completely drained. Only then we stopped, gasping for air.

"You are as good as always, my Lord!" Rhys observed with a serious expression. "Do you think you need any more training?"

I could feel the strength of my body but still lacked the experience to control it. Quick reflexes were great, but I needed their connection with my mind if I wanted to win any battle.

"I think we will keep occasional training, depending on the weather," I told him and handed back the wooden sword.

Rhys nodded. I whistled to Bysh, and we started downhill, stopping by a clear stream to drink and wash the sweat from our faces.

The journey back to the castle was quick and silent. We picked up the pace, and I only followed Rhys. He hailed somebody when we reached the gate, which was barely visible from the forest. The armed man looked down from a narrow arrowslit high up in the wall and shouted back. The gate opened, and we were in the city again.

I instantly noticed a strand of grey smoke rising from the top of the cliff, which loomed high above the town like the hand of a giant. My order had been carried out scrupulously. The flames on the palm were visible even from here.

We took a path back to the castle, and, a few crossroads later, we bumped into the seemingly endless stream of people rushing down the street. Rhys tried asking questions, but it seemed nobody knew anything. We joined the flow.

I whistled to Bysh. The dog had no collar, and I wanted to keep him close. A few angry faces turned to me, but with instant recognition, all chose to remain silent. There was a strange agitation all around. Nobody talked, but a feeling of growing menace hovered as the crowd grew.

We rushed down towards the castle. As we went, more people joined us from the side streets. Was it another show of Kyaal's? Who was being executed this time? I knew I had to put a stop to it.

Rhys touched my shoulder and silently indicated a door on the left. I nodded, and we slipped through, leaving the moving crowd behind.

"It's a shortcut," explained Rhys closing the door behind us. "It is faster and might be safer."

We passed through a small, peaceful garden. Rhys took a narrow path to the left, alongside the outer wall. I followed him closely. We emerged to the quiet backstreet, heading west. Bysh cautiously sniffed the air, and I saw hair on this coat rising. We passed a few tightly shut doors, and Rhys turned left, taking a narrow path between two houses.

"Sorry for the dirt, my Lord," he whispered, "but this is the shortest way."

Bysh slipped after him, his fur still raised, and I went after them. The path was damp and slippery and smelled of urine and fungi, but a hundred paces later, we emerged through the small door next to the gate. The crowd was gathering there, in front of my balcony, and I could hear some women crying. A hushed murmur passed around as we appeared, and people instantly stepped aside to let us through.

"It's a curse!" a woman cried out. "We shouldn't have that boy executed!"

This time, it wasn't anything to do with Kyaal – the fat priest was nowhere in sight. A large body of the dead animal was in the middle of the yard, right in the place where Abinaer had lost his head a few days ago. The dead beast was as big as a bull, and had an eagle's head on its shoulders, crowned with shiny brown feathers. It had the tail of a lion and strong back legs, partly covered by enormous brown-and-white-feathered wings. The front legs distantly resembled talons of a bird of prey, with large claws that were still squeezing a dead, bloodied lamb. It looked like those creatures on the ring I had found in the forest, and I realised at last, that I had a dead gryphon under my balcony.

"What happened?" I asked calmly.

"It fell from the sky..." explained the old man next to me, seemingly scared to death. "It nearly hit me."

"It's a bad omen!" a woman cried. "It's a terrible omen!"

A black shadow flashed next to me, and people rushed aside as Bysh, growling and barking, attacked the dead creature. The crowd gasped, but nobody found enough courage to restrain the dog.

I turned back to Rhys.

"Is it really dead?" I asked.

The crowd hastily retreated, leaving me, Rhys and Bysh standing alongside the creature.

Rhys stepped forward, shielding me with his body, but Bysh continued to circle the unmoving figure, growling, biting and barking.

A faint, barely visible glistening mist was rising from the dead animal and vanishing in the cool breeze. A few minutes later, it was gone, and Bysh stopped barking and returned to my side with pride glaring in his eyes.

I probed the dead animal with my boot. No wounds were visible, and I couldn't see any blood.

Shouts came from the crowd: "We are doomed!" and "Gods have cursed us!". And a woman kept on repeating: "It's a bad omen!"

I glanced around. Some of the women were softly sobbing, and some of the men were exchanging glances in growing agitation. I knew I must give some direction to the crowd, or the crowd would start to direct itself. I turned to Rhys and calmly ordered him to take the dead body out of the castle and burn it.

I didn't wait to see how my order was carried out. The crowd parted as I passed, doing my best not to fix my gaze on anyone. Bysh followed me.

Back in my chambers, I spread out on the bed, resting my aching body. It was silent outside, but the feeling of dread still was in the air. I didn't believe in superstitions, but that dead animal scared me. What other monsters were swarming in those woods around? Minutes became hours before a gentle tap on the door interrupted my contemplations. It was Carwyn with a food basket.

"The men have just returned from the mountain. They did as you commanded, my Lord," he told me while arranging my food on the table.

"Splendid," I said and sat up. "Where is Milo? I want to see him before he goes."

"He is in the temple of Qu'mun, my Lord…"

"What?!" I sprang from the bed like a tiger.

"I have been told that priest Kyaal joined them on the mountain and held a lovely ceremony for the deceased, my Lord," Carwyn looked frightened. "My men said that he had ordered Milo to accompany him."

I moaned. *This could not be happening! It couldn't be true! He couldn't really be about to die!*

"Get me a dozen armed men. Now!" I ordered firmly, adjusting my waistcoat. "We are going to the temple. We will bring Milo back!"

"I will fetch some jaegers…" Carwyn ran out of my chambers.

We had to act quickly. Could we take horses? I couldn't ride a horse properly – but I had to do it anyway! I had a very grave feeling that Milo was in the great and imminent danger. And this time, it was entirely my fault: I had asked him to show the Grave; I had put him at risk.

"Get the horses!" I ripped the door and shouted to the retreating Carwyn, quickly making up my mind and gathering courage.

He stopped only briefly, turned to face me and nodded. I closed the door and leant on the wall. I wasn't ready for this, but the exercise with Rhys this morning had planted a tiny seed of self-confidence in my soul. *I had to do this! I had to! If I didn't, the boy would die.*

I took a deep breath and opened the door again. The corridor was empty, and I turned to the right, heading in the same direction as Carwyn.

I found myself amid erratic movements in the yard. The men were shouting and running around, the women and children were getting out of their way and screaming with fright. I saw Carwyn talking to the armed guard and agitatedly gesturing in my direction. Moments later, men in full armour were lined up behind me; on horses, as I requested. I paled when the stableboy brought me saddled and shining stallion from the stables, but I managed to stand firm anyway. The horse looked frightening to me, but luckily, the beautiful animal knew the ruler of this land already, and a simple pat on his neck was sufficient to calm him. The boy helped me to mount, and I took reins in my right hand. The men were waiting for my orders; I had to think quickly. I wasn't sure if I would be able to retrace the way to the temple while riding a horse. I had got lost more than once on foot last time.

"We are going to the temple," I told my men.

Nobody moved. I pointed to the nearest man.

"You lead the way," I ordered and pointed at two more. "You

and you – guard my flanks. The rest will follow us!"

The orders set the whole party into motion, leaving behind the gasping and screaming crowd. I had no time for explanations; we had to save Milo!

The street was nearly empty. It led uphill, winding slightly as it passed between the red-roofed buildings. A few times the leading rider had to shout orders to get random pedestrians out of the way. We passed several squares and stopped at the foot of the long balustrade staircase, which led through the intricate gardens to the temple high above the city – the rest of the way we had to cover on foot. I dismounted and left one man behind to watch the horses.

The ascent was difficult. I was drained of energy after my vigorous exercise with Rhys. I went as fast as I could, and the men followed me dutifully, adjusting to my pace. They still bought the story of my poisoning.

The top of the staircase was empty and painted blood-red by the setting sun. I opened the door and stepped into the dusk of the entrance hall. The men followed me.

It was dark and quiet, and I spotted Obie at the far end of the corridor, slowly approaching.

"Greetings, my Lord," said the androgynous figure, still halfway to us. "Sorry for the delays: we weren't expecting any visitors. What can I do for you and your brave men?"

"I want to see Milo," I said. "Immediately. Alive."

Obie paused.

"Milo? Who is Milo?"

"Don't play with me!" My voice was surprisingly harsh.

"Are you threatening the Great temple of Qu'mun with those few men?" asked Obie calmly, gesturing with disdain.

"No," I told him; my eyes drilling into the ageless face, my voice low. "But those few men will be more than sufficient to send you directly to Qu'mun if you won't cooperate. Then we will find what we are seeking."

Obie considered my threat, suddenly less confident.

"Where is the boy?" I demanded.

"Oh." Obie took half a step back. "That boy! I never thought you were interested in the Silent, my Lord."

"You may pay dearly for your insults," I squeezed through my teeth, slowly approaching him. "I need Milo right now. Alive!"

"That might be a problem," said Obie retreating. "He is halfway through the ceremony of Initiation already."

A sudden chill squeezed my heart. We might be too late.

"Take us there. Now!"

Obie appeared slightly shaken while bowing to me and wasting a few more seconds.

"Follow me, my Lord."

I gestured to my men.

We swiftly passed through the dark corridor, which last time was filled with ecstatic moans and screams, but now laid quiet and empty. We crossed another hall before Obie hesitatingly stopped in front of a tightly shut door.

"It is here," whispered the sexless creature, looking away. "You shouldn't interfere with the ceremony."

I pushed Obie aside and opened the door.

The room was small and windowless, as I expected.

"Who dares to disturb the Initiation?!" Kyaal asked angrily as I entered.

The massive wooden table was in the centre of the room, obscured in part by the mighty curves of the priest. He didn't look back, still busy with whatever he was doing. I noticed the naked body of Milo, prone and tied to the table. His dark eyes were popping out of their sockets as he moaned in pain, a dirty plug in his mouth. His pale skin was covered with blood, but he was still alive!

"What are you doing?" I asked – or screamed; I don't remember.

"Nobody in the temple knows psalms better than me," said the priest, rising from Milo and turning to face me – a bloodied rag in one hand and an elegant stiletto in the other. Noticing my men filling the room, he hesitantly added "my Lord..."

I quickly glanced at Milo's back where words of a psalm were carved, cut deep into his skin.

"I told you: this boy is under my protection." My voice was calm and steely. "How dare you to disobey me?"

"Qu'mun wanted him back, and he returned to me," Kyaal shrugged. "I am just a humble servant."

His face was covered in speckles of blood, frightening in the quivering light of the candles. The priest's lips were colourless and pressed tightly, while his bitter gaze drilled holes in my face. I took a few more paces forward, getting closer to him.

"Now, would you let me finish the job, my Lord?" he said, placing himself between Milo and me.

"Are you threatening me?" I asked and surprised myself by placing a hand on Kyaal's chest and pushing him aside – my body began to behave like a robotic doll, frightening me and making me feel like a mere observer of my own actions.

"Not every erection ends in sex, my Lord," Kyaal whispered with a cunning smile. "We can still reach an agreement which will be acceptable to everyone. It's up to you to decide, of course, but may I suggest you be more attentive to the Order. I heard the Nightcrawlers were seen in the mountains. The life of a boy means nothing compared to the kingdom."

"Step aside!" I hissed through my teeth.

He didn't dare to interfere any longer. I took the plug out of

Milo's mouth. The boy just moaned, unable even to cry.

"Your handwriting is terrible..." I observed, taking the stiletto out of the priest's hand and gesturing to my men. "Release him!"

My order was carried out immediately. They cut Milo's bonds and lifted up his naked body, but the poor boy couldn't stand on his limping legs and collapsed on the floor.

"Find something to cover his back," I ordered, still facing Kyaal. "We will carry Milo. I am not leaving him behind."

Not a muscle moved on the priest's face. We stood like two chunks of ice confronting each other, despite the chaos around and the loud protests of Obie in the corridor.

"I hope you know what you are doing..." hissed Kyaal through his teeth.

I kept my sullen silence, but deep inside my heart was trembling with fear. I had no doubt that I had just acquired a deadly enemy. I had yet to find out how powerful that enemy was.

I turned around and left, casting the stiletto away in disgust. Three men were carrying poor Milo, while others guarded our flanks as we made our way back to the exit. Nobody dared to confront us or follow.

The grey wings of the early dusk wrapped us up as we emerged from the temple and started our long journey down the endless staircase. Milo moaned from time to time, and occasional drops of blood still were dripping from his carved-up back. The wounds were painful. I hoped he would recover, but we had to find a healer – and do that fast. Only then did I notice that he was wrapped up in Obie's robes. Secretly, I smiled to myself. This added one more enemy to my growing list.

They placed the poor boy on a horse, and we swept away as quickly as shadows.

Carwyn met us in the yard, lighting our way with a torch.

"He needs a healer," I stated this as a simple fact.

He cast a quick glance at Milo's still-bleeding body and nodded silently. I slipped off the horse, keeping a grip on the saddle, my strength slowly draining away. It had been too much of everything for me. I needed some rest.

I didn't wait to watch how they carried Milo away. I knew he was safe here.

Bysh approached me from nowhere, touching my hand with his head and demanding cuddles. At least he was happy to see me and not concerned at all by any of the new enemies I had managed to acquire.

I patted his head and went inside, navigating the corridors and staircases of the castle. Bysh followed me to my chambers, ready to guard me as I slept.

I reached my room and laid my aching body on the bed. The next moment I was sleeping soundly. Dinner waited on the table, untouched.

My aching muscles woke me up well before the alarm clock sounded. I stretched on the bed, trying to recall everything I had learned while exercising with Rhys when I suddenly realised that the training had been in my dream. Despite that, the aches in my muscles were real. I got up, dressed, swallowed two pills of painkillers with my coffee and went out.

As soon as I lifted my eyes, the grey skies above south London blasted me into a dark mood. At least it wasn't raining. The train was on time, and several minutes later, I found myself rushing towards Kent, in a state of the darkest morning melancholy.

Julie met me in the corridor, nervous and impatient. I was about to start smiling at her when she grabbed my elbow and nearly dragged me towards my room.

"What happened?" I asked.

She forced me inside, casting suspicious glances down the

corridor.

"Mrs Patel ordered to bring you at once when you get here," she whispered. "I think you have been late too often recently."

A wave of weakness nearly knocked me to the floor. I quickly realised that this might be my last day in the office.

"Have you finished looking through those papers I brought you?" asked Julie.

I looked over my messy table – yes, they had been sorted and stacked. I only had to print out the report. I dropped onto a chair and turned on the computer.

"Hurry, please," Julie kept her voice low.

Several colleagues passed down the corridor, greeting us politely. We managed to turn our faked smiles on and off, while desperately waiting for the computer to boot up. Finally, the printer spat out the required pile of papers, covered with figures, graphs, and tables. Julie helped me to collect everything and pressed the pile into my hands like a lifebelt, while, on slightly shaky legs, I approached an iceberg in the form of Mrs Patel's office.

Julie tapped the door, then opened it and stepped aside to let me in. I had never been inside before and quickly glanced around as if sticking my head into a trap. Mrs Patel's office was painted white, and there was a soft, light grey carpet on the floor. The furniture was black.

"Good morning, Mrs Patel," I greeted her, smiling widely.

Mrs Patel was standing by a large window, when I entered, and looking over the greyish rooftops of the sleepy town. She turned to face me, and for a few moments, she only silently stared at me. My silly smile faded.

"Come closer, let me have a look at you," she said, without returning the greeting.

I approached on shaky legs, feeling stupid with the pile of papers in my hands and nice graphs printed on the sheets at the top. She didn't say a word; she simply took my elbow, dragged me closer to the window and began inspecting my face. Her eyes were so dark that it was impossible to separate the iris from the pupil. That made her gaze even eerier and more frightening. I had no idea if she found what she was looking for, but traces of concern didn't leave her face. She released my elbow and gestured to the chair in front of her table. I dutifully placed my bottom on the seat, keeping the papers on my lap. I felt like an insect under a microscope. Mrs Patel kept her gaze on me before taking her seat at the table.

"Are you sleeping well?" It was a completely unexpected question.

I shrugged, unsure how to react.

"You look tired," she stated, picking up a sharpened pencil from her desk. "And you are almost always late. Are you sleeping well?"

"I am sleeping well enough, thank you, Mrs Patel," I forced out, still feeling shaky. "I am very sorry for being late. I am too dependent on trains, and sometimes the circumstances are out of my control."

"I see..." she held the pause, still pinning me with her gaze. "Have you ever considered moving closer to your work or finding a job closer to your home?"

"I have," I admitted. "I enjoy working here, Mrs Patel. But I have a very unfortunate tenancy agreement, which would cost me a lot of money to break. It ends this autumn. I will have to travel until then, I am afraid."

She turned over the pencil in her fingers, seemingly making her mind. The uneasy silence extended into minutes. Mrs Patel's face remained expressionless, and for some time, I wondered if she had forgotten about my presence.

"Very well, young man," she said at last. "Sometimes, circumstances are stronger than you, I agree. Your apology is accepted. But I can't make your working hours shorter. You must stay longer if the train timetable forces you to be late to the office. Is that clear?"

She placed her pencil back on the table.

"Yes, Mrs Patel," I nodded quickly. "You can trust me."

"You may go now," she said.

I stood up and approached her table.

"Thank you." I attempted to smile, placing my papers on her table. "You will not be disappointed."

"Leave that to Julie." She dismissed my pile with an impatient gesture, then stood up and turned back to the window.

I quickly got out and closed the door behind me.

Julie was waiting for me in the corridor.

I approached her, and she asked: "Have you been fired?"

"No," I said, not willing to get into details. "She told me to leave these with you."

I placed my reports in her hands and returned to my computer. Julie didn't follow.

The rest of the day, I felt shaky. Those dark eyes kept on haunting my mind, and I still felt like an insect, probably, in a Petri dish this time.

On my way home I bought my dinner from a Caribbean takeaway.

I ate while watching the news on TV. Then I slipped under the covers and drifted away.

An eerie thunderstorm was soaking Chadrack with gale-force winds and heavy rain outside the window. It was chilly and unpleasant. Bysh was standing in front of my bed and slowly wagging his tail. I got up, dressed and greeted him. He licked my hand.

Later, Carwyn came in with a water bowl, along with several boys carrying towels and a food basket. I asked him to light a fire in the hearth next to my bedroom.

"You forbade to use that hearth, my lord." He raised his eyebrows in surprise. "As far as I can remember, it was never used. Do you want to use it anyway?"

I didn't expect this, but there must be some practical reason for the taboo, one still unknown to me.

"No, let's leave it as it is... I am still so absent-minded. It must be that poisoning. Then light a fire in the dining room; I will have my breakfast there."

"As you wish," he waved to the boys and they swiftly vanished.

"How is Milo?" I asked Carwyn when kitchen boys left.

"He is badly hurt," said the old butler. "But he'll recover. The healer is taking care of him, as you commanded, my Lord."

"Thank you, Carwyn."

He bowed his head in acknowledgement and left.

I washed my face and combed my hair, and then left my chambers, escorted by Bysh.

The dining room was a much smaller version of the hall next to my bedroom with two tall windows framed by dark blue curtains. An impressive collection of antlers was on the wall above the hearth, and the room was filled with the soft crackling of burning logs and pleasant warmth.

Bysh stretched his body on the floor in front of the burning logs, and I decided to check what Carwyn and the kitchen boys had brought me for breakfast. The fish pie was marvellous. Then I had some ham with fresh bread and cheese, and I washed everything down with some superb red wine.

My muscles were still painful after all that running, stair climbing and training the day before, and I welcomed the break with gratitude. I picked an apple from the fruit bowl and carefully placed my aching muscles on a comfortable couch in front of the hearth.

The weather raised hell outside of the castle. Thunder rumbled almost continuously, accompanied by bright flashes of lightning. I was enjoying the warmth and soft crackling of the burning when a gentle tap on the door brought me back from my sweet daydreams. Bysh raised his head, cautiously sniffing.

"Come in!"

It was Rhys. He came in with a large brown leather sack.

"What is that?" I asked.

"Forgive the intrusion, my Lord. Yesterday you ordered the dead beast to be burnt," he said, holding his sack.

"Yes, I did. Any problem with that?"

"No, my Lord. The beast was too large to burn in one piece, and I had to cut it in half. You may wish to have a look at what I found inside..."

I had no desire to look at any bloody offals, but the serious look on Rhys' face was too concerning.

"Show me..." I stood up, and he started to unwrap his load.

First, I saw a bird-like head covered with bloodied white and brown feathers. Then I caught sight of bat wings, covered with downy fuzz, and a lion's body and tail! It was a baby gryphon!

"Would you command to kill it?" asked Rhys.

Gryphon raised the head and looked around, eyes still poorly focusing, then trembling, rose onto its feet – front like an eagle, back like a lion – and took a few unsteady steps. Bysh began to bark – angrily at first, then more out of duty.

Gryphon hissed at him, then stumbled and fell. The creature was utterly helpless. Bysh came closer and started to sniff it.

I tapped my hand on his back, trying to hold him, but the dog was already more curious than angry. Then he began to lick the baby gryphon, clearing his feathers of blood.

Gryphon hissed at first, trying to crawl away and then calmed down a few moments later. Bysh lay down, and the baby snuggled alongside him, trembling. I laughed at the view, and Rhys smiled approvingly.

"Looks like this time Bysh has made a decision, my Lord," said Rhys.

"Let's try to feed it," I nodded. "Do we have some fresh raw meat?"

"I'll ask in the kitchen."

I moved my chair closer to the animals. Bysh looked at me, concern in his eyes, then started to lick the baby again.

Rhys returned with a few chunks of raw lamb liver and began to cut it into smaller pieces. Bysh gulped one down without even chewing it.

Rhys offered a piece to the gryphon.

"How would you like to call it?" he asked.

"No idea… Gwyn? Will it be appropriate?"

"Yes, my Lord!"

"I'd like you to take care of him," I told Rhys.

"Yes, my Lord, it will be as you wish!"

Gwyn, the gryphon, managed to gulp down a few pieces of liver. The remaining chunks ended in Bysh's mouth. They both stretched out on the floor next to each other, enjoying the warmth of the hearth.

"I will ask Carwyn to place your things here. The baby needs warmth and care."

"Do you want me to stay here with him, my Lord?"

"Yes."

"It's a great honour!"

We watched the baby gryphon sleeping next to Bysh. The tiny body still shivered at the sound of thunder.

I gave orders to Carwyn when he popped in to pick my empty plates. He didn't seem very pleased with the animals around but obeyed without objection. More logs were brought in and placed near the hearth. The weather was still nasty, and it was crucial to keep the baby warm.

I stood up and picked up the burning candle from the table, as I had some solo exploration in mind. Rhys didn't say a word when I left.

I sneaked back to my chambers. The mystery hearth where the fire was forbidden had whetted my appetite for a thorough investigation. I knew it might merely be a blocked chimney, but it might be something else. I was going to find out.

The hearth was enormous – a fully grown man could walk in only having to slightly bend his head. As I approached, the possibility of a blocked chimney was instantly blown away along with the flame of the candle. I could clearly hear the wailing of the wind.

I started a careful inspection of the hearth, hoping to find some secret place with hidden treasures but found no clues – the stones had old burn marks, but any traces of ashes had been cleaned away. I tried to find any loose stones – found none. I wondered what treasures might be hidden behind those walls, what secrets? The hearth had a purpose; I just had to find it.

I stepped inside, and the wailing grew much louder. I could feel the wind in my hair, rushing up the chimney where the deafening rumbling of occasional thunder was shaking the walls.

I carefully inspected all the stones around the perimeter and found nothing suspicious. Still, I had no idea why this hearth could not be used.

I grabbed a chair and stepped on it, trying to reach further into the chimney. Three walls were flat and completely even, while on the wall facing the room there was some kind of strange carving. I couldn't use any light – candles or torches would be simply blown out by the wind. I had to trust my tactile sense only.

I felt the carving, which was sized and shaped like a human

palm – mine fitted perfectly. It looked like a keyhole, and my heart pounded faster with the sense of approaching mystery. I had to figure out how to activate it. I tried pressing several times without any success. I tried different force, tried to push it with quick bursts and for prolonged periods, hoping it would part the wall or open a secret chamber like I had seen in movies – but nothing worked. I felt the outside of the palm-shaped imprint – there were two other carvings, one on each side, both of strange shapes I couldn't recognise. Again, I traced them with my fingers and tried pressing, and again without any success. Something crucial was lacking.

I got out of the hearth, bringing the chair with me, and sat down. The mystery remained unsolved, but I couldn't ask Carwyn. It was a secret, a riddle which I had to solve on my own. The old butler might be unaware of what was hidden in my chambers.

I went to my bedroom and washed my hands. Outside, the storm still was raging as fiercely as before. When I returned to the dining room, Rhys was sitting on the floor naked to his waist. Baby Gwyn was wrapped in his shirt and slept peacefully on his lap, and Bysh had placed his head next to the gryphon.

"What happened?" I asked.

"Pardon my looks, my Lord," Rhys shrugged guiltily. "The baby was still shivering, and I had to to keep him warm."

"But now you are shivering," I observed casting a quick glance at his muscular torso.

"I am not important, my Lord," Rhys said without any irony in his voice. "I don't want to wake up the baby."

"As you wish," I shrugged. The local customs were strange, indeed. I couldn't understand how some useless animal might be more important than a human. Anyway, it was his peculiar decision, not mine. I filled two goblets with wine and handed one to Rhys.

"It's a great honour," he whispered, accepting.

I returned to the hearth and sat down, sipping the wine. Rhys tried his goblet while gently scratching behind the Bysh's ear.

"You get along well with the animals," I observed.

"I am you jaeger, my Lord," Rhys smiled.

"Tell me more what are you doing in those forests," I thought it was a safe question, not revealing my ignorance. "Have you seen many animals like this one?"

"No. This one is unique," he carefully adjusted his shirt wrapped around the sleeping gryphon. "It's mostly rabbits, foxes and deer in the woods, my Lord, and fewer wolves and bears."

"Bears? Where have you seen a bear?"

Rhys shrugged, and I secretly smile behind my goblet of wine. The jaeger was an excellent source of information I was seeking so desperately. I knew I couldn't fill all gaps with this talk. Rhys was a simple and nice guy, but his knowledge was mostly about this country – Chadrack. He knew nothing about the neighbouring countries and their rulers. Most of the time, he spent in the woods, and quite enthusiastically shared his knowledge with me.

We chatted for a couple of hours until baby Gwyn stirred and woke up. Rhys gently lifted the creature, and I volunteered to take care of Gwyn while he ran to jaegers' quarters to get a new shirt and to the kitchen for some raw lamb liver for the gryphon.

The storm still was raging outside though thunderbolts hit in greater intervals. The creature shivered on my lap and didn't even try to leave the protection of Rhys's shirt. My clumsy attempt to comfort him wasn't appreciated. Gwyn jerked head away, and for a few brief moments, his eyes lighted with countless colourful sparks like two opals. The vision faded as fast as it appeared, and I even wasn't entirely sure if I had seen anything.

Rhys returned probably ten minutes later, still half-naked, with droplets of rain in his hair, his dry shirt under his left arm and a bowl with raw liver in his right hand. Bysh greeted him at the door and got a piece of the liver as a reward.

"I ran as fast as I could, my Lord," Rhys said, still breathless.

"He made no trouble," I told him while returning the wrapped gryphon. "The beast must be hungry."

"I will feed him at once, my Lord," Rhys muttered, got down on the floor and placed Gwyn on his lap.

A few minutes later, Carwyn appeared with kitchen boys and brought my lunch. He only rolled eyes at the sight of Rhys feeding Gwyn.

"We could light a hearth in another room, my Lord, if you would like to dine away from that beast," he said, halting his boys. He didn't specify if that beast was the gryphon or Rhys.

"I am fine, Carwyn," I told him. "Leave it here."

Rhys finished feeding the gryphon and dressed while the old butler directed kitchen boys in arranging my food.

"Have a seat," I gestured to him when Carwyn left. "It's enough to feed a squad."

"It's too great honour..." Rhys mumbled, but I repeated the gesture, and he didn't dare to disobey.

We dug into roasted lamb with fried parsnips and rich gravy, as Gwyn slept peacefully on Rhys's lap, still wrapped in a shirt. Bysh sat down next to me, listening as we continued our talk.

I learned much that day. Rhys was a talkative young man, and I spent the evening trying to figure out how this society was built. We fed the baby gryphon twice and had dinner together before I retreated to my chambers still more questions in my head than I had answers.

It was late when I finally slipped into my bed and closed eyes. Before long, I was gone.

I almost overslept my alarm clock again.

The morning rush started on a high note. I hastily brushed my teeth, shaved, combed, slipped into my trousers and ran out. The weather was refreshingly chilly, wiping out all remnants of my sleepiness.

I hurried downhill, bought my return tickets and ran over the steps to the platform. Just in time – the train was already approaching.

My usual seat near the window was empty. As I entered, a young mother took her softly protesting daughter off the train, apparently in a hurry, leaving her pencils and drawings scattered on the table. I sat down and watched the train filled with more people at every station we passed. I stacked the little girl's pictures in a pile, looking at the trees, houses, flowers, cats, dogs, unicorns and dragons in the drawings as I did so. They were far from perfection, and the lines were shaky due to the movement of the train. I absent-mindedly looked through the window with a smile, remembering the baby gryphon playing with Bysh. Gwyn was a strange little creature, and I wondered what he would look like when he grew up. I picked a pencil and started to correct the little girl's dragon drawing, adding a more gracious eagle head and remodelling the lizard legs into a lion's body...

At Swanley, a grim-looking, thick-set red-haired man squeezed into the empty seat next to me. His ginger beard was still covered with breadcrumbs, and he clutched a paper cup and noisily slurped cappuccino.

I caught a few prying glimpses from his sky-blue eyes under thick ginger eyebrows. Was it my paranoia again?

He left at Kemsing, but I could feel his gaze on me from the platform until the train started to move and left him behind.

A busload of school children boarded the train at the next station, filling it with childish talk, laughter and quarrels. It was noisy, and I was happy to get out shortly after that when we reached my destination.

The day at work was busy, without anything particularly worth mentioning.

On my way home, I looked out of the window and counted bunnies, foxes, and pheasants as more and more people boarded the train.

After Kemsing, a sense of being watched returned. I looked around – the same redhead was just a few seats behind me with his grim looks and his coffee. I tried to ignore him, but the sense of unease was firmly rooted in my brain, paralysing all my other senses with fear.

I peeked at him on several occasions, and every time my eyes met his cold blue glance. I started panicking and jumped out of the train a few stations early, unable to bear it any longer. I rushed through the platform, searching my pockets for an Oyster card. The bus stop was just in front of the station, and I began studying the timetable, but that sense of unease followed me like a dark shadow.

The redhead was behind me, finishing his coffee and throwing the empty paper cup away. I boarded a bus, and he got in after me.

I went upstairs on the double-decker while the redhead stayed near the door. All way through the narrow streets of the south-east, London, I was hoping that he will leave at some stop. He didn't.

I got off the bus, and the redhead steadily, like a ginger nemesis, went after me uphill keeping a very short distance.

I didn't even notice at first when a black car stopped next to us, but suddenly several men, including the redhead, grabbed me and pushed inside the vehicle. I had no chance to scream as a plug was shoved into my mouth, and a black linen bag placed over my head. I was tied and squeezed between the two massive bodies. The car rushed forward at increasing speed, only briefly stopping at crossroads and traffic lights.

I tried to count the number of times we stopped and turned but soon lost track. I was scared to death!

My kidnappers were silent. As far as I could judge, we rushed along a motorway, but I was unsure which one or even which direction we were going in. After what seemed an eternity of hectic driving, I felt us take a rather sharp turn to the left, and the car entered a tangled network of streets again. After a few more turns and speedy runs, we stopped.

I was dragged out, still blinded, and almost carried through the narrow corridor bumping into the walls before being dragged upstairs. They pushed me down and tied me to a squeaking metal bed without any mattress. Only then did they remove the bag from my head, and I got a quick glimpse on my kidnappers – the redhead from the train aided by two smaller, but rather thick-set and muscular men of Asian appearance.

They talked among themselves, quietly and quickly. I couldn't make out any words, but it seemed like they were having a small argument, as the redhead kept shaking his head and making a few hushed remarks.

"Let's tag him and wait," said one of the Asians angrily, and they all turned to face me.

The redhead went through his pockets, searching for something, while both Asians came closer to my bed. The next moment, they grabbed my head, holding it firmly, and pulled up my hair. Suddenly seeing a sharp knife in front of my left eye, I screamed.

"What do you want? You've got the wrong man! I don't know anything!" I struggled, but my bonds remained securely tied.

They paid no attention to my efforts. The knife moved a little upwards and then sharply descended down on my forehead, making a quick and deep cut just below the hairline – all way down to the bone. I nearly screamed my lungs out, but nobody cared.

Blood gushed out of the gaping wound and ran down my left temple, but neither the redhead nor the Asians bothered to stop it. They released my head and left, leaving me tied up and alone.

I started crying out of sheer desperation. All this brutality made no sense. I was another no one – a grey person like millions of others, quietly living my lonely life. I had no friends or enemies, I had no debts, I knew no secrets. My bank account was far from swollen. Why had they captured me? They hadn't asked me a single question! Hopeless tears ran down my cheeks, mixing with the blood. I stopped when I had cried all my pain out. The bleeding stopped long before that.

From my fixed position, I could only see the empty room. I tried to move, but couldn't. My shoulders, elbows, wrists, hips, knees and ankles were securely tied to the metal bed. All I could do was breathe and wait.

Darkness was slowly descending on the earth, sneaking through the only window and filling the room.

I was alone, tied up and unable to move. There was nothing left to do but to drift with the darkness.

Fear was still holding my heart with a deadly grip in Chadrack. My pillow was stained with blood, and I could feel blood clots in my hair as well. My position was hopeless – I was kidnapped and tied up in the real world. I was desperate and trembling like a rabbit, but what possible solutions to my situation could the dream world provide?

Carwyn tapped the door and came in with the usual morning bowl of water and fresh towels. He froze midway noticing the dried blood on my face.

"I fell in the dark," I explained. "I didn't want to disturb anybody. It's nothing serious, indeed."

"May the Gods save and protect you, my Lord!" He looked very concerned. "That poison was stronger than I thought! Do you need any help? Do you wish to see a healer?"

"This might be a good idea, Carwyn. He could dress my

wound. It's not a big deal, I am sure."

He placed his stuff in its usual place.

"I will be back as soon as possible!" he said, leaving hastily.

I washed my hair and my face. The wound on my forehead looked small – just a cut – but the gaping hole in my soul was much deeper. *Why they did this to me? What would happen next?*

A few moments later, Carwyn reappeared, followed by a grey-haired man, apparently the healer.

He silently examined my wound and happily confirmed that it was just a superficial cut. First, the healer washed my wound with plenty of water and then produced some fresh linen bandages from his bag and started to wrap them around my head. Before long, I faintly resembled an Eastern trader with a clumsy white turban. He assured me that I would be back to normal in a few days. Then he offered me another bloodletting to help wash the poison out of my body, which I politely declined.

He left without any further comments.

I ate my breakfast, still thinking of my poor body strapped to a metal bed somewhere in the suburbs of London. I couldn't think of any reason why I had been kidnapped. And I was afraid to even think about what might happen in the morning. This scared me to death.

I paced through my chambers, unable to focus on anything.

Around noon, a quiet tap on the door brought me back to

Chadrack.

"Yes?"

Carwyn came in, looking somewhat nervous.

"The man named Melvyn has just returned from Mordak and humbly asks to see you as soon as possible."

Who is Melvyn? I had no idea.

"I will meet him here."

Carwyn nodded and left. A few minutes later, he was back with the scar-faced man in his forties, apparently Melvyn. The man was dressed in dark brown trousers and a black fur jacket – too warm for the season. His long greasy black hair somewhat covered the nasty red scar on his left cheek.

He paid his respects and remained silent, waiting until Carwyn left.

"What is it?" I asked, casually.

"I did all as you have commanded, my Lord," he said.

I had no idea what the man was talking about. Was it another minefield left behind by my predecessor?

"Tell me more," I told him. "I want to know everything, even the smallest details."

I took a seat, hoping the man would not become suspicious of my request, and indicated a chair for him in front of me. Melvyn sat down, appearing tense under my gaze.

"I don't know where to start," he nervously forced a crooked smile.

"Better start from the beginning," I advised, still without the slightest hint of the subject.

"I crossed the Braaid as you commanded, my Lord," he began, placing hands firmly on his knees. "It took nearly two months for me to get into the castle guard. I had to pay a few generous bribes for this, and I paid with our coins, as you suggested. It worked. Our money is highly valued. I was able to do that on my third night watch, and then I had to flee the castle. But I did everything as you commanded, my Lord."

What exactly had he done? I felt a growing disgust, mixed with fear.

"I need all details," I said and poured some wine into my goblet while trying to hide the slightly shaking hands and confusion.

"It was deep night, just after the second call," he said, with a nervous smile. "I entered her chambers while she was sleeping. She tried to scream, but I plugged her mouth and tied her to the bed."

I nearly dropped my wine. Had I commanded this to be done? Who was that poor girl or woman?

"Then I raped her and cut her throat," he told this as a matter of fact. Melvyn paused, expectantly, for a few moments, but I was too shocked to say anything. "I plunged your dagger into her belly, as you wished, and left it there. They will have not have any doubts that Chadrack is behind this. I did everything, my Lord. They will not be able to ignore this any longer."

What a monster was inside my body before me? Who was that poor lady?

"Are you sure she was the right person?" I managed to ask, suppressing the tremble in my voice.

I had a feeling that I was rushing directly into a fire, carefully and ruthlessly built and lit by my former self. I had no knowledge of the traps waiting for me; I felt like a fly hopelessly caught between the anvil and the hammer.

"Yes, my Lord," Melvyn showed his best toothless smile. "I was guarding chambers of the young princess. Mordak will not forgive this – have no doubt of that, my Lord. War is now imminent!"

That was far worse than I expected. *War?* Why did Chadrack need this? Why did that poor innocent soul have to die?

"Are they preparing the army already?" I gasped without thinking.

"Not until winter, my Lord. They don't have enough ships to bring their army across the Braaid," Melvyn grinned.

"Not enough ships to cross in one go – but can they use those ships as ferries and transfer their army with several round trips? What do you think?"

"I am not sure. Bedwyr would know better: he is the general of your army. In my humble opinion, we'd better start preparing, my Lord..."

"I will discuss that with Bedwyr," I gulped the wine unable to think clearly.

Melvyn was silent and waited, still smiling wickedly.

"My lord, could I now return to my wife and kids?" he asked since I wasn't saying anything.

"Yes." I dismissed him without casting a second glance at the man. My imagination was already painting horrific images of blood, suffering and destruction. I placed the goblet back on the table and silently stared at it as if hoping to find some answers there. *Luckily, the war was not tomorrow... Maybe I'll be able to somehow sort it out by winter if I'm lucky enough to live until then.*

I was full of grim thoughts when lunch arrived. Carwyn poured me some wine, and I downed it in a single gulp.

"Is Bedwyr around?" I asked.

"No, my lord. He is in the field camp, training your army."

"When will he be back? I'd like to speak to him."

"I haven't heard that he is making any plans to return. Should I send for him now?"

"Yes, please..."

I spent the whole afternoon studying the map on the wall. The Braaid was a huge river which served as a natural border between Chadrack and Mordak. It began somewhere in the mountains, outside of the area depicted in the map, and its waters rushed down to the inland sea. It was a significant obstacle to moving a large army swiftly. Maybe the general would be able to tell me what kind of fortifications we had along the coast of Chadrack. Would they be strong enough to keep the Mordak's fleet from getting inland? I was desperate to speak with Bedwyr about this. We might still have time to build better defences...

I was in the darkest of moods, counting the minutes until my return to London – knowing these might even be the last minutes of my life – and paced my chambers like a caged lion. Nowhere seemed safe. War was coming... *War...*

I was unable to touch the food Carwyn had brought me and slipped into bed with a troubled heart, still wondering how things would turn out in reality. Right now, I wasn't even sure which reality was the true one – London or Chadrack.

I woke up shivering from cold and fear. My back ached from the night of forced immobility. My limbs were tied, and all I could do was try to contract and relax the muscles, making use of that minimal range of movement my bonds allowed me. This activity kept me busy for some time, and the ache became duller, though still annoying.

The house was silent. A good half an hour passed before I heard footsteps in the corridor. The door opened, and the large ginger man appeared in the doorway with his two aides. This wasn't a surprise – I hadn't expected to see anybody else. He produced a knife, the same one as before, and I started to shout, calling for help. He only smiled eerily and stuffed a linen plug into my mouth.

"The best thing for you right now would be to keep silent, my friend..." he added, still smiling.

I expected more interrogations, more torture, but nothing happened. The redhead cut some of my bonds loose, but then tied others elsewhere. They put the black linen bag on my head again, then lifted me up and dragged out of the room. I bumped into the walls of the corridor again, and a few steps later, I felt a gust of fresh wind.

Within a minute, we were driving again. I didn't attempt to count the number of times we stopped and turned – it was utterly useless. Nobody said a word as we drove. An hour later, we stopped abruptly. Strong arms lifted me up and pushed me out of the car. I landed on the pavement, the bag still on my head, then I heard the car door closing and the roar of the engine fading into the traffic sounds. It seemed that I was left alone. But where was I?

It took several attempts before I succeeded in spitting out the linen plug, but I was still unable to see anything.

"Help! People! Anyone!"

I heard the tap of approaching horseshoes through the sounds of rushing cars. They stopped next to me.

"Are you okay, sir?" a soft female voice asked.

"No, I am not! Please, free me..."

Black linen slipped away, and I got a glimpse of my saviour. She was a police officer with long curly ginger hair, green eyes and a concerned look; her saddled horse stood nearby.

I glanced at the busy street around, trying to figure out my location. I was on the pavement between the two bus stops near Marble Arch. Several more mounted police officers quickly approached us from Hyde Park.

"Call an ambulance; we need a medic!" she told them.

"I don't think that wound is serious..." I started to protest.

"Let's just make sure it isn't," she said.

She took a small knife out of her pocket.

"What is your name, sir?" she asked, cutting the ropes which were binding my wrists.

"Kyle Firestone."

"What happened, Mr Kyle?"

The wailing of the approaching ambulance reached us from a distance.

I described the events of the day before with the red-haired man from the train while she cut the bonds around my ankles. I was interrupted by the arrival of the paramedics, who casually inspected my wound, while the police officers remained standing a few steps away.

My diagnosis of "nothing serious" was confirmed on the spot. The young guy in a green uniform placed a thin sticking bandage on my forehead and wished me a speedy recovery.

The ambulance left, and I was back in the hands of the police officer. We went through as many details as I could remember, but there weren't many. I had been blindfolded while in the car and had been unable to see much when tied to the bed.

"Have you been robbed?" she asked after I described the tortures I had been through.

I searched my pockets and found that my wallet and mobile phone were in place. The money and cards in my wallet hadn't been touched either. It wasn't a robbery. But I still didn't have the slightest idea what the intentions of the kidnappers had been.

She smiled, assuring me that the police would do everything possible to investigate this crime, and she gave me some legal papers to sign, which I did with my still slightly trembling hands.

"If you remember anything more – any details, even those which might seem irrelevant to you, please, call me and let me know." She handed me the card, bearing the emblem of Metropolitan Police.

"Of course!"

"Do you need any further assistance from us?"

"No, don't worry. I can handle this..."

She waved goodbye, then took reins of her horse and went towards Hyde Park. I was left on my own.

First, I called the office, briefly explained about the kidnapping and said that I would be taking a day off. Then I staggered to Marble Arch tube station and took the Central Line train. The morning rush hour was over, and I felt uneasy in the half-empty carriage. I cautiously scanned every passenger boarding it, but nobody paid any attention to my humble self. I finally calmed down when I switched to the DLR, where I caught myself secretly smiling. Life still went on!

I switched to the bus. A short journey later, I got off and started the final leg of my trip home – uphill. A sudden chill ran up my spine, as a black car slowly drove past. A wave of panic flashed through me, and I instinctively jumped away. For five long minutes, I stood trembling, pressing my back against a nearby wall, trying to calm down. Large drops of perspiration appeared on my forehead and ran down my cheeks as my heart performed a crazy tango in my chest.

"Are you okay?" a black woman stopped a few feet away, looking at me with concern.

I nodded and even managed a weak smile.

She didn't seem very convinced but kept on going, mumbling.

I waited until the panic eased a little, and then began to stagger uphill along the pavement, trying to stay as far away from the road as possible.

It was the longest and the most challenging journey – ever. My mind shrank to a single point as I perspired profusely, but somehow I managed to take step after step until I reached my flat and shut the door behind me.

Only then, slowly, the panic faded away.

I washed the remnants of clotted blood from my temple. I tried to persuade myself that nothing serious had happened, but failed. I didn't understand a thing about those recent horrors, and the terrifying thought that the whole thing might be repeated began to take root, poisoning my soul.

I inspected the contents of my fridge and ordered a pizza. The rest of the day I spent in bed watching TV, my thoughts far away and still no plan on how to go on with my life.

Bedwyr entered my chambers just after breakfast. He was a tall man in his forties, thick-set and muscular, with sharp eagle eyes.

"You wished to see me, my Lord?" he asked calmly.

"Yes, Bedwyr. How is the army?"

"Our fresh recruits from last year are still in training, but the rest of the men are ready and eager to do something heroic under your command."

"Remind me, how many ships do we have?" I asked.

"Well… there are a little over fifty on the water and about three dozen in docks."

"Are they prepared to defend our shores?" I asked.

"Of course, my Lord." He looked surprised by the question.

I briefly told him Melvyn's story, omitting the embarrassing details related to the orders given by the ruler of Chadrack. All he needed to know was the fact that the heiress of Mordak was dead, and that the war was about to begin since Chadrack was implicated in her death.

"We need to send a few more spies to confirm the story," I told him. "We may need better fortifications to protect our land."

"I will do as you command, my Lord," said the general. "Your army will be ready to repel the intruder."

Were we indeed stronger than the enemy?

"How big is Mordak's army?" I asked him. "Will we be able to fight them back if they attack with all their might?"

"Their army is nearly as big as ours," he said calmly. "But you have always been a better commander than Prince Seisyll, my Lord."

I nearly fainted. We were doomed! How could an office rat lead an army?

"I need your advice, Bedwyr," I said, hiding my trembling hands behind my back. "How can we build a better defence in case Mordak dares to attack us? What do we need to do for that?"

"We have everything, my Lord," he assured me without hesitation. "We have our brave soldiers, we have our ships, we have our land behind us, and we have you leading us – we can crush any attacker army which threatens us."

I couldn't share his optimism. I was hoping for some suggestions on how to avoid the clash, but as a soldier, Bedwyr was used to obeying orders, not making diplomacy. *Damn, this time, it was diplomacy I needed!*

For nearly an hour, we inspected the map and discussed all possible routes for troop movements, placement of ships and ways of retreat in case of unexpected resistance. He assured me that our military was big enough for an adequate defence of our land, but I still didn't feel confident.

"Is there any route from Mordak through the mountains?"

"No, my Lord. The gods closed this path. The mountains are too high and too steep – vertical walls of rock and ice," he explained that as a well-known fact, still politely.

Then we discussed several southern routes for possible attacks. All of them included ships and the river Braaid.

I grew suspicious with his overconfidence and felt an urge rising to inspect Chadrack's army myself. A few days in a field with the military would do no harm but give me some peace of mind.

I told Bedwyr to saddle a horse for me. His face expression didn't change on hearing my intent to do the inspection. "Your Knight will be ready, my Lord," said the general.

I dismissed him and poured some wine into my goblet. I was amused by my hasty decision to dive into the unknown – it was very unusual for me, but I felt cornered. The recent events in London had left me without any shelters where I could feel secure. Was the army good enough to defend me? I had to be sure. I couldn't trust his words only.

I gulped my wine and went to visit Milo – I hadn't seen the poor lad since we brought him from the temple, and it was about time to check for any success of the healer.

I peeked into the corridor and stumbled into Dahryl, who was still guarding my door. He jumped to his feet as I asked him to show the way to the healer's chambers, and we left. We passed several corridors on the same storey before we reached the closed door with strange, sharp odours leaking through it.

Dahryl opened the door for me and remained on guard.

The room was quite spacious, with several long shelves crowded with phials and glass containers filled with dried herbs, roots and fruits. I even noticed some dried lizards.

There was a low couch next to the window. Milo was laying prone on it, naked to his waist, while the healer worked his miracles on the wounded lad's back. He stopped and moved aside as I entered.

Milo looked at me and smiled weakly. As I approached, he attempted to rise, but I quickly stopped him with a gesture. The skin on his back was black, and I turned my puzzled eyes to the healer.

"What happened?" I asked my voice firm and demanding an immediate answer. "It wasn't black the last time I've seen him."

"I covered it with the ashes from a dragonroot, my lord," said the man. "This will prevent any bad phlegm and pus. A few of the cuts were quite deep."

"How bad is he?"

"He will be fine, I think," the healer shrugged. "The wounds are painful, but not that swollen already."

"Good. Feed him well," I said, taking a chair and sitting down next to Milo. "Would you give me a few minutes to speak with him in private?"

"Of course, my Lord!"

He bowed and went outside.

"I am sorry for all your sufferings, but why did you go back to the temple?" I asked Milo when we were left alone. "I don't understand this."

"I had no choice," he said weakly. "Forgive me, my Lord, but I thought it was your intention to bring me back to the temple. I felt doomed until you came to rescue me."

"I would never give such an order," I told him firmly. "You were under my protection, and I meant no harm to you. What happened at the Grave?"

Milo attempted to rise again but stopped, frowning with pain.

"It would be better if you refrained from trying to stand up for some time," I advised. "What happened there? I need to know."

"We made a pyre with lots of wood, and placed bones and

other human remains on top," said Milo. "Then, the priest appeared. He was angry about the fire at first, saying that the land belonged to the temple, but then he saw me and the bones. The men told him that they were carrying your order, and he had to obey as well."

"I assume he didn't like that," I observed.

Milo attempted a smile.

"The priest made us pray aloud," he said. "Then he took my hand and announced that I was a thief and had been sentenced to serve in the temple and that he was taking me back."

"And nobody even tried to stop him?"

"He is the high priest of Qu'mun; how could they challenge him?" said Milo. "They couldn't do anything."

He moved his hand, then frowned with sudden pain.

"I will never be able to thank you enough, my Lord," he said, after a short pause. "You saved my life."

"It was the least I could do," I said. "Now, get stronger – don't make my effort in vain."

"I will," promised Milo.

"I am leaving for a few days," I told him. "And I will give clear orders to your healer and Carwyn to keep you safe and indoors. No contacts with the temple. I will visit you when I get back."

I still saw a glint of fear in boy's eyes. I didn't wait for his answer – I stood up, crossed the room and summoned the healer.

My orders were few and simple, and Milo heard everything I told him.

I instructed Dahryl to guard the healer's chambers and make sure no one even remotely related to the temple would be able to enter. I guessed my complicated relationship with the high priest of Qu'mun was no longer a secret. Then I retraced the way back to my chambers.

Later, when Carwyn showed up with lunch, I asked him to bring some proper clothing to visit the army camp. He returned almost immediately, carrying dark brown leather trousers, a blue shirt, and a black leather jacket. The helper boy brought a wide leather belt with a large sword attached.

"Rhys has asked for your permission to move closer to the eastern garden, my Lord."

"Why does he need that?" I asked while getting dressed.

"He thinks that the gryphon would feel better with more fresh air and more places to play. The garden is the least crowded..."

"Are there any suitable rooms nearby?"

"Yes, my Lord."

"He may move then," I said and put on my belt. "I placed Dahryl outside of the healer's chambers. I want that boy safe, and I would like someone there guarding him day and night – I don't want any more surprises from the temple."

"Don't worry, my Lord," the old butler nodded. "We will do as you command. The boy will be safe in the castle."

I thanked him, and he left.

I was dressed and ready. The sword made me a little clumsy, and I hoped it would remain unused. *Was I supposed to feel safe with my general and my army?*

It was pleasantly warm outside. I crossed the yard and headed over to the group of men led by Bedwyr. The same black stallion I rode last time was saddled for me again. The beautiful animal, named Knight, was calm, but I cautiously circled him and tapped his head, trying to make friends before mounting. It wasn't necessary. He knew me.

Feeling a little clumsy, I was helped to the saddle, and we moved out through the gate. Two men were riding in front. Bedwyr and I were guarded by two riders at our flanks. Our rear was supported by four horsemen and a big-wheeled waggon with supplies, pulled by two bulls.

The winding road ran alongside the right bank of the river, in the cool shade cast by tall green trees.

"How far is the camp?" I asked Bedwyr.

"Only a few hours away, if we hurry," he explained. "But with the waggon slowing us down, it will take longer – we will be there by nightfall, though..."

We rode a few miles down the road and then crossed a stone bridge over to the left bank. There was no wind apart from occasional cool breezes created by the turbulent waters of the nearby river.

Knight suddenly started to neigh, widening his nostrils, and Bedwyr raised his hand, halting the party. Everybody waited, holding their breath.

We listened carefully, but it was the usual soft noise of the wind in the woods only. Suddenly, ravens shrieked in the distance. Bedwyr barked a short command, and two riders from the rear rushed ahead, while others remained silent and motionless.

Long, tense minutes passed. I silently cursed my stupid decision to leave the safety of the castle, but it was too late to change anything. The big unknown was just in front of us. I suddenly realised how small our party was. We would be crushed in no time if some unknown enemy would choose to attack. I noticed little drops of perspiration on the foreheads of the men on our flanks. Nobody moved.

The sound of the ravens grew much louder, and before long, we saw a flock of them circling in the skies above. One of the scouts returned.

"It is safe!" he reported from a distance. "But you have to look at that!"

We started to move slowly onwards, more cautiously, following the road winding next to the river. A few turns later, we reached a clearance. Our second scout was waiting there, and several dozen ravens were circling in the sky above.

The wooden cross stood at the far end of the field, facing the road, and I gasped, realising that there was a man brutally nailed to the wood there and, apparently, dead. The black raven was sitting on his head and pecking at his empty eye sockets. I instantly recognised the scar on his face – it was Melvyn! Bedwyr urged his horse closer, and I rushed after him. Melvyn's face was dark and spooky, with half-bitten part of his tongue hanging from the left corner of his mouth and the word "TRAITOR" carved on his forehead.

Bedwyr chased the raven away and ordered his men to take the body down.

Yes, it was Melvyn's body, indeed. But I was very confused by the message on his forehead. Who had killed him? Who had felt betrayed by him? It could have been a message from Mordak – if that were the case, I would understand – they must be angry after all that he had done. But who killed him if not? Had he betrayed us?

Bedwyr ordered for a grave to be dug and the body to be buried. We had no time for proper cremation. We left the scouts with this grim task and moved on, in sullen silence. The eyeless face with its carved message kept on haunting me; the day was no longer pleasant and joyful.

It was the early evening when we reached the army camp, based in a vast valley, framed by woods on all sides. Somewhere to the south-east, below the horizon, was the distant blue ribbon: the mighty Braaid – our biggest obstacle, a natural border and a natural means of defence.

They set up a tent for me alongside Bedwyr's. I asked for a few guards at my tent and requested not to be disturbed. I was off to the land of Nod as soon as I put my head on the pillow.

The morning was sunny in London, promising a beautiful and peaceful day. I woke up well before my alarm clock went off, and spent a lazy few minutes looking at the clouds and planes passing in the sun.

I got up, brushed my teeth, combed my hair and got dressed, and still had some time left for a nice cup of a morning coffee. I looked at the fluffy clouds passing by while blissfully sipping my hot brew.

This tranquillity was disturbed when I noticed the time, and I had to start moving. I decided to take a bus to the train station, wanting to avoid another panic attack by skipping the unfortunate spot on the street where I had been forced into that car.

The weather was pleasant, and I finally succeeded in putting all my worries aside.

When the double-decker arrived, I went upstairs, almost happily. All of the upper deck was empty, so I placed my bottom on the seat at the front, enjoying the excellent panoramic view of the street.

It was too early for morning traffic, and the bus was going quite fast. A few stops later, my heart suddenly dropped – my red-haired kidnapper was waiting for the bus! He boarded but stayed on the lower deck and didn't notice me (I hoped!). *Was he stalking me again?* I had to lay low, to hide. If he were after me again, I was sure this time I wouldn't survive the night.

I almost sank into my chair, perspiring heavily and only regained my ability to think a few miles later. The front seat was too exposing, and I would never notice him leaving the bus from the back door. *I must go to the back of the bus!*

Several more people boarded the second deck on the next stop, allowing me to relocate to the seat in the back row without attracting attention to my footsteps. I sank into a seat next to the window, which gave me a better view of the pavement and of the people boarding and alighting from the bus.

I was paralysed with fear and missed my stop long before. Going down and risking the redhead seeing me was unthinkable. I sadly counted down what I was sure was the last minutes of my life but, just before Crystal Palace, I spotted him on the pavement again. He left the bus and was angrily talking to somebody on the phone. I sank low down in my seat, keeping my eyes over the window and praying that he wouldn't notice me. I stopped saying my prayers only when the bus began moving again, and the red-haired man vanished out of my sight behind the street corner.

"This bus terminates here!" announced the loudspeaker as we reached Crystal Palace. "All change!"

I jumped out of the bus like a frightened bunny and immediately boarded another one without even looking at its number – all I needed was to get as far away from the redhead as possible. The bus was a single-decker, and I took the back seat next to the window again.

We started downhill through the narrow, shady streets of south London. I couldn't help but flinch every time I saw a ginger head. I was still struggling to calm down.

Half an hour later, I suddenly realised that I had missed my train and I was very late! I called the office and took a few days off – trauma from kidnapping was still a sufficiently good excuse.

I finally braved to leave the bus at East Croydon train station. For several minutes I only stood there leaning at the wall and scanning at all incoming trams and buses, half-expecting to get a glimpse of the redhead getting off. I was ready to sprint away at any moment, but my nemesis didn't show up.

The station was a busy place. Finally, I succeeded in convincing myself that they would not attempt anything in broad daylight and amid a crowd. I even spotted a few policemen at the station. This lifted my mood, and I checked the timetable. I still wasn't ready to return by bus. A long journey by train through crowded Central London looked like a safer alternative. The next train to Victoria station was in two minutes. I used my Oyster card and rushed to the platform, just in time to see the train departing when I got there. *Damn!*

The next train was to St Pancras in fifteen minutes, which still was crowded, next to the Tube and well suited my needs. I pressed my back against the wall and waited. The platform was full of people, and I smiled secretly. They would not get me this time!

The train arrived, and we started to fill the coaches. I dropped down into a random seat while smiling Asian man unhurriedly lowered himself down in front of me, on the other side of the table.

He kept on smiling and staring at me, which I found annoying. At first, I felt uneasy. Then a realisation jolted me like a lightning bolt – he must be one of the redhead's accomplices! My hands started to shake. He nodded, still smiling as if acknowledging that I had guessed correctly.

"You must not fear us, my friend," he said calmly, still looking at me. "You are not the person we are looking for."

"Why? Why did you hurt me then?"

"It was a mistake. You look quite similar, and we were not sure at first."

"Who are you? Why are you doing this?!"

"I can't tell you that. Let me keep a few little secrets. You are simply not the one we need. Carry on with your life!"

Then I asked a stupid question. "What would you do if I did happen to be that guy?"

Few seconds he looked at me calmly, still smiling.

"You don't want to know that, my friend..."

My throat went dry.

"Why are you stalking me now? If it was a mistake, just leave me alone!"

"It's only a coincidence, I am not stalking you. I am going my way, and you may leave wherever you like. I am not after you, my friend."

I was shaking. He indifferently picked up the newspaper from the table and started to read, clearly indicating that this conversation was over.

I couldn't take my eyes off him, but he never looked back. Soon the train squeezed between several glass-and-steel buildings and stopped on a wide bridge, known as Blackfriars station. I stood up. He kept on reading. Forcing my limping legs to move, I left the train. I continued looking at him until the coach door closed, and the train began to move, rapidly vanishing from my sight.

I felt sick, still paralysed by panic. It took my last few bits of strength to reach the nearby bench. I sat there for nearly half an hour, gazing at distant Tower Bridge with unblinking eyes. Trains passed in front of me in both directions, and the Thames flowed peacefully just below, taking my fear away bit by bit.

Finally, I stood up, but I only had sufficient willpower for the shortest trip home. I didn't look at anyone on my way, moving more like a rag doll rather than a human being.

I crawled up the squeaking stairs and open the door. I went in, closed the door behind me and then collapsed in the corridor...

Bedwyr was gently shaking my shoulder.

"Wake up, my Lord... We have a situation here."

I moaned, still confused, then opened my eyes. "What happened?"

"You need to have a look at this, my Lord..."

I silently protested while dressing, and we went out into the chilly night. The camp was flooded by hushed murmuring, and it seemed that nobody was sleeping.

I turned around, still wondering what was going on. The sky was cloudy, but that wasn't so unusual that it would be keeping everyone awake. The grim dark wall of the forest was silent as well. Then Bedwyr pointed it out for me – a distant blood-red aurora in the south-eastern sky, hovering high above the black shadow of the woods.

"What is that?" I asked Bedwyr.

"It might be Hythe, a riverside town in Mordak... or it might be Ikent, our own riverside town. It is impossible to tell from such a distance."

"And the Braaid is between them? Does that mean the war has begun?"

"I can't tell for sure. It might be just a big fire, but something is going on."

"Send scouts! Right now! We need to know what's happening!" The orders dropped out of my mouth without me even realising it.

Bedwyr nodded and disappeared into the darkness. Seconds later, I heard his voice shouting orders.

I stood in the night for some time, watching the shivering reflections of the distant flames on the low clouds. Then the chill got to me, and I returned to my tent.

I told my guards not to bother me again until dawn and slipped into my bed. The soft murmur lulled me to sleep almost instantly.

My left shoulder was aching when I woke up. I was lying flat in the corridor and felt exhausted. I tossed off my shoes and washed my face, still unable to think. I had had too much of that strange dreamland, but it kept on returning persistently, too real to be ignored. This constant feeling of being stalked was driving me out of my mind, and now the war was plaguing my dreams. Life became so confusing that I started to wonder which part of it was real. Was I only imagining things and fantasising? It seemed I didn't have any influence on my dreams or my life anymore; everything was mixed up and dragging me out of my comfortable shell like a powerful hurricane. It was just too much for me!

It was well into the late afternoon already. My aching stomach begged for some food as I inspected the contents of my fridge – empty as usual. A call to the pizzeria solved the most immediate problem, but I didn't felt strong enough to go shopping and ordered my groceries online.

My pizza arrived half an hour later, and I ate it while watching TV. I tried to convince myself to calm down back to normal, but the recent encounter with my kidnappers had sapped all of my strength. I couldn't imagine doing anything but watching some stupid movie.

My grocery arrived a few hours later when I was almost asleep. I filled up my fridge and then made myself a cup of tea. All my thoughts kept returning to the imminent war. I hoped it was just a big fire. I hoped it was just a big fire in the neighbour's backyard. I hoped...

A child was sobbing somewhere. The sound interweaved with the soft murmuring of adult voices – many adults. I heard the harsh, low tones of men speaking quietly among themselves, not attempting to comfort the child.

I only levitated in my semi-conscious state somewhere at the edge of a dream and listened to the sobs. *What was going on?*

I sprang out of my bed, pushing away my confusion. It was a field with the army around me. No child was supposed to be here.

I quickly dressed before going outside. I was met by the grim faces of my army and the early morning light.

"We caught a spy, my Lord," said one of them, holding the end of a rope.

The other end was tightly bound to the wrists of a child – a girl in her early teens.

"Are you kidding me?" I asked the man. "Where is Bedwyr?"

"The general is checking the perimeter," he answered. "We caught her stealing food."

The girl was slim and fragile. Her dress had been torn in several places and was stained with blood. She lifted her frightened eyes to me and started to cry again.

"Kneel before Kyleb, Prince of Chadrack," the man urged her, tugging the rope he was holding, and the girl slumped to her knees.

I froze just for a second. Finally, I found out my name and title in this dream world, but I had no luxury even to think about that.

"Give me that rope," I said. "And find Bedwyr."

The crowd started to dissipate, and soon I was alone, holding the rope in my hands. The girl was still kneeling in front of me.

"Get up," I told her. "Don't be afraid. Nobody will hurt you."

The girl flinched as I spoke but obeyed. I led her to my tent.

As we went, I addressed one of the guards, ordering "bring me some food."

I left her standing at the entrance.

"What is your name," I asked, searching through my garments.

"Neve," said the girl.

She started to sob again as I turned back to her, holding my dagger.

"I will not hurt you," I told her taking hold of the rope. "I have to cut your bonds. Where are you from, Neve?"

"Ikent, sir," she said, and my hand holding the dagger began to shake.

I had to take a few deep breaths to calm myself and cut the rope without injuring her. She rubbed her wrists, and I gestured to a small bench for her to sit down. I had a feeling that I might have my answers before the scouts returned. I took a chair and sat down in front of her. Neve raised her frightened eyes to me.

"Neve, please," I said softly, "tell me what happened. Why are you here, in the middle of the forest, alone?"

Neve rubbed her eyes with her dirty fist and looked at me.

"They burned the city. They killed my little brother and my mum too," she said, her voice barely audible.

"Who?" I asked, trying to keep my trembling voice soft.

"Ghouls." Neve started to cry again.

I had no idea how to comfort her, but her answers raised even more questions. Who were these ghouls? Were they related to Mordak? Why had they attacked Ikent?

I sat in front of her, helplessly rubbing my chin when a man brought a food basket.

"You must be hungry, Neve. Please, be my guest..." I smiled, placing the food basket in front of her.

She stopped crying for a moment and looked at me, her eyes

big.

"Can I take a piece of bread?" she asked.

"You may take whatever you like," I assured her, moving the basket closer for her to inspect. "But please, don't cry."

She nodded, taking a slice of bread and a pear. I smiled encouragingly and watched her as she started to chew.

Suddenly, the tent door flew open, letting in Bedwyr. She flinched.

"You have started to interrogate the spy, my Lord?" he asked.

"I see no spies here," I said. "Only a frightened, hungry child. Our child. She is from Ikent."

Neve's eyes darted from one to the other, and she began to cry again

"Please Neve," I said, moving closer to her. "Don't be afraid. I won't let anybody hurt you."

Bedwyr took a seat but kept his distance.

"Don't rush, Neve," I continued. "Eat whatever you like. Later you will tell us how this happened. We need to know who was responsible, so we can avenge your family."

"Has Ikent been destroyed?" asked Bedwyr when she calmed down.

"Yes," I answered for her. "By ghouls."

"What?!" Bedwyr sprang to his feet, frightening Neve again.

"Please," I turned to face him. "We have a child here. It's not her fault that the town had fallen; don't scare her."

"Sorry, my Lord," he sat down. "But never before has our city been lost to ghouls. Did they come by ships or by land?"

"Ships," came the quiet answer from behind my back. "With scarlet sails."

"Damn." Bedwyr had difficulty to contain his anger. "They have never harvested that far north before."

It was my turn to be confused. "Harvested?"

"Porlok has always been plagued by them. I have no idea if your sister had ever mentioned this to you, my Lord," he said, nervously clenching his fists. "Now they have started to harvest our lands as well."

"What exactly are they harvesting?" I demanded.

"Every living soul they lay their eyes on," he said. "They kill everybody and everything – people, cattle, dogs, birds – and take the meat away on their ships. It has just never happened on our land before."

A burst of sobbing behind my back interrupted him.

"Could we discuss this a little later?" I asked him, turning back to Neve. "We are upsetting the child."

"I am not a child," said Neve, rubbing her eyes dry.

"Then tell us what happened," said Bedwyr calmly.

Clutching a half-eaten slice of bread, Neve raised her watering eyes to me.

"I was playing with my friends on a hill just outside of the town when we saw ships with scarlet sails coming into the harbour," she told us.

"How many ships?" asked Bedwyr.

"I don't know," shrugged Neve. "Many. Too many. The harbour is small in Ikent."

"What happened next?" I asked.

"My friends went down to the harbour to have a closer look. I stayed on the hilltop. When Ikent started to burn, they ran back to warn me. They screamed something about ghouls, but the creatures got them. I ran into the woods and climbed a tree. The creatures followed, but didn't notice that I was high above them, clinging onto a branch," she told us in a quiet voice. "That is what happened."

"Did you get a good look at the creatures?" asked Bedwyr.

Neve nodded. "They are horrible. They look like men but are darker and skinnier. One of them had my little brother's head hooked on a rope."

A few minutes of silence followed. Bedwyr stood up and started to pace around the tent, clenching his fists. Neve sat in front of me, frightened; there was no hope in her watering eyes.

"Ikent has been destroyed, and the family of that child haven't survived," I addressed Bedwyr, carefully selecting my words. "What should we do?"

"Avenge them!" Bedwyr's response was quick, like the blow of a sword. "If that is the case."

"What should we do with this child?" I asked again, keeping my eyes on Neve.

"We can't take care of children," said Bedwyr. "We are an army."

"I am not a child," she said firmly. "I am big enough to take care of myself."

"You are not big enough to fight with the army," I told her. "Do you have any relatives who we could send you to stay with?"

Neve shook her head.

"We can't babysit her," said Bedwyr. "Our town has been destroyed. We need to stop the enemy and avenge our fallen!"

I turned back to Neve. She looked like a frightened rabbit which had been chased by a wolf and ended up in a hole with a fox. It was dangerous for her to be here. I couldn't send her away; she had no surviving relatives. But I couldn't assign her a babysitter either – every fighter was needed in the field. We had no idea how big the army that we were about to confront was.

"Do you like animals, Neve?" I asked.

She nodded slightly, keeping an eye on Bedwyr.

"I have a beautiful horse," I said, "and I need someone to take good care of that horse. Would you be interested in doing that job?"

Bedwyr was about to make some objections, but a glance from me silenced him.

"I would love to do that, sir," said Neve quietly.

"Well," I turned back to Bedwyr. "Everything is solved. She works for me now. Could you organise this, please? I want her safe and well-fed. And could somebody show her where my horse is?"

"Yes, my Lord," said Bedwyr, getting up.

"You may take the food, Neve," I said, handing her the basket.

"Thank you," she whispered.

Neve followed Bedwyr out of the tent, glancing twice at me on her way.

I was left alone, not sure how to cope with this new menace. Who were these ghouls? Who was behind them? I closed my eyes, trying to remember the map on the wall back in the castle, but I couldn't recall any land or kingdom called Ghoul. Who were they? Why were they attacking Chadrack? I had to find out since it seemed we would be heading to battle quite soon.

Bedwyr returned a few moments later.

"All has been done as you commanded, my Lord," he informed me.

"Thank you," I said. "Now could we address more pressing matters? Tell me what you think."

"I don't know if we can trust the child," he said with some hesitation. "They sometimes confuse reality with their fantasies."

"But everybody saw the flame reflections in the sky," I said. "Something is going on there."

"Yes, my Lord, I have no doubts about that," he paused. "I just don't think it's ghouls we are dealing with. That just sounds too weird."

"Still, it could have happened, even if it had never happened before," I said. "What makes you think it isn't ghouls?"

"Chadrack is too far upstream from the Forbidden Islands," he said.

"I need a map." It was a simple request.

"Then may I suggest to transfer to my tent?" asked Bedwyr. "Maps are there, and I could order for your breakfast to be brought to my tent as well, my Lord."

"Let's go." The situation was slowly heating up, and I needed some guidance before it reached the boiling point.

We left my tent, and Bedwyr barked a short command to his officers as we went. A sense of growing menace was hovering over the camp, few people were talking, none were laughing. Grim eyes followed our path to Bedwyr's tent; everybody understood that war or at least a battle was on its way.

The general had a more spacious tent than me. There was enough room to hold an impromptu table made out of a dray, several benches for officers to sit when he was holding meetings and a large case with books, papers and several rolled-up maps. The tent was empty, with general's bed neatly made in the corner.

Bedwyr opened the case and took out a smaller version of the map of the realm that hung in the castle of Chadrack next to my bedroom.

"Here, my Lord." He pointed to the lake. "The Forbidden Islands are here. It is hard to believe that they were unable to find any food closer to the Bloody Sea."

It did indeed look like a long way.

"I am certain they would be repulsed by Ash and Lyme – Ash's defences are strong, and elfin magic protects the shore of Lyme. Nobody in their sane mind would ever mess with Patna and your sister Hel, my Lord. But why they did they skip the southern coast of Mordak and Porlok? Why Chadrack?"

These were good questions based on sound logic. I couldn't help him with any answers, but I saw a possibility here to fish for some knowledge and fill in some of my gaps as well. I just had to move very slowly and carefully.

"Are you suggesting that Mordak and Porlok are their usual harvesting grounds?" I asked overlooking the map.

"Those are only rumours," said Bedwyr. "But we have never had a ghoul problem before."

"It may be that we are having one now," I told him.

"I still find it hard to believe that girl," shrugged Bedwyr. He gestured at the map. "And that is the reason why."

"That is a good reason," I sighed. "But it is based on assumptions. You can't exclude the possibility that she is telling the truth. Maybe they encountered some danger south of Chadrack, something that we don't know about."

"Danger, my Lord?" Bedwyr squinted at me, cautiously. "Wyverns?"

The suggestion sounded laughable and silly, at first. I couldn't believe that this once-peaceful land of a dream could hold any fire-spitting beasts. It was just too much for me.

"Why not dragons?" I asked, a hint of irony in my voice.

"They are extinct, my Lord," said Bedwyr seriously. "Unless the gods have chosen to resurrect them, but I don't know anything about that."

A chill ran down my back, and I froze, considering the thought.

"Let's hope it's not the case," I said. "Maybe it's just that the usual harvesting grounds of ghouls have been depleted."

"That might be true," agreed Bedwyr. "But it could still be an attack from Mordak. The girl may have got it wrong."

"That's why we need to wait for our scouts," I agreed. "Let's get that information checked before making any move."

"As you wish, my Lord." Bedwyr's face was expressionless.

"Your decision is very wise."

But I wasn't ready to stop yet.

"Tell me more about those ghouls, Bedwyr," I asked, gesturing at the map. "I guess they are the reason why these islands are called 'forbidden'."

"Yes, mainly," said my general. "Those savages live in the northern island. It's nothing but bare rocks, and their survival depends on bringing flesh from harvesting expeditions. The northern shores of the Bloody Sea have been plagued by their attacks."

"What is on the southern island?" I asked.

"The Red temple," answered the general. "And it is the main reason why the islands are forbidden. It is guarded by Gods, and those savages just take advantage of this by staying on the island but away from the temple."

That explained nothing, but I was afraid to inquire any further. The pantheon was supposed to be the essential knowledge for everybody in Rehen, and I had no intention to expose the gaping holes in mine.

"You said Ash, Lyme and Patna have their own strong protection against them," I pointed at the map. "Why couldn't Porlok unite with Mordak and stop them from entering the Braaid?"

Bedwyr stood silent for a few long seconds and then slowly

began to speak, carefully considering every word which left his mouth.

"It is known that your sister Keely has never had good relations with your brother Seisyll, my Lord," he said. "And the issue of Chadrack had always been a source of disagreement between them."

Instantly I found myself waist-deep in the swamp of the realm's politics, afraid to step any further. I had no idea what "the issue of Chadrack" was, and I couldn't just ask. I bit my lip, regretting that I had voiced this question, making my ignorance clear. I must choose my questions and suggestions more wisely, I realised.

"Yes, I remember that." I vaguely gestured over the map. "What do we know about Mordak's defences to the south?"

"They are non-existent," said Bedwyr firmly. "Since their war with Hooh, Mordak has based its army in the capital. Their southern shore is an easy target for ghouls. That is another reason why I doubt the girl's story."

"Maybe the southern shore is depleted already. If ghouls used to harvest there and, maybe, there is nothing left." I shrugged, offering another assumption. "When our scouts are due to return?"

"Tomorrow," said Bedwyr.

"We will wait until then," I decided. "It wouldn't make a

great difference who is our enemy. In any case, we must avenge Ikent."

"If it's Mordak, we will be getting into a full-scale war, my Lord," observed Bedwyr. "If it's ghouls, our military campaign will end in Ikent."

"That's true…" I said vaguely, studying the map.

A man came in with the food for us, and Bedwyr had to remove the sheet from the table to make a place for our breakfast.

"The intruder must be destroyed," I said, pouring myself some wine. "I don't want any prisoners taken. Let's give them a taste of their own medicine. It doesn't matter if it's ghouls or the army of Mordak. I want them dead."

"I share your anger, my Lord," said Bedwyr. "It will be as you wish."

We spent the day on planning strategies and the best ways to fight the enemy whoever was holding Ikent. The primary task was clear. We had to free our people, if they were still alive, to annihilate our enemies, and to prevent further attacks.

We were interrupted only by a man bringing in more food.

Later in the afternoon, when the strategy was finally ready, we held a meeting with the officers. I only sat in the corner, quietly observing how Bedwyr was giving commands and distributing tasks. We were willing to move first thing in the morning. We only needed a word from our scouts to make final adjustments.

It was dark outside when I left Bedwyr's tent. The camp was agitated and full of movement. I heard officers urging their soldiers as the formations regrouped according to our plan.

The skies above the forest remained dark and clouded. The flames from burning Ikent were gone.

I slipped into my bed, listening to the muffled sounds of the turmoil outside. My heart was fluttering like a bird in a cage, trying to escape the waves of fear. I didn't know which wave it was that knocked me down.

First thing in the morning, I made myself a big mug of strong hot coffee. *What to do next* was the only remaining thought in my head, circling like a swarm of angry wasps. I couldn't make myself believe what that Asian man had said. By keeping me alive, they were only exposing themselves to even more threats. I couldn't understand why they had kidnapped me, and I had no idea why they had released me either; I couldn't see any logic in either action. Was it safe for me to go outside?

The redhead and his accomplices were still in the neighbourhood, and I had no desire to fall into their hands again. Feeling helpless, I suddenly remembered the card that the police officer gave me – I should call her! The situation has changed, and maybe she would be able to catch them? I would feel much safer if those dangerous men were locked up behind bars.

I looked through my wallet, but the card with the emblem of

the Metropolitan Police wasn't there. *Damn!* I went through my pockets, then searched the pile of old adverts and newspapers – it wasn't there either. I clearly remembered taking the card, but where had I placed it? I was certain I had put it in my wallet.

I looked everywhere again, but the card still was missing. I nearly cried in desperation. I had lost it! The card must have dropped out of my pocket. If it were on the street, the card would be lost forever.

I paced through my tiny flat and cursed my fate. I was on my own now, and I had huge problems on both planes of reality. I couldn't decide which threat was bigger. I had to address them all.

Taking a few days off from the office allowed me to temporarily forget my fears and my bothersome paranoia. Still, those fears kept hovering in the back of my mind like an ever-present sword of Damocles.

I was in the middle of my second mug of coffee when my phone broke the silence. Julie's voice at the other end of the line was breathless.

"What happened?" I asked, putting my coffee down on the table and lowering myself onto a squeaky chair.

"Mrs Patel," she gasped and then whispered into the phone. "She asked for your home address and left five minutes ago. Just to let you know, she might be coming to visit you."

I was speechless for a few seconds. This was unthinkable!

"Were there any disasters in the office during my absence?" I managed to ask.

"No," said Julie. "Everything has been normal. This is very strange."

"Thanks, Julie, for warning me," I acknowledged. "I think I should buy some biscuits."

"You might need them," she sighed. "Phone me with the news later. I have to go."

I thanked her again. For several minutes I only stared at my coffee, unable to move. Extreme anxiety was slowly crawling up my ankles, rising to my knees and freezing my hips. I looked around at my mess, and my heart started to pound – I had to act quickly! *I might not even have an hour before she gets here!*

I jumped up, spilt my coffee, cursed aloud and then started to hide things under the sheets, intending to give my miserable small flat a more respectable appearance. Hectic running took up nearly half of the time. I washed my pile of cups and plates, then put my dirty socks in the washing machine. The bed was made, and the floors were scrubbed.

I sat down for only a brief second, and then remembered the biscuits. A short trip to the nearest grocery solved the tiny problem but consumed my remaining time. When I returned, I found a big black car parked next to my door and Mrs Patel was pressing my doorbell already.

"Good morning, young man," she turned to face me. "I thought you were in some distress?"

"I was only getting some biscuits for my morning coffee," I said, biting my tongue before it spat out Julie's warning.

"May I come in?" she asked.

"Of course." I opened the door for her. "I only wasn't expecting you to visit."

We took the squeaking stairs in silence. She passed the corridor, stopped at the door to my bedroom and looked around.

"Nice flat," she observed. "Tidy."

"Would you like a cup of tea or coffee?" I asked.

"Tea will be alright," she said, still looking around. "No milk and no sugar."

I was busy preparing the drinks and arranging biscuits. She took her time inspecting my flat. The situation was more than strange. I doubted that she had ever checked up on any absent or ill office worker in person before, but I was too scared to ask.

"The tea is ready," I said, placing drinks on the tiny kitchen table. "I do apologise that there isn't a more comfortable sofa. I am renting this flat without any furniture."

"I see..." she came closer. "I was told that you had been kidnapped and injured. May I see your injuries?"

I had no time to answer or protest. Mrs Patel took my face in her hands and brushed my hair aside, then looked at my healing scar with her black eyes. I was afraid to even blink. I felt like a guinea pig in the hands of a curious scientist.

A minute later she released me, still wearing a poker face, and sat down at the kitchen table. I noticed that she didn't ask if I had any other injuries.

"I am not lying, Mrs Patel," I said, sitting down in front of her.

"Tell me more about your kidnapping," she asked, her dark eyes still on my face.

I wasn't prepared for such a questioning but had no choice as to take a deep breath and deliver the entire story the same way I did to that police officer back near Hyde Park. Mrs Patel listened without interrupting me.

When I finished, she continued to sit in silence. I expected a few questions, at least, but she only stared at me without a word.

"What else I can do for you, Mrs Patel?" I asked when the silence began to extend into minutes, only disturbed by the traffic outside my window.

"That's all, young man," she said, standing up. "I have seen everything I needed."

She left her tea untouched.

"You may take as many days off as you need for your recovery," she told me on her way to the door. "Good luck."

She left and closed the door behind her. I heard the stairs squeaking under her feet, then the sound of a closing front door. This was the weirdest visit I could have imagined – and it raised even more questions.

I looked through the window. A man, dressed in black, was politely opening the back door of the car for Mrs Patel. She climbed inside. Just for a brief moment, that man raised his face up and his gaze locked with mine. Suddenly, I felt sick – the man looked like one of the Asians who had kidnapped me. What could that possibly mean?

The man waved to me and smiled, then climbed into the driver's seat and closed the door, starting the engine. The black car leapt forward, squeezed into the continuous line of moving traffic and was gone in an instant.

My legs failed me, and I sat down on the floor. My brain couldn't understand this. Was Mrs Patel behind the kidnapping? But they had said I was the wrong person. Maybe that's why she had given me as much leave as I needed. Was she scared?

The overwhelming fear squeezed my brain into a black dot, and it almost ceased functioning. I cursed myself for losing that card again, but it was too late for regrets. A call to that policewoman would have been very helpful. I was sure it was some kind of conspiracy, but I couldn't prove this by myself. I had no clues. *What to do next?*

More than an hour had passed in hesitation and slowly fading fear until the phone call shook my brain back into reality. It was from Julie again.

"How was it?" she asked.

I admitted the obvious. "Scary."

"Had she fired you?"

"No," I told her. "She allowed me to take a few more days off as I need to recover."

I immediately decided against disclosing the possible involvement of Mrs Patel in the previous unfortunate events.

"Weird," said Julie. "I've lost my twenty quid bet to Tom. I thought you'd be fired."

"I am sorry…"

"Don't be." She attempted a nervous chuckle. "I am glad you are still here. When are you planning to come back to the office?"

"I have no idea," I said honestly.

At that moment, I wasn't sure if I would ever be returning, but Mrs Patel's offer gave me a convenient opportunity to postpone the solution of the issue. Julie sighed and wished me a speedy recovery. After a short goodbye, she hung up, leaving me still lying on the floor, but coming back to my senses.

In fact, I realised, I could address this question in a week or two's time, when I had finished dealing with my more pressing issues. There was a war on my doorstep in Rehen, and I remembered my desperate need for some knowledge about military matters.

The rest of the day was taken up by pizzas and the Internet. I took in as much information as I could find about great and successful military campaigns, and about strategic planning. The data was too abundant, but I had no time to start sorting it – I just read what met my eyes.

My head soon felt swollen and aching, but I couldn't help but go on – reading about tactics in small fights and strategy in big wars. I wasn't even sure if the words I was reading would be of any use. I only had to keep my brain busy.

Later that evening, I fell asleep next to my laptop computer.

Bedwyr touched my shoulder and dragged me out of the depths of my dream.

"What is it?" I asked, still sleepy.

"I have just been informed that one of the scouts is back," he said. "Sorry for waking you up, my Lord, but I thought it was urgent."

"Bring him in," I said, rubbing the remnants of sleep from my eyes and getting up.

The general barked a command through the door, triggering mild confusion outside. I had only a few minutes to dress before the man entered my tent.

I silenced his long introduction with "have a seat," then said, "tell us how many ships are in the harbour."

"Three dozen." The man looked puzzled. "I haven't told anybody they came on ships."

"Ghouls or Mordak?" asked Bedwyr from behind me.

"Ghouls," said the man.

"How bad was the attack?" I asked. "Any survivors?"

"No, my Lord," said the man. "Ikent has been burnt to the ground. We were ambushed while trying to sneak out of the port. I am the only survivor."

"How far they had moved inland?" asked Bedwyr.

"Not too far," said the scout. "The burnt town is still scattered with bodies. They have been picking them up and loading onto ships."

"Damn! We don't have much time," said Bedwyr. "They will sail away as soon as they have finished loading."

"And I have seen smoke rising from the other side of the Braaid too, my Lord. It might be that Hythe was under attack as well," said the scout.

"Hythe?" I looked at Bedwyr.

"It's a town in Mordak, the other side of the Braaid," he said disdainfully. "Not our problem."

We dismissed the scout.

"The girl was right," admitted Bedwyr.

"Let's fight our battles," I sighed. "We'll have time to search for explanations later."

"Yes, my Lord." The general left my tent.

I heard him issuing commands outside, and the army was set

into motion. First, the squad of two hundred horsemen left. They were going to scout out a secure campsite closer to Ikent. Then the main body of infantry left, carrying their guns and provisions.

Bedwyr and I were still waiting with another four hundred horsemen behind us, ready to depart any minute.

The morning was chilly, with low clouds, light rain and fog. I wrapped myself in a warm cloak, shivering, mostly from fear. I was standing on a hilltop alone, looking at the troops marching by and then disappearing behind the milky strands of thick fog – slowly, one by one.

Bedwyr was at the foot of the hill, sitting on his horse, surrounded by a few officers, as he orchestrated the departure of the troops. His infrequent orders were passed down the line by hushed voices, as the campsite slowly drained of people, leaving nothing but cold fireplaces behind.

We waited for another hour. Bedwyr planned to make sure that we would have safe passage and there would be no nasty surprises waiting for me behind the white curtain of fog. The horsemen ahead of us were supposed to scout out the territory and build a camp for the Prince of Chadrack. The forces around me were impressive, but that didn't boost my confidence. I was still trembling. I was still afraid.

"It's time, my Lord," Bedwyr told me at last.

I had thought that we would never be ready. Two men

brought my black stallion and helped me to mount. I grabbed the reins and Knight started galloping down the hill, along with Bedwyr, surrounded by other riders. The battle was waiting for me, but I wasn't prepared for it; I never would be...

The way was long and strenuous. The forest seemed never-ending, with no roads in sight. I had not the slightest idea how the riders decided which way to go; all I could see was a narrow band of sky above us, and, all around, dark woods filled with tall trees and thick shrubs.

We moved quickly. A few times we had to ride around broken mighty trees or strange cliffs arching above the ground like the ribs of a giant. It was a strange journey through an unknown land, a dark sense of menace hovering in front of our advancing troops. I clung to Knight, as I clutched the reins and wondered how many of them would not return from Ikent.

It was well past noon when we stopped by the creek to let our horses drink and rest.

"Will we be able to cover the distance today?" I asked Bedwyr, who was sitting on a flat rock.

"Yes, my Lord," the general said, nodding approvingly.

"What about the infantry?"

"They will arrive tomorrow morning."

I knew that. But this knowledge didn't dispel my fear. A shadow of the approaching battle was plaguing my consciousness as well, forcing me out of my mind. My body felt numb, and I had little hope that I would live through that night and survive the battle the next day.

I blamed myself – my own stupidity for leaving the castle. Now I was in the forest, heading to war.

Later, we mounted our horses and resumed the journey. The four hundred horsemen moved through the dark, creepy woods like shadows. I watched them as we rode, still hardly able to believe my eyes. *What the hell I was doing there?*

We had passed a few more arched cliffs when a cry of an owl brought the message from the front riders. This could only mean trouble. We halted and waited, listening to the sounds of the forest. I started to panic, but Bedwyr remained calm, just clutching the handle of his sword.

Then a horseman appeared from behind the wall of fog, rushing between the other riders. He stopped in front of us.

"We have found bodies, my Lord," he said, addressing me. "Bodies of the enemy."

"Must be men from Ikent were fighting back," said Bedwyr. "We might have survivors."

"No, they don't look like they were killed by a sword or a spear," the rider replied, shaking his head. "You better take a look."

I glanced at Bedwyr, a clear question in my face. *Should we*

investigate the murder of an enemy when there would be a battle
tomorrow?

Bedwyr shrugged and nodded. I waved my hand, and the messenger set off, leading the way; we slowly followed. The shadows of countless riders moved with us, blending into the dark forest.

We travelled for almost half a mile in silence before the messenger stopped in a small clearing between three massive black cliffs. The unmistakable odour of death was there. It hit my nostrils before I saw the bodies.

"These are ghouls without a shadow of a doubt," said Bedwyr dismounting.

I preferred to stay on my horse.

The creatures only looked like humans. Their faces were dark and distorted, remotely resembling canines, but with large black eyes and human-like noses. Their teeth were big, barely covered by scarred lips. They were hairless, dark grey skin covering their muscular bodies. Their crooked fingers with brown claws still clutched weapons – bludgeons, spears or swords, all covered with clotted blood. Their strange garments, made of rags and leather, were grimly decorated with human palms – some rotted to the bone, some still whole.

"I have never seen anything like this," said Bedwyr, inspecting the bodies. "Look, my Lord!"

My gaze followed to where he was pointing. The torso of the dead ghoul was warped as though it had been in a twister, guts spilling out of its torn belly. The sight was so repulsive that it almost made me sick.

"They were killed without a sword or an arrow," he said, leaving the bodies and mounting again.

"The forest is more dangerous than I thought," I said clutching the Knight's reins, my eyes still on the bloodied guts of the dead ghoul. "Whoever killed them might be still around."

"We have to move more cautiously," said Bedwyr and shouted a few commands.

Moments later, we were surrounded by fifty horsemen, arrows fitted in their crossbows, ready to shoot any moment, and we resumed our journey – now at a slower pace and carefully.

It was the longest evening of my life before we arrived at the camp in the forest next to Ikent. The sun was setting, and soldiers set up a tent for me and began preparing for the night.

Bedwyr forbade any fires, hoping to spend the night unnoticed by the enemy. He put several lines of defence around my tent, but that didn't make me feel any safer.

I chewed a few chunks of dried meat and gulped down a few mouthfuls of water. Then I slipped into my tent and closed my eyes tightly, hoping that any horrors would stay outside. The wind in the trees above the tent was the last thing I remembered before drifting away.

It was late morning when I finally woke up in my bed. The sky was clear, and sunshine shone all over London. I spent ten more minutes trying to come back to my senses and calm down, failing.

The images of the dark forest and the twisted bodies were haunting my brain. I was in my flat with the usual sounds of the city outside my window, but my mind painted blood and destruction in every spot where my eyes focused. I was afraid to get out of my bed or to set my feet on the floor. *War is coming, war is coming, war is coming…* The phrase reverberated inside my skull, forcing all other thoughts out of existence. Was I going insane?

An hour later, I felt brave enough to get up. I sipped a mug of strong coffee, trying to calm down, but the fear only increased. I slipped back into my bed and pulled the sheets over my head, in a silly attempt to shield myself from the outer world. Nothing worked.

I was afraid that our camp at the edge of the forest would be attacked by those creatures. I flinched every time I heard footsteps on the pavement outside of my window, afraid that the battle has already begun. I closed my eyes. My mind was drifting between the dream and the reality, in a crazed perpetual whirlpool, without completely reaching either side or focusing on anything. The muffled talk of the guards outside my tent was mixed together with an ambulance siren passing down the street; the lonely cry of an owl amid the forest was drowned out by the sound of a passing plane. *Was I losing my mind?*

Later that afternoon, my stomach finally forced me out of bed again. I managed to call a pizzeria. When the pizza arrived, I quickly stuffed it into my mouth, washing it down with a glass of water. Then the swamp in my bed engulfed my shaking body again. I only waited.

When the night fell on London at last, it felt like salvation. Or were the gates of hell about to open?

Twittering of morning birds brought me back from oblivion. Everything seemed quiet and peaceful, but I knew how fragile that tranquillity was.

I laid in bed, covering my head with a blanket, and hoping that the troops would start fighting without me, allowing me to quietly hide in the woods. But a few minutes later, Bedwyr entered the tent, crushing my hopes.

"We are ready, my Lord," he said. "We are waiting for your command."

I wasn't ready. Somehow, I forced myself out of bed, leaving the fragile protection of the blanket behind.

"Let's have a look," I said, getting dressed.

Bedwyr just nodded and turned around. I followed him out of the tent on my feeble legs.

I was the centre of attention of my army as soon as I got

outside. I looked at their faces – serious, grim, furious, eyes glowing with anger – and instantly understood: they weren't fighting for me, they were fighting for themselves. It was their blood that was spilt. It was their land that had been desecrated by dirty feet of those savages. It was their town that had been burnt down. They were blazing with revenge.

Bedwyr led me to the edge of the forest. The flowering meadow in front of us was peaceful and serene, with countless butterflies and bees visiting every smiling blossom. A pile of firewood in the middle of it looked blasphemous amidst this overwhelming celebration of life, but it was a part of our plan.

We slowly went through the meadow, trying to keep as quiet as possible. For some time, it looked as if it was only the two of us crossing the field, but when I turned back, shadows were emerging from the forest in complete silence – our army was following us.

We reached the hilltop, where a lone pine stood, and stopped there. The army stopped a few hundred feet behind us.

I looked down across the field. There was Ikent, or what was left of the town, ransacked by ghouls. As far as I could see were smoking ashes, stretching from the foot of the hill to the harbour, which was crowded by the dark shapes of ships, and to the meadows along the great river hiding behind the veil of smoke. Dark silhouettes were moving there, among the piles of debris on devastated land. There were hundreds of them, moving in small packs, picking things up from the ground, stacking them in piles closer to the port. I saw them quarrelling and fighting among themselves. I saw them slicing a body in half, as it was too large to carry in one piece. I saw them tossing a child's head around like a ball. There were no survivors here.

"Are they in the position?" I asked Bedwyr.

He nodded silently, pointing to our two battalions, which were hiding in the hills close to the harbour. The one further north was supposed to take the ships and secure them, cutting off the ghouls' means of retreat by water. The southern troops would have to cut their way to Porlok. The main body of Chadrack's army was behind me. They were waiting for my sign.

I looked back. Men were clutching their weapons, ready to spring into action. There was no fear in their eyes – just cold hatred. I wondered: how many recruits were from Ikent? How many had lost their mothers or fathers; lost their sisters, brothers or lovers? Clans and families were dead in the destroyed town. Our town.

I spotted a girl next to the pile of firewood, clutching a burning torch in her hand – was it Neve? The distance was too great, and I wasn't sure, but I didn't think there were any other girls in the army. I reprimanded myself for not sending her away from danger. The front line was not a proper place for a child, but it was too late now. She was here to avenge her family.

For a few heartbeats, I admired her courage, then I raised my hand. This was the sign.

Neve dropped the torch on the pile, and for a few minutes, she only looked at the fire slowly spreading across the dry wood. The logs were quickly engulfed by flames. The wood was dry and burnt eagerly, but it was smoke which we needed to signal to our troops, and there wasn't any.

A few minutes passed, but the situation remained the same. We were losing time. I turned back to face Ikent. Our troops hadn't moved.

"We need to throw some green branches on that fire!" I told Bedwyr. "It will go out soon!"

"Green branches! Bring green branches!" Bedwyr shouted back the order which was quickly passed down the line.

I saw from where I was standing how troops in the forest started to cut the green leafy branches with their swords and pass them back to the front where the fire was. From a distance, it looked like a colony of ants, bringing green leaves to their anthill.

The turmoil didn't go unnoticed. The ghouls at the harbour ceased gathering up the bodies and started to run in our direction in several large packs. From the hilltop, they looked like small bugs, but I knew how false this illusion was. Bedwyr stood next to me, looking calmly at the slowly approaching enemy. Not a muscle twitched in his face; only the right hand tightened its grip on the hilt of his sword.

I glanced back. The troops were standing still, waiting without a sound. Having finally served its purpose, the fire was now spitting a large cloud of smoke into the morning sky.

I looked at Ikent, and my heart skipped a beat. A large crowd of ghouls was already gathering at the foot of the hill, but they weren't attacking yet. They roared, shaking their weapons and trying to scare us. Our troops remained beyond their visibility. Bedwyr and I looked like two random travellers, standing on the hilltop and looking down at the devastated town – we would be easy catches for meat hunters, but the pillar of smoke behind us seemed to puzzle them, slowing their approach. Something was going on behind us, and that unknown thing was attracting the savages, from all corners of the burnt town of Ikent.

At around this time, our troops hiding behind the low hills next to the harbour started to move. I couldn't see any fighting from where we were, but before long, a blue flag was raised in one of the ships, signalling to us in the agreed manner that the port had been secured.

By this point, the ghouls had gathered their forces in the field in front of us and had formed an irregular line, which was now slowly advancing.

Bedwyr waited while our troops in the port regrouped and

took up defensive positions, while the southern battalion lined up behind the horde of savages, cutting off all possible ways of retreat.

It was time for revenge. Bedwyr turned to face the army.

"Soldiers! Let's spill some blood!" He raised his naked blade. "For Ikent!"

The army roared in response.

The dark line of ghouls stopped advancing up the hill when our army spilt over the crest like a swollen river.

Bedwyr had gone with the charge, and I leant helplessly against the pine, watching roaring troops pass on either side of me. They ran down the slope with wild cries, seeding horror in the hearts of the opposing force. I didn't see the clash nor heard any sound when our army met the enemy. I was instantly surrounded by hundred swordsmen, who had been appointed by Bedwyr to defend their prince as soon as the main body of the army had left me on their way downhill.

I still had a view of the battlefield. It was a mess. The army had gone down the slope of the hill like a wave, spiky with spears and swords. Pieces of flesh, torn limbs and heads could be seen being lifted into the air where the wave met the ghouls, but it was impossible to tell from this distance if those chunks had been ripped out of our troops or the enemy. Blood was being spilt.

Shrieks and cries filled the air, mixing with the roar of the advancing army. I shaded my eyes, trying to get a better look. It was hard to make out any individuals in all that chaos, but I managed to spot Bedwyr ripping his way through the hordes of enemies. The ghouls held their grounds only for a few minutes, before starting to retreat – first slowly, but then bursting into a run.

But another wall of spears and swords met them before they were able to reach the still-smoking ashes of Ikent. It was then that the ruthless slaughter began.

An hour later, the battle was over. The dust had settled, and my order that there should be no captives taken had been obeyed. Two squads of our soldiers went across the field, picking out the wounded ghouls and running their spears through every single one, making sure that none survived.

We had taken our revenge.

I was still standing next to the pine when Bedwyr left his wounded to the army healers and approached me. His face was covered in sweat and blood, but I was sure it was the blood of our enemies.

"You have avenged them, Bedwyr," I told him.

"It is your victory, my Lord," said the general.

I looked across the field at the piles of bodies.

"How many did we lose?" I asked, afraid of the answer.

"Less than a dozen, I guess, my lord," said Bedwyr. "Rightful anger is the most powerful weapon."

I looked up to the sky, where a flock of ravens was circling, ready to feast on the bodies scattered across the field. My heart convulsed with pity. The town had been burnt to the ground; people had been killed and dismembered, stacked up as food. Invaders had been killed too, but the fact didn't bring me any relief or happiness. I just felt empty, scared and sad. Why was this world so wrong?

"How many wounded?" I asked, afraid to be silent, feeling a sense of guilt sneaking into my heart.

"Not too many," said Bedwyr after a few moments of hesitation. "Less than a hundred, I think."

Then I remembered the child. Where was Neve? I had utterly forgotten her during the battle. Was she alright?

I was unable to spot her next to the still-smoking fireplace. Where had she gone?

"Have you seen that girl?" I asked Bedwyr, shading my eyes and looking around.

"I hope she hadn't gone to the town," he shook his head. "She could get killed during the battle. Do you want me to send scouts to look for her, my Lord?"

It took a few more seconds for me to answer.

"No," I said. "I have found her."

Neve was standing a several hundred yards away on top of a

massive cliff. I came closer.

"What are you doing there?" I asked. "You are looking in the wrong direction. The battlefield is just downhill, not in the river."

"I am waiting for the ships to come," she said, looking across the Braaid. "Sir..."

"Well..." I said. "Do you see any?"

"Yes." She pointed to the horizon. "They are coming."

"How many ships do you see?" I felt a sudden chill as I asked the question.

"Many!" was the answer.

I left my heart on the ground where I was standing – my body just sprang on the cliff in two mighty jumps.

"Here!" Neve pointed for me.

At first, it looked like there was a swarm of fleas on the face of the Braaid, although they were nearly invisible in the bright sunlight. I shaded my eyes, trying to get a better view. Yes, the ships were there – four dozen of them, at least, approaching our shores in full sail. And the sails were scarlet!

"Get me the general," I whispered to Neve. "Quick."

Neve slipped from the rock and ran to fetch Bedwyr, while I remained on top of the cliff, watching.

The ships were still far away, but the direction of their movement gave no space for doubts.

"Why is this happening to me?" I moaned. "It's unfair..."

I turned back to the field, and my eyes fell on Bedwyr, who was standing next to the cliff, waiting for me to turn my attention to him, his face still covered with the blood of our enemies. His grim glance showed a hint of concern, but he remained silent, waiting for me to speak.

"We are under attack," I told him. "It looks like the ghouls have finished their business in Mordak and are heading back to join the gang here."

I gestured to him to join me and looked back at the fleet of fleas, still in the same place on the mighty river, trying to catch a better wind in their scarlet sails.

"What will be your orders, my Lord?" he asked, looking at the fleet slowly growing from the dark waters.

I didn't like the responsibility, which was crushing me. I felt so confused – I wasn't in fact from Chadrack, but they unknowingly regarded me as their leader, their royal, the tip of their power. But I wasn't fit for the role. Bedwyr had asked me to decide, and I knew if I make a decision, my will would be instantly transformed into Chadrack's will. But I didn't feel like a royal. I wasn't able to decide their fate for them. *If only I could end this nightmare somehow.*

"What do you think?" I asked, avoiding a direct answer.

"We can't leave those who have fallen and flee," said the general. "All the people of Ikent have been loaded onto the ships already – ghouls from Mordak could easily split their crews and take the whole fleet back to the Braaid. Our people are on those ships; we can't abandon them, or their souls will haunt us 'til the end of our days. We have only sustained a few casualties in this battle. If you need my advice, my Lord, I would rather go for a fight. But I will do as you command."

I thought for a moment.

"I don't want to lose our army, at a time when Mordak is threatening us," I told him.

"You won't lose your army, my Lord," said Bedwyr. "Consider it some kind of training. If we can't drive a bunch of savages out of our land, then what are our chances against a regular army?"

"What are our chances of winning against them?" I asked, pointing at the ships, my tongue growing numb.

"That party seems bigger, but we still might outnumber them," said Bedwyr. "We may have a good chance if we act wisely."

"But we don't have a plan," I reminded him, still unwilling to rely on a chance.

"Your plan was perfect, my Lord," he smiled. "We can simply reuse it."

I was unable to share his optimism. I looked again at the fleet of ghouls and nodded.

"You are asking for a fight, general," I said, keeping my eyes on the scarlet sails. "You may have it."

"Thank you, my Lord," he said unsmiling. "I will bring you victory."

He turned, preparing to jump off the cliff.

"Bedwyr." I stopped him.

"Yes, my Lord?"

"Would they use bodies of their own dead for food?" I asked.

The question sounded ridiculous, but when he looked back, his was face serious, and there was a spark of hope in his eyes.

"Yes, my lord, it is known that they would," he smiled for the first time. "We will use ghoul bodies as bait! We need them on the solid ground!"

"Go," I told him. "We don't have much time for preparations. Kill them for Chadrack!"

The general jumped off the cliff and barked a few words to the nearest soldier. A few minutes later, he was holding a meeting for his officers in the shade of the pine on the hilltop.

I sat down on the rock. My legs wouldn't hold me any longer. Minutes later, Neve climbed up alongside me. We sat on the cold surface, looking down at the river.

"Are we going to die?" Neve suddenly asked.

"No." I tried to keep my doubts deep inside.

"I want to die," she muttered.

"Why?" I was shocked by her words.

"I miss my mother," she said sadly. "If I die, I will meet her on the Road of Gods."

"You will meet her." I took her arm. "But not today. You will meet her when you are old, and both of you could watch your children from the Road of Gods – and your children's children too. It will be more fun when you have someone you care for down here."

"Do you have someone to watch you from the Road of Gods?" she asked, lifting her eyes to me.

"No," I admitted. "But if I die today, I will watch over you. You must promise to keep that interesting."

Neve considered the thought for some time.

"But I will need some private moments, sir. I don't like anybody to watch me when I am washing," she said seriously.

"I don't want to look at you in your private moments," I said. "You only need to show me a sign that the next moment is private, and I will look away."

"What sign?"

"Well..." I smiled. "We'll need to agree on that."

She flapped her hands like wings of a butterfly.

"Would this be alright?" she asked.

"It's too complicated," I said. "What about giving me a thumbs-up sign?"

"Like this?" she asked, raising her thumb in front of me.

"Yes," I smiled, turning away from Neve, but my eyes caught the scarlet sails again, and I froze.

They grew much bigger. The enemy was getting closer, and I jumped on my feet to have a look at the ashes of Ikent. The field was deserted already; there were only dead bodies of ghouls scattered across the trampled grass.

"If you meet my mother on the Road of Gods, could you tell her that I love her and ask her to wait for me so that we can watch together?" asked Neve, holding my hand.

"I will..." I mumbled absent-mindedly.

At first, I thought I had been abandoned and left to face the army of cannibals and their fleet heading to my shore. My heart skipped several beats before I located the camouflaged army. The battalions were hiding behind the thick bushes next to the harbour. The main body of troops was now behind me again, passing dry logs of firewood along the line. The pile of green branches was in place already.

"Let's go," I said. "You will need to drop the torch and get those ghouls killed."

"I will do that, sir."

We were ready in no time. Bedwyr ordered the troops to plant a thick bush in front of the pine, where we could observe proceedings without revealing our location. Now we were better camouflaged, and I hoped that the troops would be able to rest for some time before the next wave of enemies arrived.

A few hours passed waiting. I climbed the cliff several times just to assure myself that the ghouls still were there. The wind was blowing from the land, and approaching ships had to struggle with the fast currents of the Braaid as well. That made their progress slow and our waiting unbearable. My impatience and fears grew with every passing second.

Bedwyr was calm all this time, showing no emotion.

"Maybe they will turn around," I said, standing next to my general and looking at the devastated town below. "The weather is unfavourable. Perhaps they will just quit?"

"That is unlikely," Bedwyr said, crushing my hopes. "Look at those ravens, my Lord. The ghouls would follow them at all costs."

I sighed and looked up at clouds of black birds circling over the battlefield, landing and pecking at the ghouls' bodies. He was right. It was like a red rag to a bull.

An hour later, the first ship reached the harbour, which was already crowded with abandoned ghoul ships. The rest of the fleet stayed in nearby, still unable to anchor.

We waited, holding our breath, but, for some time, we saw nothing but ruins and ashes. Then a flock of ravens rushed into the sky, their shrill cries making me flinch, and I saw them: dark creatures carefully making their way through the burnt town, stopping now and then to check something on the ground, and then proceeding cautiously. They made their way through the ruins, looking around and sniffing the air like wild dogs.

Halfway through the burnt town, they spotted the battlefield at the foot of the hill, thickly scattered with ghoul bodies. Two scouts separated from the group and returned to the harbour immediately, while others rushed forward, scaring the hungry ravens away. Several minutes later, a whole bunch of ghouls appeared from the port, rushing to the battlefield.

Bedwyr was right. They were not going to be grieving for lost friends. They began picking up the bodies, casually slicing them in half and piling them in stacks. It looked like a preparation for a shipment of goods rather than a funeral. A series of loud roars reached us from the harbour, and more ships started heading to the shore.

"They swallowed the bait," whispered Bedwyr smiling.

I didn't share his enthusiasm. Battle was nearing again, and that scared me.

Soon the overcrowded harbour was full, and ships started to line along the riverside. More ghouls poured down through the ruins, rushing to the site of the battle. The sight was so disgusting that I had to lower my gaze, trying to suppress the convulsions in my stomach.

When I raised my eyes again, I saw that something had gone wrong. Our plan failed.

We had failed to assess the capacity of the harbour; the ghoul ships had dropped their anchors along the riverside, and quite soon they discovered our southern battalion hiding behind the hills, and a full-scale battle began. But it was at the wrong site, and we were unprepared for it.

Our southern battalion was outnumbered several times; they needed quick enforcement. But between them and our main force were hordes of ghouls, preparing their own flesh for transportation. Fairly soon, the sounds of the battle attracted their attention too, and they dropped the bodies they had gathered and rushed to the southern banks, where our troops were fighting for their lives.

"Go!" I screamed to Bedwyr. "They need help!"

He left without a word, raising the naked blade high above his head. The army followed him down the slope, engaging in random fights with the scattered bands of ghouls and forcing their way south.

The clash was fierce, but the forces were roughly equal. The battle lacked the element of surprise and was disturbingly chaotic. I looked at the field, feeling completely helpless. *We might fail; yes, we might fail!* The victory was now just an ephemeral fata morgana, hovering next to the horizon. Would we still be able to reach for it?

I nearly started crying in desperation as I looked at the fighting between ruins of Ikent. I flinched when my personal guards surrounded me with their swords drawn.

"Go!" I commanded them. "They need everything we've got!"

My protection left without a second of hesitation. Minutes later, they had joined the main force trying to push their way south.

I looked at the field, hardly believing my eyes. Was this the end of Chadrack's army? *Would I die too?*

Clouds of black ravens were circling in the sky above, patiently waiting for the battle to end. More were coming from every corner, ready to feast on still-warm flesh.

I felt somebody touch my hand.

"I miss my mother so much, sir." It was Neve. "Can I go to Ikent and die today? I will promise to watch over you, and you know the secret sign already."

"No," I said, desperately looking around. "You are not going to die."

And I suddenly laid my eyes on our solution which was waiting by the river. Our north battalion was still unaware of unfortunate turns of events, and still waiting for my sign!

"Let's go," I said to Neve. "We need to light the fire!"

"Will it save us?"

"Yes."

"We don't have a torch," Neve observed. "Olby was meant to light it, but he is now in Ikent, fighting."

"We must find some embers," I dropped, rushing over to the burnt-out circle where the fire had been lit during the previous battle. "Find me some dry grass!"

The ashes were still scalding hot. I found a stick and started to poke them, unsuccessfully searching for any embers. Neve rushed over to me, her hands full of dry grass she had collected in the field, but they were useless until I found a spark.

"Find more," I said, hastily digging through the ashes. "That will not be enough."

Neve rushed back to the meadow, and I finally succeeded in finding some redness, glowing in the light wind, among the grey ashes – they were not actual embers, but it was the best I could find so far. I pressed the bunch of dry grass against it and blew gently, bending as low as I could. Then again...

A barely visible strand of smoke appeared, bringing a faint smile to my face. I blew again, silently praying and hoping. Then one more time.

By the time Neve returned with more grass, I already had a shy flame dancing. We carefully fed it another bunch of grass, then added a few small branches and pieces of dry bark. The fire grew stronger, but it was far from sufficient to give our troops a sign. But at least, it gave us some hope.

"We need more dry branches," I said, carefully adding the last piece of bark to the fire.

"I will bring some," Neve ran away, leaving me to watch the fire.

The harsh cries of ravens filled the sky, and I felt rather than heard a sudden roar behind me. I fell on the ground without thinking and rolled to the side, just in time; a huge bludgeon dropped where I had been kneeling only a few seconds before. A one-eyed ghoul as big as a mountain appeared, seemingly from nowhere, roaring at me and lifting his bludgeon again.

He looked at me, licking his lips as if measuring his bite, then he attacked again. My sword was on the other side of the fireplace, out of reach, and all I could do was try to avoid his blows, rolling and jumping around. It couldn't last forever.

We were jumping and swirling around the fragile flames like we were engaged in some weird dance. The ghoul blocked me every time I tried to get closer to the sword. He grinned widely, seeing my helplessness, but I wasn't going to give up that easily.

I took a few more leaps, this time away from the sword. The attacker followed me without a trace of hesitation. He dropped his bludgeon to my right, barely missing my shoulder, and I fell to the ground and rolled to the left, managing to get some hot ashes in my left hand. I hurled the scalding powder in his face, and we both screamed.

He threw his weapon away and grabbed his only eye with both hands, and that was my moment to reach for the sword.

I screamed again, gripping the hilt with my both hands, but the blow of my sword was strong enough to sever the head from his shoulders. The body slumped to the ground, spilling blood on my precious fire and nearly putting it out. I managed to save a few flaming pieces of bark with my sword, then I looked around. Neve was rushing from the forest with a large bunch of small dry branches. They might be our salvation, but we must act fast.

I carefully kneeled down in front of the two pieces of bark and started to feed the fire with all dry grass I had left, just to keep the flames alive. Neve brought some bare branches of pine, covered with yellow drops of sticky resin – an excellent booster for the fire.

Soon the whole bunch was flaming happily, but smoke still was too thin for our troops to see. I carefully added a few larger branches from the pile that had been prepared for the battle.

Time was running out, and I was afraid that we might have lost the battle already, but I was even more afraid to go and have a look from the hilltop.

Gradually the flames became big enough to handle a few green branches, and I started to add them to the fire, alternating them with dry logs.

"Go and hide in the forest," I told Neve. "Climb a tree, as you did before, and wait there until everything calms down."

"Are you going to die?" she asked.

"Maybe," I admitted, placing more wood on the flames. "You must stay alive."

"Remember our secret sign, sir," she said.

"I will," I promised.

I didn't watch as she ran away. I put a large bunch of green leafy branches on top of the flames instead. A large pillar of smoke shot up into the sky, and I finally felt brave enough to have a look at the battlefield.

The carnage was still going on, but I had no idea who was winning. Everything was so confusingly mixed up that it looked like a giant shapeless porcupine spreading across the ruins of Ikent, spiky with countless spears and swords. Sudden cries from the north made everyone freeze, only for a second, as our troops spotted the smoke and finally joined the battle.

I reserved my final strength for climbing the cliff. Keeping the fire burning seemed irrelevant now. I sat down and placed my sword, still covered with ghoul's blood, next to me. My left hand was painfully throbbing. There were a few nasty blisters on my palm, but I was alive.

I sat on the cliff, looking down at the apocalyptic battle and at the ravens circling in the sky above and waiting for their time. A strange apathy filled my limbs – the agitation was gone, my heart had calmed, and my body felt weak and numb. I only looked at the fierce battle in front of me, indifferently. The fight had spread across the ashes of Ikent. It wasn't a picturesque clash of two armies. It was a rather bloody mess: warriors standing their ground against other warriors.

An hour passed before the fortune clearly shifted to our side. The influx of several hundred of our swordsmen made the difference. Our troops did their best to keep the ghouls away from the port, but a large group managed to get through and boarded a ship – one of those anchored along the shoreline. They lifted the anchor and tried to sail away, but were only able to make it a few yards into the currents of the Braaid before several torches gracefully soared in an arc from the coast and landed on the ship, igniting everything around that was combustible.

Bedwyr's order had been to destroy them all.

Screams and roars filled the deck, as the ghouls made desperate attempts to fight the flames. Some of them died in those flames while others chose to meet their destiny in the deadly currents of the mighty river. Half an hour later, a giant flaming torch was flowing downstream, before slowly disappearing behind the horizon.

The carnage of the ghouls lasted for another hour. We took no captives.

Men of Chadrack were utterly exhausted after two consecutive battles. We had won, but it brought us no happiness.

I watched as healers rushed across the battlefield, searching for wounded, and I wondered how high was the price we had paid.

Later, I spotted Bedwyr climbing the hill. He was accompanied by two of his officers and looked unharmed. I climbed down the cliff to greet him.

"It was a difficult victory," I said when he stopped in front of me.

"Yes, my lord," Bedwyr responded. "Songs will be sung forever in all Rehen about the brave Prince Kyleb who won two battles in a day avenging a fallen town."

He dismissed his officers.

"The destruction of Ikent has been avenged," I told him. "Our troops are real heroes. The songs should be about them and their brave general who continued fighting amid enemies."

"I see blood on your sword too, my Lord," he said. "What happened?"

"We had a little dispute with the one-eyed ghoul about lighting the fire," I said, gesturing to the fireplace, where the headless body still was leaking blood. "I had to silence him."

Bedwyr smiled, but I frowned. My reckless gesture had

ruptured a blister on my palm. Bedwyr looked at my hand, and his smile was gone in an instant.

"A healer! Now!" he barked at the battlefield. "Our Prince is hurt!"

"It isn't serious," I started to protest. "The healers are needed more in the field."

"It is always serious," he said, watching a healer running uphill. "The whole army would rather die waiting while your wound is dressed than see your blood spilt, my Lord."

I chose not to argue. The healer washed my blisters and put on clean bandages. Then he rushed back to the battlefield, where the real wounded were waiting.

"We could have all been dead by now if you hadn't lit that fire, my Lord," said Bedwyr, looking at the bodies scattered across the field. "We are all grateful to you for saving our lives."

"How many troops did we lose?" I asked.

"It was many more this time," the general sighed. "It might be as many as a few hundred, I'm afraid. But you mustn't worry, my Lord. We have many fresh recruits in training to replace them. The army will be ready in no time, and the legend of this victory will make your enemies tremble."

I didn't answer.

The day was slowly dying. We were watching the burnt town scattered with bodies and listened to the cries of ravens flying high above when a small group of troops approached us and politely stopped in the distance.

"What is it?" I asked.

"My Lord, we have come to beg you for permission to unload the ships and conduct proper funerals for the deceased," said one of them. "We are from Ikent. Our families are there."

"Yes, of course!" I said without a second of hesitation. "Carry out proper funerals for all the deceased. It is our duty."

They left immediately.

"Stay here for a time, Bedwyr," I said to my general. "Let them mourn properly."

"That will mean a lot of cremation pyres here, my Lord." He stated this as a fact, not an objection. "Do we need to cremate ghouls as well?"

"No," I said, with disgust. "Feed them to fish!"

"It will be as you command," he said, and I knew it would.

"I want to return to the castle tomorrow morning," I said.

I had had enough of death around me. I longed to hide away somewhere in a quiet and peaceful corner and wait until everybody forgets about me, wait until the end of my days and nights.

"I will arrange a group of horsemen to accompany you, my Lord," said Bedwyr. "It is still unsafe out there. A group of ghouls escaped to the woods on southern outskirts of Ikent. They will keep wandering around until our jaegers solve the problem."

"I only want to get back," I sighed.

We stood in a shade of a lonely pine for some more time before returning to the forest, where our camp had been set up. I felt deadly tired. They brought me dinner, but I only managed to take a few gulps of water before slipping into bed. I heard Bedwyr placing guards around my tent, and then I drifted into the darkness.

This time, it was the sound of a doorbell which painfully drilled into my brain. I jumped out of bed but spent a few more minutes looking for my trousers and getting dressed. When I finally got downstairs and reached the front door, there was nobody outside, only a red-and-white paper slip from Royal Mail on the floor. It had my name on it, along with the brief statement: "Sorry, we missed you".

Puzzled, I returned to my room. I hadn't been expecting any packages. It must have been a mistake. I placed the slip on the top of my pile of junk mail. *Later, maybe...*

I could still see those battles in Rehen, all that blood, pain and death in front of my eyes. My left palm was aching slightly – although the ruptured blister didn't look too awful in plain daylight. I carefully washed it and placed a sterile bandage, then made a large mug of coffee.

The morning was peaceful and lovely, in sharp contrast with the nightmare I had just had, but my soul was trembling while I looked at the passing planes. Those dangerous men who kidnapped me were still walking around, and my boss seemed somehow connected with them – *and they knew where I lived!*

I must find that policewoman somehow.

Planes were passing low over the rooftops on their way to Heathrow, and their noise planted some restlessness in my legs. I didn't want to be a sitting duck anymore. I must go to Hyde Park. She might be there patrolling on her horse. I needed her advice. I might need a new job, a new flat, a new identity. *Would she be able to help me?*

I placed my unfinished coffee and stormed out onto the street, glancing cautiously around as I went. A sense of danger followed me like a lost puppy.

I slipped into the first backstreet, away from any cars and traffic. All way I went glancing back over my shoulder, ready to sprint off at any moment. Nobody was chasing me, and I calmed down a bit until I reached the DLR station. I smiled at the view of commuters waiting for the robotic train – never before I was happier to embrace the crowd. I switched to the Tube at Bank station and arrived at Marble Arch without incidents.

Merry sunshine met me when I emerged from the underground and strolled across the street towards Hyde Park. I kept my distance from other people and looked carefully at their faces – there weren't too many around, mainly children and their retired grandparents enjoying the sunshine. It was a weekday, and workers were spending their time in offices, in front of computers surrounded by piles of documents, without even noticing the blue sky and fluffy clouds.

I entered the park by Speaker's Corner and took one of those paths through the vast open field towards the Serpentine. There were no horse-riding police around as far as I could see.

My gaze passed over old ladies chatting on a bench and a few morning joggers stretching their legs, and then I suddenly recognised the familiar silhouette. It was that same dark man from the train! He noticed me the same instant as well and stopped with a shadow of panic passing over his face. The man turned around pretending to inspect his watch and then took off at a rapid pace towards the Serpentine, glancing over his shoulder a few times. I couldn't let him get away again. I had almost run to keep up with his pace.

When we reached the shade of the trees, I dashed forward the final few paces separating us and grabbed his elbow.

"Wait! You owe me an explanation!"

He looked frightened, mumbling something and trying to get his arm free.

"Who are you? What happened on the train?" I went on.

He tried to push my hands away, but I didn't let him free. The struggle was short – I was stronger. The man sighed before submitting to my pull. I quickly glanced around. Nobody was looking at us, and nobody was approaching. We were all on our own.

"Please..." His eyes were begging. "Let me go..."

I dragged him to the nearest bench. He didn't make any further protests.

"What do you want?" he managed to ask.

"Do you know me?"

"I do," the man sighed. "You are Kyleb, Prince of Chadrack. I have no idea what you call yourself here in London."

How could he know that much about my nightmares?

"Is this a joke? Who are you?!"

"I can't tell you that. It would be very dangerous to me and of no value for you." The man attempted to release his hand, but I only squeezed it harder. "Enjoy your dreams!"

"Are you trying to say that you are somehow connected to what I see at night?"

"Yes, I am afraid I am."

"How? Why?" I nearly choked on my question.

"I won't explain that too," the man sighed. "You won't believe it anyway."

I was still gripping his hand rather tightly, making him

wince.

"What can you explain then?"

"All you need to know is that you can't change or undo what was done. Relax and enjoy it." He almost whispered the last part, cautiously looking around.

"Why me?" I asked.

"It wasn't my decision. I am only doing what needs to be done, but I can't predict any results. It is always a tricky business to deal with a new Sleeper. You can never know how it will end."

The answer didn't explain anything.

"Who is the Sleeper?"

"You are a Sleeper now. You are a person who lives in two worlds while you are asleep. Those worlds connect through you."

My brain refused to understand this.

"Are you trying to say that Rehen is real?"

He nodded.

"No less real than this park around us... but you probably know that by now."

I knew in my guts that he was telling the truth, but it was too much for me to accept it.

"Could you release my arm? It is starting to hurt," the man said calmly. "I won't run."

Reluctantly, I let it go. The man squirmed but kept his promise.

"When it will end?" I asked him, my hope fading.

"Never," he whispered. "You must learn to live with it. This can't be undone. Just enjoy it. You are much luckier than me, anyway."

"Why is that? Somehow I don't feel lucky with all those atrocities you have put me through."

"You have free will in both worlds," he said, "while I don't have it in either."

"Don't try to trick me," I looked into his black eyes. "You are not in prison."

"It's much worse than that." He looked around carefully and started to unbutton his shirt. "Have a look!"

There was a tattoo of a snake on his chest. He shook his head as I moved closer to get a better look at the picture, which was still shaded by his shirt. The snake was sleeping on his ebony skin. I extended my hand, trying to touch the image, when suddenly the snake lifted its head and looked at me, probing the air with its tongue.

"No!" the man said, pushing my hand away. "Don't touch it!"

The snake lowered its head back to the man's chest, making barely perceptible breathing motions. He quickly buttoned his shirt.

"This is the image of God. It guides me," he whispered. "When the Serpent senses the required person, it slips into my hand and directs me. Then I must place my hand on that person, and it bites. Don't ask me how it works. I only carry the snake."

"So, this is what happened on the train?" I asked.

The man nodded.

We were silent for a good five minutes after that. I felt sorry for him, but why had the Serpent drawn me into this mess? I had the feeling that I would never get an answer to that question.

Suddenly I remembered the red-haired man. "I was kidnapped. Why?"

"I know," said the man. "I heard rumours about this. You were lucky they caught the wrong Sleeper, or that they even weren't sure whether you were the Sleeper. If you did happen to be the one they needed, you would be dead now. The hunters are ruthless..."

"Who sent them?"

"I don't know. It is very complicated, and you never can be sure. It could be anybody in either of the worlds, somebody rich or powerful enough to hire hunters."

Two old ladies passed our bench, and we grew silent, but he didn't attempt to run away.

"Are all people in Rehen Sleepers?" I gasped, recalling my troops who died in the battle with the ghouls. It was a ruthless slaughter, and I couldn't even imagine the consequences if that slaughter was somehow reflected here, on Earth.

"No, of course, not. Sleepers are rare," he glanced around cautiously again. "And I would advise you to keep quiet about this Sleeper thing if you want to live long enough. The dangers are plentiful."

"I was very quiet... How could they find me?" I asked.

"You made some mistake, something that indicated your knowledge of Rehen when you were here, or your awareness of this world when you were in Rehen."

I sat silently, but I couldn't remember anything. I shook my head.

"You need to be more careful."

I was digesting the scarce information, trying to remember my most nagging questions. My brain was silent, and my head was empty.

"Who are the Nightcrawlers?" The question slipped out of nowhere.

"Oh," the man looked puzzled. "Have you met them already?"

"No," I shrugged. "I only heard that somebody had seen them."

"Where?"

"I don't have that knowledge. I am new in Rehen, remember?"

The dark face of the man darkened even further, and he

looked at me with a noticeable pity in his eyes.

"I am sorry to involve you in this," he whispered. "That means you are in great danger."

A wave of chill ran down my spine. What danger could be greater than wars with ghouls, hijackings, confrontations with the Temple, the tricky situation with Mordak? Enemies and threats were piling up in front of my eyes and multiplying at tremendous speed. *What else was waiting for me there?*

I persistently repeated my question. "Who are the Nightcrawlers?"

"They are ancients who lived in Rehen before the Gods descended from heavens," he said in a whisper, as if afraid of what he was saying.

"Don't feed me those fairy tales," I interrupted him. "I need some real information."

"You can't even imagine how *real* it is," he said, still whispering.

"Well..." I wasn't sure how to react to the news of these menacing night creatures and Gods descending from heavens. It sounded like madman's delusions. "How would I know it's one of them when I see one?"

"You'll know, have no doubts," the man whispered. "Don't ask me more. I have said too much already..."

Three gentlemen ended our whispering and sat down on a

nearby bench, talking loudly, yelling and laughing.

"May I go now?" the man asked.

"How could I contact you? You dragged me into this, then have a bit of responsibility. I might need some guidance." I tried to find a hint of compassion in his black eyes.

The man shook head vigorously. "No way. No more contacts. It is too dangerous for both of us."

He rose and slowly went towards Speaker's Corner. I remained on the bench. My heart was fluttering while my mind wandered in the country of doom and dwelled in the trenches of self-pity. Long minutes passed before I realised that he had gone. The sunny and pleasant day suddenly became not so pleasant, although it was still bright.

I hadn't seen when those noisy gentlemen left. The sun reached the zenith and began its slow climb down towards the evening, but I still sat on the bench, staring at the neatly cut grass in front of me, and still unsure of what to do next.

It was dangerous for me to be noticeable – I clearly understood that. But nobody knew me before – *how those hunters found me?* I was the merest grey rat without any personal life in the office; on the morning train, I was just another faceless passenger; on the streets of the big city, I was just another "no one," strolling away.

The real meaning of the scar on my forehead was clear. It

made me recognisable in both worlds. I must hide it. *Maybe it would be best to flee somewhere in the countryside?* I spent another hour considering the thought and then rejected it. I would be a sitting duck in a small town where everyone knew everybody. The most significant advantage of a big city was its crowds, where I could get lost among other faces. Nobody looked at me twice. But despite that, I still kept on bumping into the redhead and his companions. Those hunters told me that they are not interested in my humble person, but there might be other hunters around. And if I would succeed in making too many influential enemies in Rehen, they might hire them!

I must hide! I must camouflage! That was a matter of survival. But would it help? My body grew numb when I remembered Mrs Patel. She knew my home address. I wasn't sure if she was a threat to me, but she was acting weird.

For some time, I contemplated moving to another place, but that was damned expensive with all those penalties for early termination, costs of new flat rent and those deposits. It was well over my budget, and it was useless as long as I stayed in the same office – my new address will be known there as soon as I inform my bank about the change. I could, as effectively, give Mrs Patel the new address with my own hands.

A new job wasn't salvation either. I was sure the new boss would ask Mrs Patel for references. The wisest thing would be to follow the advice I had been given: to lie low. I was still entirely unaware of the rules of the game I was involved in. Possible war with Mordak could substantially raise the price on my head if my enemy knew I was available here. That thought chilled me to the bone.

I wasn't entirely sure if Mrs Patel was related to my kidnappers. Her driver might only look similar to those Asians; I wasn't sure about that either. That impression might be only a trick of stress on my imagination. But indeed, she was acting rather strange lately.

I spent a few more hours in hesitations, seeing nothing and nobody around. It was cruel to sentence me for a lifetime in danger, for eternal hiding from hunters and fighting monsters, and I clearly realised that my life might get very short. Fear was driving me mad.

The early evening breeze brought some chill from the Serpentine, cooling my aching head. The problems remained unsolved, no decision was made, but it was time to return home. I stood up, got back to Marble Arch and merged with the crowd. Suddenly, I was no longer in the mood for any adventures. I took the Tube home; nobody bothered me on my way.

The air above the vast field was thick with funeral smoke.

My breakfast was spartan – no coffee, as usual. Bedwyr showed up shortly afterwards and told me that everything was ready for my departure.

"The ghoul fleet is still in the harbour, my Lord," he said coldly. "What are your instructions? Shall we set fire to their ships?"

"No, don't destroy them," I told the general. "I understand how much hatred you have for these bloodied ships, but with them added, our fleet almost doubles in size. And the people of Mordak know their shapes very well. Organise small crews and start patrolling the Braaid in the ships; let's trick them into thinking a ghoul invasion is about to come to the north. This will keep them busy and buy us time to build up our defences. Just don't go too close to their shores."

Bedwyr chose not to comment further on this. "It will be as you say, my Lord."

We went outside, but I was unable to cast another glance at the battlefield, scattered with pyres, or at the ashes of Ikent. It was too much for me. I only wanted to get back to safety and quietness.

Neve brought my dark stallion, and we were ready to go.

Several miles of woodland without visible tracks lay between us and the nearest road to the capital. We had passed this way last time, in the dusk, although I barely remembered it. I looked at the creepy forest, seeing dark shadows lurking everywhere.

"Let's go," I commanded, and five horsemen rushed ahead of us, scouting out the way.

The main body of riders assigned to my protection gathered around me, guarding my flank and rear. We didn't expect any real threat, but with the ghouls still on the run, it was a better idea to play it safe. The way was slow and arduous. We kept bumping into thick, impenetrable shrubs and fallen trees and several times had to find our way around towering cliffs or deep ravines.

Minutes later, I thought we were lost, but men in the vanguard seemed quite confident and followed tracks only visible to them without any trace of hesitation.

We were deep in the forest, away from the camp, when the vanguard suddenly halted. One of them raised his hand and stopped all the party. The men around me drew their swords ready and prepared to defend me. The forest was deadly calm and still, and I couldn't understand what was wrong.

We waited for several more minutes, and then I heard it – the sound of breaking branches. I looked around but saw nothing; the horsemen had closed in around me, swords drawn and crossbows ready. The tension grew as the still-invisible source of the disturbance moved nearer. Strangely, it seemed to push through the tops of crooked trees in front of us. Then it passed above the nearest treetop, and somebody gasped behind me. It was a large black bear, slowly floating in mid-air and breaking occasional branches as it moved.

"What the hell?" whispered someone.

The bear was dead – I could clearly see from this distance that its eyes were glassy and tongue was sticking out, ripped up by collisions with sharp branches. Its fur was missing in some places, and there was a large gaping wound in its side, exposing pieces of guts. But nothing could explain the strange demeanour of the dead body floating high above our heads.

We stood there, holding our breath soundlessly, until the bear slowly passed above us to the right, then squeezed through the branches of the mighty oak tree, leaving a few pieces of fur hanging randomly here and there, before disappearing from view completely.

For some time afterwards, we were able to hear some retreating noise, then everything was still again.

I kept my eyes on the treetops until my neck started to hurt. The men around were waiting for my decision. I was sure, Bedwyr would have sent a squad to investigate, but it was too much for me to chase the dead meat. I only gestured to move forward. Nobody argued or commented on that.

A few miles later, we reached the main road and turned right. It was much easier and faster. The rest of the journey was uneventful, and we reached the castle well before nightfall.

I went inside as news about the battles with ghouls and fallen Ikent spread, and women started to scream and wail for their lost loved ones. I needed some rest. My dinner was lonely, but the food was plentiful.

The next morning, I called the office and took my annual leave. The recovery from kidnapping was still a good excuse, and Mrs Patel's promise to let me have as many days off as I required still in power. I needed some time to organise my life.

I stopped shaving, hoping that a short beard will make me less recognisable among the abundant hipsters of London. Longer hair and a baseball cap would hide my scar for some time, at least.

I sipped my strong morning coffee as the plan of action slowly took shape in my still-cloudy brain. I couldn't live in constant fear. I must fight back. I knew I had to train and keep my body strong to be capable of defending myself. I must get some training! I was alright with the sword on Rehen, but I wasn't sure how my body would react there.

A quick internet search gave me a few nearest options to choose from. I hated boxing and rejected several clubs on that basis. Gyms purely for narcissistic body toning were of no use either. I found a nearby martial art club which seemed worth trying; it didn't have a webpage – only an address and telephone number were available.

I never was keen on sports, but this time, it was a matter of survival. I must be able to fight back.

I put on my baseball cap and spurted downhill, testing my physical strength. It wasn't great. Several hundred yards later, I was sweating like a pig and gasping for air. Maybe I was pressing too hard? Anyway, that required some improvement.

The weather was beautiful but windy. The cool shade of tall trees met me at the entrance when I finally reached the required address. I went inside before my determination evaporated. There was a young black lady at the reception who kindly led me through the tricky process of registration. I quickly paid, and she gave me a list of what I would have to buy before I started.

I thanked her and left, and the crowded street embraced and engulfed me. Seconds later, I was just another anonymous face, walking in an unknown direction. I did my shopping and headed uphill.

I spent the rest of the day at home.

That morning in Chadrack was soundless. The battle with the ghouls claimed its victims, and the losses had touched almost everybody. The air was filled with grim, silent mourning of men and occasional hushed weeping of the women. Many had relatives in Ikent, but Neve appeared to be the sole survivor from the town.

The ghouls wandering somewhere on our soil were big enough blasphemy and menace in everybody's minds. How many more lives this would claim? The ghouls were acting like pirates – those battles weren't part of any real war, but it clearly pointed to gaping holes in our defences. Ikent was left exposed without any military presence at the borders. And I was afraid that the same problem was lurking along the entire length of Chadrack's shore.

I sneaked out of my bedroom and looked at the map in the hall. The presence of two large parties of savage cannibals that far to the north was worrying – several large towns of Chadrack lay north of Ikent on the banks of Braaid. If their defences were as non-existent as those of Ikent had been, we might have a serious problem.

I gulped down my breakfast and decided to find out how Rhys was doing with the gryphon. Carwyn helped me to find their new location, and, naturally, Bysh was there as I entered the room. Rhys was feeding the baby gryphon with chunks of lamb.

"How things are going?" I asked.

"Thank you, my Lord! Gwyn is growing faster than I thought. Look, he has some feathers on his wings already..."

"Great. I hope the gryphon is well-behaved? We can't keep an aggressive animal..."

"Don't worry, my Lord. He's clever. You will have no problems with him. Gwyn! Come here!" Rhys extended his hand, and the baby gryphon stood up on his lion's legs and carefully touched Rhys's arm with his eagle's talons.

The wings were folded up on the creature's back and quivered when Rhys stroked his back. Gwyn cocked his eagle head and started to purr like a small kitten.

"What do you know about gryphons? You know these woods best – what kind of animals are they?" I asked while Rhys fed another piece of lamb to Gwyn.

"Not much," Rhys shrugged, keeping his eyes at Gwyn who

was fooling around with Bysh. "They are predators and extremely rare. You have seen the mother, my Lord, and you can estimate how big Gwyn will be when he grows up. Males must be slightly bigger, I think. Legends say they are more intelligent than humans."

We were watching Gwyn rushing around the room and playing hide-and-seek with Bysh when a tap on the door brought everything to a halt.

"My lord, your sister Keely, Princess of Porlok, has sent an emissary to you," Carwyn announced peeking through the half-opened door.

"What does she want?"

"She seeks your hospitality. She is still several miles away, waiting for your decision."

"I will meet her in the throne hall as soon as she arrives."

"Yes, my Lord," Carwyn nodded. "Do you want a formal state reception?"

"That would be appropriate, I guess," I shrugged. "And I will need your assistance with this."

"You have no reasons to worry, my Lord," Carwyn assured me. "Everything will be as you wish."

I didn't share his optimism. I had no experience of receiving heads of neighbouring countries.

"I'll meet you there," I said to Carwyn, and he left

immediately, closing the door behind him.

I sighed and shook my head. I was back in the land of doubt, swamped by uncertainty.

The gryphon stopped abruptly in the middle of the room, shrieking like an eagle. I flinched, as his cry was unexpectedly echoed by the harsh shriek of a raven. A large anthracite bird slipped through the window like black lightning and attacked Gwyn. The gryphon swirled around the room crying as loud as he could, trying to escape the blows from the black wings, pecks from the beak and scratches from the talons.

I grabbed a chair, attempting to hit the bird, but missed several times. Bysh leapt after them, barking loudly, but the raven managed to escape his jaws and continued chasing Gwyn.

"Gwyn! Come!" Rhys cried out, spreading his arms.

The poor gryphon made a few evasive manoeuvres before jumping on Rhys' lap. The fierce attack focused on Rhys while he did his best to shield the gryphon from raven's blows with his body. The black bird circled around the room several times, giving me a few opportunities to strike with a chair, but I missed all of them.

Rhys wrapped his arms around Gwyn and buried face in his hands, trying to prevent direct blows to eyes, but I noticed streaks of blood leaking through his fingers already.

Finally, Bysh managed to grab the black intruder and tore it apart with his mighty jaws. I gasped in the abrupt silence; my heart still continued to race.

The door burst wide open and worried Carwyn appear in the doorframe.

"What happened? We heard the noise!"

Gwyn was intact, but blood was bursting from the deep wound on Rhys' cheek. Bysh and I had no injuries.

"We need a healer to take care of Rhys!" I ordered.

Carwyn vanished without a single word and moments later returned with the breathless healer who was carrying his bag of supplies. The wound looked nasty, but it wasn't as deep as I anticipated. The healer washed away the blood and put some smelly ointment on the wound and placed bandages.

"Please, keep Gwyn here, out of anybody's sight, while the Princess is staying. I don't want any trouble," I told Rhys. "I must go now."

"I will, my Lord," he said, frowning with pain.

I left the room still shaken and stormed to my chambers. It seemed like the whole world (both of them, in fact) were united in an evil conspiracy against me, tossing at me one disaster after another.

I wasn't ready to meet my so-called sister. I knew it might be an awkward encounter. Of course, she would have some childhood memories, she would have extensive knowledge of life in Rehen – and she knew our parents… I had no knowledge of those things and would be quickly drowned in the political undercurrents hidden beneath the calm surface of the realm. I had no knowledge of any of the country's customs or current policies either. She might mention names I had never heard before. She would surely ask me questions! *I was doomed!* There was no way I could avoid exposure. *Would she buy the story about my poisoning?*

I paced my chambers several times, then briefly checked my appearances and left, still unable to take my nervousness under control.

The corridor was empty, and I sighed, trembling like a rabbit. *Would she be able to crack my defences?* She might be. *Would she dare to challenge me?* I had no idea.

I knew I must calm down, place a lock on my tongue, go with the flow and see what happens. I didn't like the idea, but there were no other ways out of this situation.

I took the stairs down and entered the throne chamber. It was full of people, with nobles lining the aisle on either side, preparing to greet the Princess. I wondered how Carwyn had managed to organise this at such short notice.

Instantly all eyes were fixed on me, and all conversations died away into silence.

My palms were sweating as I slowly went down the aisle to the throne, trying not to make eye contact with anyone. Men bowed as I passed and ladies curtsied.

I sat down and waited. Nobody spoke a word.

A few moments passed before Carwyn appeared in ceremonial garbs with a white staff in his hand. "Princess Keely of the House of Porlok has arrived!" he announced.

A soft murmur passed over the nobles.

Minutes later, she came in, wearing a long, dark red gown. She was tall and graceful, with long curling ginger hair. Her eyes were large and green, and a serene smile danced on her lips. I rose from my throne as she approached.

"Welcome, Keely, Princess of the House of Porlok! Welcome to Chadrack!" I echoed her official title after Carwyn's announcement.

"Skip those formalities, dear brother Kyleb!" she smiled, approaching the throne. "I am delighted to see you."

"Be my guest, dear sister!" I smiled, too, but my soul was trembling inside. I was afraid to make any mistakes.

She gestured to her accompanying retinue, and they parted letting through a gracious figure, dressed in a long, nearly transparent crimson gown, her head covered with a lightly glistening purple veil. Keely took her hand and stepped on the dais, still smiling.

"I have brought you a gift, dear brother," she said, stopping in front of me.

My nervous smile faded, suddenly feeling a trap. I had no idea how to react.

"It is very kind of you," I managed to mumble when Keely uncovered the veil and let me inspect the gift.

"She is Saqia. She comes from the south," said Keely. "A very rare breed."

Saqia was a young woman in her early twenties with handsome features – a small nose, puffy lips and a small chin. But the strangest thing about her was her blue skin and pale blue, almost white eyes. Her shiny black hair was nicely done up, held in place by a few glistening red pins. A shy smile was playing on her lips, barely covering two even rows of pearl-white teeth.

I was petrified, but not because of the beauty of the gift. I was sure everybody was waiting for me to make a mistake. I helplessly glanced at Carwyn, who was standing behind the Porlokans. His face seemed carved of stone, but I saw his eyes slowly moved down as if for acknowledgement. *Or was it only my imagination playing tricks on me?* Time was slowly passing like a thick, sticky wine, bringing dizziness into my head. Keely stood next to Saqia, still smiling, and waited for my reaction.

All eyes in the hall were on me, and I felt frozen, like a tiny ant in a piece of amber.

"It is very kind of you," I forced out, at last, attempting to regain my senses.

Impatient murmurs passed over the nobles, and I distinctly understood that my time allowance for inactivity was gone – I had to do something. I couldn't reject this offer – that would undoubtedly insult my beautiful sister and head of the friendly neighbouring country. But I couldn't accept it either.

Smile slowly faded from Saqia's lips, and I made up my mind. I stood up and took a few steps forward in complete silence.

"Don't you like her?" whispered Keely.

I was sure that her whisper was loud enough for the front row of Chadrack's nobles to hear.

"She is gorgeous," I told her. "You are very generous, dear sister. I am simply speechless."

I took Saqia's hand, briefly glancing into her nearly white eyes, and noticed a faint smile returning to her lips. I allowed myself the luxury of a few more heartbeats in silence. Then I passed Saqia to Carwyn with orders to accommodate her in the castle so she could rest from her long journey. She was quickly moved along the line to some lesser-ranked butler, but I knew that my order would be carried out.

I returned to the throne and offered my sister a seat next to me.

"I must apologise for the men from Porlok who you caught on your hunting grounds, dear brother. It was unintentional and purely accidental. They said they were lost." She smiled, turning back to me. "They meant no harm. Thank you for your kindness and for sparing their lives. I must confess, wanderers like that wouldn't be so lucky in Porlok. However, the escort was a little bit excessive. You could just have pointed the way."

"It wasn't difficult. I only wanted to make sure they reached Porlok safely. These are troubled times." I said; the nervous note in my voice fading.

She gracefully nodded.

"I have just learned you have recently had some problems with ghouls?" she asked.

"The rumours are true," I said. "One of our towns was entirely destroyed, and every living soul there was killed. The battle was difficult, but we defeated the intruders. They all are dead now. Well, nearly all…"

"Please, accept my condolences for the destruction of the Chadrackan town," she said seriously. "Could the House of Porlok be of any assistance in your fight?"

"I greatly appreciate your offer, dear sister," I said aloud.

Murmurs rolled through the hall as soon as I finished speaking. Had I said something inappropriate? She smiled again.

"Could we end this farce and have a more private conversation?" she quietly whispered, a heavenly smile still on her face.

"Forgive my insensitivity, dear sister," I thundered. "You

must be exhausted after your long journey. Could I offer the Princess of Porlok chambers to rest? Will you join me for lunch, dear sister?"

"Thank you, dear brother, Kyleb. I will..."

"We will dine at noon," I announced and added almost inaudibly. "But I will meet you in your chambers before that."

She nodded and gracefully rose to her feet. I watched her retinue parted to let her through while Carwyn showed the way. A wave of bows and curtsies passed the nobles with no acknowledgement from the Princess. I noticed some women making quick hand signs as Keely passed.

I left the throne hall soon after her. The official reception was over.

Rooms of the Princess were next to mine. Jaegers were guarding my chambers, and two Porlokan knights stood at Keely's door but stepped aside as soon as I approached. I had no time for hesitations but gently tapped the door before entering.

"Come in!"

She was standing by the window and looking outside but turned around to face me as I entered. I stopped, then took another unsure step, but she rushed towards me.

"I am so glad you are alive, Kyleb" she whispered, embracing me. "I heard you had been poisoned."

"That's true," I said, gently touching her shoulders. "It's no longer a secret. Don't worry, I am fine."

She lifted her eyes and for several long moments, carefully studied my face as if trying to find any traces of poison on it. Then she kissed my forehead.

"Poor brother... this country of bastards doesn't deserve to be ruled by you!" Her eyes were wet, but the next moment, she took her emotions under control, shook head and released me.

"I have no other country to rule," I observed, following her as she walked back to the window.

"That's not true, and we both know that," she grunted without looking at me.

I froze. *What did she mean by that remark?*

"How much longer are you going to wait? Next time they will use a sword or arrow, or a stronger poison. What are you waiting for?" Keely fixed her gaze on me again. "Don't you think it's about time to make a move?"

I was afraid to break the silence. I had no idea what I was supposed to do.

"Say something, Kyleb," she whispered.

"I am thinking," I dropped the vaguest phrase I could think of. "I'm still unsure of how to proceed."

"Don't play the fool with me, Kyleb," she said. "You know Mather – he will try harder next time, and you may not survive it. The whole realm is trembling under him. It's been five long years since the tragic death of King Grehlard, and everyone is already sick of his bloody regency. You are the eldest of us, Kyleb. What are you waiting for?"

My head felt dizzy when the meaning of her words finally started to shine through the thick fog of aposiopesis.

"I don't think I am ready to do this, Keely," I whispered, a panic attack slowly overwhelming me.

"That's no excuse," she told me firmly.

"Maybe Mather knows something that we don't?" I suggested, my hope fading. "Maybe the King is still alive?"

"Don't be silly, Kyleb," she shrugged. "No one has ever returned from the Road of Gods."

I slowly shook my head, frowning. My heart fluttered each time I crossed a yard full of people, and now she was implying that I must sit on the throne of this realm! I nearly fainted at the thought.

"Do you know something? If you have some important knowledge which is holding you back, please share it with me." She gently took my arm. "Please..."

I thought I had finally found a serious-sounding reason for my inaction. "Do you think Mather will simply step down when I wave my finger?"

"He has no right to sit on the throne, and he knows that!" Keely hissed through her teeth. "I am sure you will have many supporters if you stake a claim."

"More than he has?" I asked, meeting her gaze. It was a pure gamble since I had not the slightest idea what the balance of power was.

"You know, that's a difficult question, Kyleb," she admitted. "I can only guarantee the support of Porlok, you can be sure about this. I think Devona would dare to join an alliance as well, but you will have to ask her yourself. With the lands on the right bank of the Braaid united, Seisyll and others will be forced to follow you if you claim your right. Everybody has had enough of the usurper."

Now I felt lost. I didn't know the game. Was it Seisyll of Mordak she was referring? *Seisyll would never forget what had been done in my name!* I was slowly drifting into foggy and muddy discussions about things I had no idea, events I had no memories of and people I didn't know.

"I need more time to think about that," I said vaguely. "This matter needs some careful planning."

"Promise me, Kyleb, you will look at the issue seriously," she said. "We can't let it go on for too long. I promise you will always have my full support."

Luckily, I was saved by Carwyn's announcement that the lunch was ready.

"Could I share my food with my lovely princess?" I asked her.

"Yes, dear brother, with great pleasure!" she answered, laughing.

I took her hand and led her out to the corridor.

The dining room was filled with warm candlelight. Roasted pork, roasted pheasant, fish stew, freshly baked bread, cheese, fresh fruit and, of course, the wine was waiting for us on the dining table.

I moved the chair and seated Keely and then positioned myself at the other side of the table, in front of her. Carwyn served us the meal. We ate silently, exchanging a few formal remarks only. After a dessert of fruit, Carwyn left us alone, and I poured out two goblets of wine for us.

She accepted the drink and smelled the bouquet.

"What a beautiful elfin piece of art you have there, dear brother. The wine is excellent," she observed. "I am closer to Lyme, but I have never tasted anything like this masterpiece."

I sipped the wine, which was a little too sweet for my liking, feeling silly as I had no knowledge of the elfin arts. She tasted the wine again with a content smile and placed her goblet on the table.

The drink had untied my tongue, and I felt brave enough to ask about the gift. "I have no intention to sound ungrateful or anger you, dear sister, but why you brought that blue girl to me?"

She chuckled.

"I was expecting a question like this," Keely said with a smile. "She always attracts attention and prompts questions, but this one is easy to answer – she is there for your amusement only. She will do whatever you ask, and she is well trained in doing it if you know what I mean."

"Don't you think I can take care of my own desires?" I dropped without thinking.

"Don't judge me harshly," she said, apologising. "I had no intention to insult you. Do as you like. If you don't need her, you can just send her back to me anytime."

"And you will be able to present her to somebody else?"

"Yes. Why waste such rare beauty?" she sighed.

"Then I will keep her," I made up my mind. "But I am not sure if she will have much work here."

"Don't pass her to the temple of Qu'mun," she asked flatly. "Please…"

"I won't," I promised.

Keely smiled before raising her goblet.

"I think we should drink a toast. To the future alliance!" she offered and added after a short pause. "To the new King of the realm. To grace and glory!"

It was a very subtle reminder of our previous conversation and the persistent pressure she was piling on me. Keely smiled, and only then I noticed the giant sparkling ruby on her finger. The ring was decorated with a familiar pattern of two gryphons. Was that the Ring of the ruler of Porlok?

"To grace and glory," I echoed, skipping the first part of her toast.

We drank the wine. The aftertaste was strangely bitter this time.

"The food was marvellous, dear brother," said Keely and placed her goblet on the table. "Now, would you permit me to visit the Well of Power and pay my respects, as I always do?"

"Of course, sister," I nodded, still unsure what she meant.

I was puzzled by her request. *Was this some religious ceremony?* The Well of Power sounded like a mystery, and I was keen to explore it.

"Do you mind if I accompany you? I promise to be very quiet and won't interfere," I winked.

"Not at all!" She smiled mysteriously. "Can we go now?"

I shrugged. It was very unusual for me to dive head-first into the unknown, but Keely knew much more than I did, and I couldn't waste the opportunity. I stretched a silly smile across my face and got up. Keely rose as well. I had to mumble a few polite nonsenses and open the door for the Princess to trick her in leading the way. We turned left and went down the corridor, keeping the small talk. I trailed a few paces behind, complaining about "that damned poison".

"Are you sure you can cover the whole way?" Keely looked at me, concern in her eyes.

"I think I can," I assured her having not the slightest idea where we were going, "at a slightly slower pace than usual."

The Princess found my remark amusing. She was softly chuckling as we passed the corridor and took the stairs down, and then she unexpectedly turned outside. I held the door for her.

Porlokan knights in the yard rushed after their Princess, but Keely stopped them with a gracious compelling gesture. She was still smiling when we went towards the gate. I didn't permit my smiling mask to slip, but deep inside the worry was growing. *Where is that Well of Power?*

We got outside of the city walls and crossed the bridge. I briefly glanced back as the gate was closing. Several armed men were on the wall, calmly looking as we went. *Was it a trap?*

Leaving the safety of the castle seemed like insanity, especially with ghouls still on the loose, but Keely seemed very confident about what she was doing. Warm sunshine greeted us with gentle waves of a calm breeze, as my sister unhurriedly took the path to the waterfall. I followed her, a step or two behind.

"Tell me, Kyleb, was it your military strength that enabled you to prevail in the battle with the ghouls or did you used your Ring instead?" she asked without looking at me.

I was puzzled by her question. How could a piece of jewellery have any combat use in a battle?

"No," I shrugged. "The victory was down to my troops alone..."

"Then I am very impressed by the military power of Chadrack," she said seriously. "That ghoul thing is poisoning any joy of life."

"Why don't you place more of your military forces on the riverbank?" I asked. "They are coming on ships, I guess?"

"My military has more important things to do than deal with attacks from those pitiful savages," she sighed.

"What is more important than that?" I asked, surprised.

"I am sorry to be a messenger of doom, Kyleb," she said, then stopped and looked at me. "The Nightcrawlers are in Porlok already. Have you seen them in Chadrack?"

"No," I mumbled. "I sleep at night..."

"I appreciate your humour, brother, but this is serious." She began to ascend the stairs carved into the rock.

"I heard rumours that they were spotted somewhere, but I hope it wasn't in Chadrack," I said. "Have you seen them?"

"No, I haven't," Keely responded after a short pause. "I've sent my army there. We suffered terrible losses. My scouts followed them downstream the Ciwc almost to the shores of the Braaid. I was too afraid to have a look myself. Believe me, the ghouls are nothing compared to this."

"What are you going to do about it?"

"I don't know, Kyleb." She turned to face me, looking very fragile. "Devona has burnt her bridges, and now it seems I am on my own. They might let me down under the Hammer. I am so scared."

Notes of genuine dismay were in her voice. My heart skipped several beats as I tried to hide my rising panic. *What kind of terrible monsters was plaguing this land? What was threatening my sister?* I felt her fear echoing in my soul.

"I will support you, Keely," I told her, but there wasn't much confidence in my voice.

"We don't have much time, Kyleb," she said. "Don't put your claim on a long shelf. It might be much safer on islands in Wagorn, and I would gladly follow you there."

Before long, the rapids had been left far below, and we approached the roaring waterfall.

"Why did you chose not to use the Ring? Any particular reason?" She seemed concerned.

I shrugged. I had absolutely no idea what Keely was talking about.

The beautiful valley slowly unfolded in front of our eyes as we ascended the mountain. It was impossible to speak due to the loud thunder of the waterfall, and I was glad about that. I had no taste in talking about things I didn't understand.

We reached the top of the stairs and stopped there for several long minutes, catching our breath. Keely was leaning on me.

"You are stronger than I thought, Kyleb," she grunted.

Then she turned to the waterfall. I followed. Ignoring the dangerous proximity of turbulent water, she went straight over to the black rock at the base of the falls. She was very self-assured, and I was sure it wasn't her first time there.

I stood a few paces behind her while Keely silently inspected the wet surface of the dark rock until she found a barely discernible carving in the stone, shaped like a human palm with two figures of gryphons on either side. Keely placed her hand on the carving, and I caught a glimpse of a strange glow from the Ruby in her Ring.

The cliff trembled and parted, revealing a narrow set of stairs leading down to the depths of the mountain.

Keely stepped inside without a trace of hesitation. I was forced to follow her, my heart pounding insanely. *It felt indeed like a trap!*

We took just a few steps before the rock trembled again, closing, but the darkness didn't follow. Myriads of strange crystals were scattered across the ceiling of the narrow tunnel, emitting a pale green light. Keely's dark red gown blended in with the colour of the walls, creating the eerie impression that her ginger head was floating in mid-air in the greenish ghostly light of the crystals. The walls gently vibrated under pressure of the waterfall, but the sound here was muffled and not as deafening.

We descended the slightly spiralling staircase into the depths. Keely was watching her steps, and I didn't dare to bother her with the questions which were now boiling inside me. We left the loud rumbling of the falling water far behind and continued to descend in complete silence.

It was a long way down. We made our way through the darkness in a bubble of greenish light. The monotony was killing me, but Keely remained silent and focused. I felt tired already and had the uneasy suspicion that we had passed beneath the foot of the mountain long before, but I was afraid to disturb her concentration and ask.

The staircase seemed endless, with no side tunnels to be seen. I was glad when it finally ended in a large grotto. Keely stopped unexpectedly, and I nearly bumped into her. The light was much brighter here, but it was not only from the green crystals. Pink and purple shadows were playing among them, creating the stunning illusion that the walls were swirling in a strange perpetual dance. The source of this weird illumination was at the very centre of the grotto, pulsing deep with purple light like a living heart. The Well was framed by a rather eclectic collection of black boulders and flat but oddly shaped red rocks. Despite all the fancy movement of lights, the most bizarre thing about the grotto was the deadly silence. I could hear my heart beating. It was nearly in unison with Keely's for a few seconds, then mine skipped a beat.

Keely approached the Well.

"Its power always makes me tremble," she said, extending her hand.

The Ruby flashed bright red, like an ember in high winds, and the Well stirred into motion as if a giant jellyfish had awoken in its depths. A few purple thunderbolts jolted the Ruby, raising a flock of red sparks, but Keely only smiled and touched the surface of the Well.

Something was going below the surface as the light was intensifying. The Well was swirling and bubbling; coloured sparks were flashed on its surface and then sank back into depths. The Ruby now shone like an evening sun, completely submerged under the purple veil.

Keely was calm and confident in whatever it was she was doing. I observed her from a distance; not a muscle twitched on her face even though the purple lightning jolted her Ring several times. The mesmerising whirlpool engulfed us completely. The time seemed frozen when I looked at my sister in the very centre of the swirling lights. Her palm, submerged under the purple surface, seemed black, while flashes of her Ruby were even more intense.

It ended abruptly.

Keely withdrew her hand from the Well and looked at the Ring with a content smile. The rays of purple light retreated under the surface, resuming previous slow mesmerising dance.

"Your Well is much stronger than mine," Keely said, admiring her glowing precious stone. "And where is your Ring, Kyleb? I thought you were going to use it."

"I left it in a safe place in the castle..."

"Are there any safe places in Rehen?" she chuckled, then added, "any safe places for the Ring?"

"I think that one is safe," I insisted. I was sure nobody would dare to touch the leather vest in my bedroom or search through its pockets.

"You know better." She didn't seem convinced but had no wish to argue any further. "Let's return."

The way back was challenging. I was utterly exhausted when we reached the top, and the black rock parted again when my sister touched it.

Still, a long way down was ahead of us. The evening dusk was landing on the ground already, and, high above us, the silver contours of the magnificent globe were lit up.

We started to descend, slowly moving away from the falls. It was dark already when we crossed the bridge next to the castle.

"Would you extend your hospitality for a night, dear brother?" asked Keely. "I hate to travel at dark."

"Of course, sister. It is a pleasure to have you here. I'll make sure your men are well accommodated too."

Then we had tea and biscuits with Keely, neither of us talking much. I had a lot of questions swirling in my head, but my sister ate silently with her absent-minded gaze wandering around delicacies Carwyn had placed in front of us, without focusing on anything. She must be deadly tired, I guessed. She finished her biscuit and left for her room, her Ring dimly glowing in the dark.

I went to my chambers. My hands were shaking when I searched through my garments and cursed, more than once, for my carelessness with the jewel. I realised that it wasn't just a ring but the Ring – an attribute of power and a symbol of the ruler. *And I left it in some goddamned pocket!* I rushed around my bedroom like a panicking lion until I slapped the vest I was wearing. I sighed while retrieving the Ring, then turned it in my fingers and smiled like a child. The jewel was casting blue sparkles in the shivering light of candles, but I saw none of the glow I had seen in my sister's Ring. That was strange, and I slipped the Ring back into the pocket of my vest. I was too tired to think clearly.

Undressing, I closed my eyes and envisioned the purple Well under the mountain. I must go back, alone – I realised that the Ring was a key. It was a big and very intriguing mystery, but at least I had some clues about where to start. I was deadly tired and fell asleep as soon as I slipped into bed.

When I woke up in London, the leg muscles were still dully aching after my long wanders through the underground tunnels in Rehen. I stretched in my bed, still enjoying the lazy morning moments, then got up, brushed my teeth and made myself a cup of strong coffee.

The morning was peaceful and refreshing. I took my time to get in a proper mood preparing for my first training session in the martial arts club. I collected my acquisitions from the day before, then put on my trainers and the new baseball cap and left the house.

It had been raining all night, and the pavement was still wet and slippery, but a few bright rays of the sun were already probing through the tumultuous clouds.

I rushed downhill, trying to make it to the club by the appointed time when a sudden wave of coldness washed over me as I reached the place where I had been kidnapped, but somehow, I managed to suppress my rising panic and moved on. Cars and people passed by as usual, and I did my best to ignore them.

I arrived at the club, slightly breathless, and the reception girl met me with a nervous glance.

"I am very sorry, sir. Your instructor just called to say that he has been injured, and he needs a few days to recover." She looked quite embarrassed. "Of course, we will not charge you for those days and will give you a discount for the rest of this month if you choose to stick with us."

"Do you know what happened to him?" I asked.

"Honestly, I have no idea. Maybe he has sprained something – or maybe it's something else. I don't know. I am sorry."

"Okay, never mind. Could you phone me when he recovers? And I will be counting on that discount."

"Yes, sir, of course!" she said. "Maybe you would like to consider joining one of our yoga classes while you are waiting?"

I politely declined her offer and left. *Damn! It was a pity.* I was highly motivated to start that day, and I am not that keen about sports. I hoped my determination would not evaporate over the next few days while I waited for the instructor. The day had been utterly wasted. I felt lost and wasn't sure what to do next.

I needed some groceries, so I popped to the nearest store on my way back. Ten minutes later, I was done and out on the street again. Damn, still a lot of empty time to kill until dusk. I didn't like the aimless wandering around, especially when the risk to run into those hunters was high.

I quietly returned home, then I washed my laundry and dusted. Later I made some salad and fried chicken. The food in Chadrack was much more satisfying, but I wasn't sure if what I had eaten in my dream gave me any nutrients here in London.

I spent the rest of the day thinking of my beautiful sister and the Well of Power under the mountain.

Carwyn tapped the door politely.

"The Princess wishes to leave as soon as possible, my Lord."

"Why?"

"She didn't explain."

"Serve us breakfast, Carwyn. I will not let her go starving."

He nodded and left.

I quickly splashed some water on my face, dressed and combed my hair, then tapped the door of Keely's room.

She was leaning at the window as I entered but turned to greet me.

"I heard you are leaving?" I asked.

"Yes." She told me with a faint smile on her face. "I'd love to stay, but affairs of the state are pressing, and the journey is a long one."

"Would you grant me the pleasure of sharing my breakfast

with you?"

"Of course, Kyleb. I only hope it won't stretch into a late dinner?"

"I am not trying to keep you here, Keely. I only don't want you to travel with an empty stomach," I said apologising.

She laughed and thanked me for my troubles, and we went to the dining room. Carwyn was serving the breakfast already.

We ate in silence, apart from a few polite exchanges. I had nagging questions about the rest of our family in Rehen, but Keely's thoughts seemed wandering away with occasional concerned look crossing her face, and I was afraid to ask, afraid to expose the ignorance and afraid of being rejected by her. I would have to find everything out some other way.

We finished our meal, and Keely left after briefly saying her goodbyes. I returned to my balcony just in time to see her mounting the horse. She waved at me, giving me a quick smile, and then the whole party left through the open gates.

I returned to my bedroom, silently summoning up all my determination. I wondered if the Ring could open that secret lock in my room. I reached into my pocket and got it out into the broad daylight. The Sapphire I found in the forest looked exactly like my sister's Ruby, and the gryphon design was the same. I wasn't sure if this was the right thing to do, but I couldn't think of any other way to find out if this Ring had the same power to open secret passages. I had a suspicion that it might turn out to be of paramount importance.

I quickly slipped it onto the ring finger of my right hand, and a sudden spark flashed in the depths of the Sapphire, jolting my neural system. It fitted just fine, and I instantly felt some strange sense appearing as if I had plugged into some kind of omnipresent ethereal network; it was feeble, though. Faint images flashed through the surface of my cognition without penetrating any deeper layers, until they fitted into their right places somewhere in my mind and waned.

That felt encouraging. I grabbed the chair and placed it in the hearth. My heart was racing as I reached into the chimney, where the carving was. This could be dangerous. I had no idea what kind of secrets were hiding there and hoped I would not end up letting loose some bloodthirsty monsters.

The carving was where I remembered it was. My palm fitted just fine, and I even saw a weak blue spark in the Sapphire, but nothing happened – none of the walls parted.

"Open, Sesame," I murmured, pressing harder, but the result was the same.

After several more unsuccessful attempts, I quit and took off the Ring. It wasn't as simple as it seemed. I envied Keely for the ease with which she had opened the passage; I lacked the knowledge to do the same. Or maybe the carving in my chimney was faulty. I had another hand sign to try at the top of the waterfall, where I had seen my sister walk through the solid rock.

I replaced the Ring into my pocket and stormed out, my heart beating in excitement. I put on my poker face, adopting a mask of bored indifference and slowly crossed the yard. The people I saw on the way greeted me, although there weren't many of them. I waved to the guards and then stepped through the open gate. Bright sunshine followed me over the stone bridge, and, as soon as I was out of sight of the guards, I began moving faster.

At first, I nearly ran up, taking several steps at the time, but exhaustion forced me to slow down. The ascent was steep and strenuous, and I had to stop and catch my breath several times. Gusts of lazy wind sprinkled cold drops of mist from the waterfall on my face, and the rest of the way I went at a slower pace, trying to avoid tricky spots of damp on the stairs.

I was breathless when I finally reached the top and had to spend ten long minutes trying to slow down my racing heart. Then I put the Ring on again.

The palm-shaped carving was barely discernible on an uneven surface, but I clearly remembered the place from the last visit with Keely and quickly found it. I placed my hand on the shape the same way as did my sister and closed eyes, trying to focus and strengthen my desire to part the rock. Nothing happened. I cursed and punched the rock in desperation, then closed my eyes, trying to force all distractions out of my mind, and focused on parting the cliff again. Long minutes passed in vain; the tension nearly ripped my skull apart until I finally sensed a subtle tremor. I opened my eyes just in time to see the Sapphire faintly flashing blue as the dark wall of stone trembled and opened. I rushed inside with a victorious smile and began a quick descent down the tunnel. Then the rock closed behind me, leaving me in nearly complete darkness. The green crystals above, which lighted the way last time, were barely glowing.

I had no idea what happened and hastily jumped back to the entrance. My hand trembled as I desperately tried to locate the carving on the inner wall, but in this poor light, it was impossible. I had been exhausted on our way back the day before and paid no attention to how Keely had parted the rock. I couldn't remember where she placed the hand with the Ruby. I ran my fingers along the walls, feeling its cold, uneven surface, but my tactile senses were useless. *I was trapped!*

The only way still open was the ghostly, barely visible passage leading downwards. Cautiously, I started to descend, trying to hold onto the walls and keep my balance.

Long hours passed as I slowly made my way down. The crystals above were barely flickering, and their faint glow was far from sufficient to reach the stairs. My feet were stepping in complete darkness, and I was afraid I would stumble on something. It was a very different experience from my previous descent with Keely, which seemed a real pleasure comparing with this torture.

I had no other choice but to continue.

Suddenly I heard a muffled chuckle somewhere below and froze instantly. The chuckle repeated again, and I spotted two purple eyes glowing in the darkness, probably twenty paces in front of me.

"Prince Kyleb, you need to make more frequent visits to the Well." The voice in the darkness crackled and hissed, like the autumn wind in dry leaves. "You are lucky. It is almost impossible to open the passage when your Ring is in such a state. You must be ashamed..."

"Who are you?"

"Who am I?" The voice chuckled again. "You are funny, Prince Kyleb. You haven't been here for so long that you can't remember me? I am Hawa, the Keeper of the Well!"

"Yes, how silly of me; now, I do remember. But I didn't see you yesterday, when I was there with my sister," I did my best to sound polite; I wasn't sure who was lurking in the darkness behind those purple eyes. "Could you do something about the light?"

"It's your job, Prince. You are the one with the Ring. The Sapphire is completely exhausted, I see. You have to charge your

Ring in the Well, or you will find yourself in darkness. Let's move on! Quick!"

I resumed my slow descent, while Hawa went far ahead, mumbling something and urging me onwards. He was invisible in the darkness below and moved much faster than my trembling legs could manage. I was sure he didn't need any light to see.

"Wait!" I stopped. "I need a little rest."

He looked at me. I could see his glowing purple eyes turned to face me.

"You used to be stronger, Prince Kyleb. What happened?"

"I was poisoned not long ago," I lied. "I had no chance to recover completely."

"I see..." His eyes grew bigger as Hawa came a few steps closer. "Poisoning is a serious matter..."

I took a few deep breaths while he waited.

"Let's go!" The Keeper turned away in the darkness, and his eyes disappeared.

I resumed my slow descent, leaning at the wall to keep my balance.

"Who poisoned you?" asked Hawa without looking back.

"Cook Abinaer." I decided to make as much of the story as possible.

"What? Doesn't that sound silly?" he chuckled. "I would like to know which of your beloved relatives sent you that poor cook and his poison. I suppose you tortured him? What did you find out?"

"They tortured him without me. I was too sick. They obtained nothing more! He just confessed."

"Dilettantes!" the Keeper said disdainfully. "Torture without obtaining information is wasted torture."

"Yes. But it's too late for any regrets now – the cook had been executed already."

"Fools!" Hawa said casually. "And what was the effect of that poison? Were you paralysed? Did you bleed? Did you have stomach cramps? Did you lose wind?"

"No, I was confused. And part of my memory appears to be lost."

"I've never heard of such a poison! That's fascinating. It must be something new and exciting substance. Tell me more!"

"There's not too much to tell: I don't remember many things; I don't even remember my family." I was bluffing. "And I don't remember how to use the Ring properly!"

"It's very simple with the Ring. Everything will come back when you dip your Ring in the Well. And your family will let you know about them sooner or later, I am sure. Don't worry." Hawa chuckled again. "Your toughest task will be to find out who you can trust. Yesterday I saw you visiting the Well with Princess Keely. Do you trust her?"

I shrugged in the dark.

"She appears to be a trustworthy person..."

"Appears to be... Exactly!" Hawa looked back at me as his eyes eerily glowed in the darkness. "You never know whom and when you can trust... Everybody only appears to be trustworthy."

The Keeper mumbled something, and we kept on descending.

"What about Seisyll?" I decided to keep on fishing for any possible piece of information.

"Seisyll?" He paused as if having trouble remembering the name. "It's been a very long time since I have heard about him... He was a very nice young man, funny and appeared to be honest..."

"Can I trust him?"

"You are funny, Prince Kyleb!" he chuckled again. "You are a grown man, and you still think you can trust anybody?"

"What about my father?"

He fell silent.

"It must have been a very strange poison," he exclaimed at last. "Don't you remember that King Grehlard is dead?"

"I know the fact." This time I was genuinely curious. "But what exactly happened?"

"It is such a well-known story, and you don't remember it? He fell into the Well, drunk as a pig! The body wasn't recovered, but where is the need for a better grave?"

His laughter reverberated in the darkness.

For some time, we kept on descending in silence, but the Keeper's weird laughter was still ringing in my ears. He was very strange, but he proffered some information. I only had to find out how accurate those bits of knowledge were.

"Do you know anything about the rest of my family?" I finally dared to ask.

"It is such a pity that the cook is dead! I would like to know what kind of poison he gave you... Such a blank memory! It must be an incredible substance."

He went on for some time, thinking.

"I am not an oracle, and I cannot tell you much, but your family are well-known. It's crazy that you don't remember this. You have five sisters: Ailis, Bedelia, Devona and Keely; and five brothers: Ninian, Yasar, Seisyll, Cadeyrn and Bradan."

"You said five sisters, and mentioned only four," I objected.

"Oh, I skipped your sister Hel! She is High Priestess of Patna," said Hawa.

None of the names flashed any spark in my memory. I had met Keely only, but I had no memories or knowledge of anything related to her until that meeting. I had no knowledge or memories of the rest of the family either.

"I don't remember them..." I admitted after a period of silence.

"Good heavens!" exclaimed the Keeper. "I would like a drop of that poisonous substance – such wonderful, blessed oblivion!"

He laughed again.

"You must promise me some of that poison if you find it!"

"I promise."

We walked less than twenty steps in silence before I asked: "do you have any idea about whereabouts of my brothers and sisters?"

"Oh, no! How could I know that? I dwell underground; how could I possibly know where they are – you need to find out that for yourself!"

I had a large family scattered throughout this dream world. However, I had no idea how to find them or how to react when I did find them or how dangerous or friendly they might be.

"Well, almost there..." he exclaimed from below.

We were nearing the grotto where the Well was as I noticed the purple glowing below. In the faint light, I couldn't make out any features of the Keeper – only an indistinct shadow entered the purple opening. I followed.

The Well looked nearly the same as it had yesterday; the mesmerising show of purple lights was swirling on the walls, but the greenish crystals of the grotto were dark. Then my gaze stumbled across the giant, hairy spider. Its face looked almost human, but grotesquely melted and wearing a sad expression. In the ghostly purple light from the well, his glowing purple eyes looked eerily like empty eye sockets. I froze, feeling the hairs on my back rising.

"What?" he chuckled, turning around. "You have forgotten what I look like as well, I see. Definitely! Don't worry, Prince Kyleb, I'm not going to eat you, unless you are not true Prince Kyleb."

The remark brought a wave of chill down my spine, and I shivered. The expression of horror on my face was too evident, and Hawa chuckled.

"What do I have to do?" I asked, now visibly trembling.

It felt like the point of no return – would I be able to wake up in London after this? Or would I'll be stuck here forever?

"My poor poisoned Prince!" An evil grin was now playing on his twisted lips. "Just dip your hand into the Well, and the Ring will do the rest!"

I did as instructed, and the universe exploded.

The whirlpool of purple light sucked my mind out of my skull and then spat it back. The Sapphire in the Ring on my hand kept on pulsing, sending blue rays to the purple surface, and the Well responded, extending trembling tentacles and carefully touching my palm. I was unable to close my eyes and flinched every time the purple thunderbolt hit my Ring.

Before long, my hand was entirely engulfed by alternating

blue and purple light, sending rapid neural discharges to my brain. I stood watching the thunderbolts as in a trance. Then everything stopped. I knew that it was time to withdraw my hand.

"How do you feel, Prince Kyleb?"

"A little tired but well," I responded. "Thanks for asking."

"Pity..." said Hawa.

"Why?"

"I would feast on you if you were not the real prince..." He smiled wryly.

"How would you know that?"

"The Well would have fried you by now," he explained.

"Next time I will bring you a rabbit," I promised.

"Then see you next time!" the Keeper grunted angrily. He moved aside from the tunnel opening, and slowly crawled off to some dark corner at the far end of the grotto.

I cursed feeling frustrated at the thought of what a long way I had to go up the steep stairs when a blue spark suddenly departed from my Ring and slowly floated to one side as if inviting me to follow. I hesitated at first, but then my curiosity got to me. The spark drifted past the Well to the far side of the grotto, away from the tunnel opening. I quickly glanced around, but Hawa was nowhere in sight.

The spark floated above the winding path, then touched the

surface of the rock and disappeared into the wall. I approached closer to have a look. It was a barely visible carving of the palm with two gryphons on both sides. I was reluctant to follow the hint, but another spark left my Ring and touched the carving as if urging to give it a try.

My Ring was leading the way, but I had no idea where. The Sapphire flashed blue when I touched the cold surface of the rock, and a dimly lit tunnel opened. I sneaked inside, and the wall closed behind me. The path was slightly winding, bending around two massive stalactites before ending abruptly several hundred yards later. The wall was brightly lit by green crystals, and it was no trouble to spot another palm-shaped carving in front of me.

I opened the passage and stepped into the hearth. The wall slowly closed behind me as I walked forward.

I was back in my chambers. That was why it was forbidden to build fires there!

I went straight to the balcony. The yard was already immersed by the dusk, and the sky was putting on its magnificent nightly show. But I wasn't alone in admiring the view.

Saqia was there, standing on the balcony. She turned around as soon as I entered, smiling. She was dressed in a misty, almost transparent gold gown, leaving little to my imagination. Her blue skin in the evening dusk looked almost black.

"You forgot your gift, my Lord," she whispered, slowly

approaching. "So, I decided to visit you instead – just in case you would like something…"

I nervously smiled back but stopped at a distance. I wasn't in the mood for any gifts and hated to be pushed to do things. The fact itself seemed unthinkable.

She came closer, close enough for her sweet perfume to hit my nostrils. I wasn't sure what kind of scent it was – the sweetness was floral with a subtle hint of lemon and melon, and a trace of cinnamon. Her chest moved smoothly when she took a few deep breaths and came even closer.

I was still unable to think of any decent excuse.

"I am your gift, my Lord," she whispered, raising her chin and looking directly into my eyes. "Unwrap me…"

Her pale blue eyes had a ghostly appearance in the light of the dying day. I took half a step back, still searching for possible excuses. I had no intention of hurting her feelings.

She took my hand and pressed it to her right breast. It was warm and firm under my fingers. My palm rested there for a few heartbeats too long, while her fingers gently rubbed my Ring. She parted her lips, slowly inhaling, expecting a kiss.

I quickly stepped back, withdrawing my hand and leaving her gasping.

"What? Why?" She looked at me, seemingly frightened and confused. "Have I done something wrong?"

I shook my head.

"I am too tired for any games," I told her.

"You don't like me?" Her words sounded more like a statement than a question.

I stepped back a few more paces. Something just didn't feel right here. She was too persistent, too pressing, and I felt uneasy under her ghostly gaze.

"It is nothing wrong with you," I said, as my thinking became calmer. "Just go back to your chambers. I need some rest."

Saqia followed me with her ghostly gaze as I moved to the far side of the balcony and leant at the wall.

"Will you send me back to Princess Keely?" she asked calmly.

She didn't attempt to approach me again. Clouds were gathering in the west, most likely bringing rain. I followed them with my gaze for a long few moments before answering.

"No," I said. "You may live here. But that doesn't mean that you will have automatic access to my chambers."

"Then I hope you will order my presence someday," she said. "You will not be disappointed."

I remained silent, watching from a safe distance how Saqia turned around, picked her dark cloak hanging on the balustrade and covered her shoulders. Then she left without any further words.

The sound of her retreating footsteps and the closing door

reached me from across the hall. I waited a little longer before returning to my bedroom. On my way back, I ran into Carwyn.

"Would you like your dinner here or in a dining room?" he asked.

I told him I would prefer it where I was.

I took off the Ring as he left and slipped it into my pocket. I remembered Keely's advice and decided to find a safer place to keep it.

Later Carwyn returned with a food basket. I ate alone.

When I slipped into my bed, my only thoughts were about whether I would still wake up in London after my experience with the Well. Then I drifted away to find out...

The phone was screaming into my ear with all its might. I only blinked, slowly realising where I was, and then I answered the call. It was the receptionist from the martial arts club. She casually informed me that my instructor would be coming back to work and that she could book a session for me if I were still interested. Of course, I said that I was. It was something I really needed, something essential for my survival. And I had paid for it already.

Only then the realisation broke through the fogs of a dream at last, and a broad smile split my face – I was in London! The Well of Power didn't change the rules, and I was glad to be back in my grey corner where I could hide from the world.

I lazily sipped my morning coffee, gazing at the planes passing over the red London rooftops. Then I remembered the mysterious undelivered package, which was waiting in the post office for a few already. Maybe it was time to check it?

I quickly looked through my pile of adverts and old newspapers until I found the red and white Royal Mail paper slip and inspected it again. Yes, there was no doubt – my name and address were shown correctly.

I finished my coffee, quickly brushed my teeth, got dressed and went out.

The morning was fresh and windy. I had no reason to hurry, but the wind rushed me downhill with sharp, chilly gusts. The streets were nearly empty, as I had overslept the morning rush hour. I took a short bus ride, trying to avoid the unpleasant weather.

In the post office, a still-sleepy gentleman took my paper slip and presented me with a small carton, smaller than a shoebox.

I got out and inspected the label; it had my name printed on top of it, but I couldn't find any return address. The sender clearly wished to remain anonymous. It was a strange package, received from a stranger.

Back at home, I felt an almost irresistible urge just to throw the box away, toss into the garbage bin without even opening it, but then curiosity got me over.

I shook the package, listening carefully. Inside something moved slightly, something big enough to fill almost the whole space of the carton. I pierced the sticky tape with a knife. Nothing came out. Whatever was in the carton was elongated, buried under several layers of a bubble wrap and sealed with sticky red tape. I had no idea what it could be. I carefully took it out, weighing in my hand – it was less than a pound. Still, it was a mystery.

I pierced the wrapping with a knife and instantly dropped everything on the floor when the most sickening, foul stink of decaying flesh hit my nose. My stomach turned into knots, and I rushed to the loo, vomiting on my way.

Minutes later, I was sitting helplessly on the floor, fighting the impulse to wrap it back up without even looking again, and immediately dump it in the garbage. Was it a dead rat? But someone had bothered to deliver me this very twisted message, and I decided I should find out why and what precisely that message was. I had no idea who could have such a perverted sort of humour. Maybe the message itself would provide some clues as to the sender's identity; I only had to force myself to take a look at it.

I took a damp towel and wrapped it around my nose, then collected all my courage and returned to the kitchen, where the stinky package was lying on the floor. First, I opened all the windows, and the fresh wind instantly swirled inside, carrying some of the foul odours away. Then I poked the package again, using the knife and peeling off layer by layer until bloody and rotten human hand slipped out of the wrapping. The skin was broken in several places, and stinky yellow fat and white knuckle bones protruded through the gaps. This made me sick again.

My second visit to the loo was less convulsive but still exhausting, and I needed another towel.

On my way back to the kitchen, I picked up the phone and started to dial the police when my gaze stumbled on something flashing brightly on the putrid hand. Was this the message, presented in a mysterious and sick way? I carefully removed the wrappings away from the rotten fingers, and it was there – the golden ring, covered with clotted blood, on the ring finger of the severed hand. I instantly recognised the pattern of two gryphons holding a precious stone.

The police were out of the question. The ring clearly was connected with Rehen somehow, yet I only couldn't understand how. Could it belong to one of my Rehen relatives? Or was it just someone's idea of a sick joke? If so, that someone had a firm knowledge of what he or she was doing – the ring looked the same as my Sapphire Ring. The only different thing was the blood-covered stone; it wasn't blue. Why had someone bothered to make a precise replica of the Ring and send it to me? I was sure it was a copy. Transfer of anything material between the real world and Rehen was impossible; only a mind could travel between them. Or was it possible? I had nobody to ask...

I had the unpleasant task of removing the ring from that swollen finger somehow. I covered my hands with several layers of used grocery plastic bags and grabbed the stinking hand. The ring was stuck deep into the flesh and wouldn't come off. I tried for several minutes without any success, realising with increasing horror that the only way was, in fact, to cut the finger off.

My eyes were watering from the horrible stink. I held my breath while putting the hand on a towel, then pressed my knife through the knuckle. The first attempt was unsuccessful, but I kept on trying until the blade finally pierced the joint. I had to make a few cuts in the skin to free the ring, which was buried deeply in the swollen tissues. When it finally came off, I tossed it into the kitchen sink, wasting no time for a closer look. The unbearable stink was still transfusing my tiny flat, and I had to deal with it before the neighbours became curious and started asking questions.

I placed the severed finger in the palm of the rotten hand, then carefully wrapped it in a dirty towel and plastic grocery bags, securing everything in place with sticky tape. I had no way to check if the package was leaking any smells – my whole flat was stinking already, so I just wrapped everything more tightly, adding layer after layer until I had used all of the bags I had.

Now I had another problem. I couldn't just dump the stinking thing into any bin. That would undoubtedly attract foxes, and if somebody spotted a cheeky vixen running around with a human palm in its mouth, it would lead to an investigation. Then I would have to hand that replica ring to the police, ruining my chances to conduct my own research. I was sure the clues must be somewhere in Rehen; I only had no idea where to start looking yet.

I stuffed the stinky package into my rucksack and started scrubbing the floor. A fresh wind through the open windows blew away most of the terrible stench, and I was ready to go. I must get somewhere outside London and bury the hand in a field.

The journey was a hard one. I went downhill, avoiding all crowded spots, which was tricky in the busy streets of London. I couldn't board a bus with my smelly load. At several road crossings, I nearly ran risking to get hit by a car, only to make sure that other people won't stay alongside me for long enough to grow suspicious.

At the train station, I quickly bought a ticket to Sevenoaks and went down to the far end of the platform. Luckily, the weather was windy, and the stench, if it did leak out, was quickly carried away.

I skipped three trains – they all were too crowded for my purpose. I only waited at the far end of the platform, standing in the wind. The next train was nearly empty, and I gladly boarded, feeling quite chilly already. Despite that, I opened a few windows to get the wind inside and placed the rucksack under my seat.

A few stations later, an elderly woman got on and ambled past my seat, leaning heavily on her stick. She lowered herself down next to the window, a few rows behind me.

Just seconds later, she frowned and exclaimed angrily "what is that smell?".

"Dead rat, I suppose," I replied calmly, keeping my eyes on the moving scenery outside of the window.

"For God's sake," she mumbled, getting up. "Do they ever clean these trains?"

She hastily moved to another carriage, and I rush to open a few more windows when I was left alone. That kept the stink at bay, earned me a cold and wasn't necessary after all since no one else boarded the carriage.

I got off the train several stations later, in Kemsing. The weather was grim but less windy here. The station was empty, and I walked down the steps and headed south across a meadow scattered with flowering scarlet poppies. I kept on glancing around, but it seemed I was the only wanderer crawling across the field. Nearly half a mile later, I stopped under the mighty oak. The place seemed sufficiently remote.

I dumped my smelly rucksack on the grass and looked around again. There was no one in sight, only a hawk testing wind high above me and stalking mice. I picked a dry stick and started to poke dirt until I had dug a shallow hole, sufficiently big for the wrapped hand. I placed the package in with all those groceries bags and pushed the dirt back. It still didn't look secure. That putrid hand was human and deserved some dignity. I collected the largest stones I could find nearby and piled them over the grave to keep the wild animals away. Then I left without looking back.

Nobody bothered me on my way home.

I cleaned my kitchen with antiseptic and scrubbed the floors twice before setting my eyes on the ring. I carefully washed it with soap and plenty of water. Still, it didn't feel clean.

The ring was adorned with the same pattern of two gryphons, but the beasts were holding a large clear gem which looked like a diamond, not a Sapphire, as on my Ring; or a Ruby, as on Keely's. Was it the real Ring or a mere replica? It was a mystery, which must get solved. I had no idea how could this ring cross the plane between the two realities? It must be a copy, but this copy brought me a message which I had to decipher.

It must be from my Rehen's family – from someone who owns the Ring with a Diamond. That person wanted to show me that he or she knew who I was – the replica was sent to my home address. This knowledge might be very dangerous for me – I must find out if I was dealing with a friend on an enemy.

Still, I had no idea who in Rehen had the Ring with a

Diamond. Maybe I should pay a visit to that monster Hawa in Chadrack?

I was too tired to wonder about it. I ordered a pizza and spent the rest of the evening watching TV.

I was greeted by a warm morning sun in Chadrack, as Carwyn popped in with a bowl and towels. Before he was able to place everything on the table, I asked him for five or six rabbits in a basket.

"Would you like them to be dead or alive?" he inquired casually.

"Dead will be all right," I replied. I didn't want to watch Hawa hunting around the cave.

I had a quick breakfast and then sneaked into the corridor to kill time while Carwyn was dealing with rabbits. The castle of Chadrack was big, with too many secrets, and I hoped that nobody would find my little exploration suspicious.

I turned right and went towards the eastern wing. The smaller staircase here was mainly used by the attendant staff as the shortest route between my chambers and the kitchen. Last time I went this way with Abinaer on my first day in Rehen. The thought was sad: I still blamed myself for the death of the poor lad.

I took the stairs down and reached a hall where several corridors met. I was hesitant as to which way to go. I recognised the one leading to the kitchen, but the three others were unknown to me. There was no one there to direct me; I had to rely on my intuition alone.

I took the first to the right, heading east. It was long and lined with gracefully arched windows facing the garden. I spotted Saqia sitting on a bench and reading something. I quietly sneaked further, hoping that she was too immersed in her book to notice me. That blue girl made me feel uneasy each time she tried her luck at seducing me. I wasn't used to such persistent advances. I'd rather take everything at my own pace.

I passed the corridor and turned left into the narrow shady gallery, green with flowering vines. The weather was serene, and white flowers of the vines gave off a beautiful aroma. I stopped there and listened for a few minutes – but I couldn't hear any footsteps; nobody followed me. I walked through the entire gallery and then turned right, crossing a small yard.

The sudden shriek of an eagle stopped me next to a small fountain. I looked up, shading my eyes, but the sky was empty. I flinched and glanced back when something touched my right calf.

"Gwyn!"

Gryphon happily ran around me in circles and dashed back to Rhys as he entered the yard. Gwyn had grown even bigger since the last time I had seen him. Shiny brown feathers now covered his wings, and his head was crowned with white.

Rhys looked gloomy and tired, with a star-shaped wound on his cheek, which reminded me of the attack a few days before.

"How is that wound healing?" I asked, feeling ashamed for not having visited him sooner. "Why have you taken off the bandages?"

"I am feeling fine. Thank you, my Lord," he replied, promptly managing a vague smile, which made him wince since his cheek still was hurting. "It will heal faster this way."

"You know better," I shrugged. "How is Gwyn behaving?"

"He is like a small child, happy and inquisitive. He is growing fast."

Gwyn was rushing around like a drop of mercury. With this playfulness, he more resembled a kitten, rather than an eagle. He was happily playing with the leather ball Rhys had made for him, tossing and catching it, throwing it around.

"Maybe you should start training him," I told Rhys. "He's going to get big, and we can't let an aggressive animal live in the city."

"You don't need to worry, my Lord," said Rhys. "He is too

intelligent to be aggressive."

"But he is a predator, isn't he?"

"Yes," agreed Rhys. "But gryphons have never been known to attack humans. It has always been the opposite."

We were interrupted by Carwyn. He appeared in the gallery with a very concerned look on his face.

"What happened?" I asked before he opened his mouth.

He started to apologise. "I am so sorry, my Lord, we have only four rabbits. Will this suit your needs? Or do you want me to send the hunters for more?"

"That's enough for me," I waved away his worries. "Don't bother hunting."

Carwyn slipped back to the gallery. "Everything will be ready in a few moments," he said. "As you wished."

Rhys looked at me, a clear question on his face, but I only wished him a speedy recovery and returned to my chambers.

The basket with rabbits had been placed already in the middle of the hall. I put on my Ring, took the basket and headed towards the hearth, feeling like Red Riding Hood preparing to visit the Big Bad Wolf.

The passage opened, and I stepped inside.

Hawa was sitting next to the Well.

He greeted me in his way. "What kind of gigantic job are you working on, Prince Kyleb? You charged your Ring in the Well only yesterday… is it down already?"

"I don't need the Well this time. I'm just keeping my promises."

"Interesting..." Hawa mumbled, inspecting contents of the basket. "That's very strange and unusual for you. But thanks, I will feast on them later. What is it you are after anyway?"

I sat down on the rock. He kept his distance.

"You are sagacious, Hawa," I began. "You know that my memories are vague. I am seeking knowledge."

"Yes, yes, I remember. Did you find that wonderful poisonous substance?"

I shook my head.

I decided to get straight to the point. "Pardon my ignorance, Hawa, but I noticed that Keely's Ring has a different stone."

"Yes, my dear Prince. The Ruby is the Master of Love. Your Sapphire is the Master of Destiny. The Emerald is the Master of Life; the Onyx is the Master of Death. Does that satisfy your curiosity?"

"In part," I grinned, hiding my complete confusion. "And if somebody puts on the other Ring? Purely by accident. Would it work the same way?"

"Rings cannot be switched or exchanged, and as far as I know, if you put on the Ruby Ring, dear Prince, it will fry you up. Did you take Keely hostage or did you simply kill her?"

"No, of course not! I am just trying to remember the nature of the Rings and avoid making any stupid mistakes."

The Keeper chuckled.

"Of course, of course!" he exclaimed, notes of sarcasm clear in his voice. "You have almost succeeded in convincing me of your brotherly love!"

"Keely went back to Porlok in good health. I mean no harm to her; I am only curious," I shrugged with an innocent smile.

"Yes, yes, I almost believe you," Hawa chuckled. "It only looks suspicious when you make too many excuses. So, the answer is no – you can't try putting on Keely's Ring, this might result in entirely different magic than you are expecting. But this didn't sound like a four rabbit question. What else do you want to know?"

I finally felt brave enough to ask him the main question.

"What about other stones? Have you heard about a Diamond Ring, for example?" I looked directly into his empty, flaming eye sockets.

"Diamond? Where have you seen the Diamond?"

"I haven't," I lied. "I am just curious."

"The Diamond is the Ring of the King," he replied after a short pause.

A sudden wave of heat ran down my spine. That grim message I had received in my London flat *was* about the King.

Maybe King Grehlard of Rehen wasn't dead if he had sent me the replica of his Ring? Or was he killed, and that was the message of the slayer of the King? What kind of perverted plot was this? Still, the message remained a mystery.

"Then that Ring must be passed to the new King," I said. "Are you sure that the Ring kills everyone except its owner? Then how will the new King be able to put on the Diamond Ring?"

"Oh!" The Keeper looked amused. "It's a fascinating problem. But as far as I remember, King Grehlard drowned in the Well while wearing his Ring, and no one had ever seen his body. The Diamond Ring is lost forever, dear Prince. You don't need to worry."

"I am not worried," I told him. "It's just a very curious theoretical problem, don't you think?"

"It's amazing how you can hit a curious problem in your state of mind," said Hawa. "But I don't have the answer now. I need to think about it. Ask me later."

"I will," I promised. "And I will bring you more rabbits next time..."

"You'll make me fat!" he laughed. "I'll have to shed my skin!"

"But you will grow bigger and stronger," I observed calmly.

"That's true..." He inspected contents of the basket again, and I spotted drops of toxic greenish saliva dripping from his fangs. "You may want to leave now." The Keeper told me quietly.

"Goodbye," I said, standing up. *"Bon Appétit!"*

I opened the passage and was immensely relieved when the walls quietly closed behind me. Hawa was a dreadful creature.

My chambers were brightly lit by the sun, and Bysh greeted me in the hall, wagging his tail. He licked my hand while I patted his head and scratched his ears.

A dark shadow suddenly passed somewhere between the midday sun and my window. Bysh started to bark, and a strong gust of wind blew in through the open balcony, bringing in thousands of shrieking crows. They quickly filled the hall, circling like a giant black tornado.

I instinctively raised hands to protect my face. The Ring on my finger flashed blue, and I sensed a few solutions. I knew what to try first. My attempt to expel the crows back failed. I drew the power from my Ring and clumsily splashed it at the birds, but it dispersed without any effect. I felt some dark presence behind the flying birds, which made my efforts as futile as blowing against the hurricane. I tried harder. A burst of eerie laughter thundered through the shrieks of crows, and I stopped my shots. It was something different I needed.

Bysh was jumping as high as he could, catching crows from the circling cloud and tearing them into pieces. But he was just one against thousands.

I wasn't confident enough using the Ring to be involved in

such a complex game, but I couldn't show my weakness either.

I grabbed the other option offered by my Ring. I pointed the Sapphire at the crows and hit them with its pure energy. The dark presence kept them circling the room, while blue sparks flashed, igniting the passing birds, and soon the circling whirlpool resembled a fiery hurricane, setting fire to everything combustible in the hall. I hid in the hearth, and Bysh soon joined me there, as the heat became almost unbearable.

The birds died in mid-flight and dropped on the floor, and the creepy vortex slowly fell apart. A deadly silence followed, disturbed only by the soft crackling of burning tables and chairs.

I got out of my hiding and looked around. Books and curtains were on fire. A smoking pile of dead birds, twice my height, was in the centre of the hall, and countless other half-fried bodies were scattered all over the place. The eerie presence was gone.

Carwyn stormed through the door. "Oh Gods, what happened?!"

"A friendly hello," I grinned wearily. "I only don't know who was behind it... We need some water to put the flames out."

"Oh..." moaned Carwyn, pale as paper. "You don't need to worry, my Lord. We will take care of everything."

I went to my bedroom, washed ashes from my face and put on fresh clothes. I left for the dining room, leaving the smoking mess and sharp, sickening stink of burnt flesh and feathers for

Carwyn.

There was notable agitation in the corridor – people were running around buckets of water trying to extinguish the fire.

"Find me Bedwyr," I stopped the boy who was running with a bunch of rags.

He nodded and ran away.

I slipped into the dining room, away from all that turmoil. The lunch was served on the table already, but my nerves still were too shaken after that confrontation. *Who was my opponent or, more precisely, who was my enemy?* It didn't feel like a friendly encounter but wasn't life-threatening either. It looked like a challenge, like a test for me. With only Bysh defending me, I was an easy kill for whoever was behind the attack. It was more like a warning or a weird way of attracting my attention. Could it have been the Prince of Mordak? It was possible, but I had no proof.

"Are we under attack, my lord?" asked Bedwyr, entering the dining room. "You called for me. What happened?"

"Looks like somebody bothered to send us a message," I told him. "But I have no idea what was that message about nor who was the sender. Any news from Mordak?"

"No, my Lord," said the general. "I sent a few spies there, as you ordered, but they haven't returned yet. Everything seems quiet so far..."

I didn't like this quietness. Knowing what Melvyn had done

in my name, this Mordakan tranquillity seemed suspicious if not concerning. They must be preparing an attack. And with strike imminent, I remembered our non-existent defences at the borders. We couldn't afford to be sitting ducks anymore.

"We must be ready for everything," I said, placing my goblet on the table. "How is the ghoul fleet? Could we use those ships?"

"They are far from beauties and slow," admitted Bedwyr, "but they can take a large payload. We could use them as transport."

"Then start patrolling our shores immediately," I told him. "Keep the scarlet sails flying; let the Mordakans think that Chadrack is riddled with ghouls. That may buy us some time."

"That's a very wise decision, my lord," acknowledged the general. "I will do as you command."

"I want you to inspect the shoreline," I ordered. "Go and visit every town and city along the riverbank. What happened in Ikent must never happen again, and it doesn't matter if ghouls or Mordakans are attacking. We can't leave our people exposed. If a town doesn't have a wall, one must be built. If the town has a wall but doesn't have enough soldiers to defend it, we must train a garrison. We must be ready."

"I will leave at once," Bedwyr nodded.

"You are acting in my name," I reminded him.

"Thank you, my Lord," said the general. "I will not

disappoint you."

He left without making any further comment.

After Bedwyr closed the door, I paced the room, and my thoughts kept on returning to my family. My distant relatives raised me in a small village in the Highlands of Scotland. I had never known my parents, and nobody ever spoke anything about them. I was lonely, orphaned and alienated. Now in this dreamland, I had several brothers and sisters, and we were rulers of this world or at least part of it. This brought strangely mixed emotions.

I had met only Keely. She was a lovely lady; it was no wonder she wore the Master of Love on her finger. What about the rest of the family? I felt bad about Seisyll and ashamed of the pain I had caused him. I couldn't understand why it was necessary. Why did Chadrack need a war with Mordak so desperately? Was Seisyll's dark presence behind the ravens?

I still had no idea what forced the ghouls to move north. Was it the Nightcrawlers Keely had mentioned? I nearly persuaded myself to pay a visit to my sister and lay my eyes on these monsters. I had the feeling that I might be forced to do this if I was brave enough to claim my right to the throne of Rehen.

I filled my goblet and slowly sipped the wine until dusk filled the room. The corridor grew silent long before. I left the food untouched and returned to my chambers.

The place was clean but still was filled with the faint odour of burnt feathers. I quickly slipped into my bed and closed my eyes.

It was just another quiet and cloudy morning in London with the soft twittering of birds outside of my window. Moments later, I jumped out of bed, suddenly remembering my martial arts session. I skipped the breakfast to keep myself agile for the stressful activity, but I couldn't resist drinking a cup of strong coffee to shake my neural system into a higher gear.

I quickly gathered my stuff in my new backpack and departed. Still, I had time and walked downhill without rushing. I did my best not to think about the cars passing by and any spying eyes behind the wheels but stayed as far from the road as the pavement allowed. I lowered my baseball cap and forced my mind to ignore them. It was clear that my return to complete sanity still was hovering somewhere around the corner.

The receptionist met me with a broad smile and let me straight to the beautiful back garden, tastefully decorated in

Chinese style. There was a low wooden platform, maybe six yards wide, in the middle with several unpaved paths winding around it. The garden was framed by tall, thick shrubs, shielding it from the outer world.

"Please, wait here," she said. "Mr Richard will be with you in a minute."

I sat down on a wooden bench and waited.

Mr Richard was dressed in blue jeans and a dark blue flannel shirt. It was a strange outfit for the training session, but I had already learned never to judge a book by its cover. He was a lean, tall young man in his thirties, blue-eyed and dark-haired.

He greeted me politely and started explaining what we were going to do. At first, I did my best to listen carefully, but then my attention began to slip to the healing, star-shaped wound on his left cheek. It looked strangely familiar.

"What is your primary purpose for the training, Mr Firestone?" he asked.

"Self-defence, mainly. And, please, call me Kyle," I mumbled, still secretly peeking at his scar.

"Okay," he nodded. "Then call me Rick. The best way to win the battle is by avoiding the battle – it is no shame to run away when facing a threat. But we will be going through several basic techniques to make sure that you can defend yourself with some very basic weapons – such as these, or none at all."

He took two wooden sticks and handed one to me, explaining how to hold it as he did so. The situation was damn familiar too! Then we stood *en garde*. His first attack was a slow *en sixte*, and I was easily able to block it.

"Have you ever trained with swords before?" he asked, backing up to the *en garde* position again.

I began shaking head but then remembered my training with Rhys in Chadrack.

"Long ago – in another life!" I replied half-joking.

The next attack was *en quarte*, which I quickly blocked as well, before attempting an attack myself, and succeeded in reaching his shoulder through his defences.

He looked puzzled but continued with the attack-defence sequence, slightly increasing the pace. In no time we had reached a quite intense level, attacking and blocking, then attacking again and blocking again.

We ran and jumped across the garden – attacking and blocking, seeking for any weak spots, then attacking again. An hour passed before we stopped, breathing heavily. I felt a strong sense of *déjà vu*.

"You are quite good," observed Mr Richard. "Are you sure you need this training?"

"Yes, I think I do," I replied, leaning on my stick. "It gives me some confidence."

"You're the one paying for it," Rick shrugged.

I took another short glimpse at his scar and gathered all of my courage.

"Rick, I'd like to ask you a strange question. Don't get mad."

He looked at me, a little concerned. "Go ahead…"

"Have you ever had a dream of a strange place, of a black stone castle and a baby gryphon?" I looked at his eyes under frowned eyebrows.

He grew pale, and I noticed him clenching his fists.

"I don't mean any harm," I added quickly. "I've been having such a dream myself!"

He immediately resumed the *en garde* position, pointing his stick at me. "Who are you?" His voice was now deep and cracking.

I didn't move.

"Calm down, Rhys!" I used the name intentionally; I was sure – it was him. "I mean no harm."

"Who are you?" he repeated, raising his voice.

"I am Kyleb, Prince of Chadrack," I whispered. That sounded silly.

He lowered his stick at once.

"Forgive me, my Lord!" Rick muttered, lowering his eyes and bowing. "I had no way to recognise you."

I had to stop him from dropping to his knees. "Please, call me

Kyle here." I smiled.

I was thrilled to see him. Rhys looked like a decent and honest guy in Rehen. I hoped he was no different here. I needed an ally, a friend I could trust.

"Yes, my..." He managed to smile, as well. "Yes, Kyle."

"Is there any place we can talk safely?"

"It is safe to talk here. Let's have a seat," he said, pointing at the wooden gazebo at the far end of the garden.

We went unhurriedly. I briefly told Rick about my kidnapping, but he had not the slightest idea of who could have been behind it.

"I am not such an important person," he shrugged. "I had a very simple life in both worlds."

"I had a simple life too," I sighed. "Before all this began."

"You sound disappointed, my..." Rick shook head and smiled guiltily, "... Kyle. How did you realise that I am Rhys? I look a bit different in Rehen."

"I would never guess if that raven hadn't tag you," I told him.

"Tagged?" Rick looked puzzled.

"You know, that all wounds and bruises on your body, which you get in one world, are instantly reflected in another world with the same size, shape and location?" I asked, and Rick silently nodded. "You took off bandages yesterday, and I saw that wound which raven made on your cheek. It was a pure coincidence to meet you here, but I recognised the wound."

"That's very clever," observed Rick. "But this is like finding a needle in the haystack. I wouldn't ever think this might work."

"This clever idea is not mine," I admitted. "I was tagged myself when they kidnapped me."

I showed him my scar, but this entire thing with tagging was new to him.

"I would never have guessed your identity if not for that wound," I told him. "I suppose you have more experience with this Sleeper thing. How long have you been visiting Rehen?"

"Since I was in my teens, as far as I can remember."

"It's just been a few weeks for me..."

"And you are being hunted already? It's not so easy being a Prince..."

"I didn't choose it," I shrugged. "I guess you didn't choose it either."

Rick sighed and then shook head. "It was long ago, but I still remember it clearly..."

Our talk was interrupted. The receptionist came into the garden, a concerned look on her face. She glanced around until spotted us sitting in the gazebo.

"I am sorry to interrupt," she said, addressing Rick, "but your next customer is here already."

"It's okay. We've finished," I assured her politely. "When is my next appointment?"

"I will check the calendar," she smiled approvingly and left.

I quickly exchanged my phone number with Rick and agreed to keep in touch.

On my way out, I stopped at the reception.

"The day after tomorrow – it will be the first slot in the morning, at nine o'clock? Is that okay with you?" the receptionist asked me.

I nodded as it didn't really matter to me and went out.

On my way back I bought a pizza to save me from having to mess with cooking. I spent my afternoon in front of the TV, barely watching it – I had too much excitement to contain. I trusted Rhys in Rehen, and finding him here was a significant boost for my confidence. We weren't a significant force – an army of only two, but with Rick trained to fight in both worlds, we could stand our grounds against the redhead.

My phone rang later in the evening. It was Rick.

"I have a slightly questionable idea, which might help to solve the mystery with your kidnapper," he said, after a few polite pleasantries. "But this may involve some issues with the law."

"I am listening," I replied.

"Maybe it would be better to meet and discuss somewhere?"

"All right."

We agreed to meet in Mountsfield Park, which was not far

from my home. I quickly got dressed and left.

Outside, the warm early evening dusk engulfed me, soothing my troubled mind. I followed the plane flying over my head before passing the street. The waiter smiled at me as I passed in front of the windows of the Indian restaurant. I nodded and went on, passing several takeaways and convenience stores on my way. Life felt different. I arrived at the rusty gate of the park and only then realised that I hadn't even glanced at the traffic.

I hid my smile with a palm and entered the park. Not a single soul was in the vicinity; I was alone and slowly walked uphill under the tall leafy trees. On the hilltop, I sat down on a bench and started to wait. The sun was setting, and a few bats, hunting for small insects, flew silently over my head like a flock of black leaves.

I glanced at my watch a few times as the dusk grew thicker. Then a lonely figure emerged from the shadows. I recognised Rick as he came nearer. He greeted me from a distance.

"Good evening, Kyle," he said, then stopped hesitantly and added with a guilty smile. "I've practised the greeting all afternoon. Still, it doesn't feel right to address the Prince this way."

"I am not a Prince," I reminded him. "A few weeks ago, I had no idea about Rehen or Chadrack. Or you... I am new in this game."

"How it began for you?" Rick asked.

With a gesture, I invited him to have a seat on the bench next to me. Then I delivered my story about the incident on the train. Rick listened without interrupting me.

"So, you were stabbed?" Rick asked.

"Well… not exactly," I sighed. "I managed to get my hands on that man in Hyde Park, and he showed me the tool."

"What was that?"

"The serpent," I sighed. "I was bitten by a snake. And what is your story? Had you been stabbed or bitten?"

Rick flashed a quick glance at my side.

"It was long ago," he sighed. "I was only twelve. My dad and I went to the park to walk our dog. We talked and joked as we always did. We walked our usual ways and were about to turn back when everything happened. That man appeared as if out of nowhere – I didn't saw him coming."

"Indian?" I asked.

"No," Rick shook head. "He was blond, white and chubby. He kicked our dog laughing, and when my dad stepped up, that man stabbed him several times. I screamed when my father collapsed, and that chubby man only spat at my side and went away. I kept on screaming, but nobody heard. It was getting dark, and the park was empty."

"I am sorry…" I mumbled petrified.

"It is not your fault, my Lord," Rick sighed. "My father died in my arms. I clutched his body all night long, soaked in his blood. I was afraid to let him go. A jogger found us in the morning and called the police. Next night it was the first time I woke up in Rehen."

"Why didn't your mother came to look after you? You were missing for the whole night…"

"My mum died at my birth," Rick said flatly. "Next five years after my dad was stabbed, I spent in shelters. I learned how to live there."

"You had quite a rough ride," I only managed to mumble. Rick shrugged but added nothing. For some time, we just sat silently, gazing at the bats. I was too shocked by his revelations, but Rick seemed had numbed his pain with time.

"Would you like to hear the idea, my… Kyle?" he asked.

"What's on your mind?" I still was looking at the bats and avoiding his gaze.

"We could kidnap that redhead and interrogate him. I know this might be dangerous, but I can't see any other options if you want to find out who is behind your troubles," he said, sitting down.

I grew silent, considering the thought. The idea was tempting, and revenge would be very sweet. *Would it be possible? Could we overcome such a large man as the redhead?* Yes, probably, the two of us could capture him despite his size and muscles. We had the advantage of Rick being a trained fighter. And I proved to be not that hopeless with sword fighting as I thought.

"What do you think?" Rick asked quietly.

Another lonely figure passed down the path in front of our bench and dissolved into the evening dusk.

"How do you plan to do this?" I asked him as this was his idea.

"Let's make it simple. Your kidnappers worked out quite an effective plan to get you. Let's do the same. We need to rent a house somewhere, a considerable distance from London, and a car too. The rest of the venture will depend partly on luck and partly on muscles."

I didn't like the idea of depending on luck, but the plan could provide an opportunity to find out the name of my enemy. I was sure that the redhead wasn't the mastermind but a mere tool, following someone's orders.

"Perhaps, we could frighten him. All I need is the name – who ordered this," I didn't realise I was thinking aloud.

Rick nodded.

"We need to think about this, Rick." I wasn't sure if it was safe to go ahead with this venture – it could result in something unexpected, such as a war in Rehen or some revenge killing. "Let's think about this seriously, and we will talk about it later. I have booked a session with you for the day after tomorrow. Or we may discuss that in Chadrack."

"Okay," he agreed. "That sounds wise."

The darkness of the moonless night was already surrounding us.

"It's time to return to Rehen," I told him. "I will see you there!"

He nodded, and I went back home, leaving him behind, still sitting on the park bench.

Later in bed, I had tempting thoughts of revenge but fell asleep with the dreadful forebodings of an impending war.

A horse was neighing under my window when my mind slowly wandered back to daylight. I glanced outside the window. A cold wind was blowing over the capital, bringing dark clouds and the overwhelming sense of danger.

I was getting dressed when Carwyn knocked on the door.

"It's the messenger from the South, my Lord," old butler's eyes were frightened. "He said it's urgent."

"Bring him here."

Minutes later, Carwyn let in the messenger. He was a young man limping on his wounded leg. I could see bright flowers of red soaking through the poorly placed bandages around his thigh. I sat him down on a chair while he struggled to catch his breath.

"What happened?"

"We have been attacked, my Lord!"

"Was it Mordak?"

"No, sir..." he said, breathing heavily.

"Ghouls?"

He shook his head. I ran out of options.

"I don't know. It was an army of dark knights. I have never seen them before. They are led by a woman."

"Do you know her name?"

"I think she looks like Priestess Hel, my Lord!"

The name was familiar from my genealogy studies with the Keeper. She was my sister, but why she was attacking me?

"Where was the attack?"

"Golcar, sir!"

"How big is the army?"

"It's only a couple of dozens of knights, my Lord, but they are mighty. They look like gods! They kill like gods! They have smoking spears, and those fumes kill as surely as an arrow. My all squad is gone, my Lord. My horse is gone. And I barely escaped with my life..."

I glanced down at his bandaged leg. A few drops of blood were dripping on the floor – that wound needed urgent attention. I dashed to the door, called Carwyn and ordered to bring in the healer at once.

A few minutes later, the healer rushed in, just in time to see the messenger fainting. I left him to perform his magic on the floor.

As I went, I bit my lip, silently cursing my stupidity. I desperately needed the general right now! Silly me, I had sent him to strengthen riverside borders only a few days ago!

I bumped into Carwyn and ordered him to send for Bedwyr immediately.

Damn! I suspected that the Dark Priestess was behind the crow attack as well. *How powerful was she?*

I stormed through the corridors of the castle, unsure how to proceed. I was afraid. *I was very afraid.*

Why me? Why couldn't she have chosen to pay a visit to Keely or some other remote land, some distant territory somewhere far far away. But maybe Keely was next on her list?

I hastily paced back and forth, and my mind squeezed into a tiny spiky ball by fear. I needed to calm down… I needed some rabbits! The Keeper might know something about my approaching nemesis. Maybe he would even know how to deal with her.

I half-ran into the kitchen and told the boy I found there to bring a basket with five or six rabbits to my room. He hurried away, and I returned to my chambers, trying to focus and to force the fear out of my head.

They had carried the poor messenger off somewhere: to the healer's chambers, I guessed. I rushed across the hall where the map was hanging on the far wall and began searching in desperation – Golcar was far to the South – at least five days' travel by horse and more than a week's march for an army. The way to the capital was along the Porlokan border, and I hoped the Dark Priested still could turn left on any of the many crossroads and pay a visit to my sister Keely.

I paced the room like a caged wild lion until the boy delivered the basket with rabbits, then quickly slipped my Ring on and stepped into the cold hearth. The wall opened in front of me and then closed as I hurried down the tunnel, occasionally stumbling on stones underfoot.

The grotto was unchanged since the last time I had been there, but I couldn't spot Hawa. I put the basket down and slowly approached the Well. Purple sparks rose from the surface, greeting my Ring, which responded with a pale blue light. *Was it time for it for another dip?*

I submerged the Ring under rippling surface of the Well, feeling power gathering around it. Then I heard a familiar chuckle behind me.

"What have you brought so soon, Prince Kyleb?" asked Hawa.

"I brought you a few more rabbits," I responded.

"That's very kind of you," I heard the Keeper shuffling towards the basket. "But feeding me is not your priority, I guess?"

"You are wise, and you are right," I admitted. "I still need more information. Do you know Priestess Hel?"

"Oh, you have met the Onyx already..." he whispered. "She is your sister, as I told you, and her Ring is the Master of Death."

I must have flinched at these words, as the Keeper chuckled.

"What does she want here?" I asked.

"That's easy to guess, knowing Hel. Probably, she wants power. She has no Well in Patna. The source of her power is the Tower of Whispers." Hawa said still futzing in the basket. "You have the most powerful Well in the realm, dear Prince. You must defend it, or you'll lose it. Or you may lose yourself defending the Well."

"Is my Ring capable of defeating the Onyx?"

"I don't know," he sighed. "It is not that straightforward. The Ring might shield you for some time, but it won't shield the whole country. You are by your Well, Kyleb. Take advantage of this, but be careful and avoid face to face confrontation. If fumes from the Onyx gets to you – you are as good as dead."

"Do you think there is any way to avoid those fumes?"

Hawa chuckled again.

"Well, just avoid it," he said. "But don't take my words for it; I might be wrong."

I took my hand out of the Well, looking at the purple drops as they fell back to the rippling surface.

"It doesn't sound easy," I observed. "I am still very clumsy in using the Ring – I don't remember many things. Priestess Hel attacked me with crows a few days ago, and I was forced to try my Ring on them without any preparation. The birds just burnt; I couldn't force them back. Could I create a similar attack to get her out of my yard?"

Hawa laughed as if I had said something incredibly funny.

"I can't believe how completely your mind was wiped out by that poison. You need some practice, dear Prince – go and use the Ring on somebody or something. Destiny can be as deadly as Death, my dear prince," he said, still laughing. "Try it!"

"I will," I promised. "But can you guide me just a little bit? There's a war coming, if I may remind you."

I failed to suppress the note of desperation in my voice.

"How can I guide you when any direction is the right one. Just choose your way and then follow it..." said Hawa seriously.

"A small hint would be greatly appreciated," I insisted.

Why didn't they have any user manuals for such complicated matters?

"Does the word 'destiny' ring a bell, my dear Prince?" The eerie gaze of purple fire was fixed on me. "And your Ring is the Master of Destiny."

I spent a few moments digesting the thought.

"Does that mean I can change someone's destiny with my Ring?" The question sounded foolish.

"Yes!" he laughed again. "At last, you got it! But be careful and don't play with the power of your Ring too much or you may end up in a total mess, Kyleb. This is very serious."

"Does it mean that being destined to die is the same as being dead?" I still couldn't believe what my tongue had just said. "Right now, I am mostly interested in the combat power of the Ring."

"Yes, yes, you got that right. It is almost the same," he mumbled impatiently. "Go and find some innocent sufferer for your practice..."

The Keeper was circling the basket already, and I understood that it was time for me to leave.

"I'll see you later then," I said, keeping my distance from Hawa. "Just don't get mad if I return with more silly questions!"

"You are always welcome, dear, especially when you bring a feast like this!"

I left without looking back.

The day was dark and gloomy when I emerged from the hearth. The hall was empty. Heaven over Chadrack was erupting with cold streams of water, and gusts of wind were shuddering windows. I stopped and looked around, keen to try my Ring on something harmless, but nothing suitable caught the eye. Hawa was right – such an experienced enemy as the Dark Priestess wasn't the most suitable candidate for a beginner's experiments.

"Lunch is ready!" announced Carwyn, peeking through the door.

I paid no attention to what I chewed. *I need some practice* – was the thought numbing everything, even the bestial fear. I hoped I still had a few days before facing her, and gaining experience was the most important thing.

I asked Carwyn about the injured messenger. I was hoping that if he was still alive, he might tell me more about Hel and how he was injured.

The poor guy was in the healer's chambers. I asked Carwyn for directions and navigated my way through the castle. The chambers were at the very end of a long, dimly lit through a narrow window, corridor. I tapped the door and entered without waiting for a response.

The healer was tending to the injured man. When I came in, he only glanced at me and then turned his attention back to the procedure. The messenger was pale; he had drops of perspiration on his forehead and was breathing deeply. His eyes were frightened and wide open as if Death herself was hovering in front of him.

"What happened?" I asked, quietly, not wishing to interfere with the procedure.

"I have never seen an injury like this," the healer replied after some time. "Look, my Lord, that wound is still smoking!"

I glanced at the bloodied wound in his leg where a small strand of faint black fumes was swirling like seaweed in a rapid current, pinned deeply among pulsing streams of blood. *This must be related to the Onyx!*

"Have you found anything in the wound?" I asked.

Healer only silently shook his head.

"And I am unable to put any stitches. The wound won't close, and it keeps on bleeding. I am starting to think about amputation..."

I sat down on a chair in the corner, observing the healer's unsuccessful efforts and silent sufferings of the wounded from a distance. *Could I change this?*

I gathered my courage and mentally reached into my Ring, setting focus at the injured soldier. A blue sphere appeared in front of my eyes, and a sequence of images flashed in it among the blue mist: the young man entering my hall, then the same man entering the castle, then furiously riding a horse through a dark, creepy forest, then catching a horse standing alongside the corpse of another man, then falling off a different horse. And then I saw it: the moment when a fuming spear pierced the backside of his frightened mare, while a tiny strand of blackness reached out and touched his leg. That was the key point. *Could I change this?* I extended my will through the Ring and tried to force his leg to move. It wasn't easy, and my mind felt trapped like sinking in quicksand. More I struggled, deeper it was sucked until I nearly smelled the blood of the dying horse. I reached my left hand into the blue sphere and pushed the soldier's thigh forward with all my might. After several vigorous attempts, I succeeded in moving it a few inches only, but the strand of the black fumes missed the soldier's leg completely, disappearing into the flesh of the falling horse.

I scrolled through the images a little further and saw the dark knight in strange, smoking black armour pointing a spear at the young man, then the grim black knights emerging from a nearby forest in a line formation. Finally, the image of a tall blonde lady dressed in black appeared. She was riding a black stallion behind the line of dark knights. She must be my sister.

I built up remnants of my will and reached out trying to divert her from Chadrack when suddenly the image blurred, emitting strands of black smoke. I was sure this was the Onyx Ring protecting her, and I was unable to penetrate its protection.

I hastily dropped the sphere, severing the connection.

"Mighty Gods!" The healer blinked, shaking head in disbelief.

The wound was gone.

"Let him rest," I mumbled on my way out.

My attempt to manipulate the past had exhausted me. I wiped the perspiration from my forehead and stormed along the corridor, feeling restless in the face of the menace. I absentmindedly wandered through the castle passing halls, terraces and gardens, my gaze empty, and only the thought of my blond sister circling through my head. Later in the afternoon, I remembered the promise I had made to visit Rhys.

I found him in the inner yard, along with Bysh and Gwyn, who were almost inseparable.

"How are you today, Rick?" I asked him and then quickly corrected myself. "Rhys…"

"Thank you, my Lord," he smiled. "I am well. Look at Gwyn – he is testing out his wings already! He is growing so fast! I would not be surprised if he starts flying in a few weeks. But you look terrible. What's bothering you?"

I sat down next to him and quietly described the situation. My sister had a deadly weapon, she was heading here, and I believed she had the intention of taking the castle!

"Then we have to get your redhead as soon as possible. He might be her accomplice!" Rhys exclaimed.

I had a nasty feeling that he might be right.

"Will you be able to rent a house somewhere south of London? Not too expensive…" I asked.

"I will try to have a look tomorrow," he nodded.

"Then I'll rent a car," I promised. "We must hurry. We might have only a few days left."

We watched Bysh fooling around with Gwyn.

"What should we do if the redhead turns out to be related to your sister? Kill him?" he asked.

"I don't know... That's a difficult question. If he is of any value to my sister, then maybe we can hold him captive to make Hel change her plans..."

"And if he is of no value to her?" Rhys was serious. "If we might be forced to kill him, we need a plan for how to get rid of the body as well."

The discussion had slowly slipped into the nasty territory. Gwyn sneaked onto my lap as we spoke, hiding from Bysh.

"How big is that redhead?" Rhys asked.

"Why?"

"I need to plan how to get rid of the corpse. Will we be able to lift him by ourselves?"

"I doubt that. He is a big guy, much bigger than me."

Rhys glanced at me, his gaze like a butcher's, estimating.

"Then we will need to cut him into pieces," he said, finally.

I felt nauseated only thinking about it.

"You will need to do that alone, I'm afraid. Don't count on me to help," I told him, stroking Gwyn's head.

Rhys shrugged.

"I had to do it several times – here, of course! Not everybody is thin enough to be put on a cremation pyre in one piece..."

"Let's be clear – killing him is not our purpose. It can be the last desperate measure only," I sincerely hoped we would not be forced to stain our hands with blood.

"I'll need to find a house with a large bath or kitchen, then. And I will need some plastic covers and meat cleavers..." Rhys started to bend his fingers.

"I don't want to know any of these details," I stopped him. "Please..."

He only glanced at me and nodded.

"I will rent a car in the morning," I said, after an awkward pause. "Let's keep in touch by phone if anything unexpected happens."

As I left him, my heart was troubled. I hadn't expected that this venture might lead to murder, but with the war approaching; this might be the only option.

I ate my dinner alone, then undressed and slipped into bed, my thoughts still somewhere in that meadow, my mind's eye on that tall blonde woman riding a black horse who happened to be my sister and who might become my executioner. I didn't like the thought and was overwhelmed by a strange mix of feelings – both love and fear. She was my family, but I couldn't force myself to face Death with family love.

Sleep didn't come easily, but when I finally felt the darkness approaching, I drifted gratefully.

I woke up to the disgusting thought that we were preparing for murder. The rising threat changed everything and forced us to take desperate measures. I hated this, but the overwhelming fear had paralysed my sense of morality. The most important thing now was to survive. I had an irresistible urge to run away, hide somewhere and wait for the danger to dissolve. But what about the other people in Chadrack? They might be doomed if the Dark Priestess gets the castle!

The redhead showed a lot of self-confidence by not killing me. The rules of this game were more than weird. I had seen their faces, I knew them, and the fact that I had this knowledge didn't seem dangerous to my kidnappers. That was very strange. Were they related to my sister Hel? Did they know she was coming to get me? If they were, their presence in London could be deadly dangerous. I still was a sitting duck.

I trembled inside and longed to wake up in some other reality or to dream another dream, one without any blood, war, danger or cruel envy. I longed for simple grey everyday life, and ordinary night-time dreams about trivial things. But I had been told I couldn't have this anymore. I had to go on.

Renting a car was easy. I selected a dark grey sedan – nothing special, just a big grey car. I didn't want to attract any unnecessary attention.

I drove around, thinking of Chadrack and making plans for how to build up defences against such a powerful enemy as Hel when I suddenly spotted the redhead walking down the street. He was carrying a plastic bag of groceries and unhurriedly strolling on the sunny side of the street, clearly enjoying himself. I hit the brakes so hard I nearly caused an accident, then I cursed and parked the car, attempting to lie low. Luckily, the red-haired man didn't notice. I passed a few blocks following him, intermittently stopping the car and pretending to read text messages on my phone.

I did my best to keep my distance but continued secretly peeking at him. I drove erratically, stopping many times and suddenly accelerating at unexpected moments. Luckily, there was almost no traffic.

Then he stopped and, without even glancing around, took out a bundle of keys and unlocked the front door of a house. The redhead wasn't hiding. He entered the house, grocery in one hand and keys in another, and then closed the door behind him.

The house looked like an ordinary family home with baskets of white and red petunias hanging from the front porch. Maybe the redhead had kids and a loving wife there, all unaware of his involvement in hijacking and maybe even killing people.

I parked several hundred yards away and waited for a few hours but without any success. The redhead didn't come out again. I noted down his address and moved on. If I stayed here much longer, I would certainly attract the attention of some concerned neighbour.

I paid for the parking and left the car in the shopping centre car park – a foolish attempt to remain inconspicuous. On my way home, I picked up a Chinese takeaway. A day heavy with planning and plotting was waiting for me, in both worlds – I had no time for cooking.

Rick called later in the afternoon. He had found an abandoned house somewhere in the forest, which would be suitable for our venue. I briefly told him about my achievements. He asked me to call the reception in the club and cancel our training tomorrow – I was his only customer, so we would be able to start stalking the redhead earlier.

I did as he told me and spent the rest of the day watching TV. I hoped the redhead would be willing to talk, but was afraid that

Rick might be right – it could be too dangerous to leave him alive. My sister seemed to have far from friendly intentions for her impending visit, and this caused me painful mental spasms. I fell asleep at some point, the TV still on.

The weather was grim in Chadrack: dark clouds covered the sky, distant thunder was rumbling somewhere off to the south, and gusts of wind brought the smell of the damp forest in through the open window.

How could I fight her? That was the only thought buzzing in my head. I wasn't ready to die, and I wasn't prepared to fight for my life, either. The image of that smoking wound was tantalising my mind. *Run!* That was my only urge – *run and hide somewhere in the caves, and wait until my sister gets bored with my castle.* But it wasn't only the castle. I slowly realised my responsibility for the city outside of my window. I couldn't fail the people. But how could I fight her?

Carwyn came in after a soft tap on the door, bringing, as usual, a bowl of water and a fresh set of garments for me.

"Bedwyr has returned as you requested, my Lord," he said,

placing everything in front of me.

"Great! Bring him in," I said, springing to my feet.

Carwyn left without another word. I washed my face and was midway through putting on my trousers when Bedwyr came through the door.

"Do we have a plan for defending the capital of Chadrack in case of an attack?" I asked my general as soon as he had closed the door.

"Nobody dares to attack Chadrack," he said firmly, without any trace of hesitation. "We have had no attacks in living memory."

"We are going to have one now," I told him. "And I presume there is no plan for defence?"

"I haven't seen any army outside of the city walls, my Lord," said Bedwyr, carefully selecting his words.

"It's not an army. She hasn't arrived yet, and I hope we have a few days to prepare."

"She?"

"My sister Hel," I said, watching for his reaction. "The Dark Priestess of Patna. Her dark knights destroyed our guards in Golcar, and I assume she is heading here as we speak."

The blood slowly drained from the general's face.

"No defence can withstand if Death is attacking, my Lord," he slowly said. "I will bring the army to the capital, but there is too little time to build any serious obstacles for your sister. We will defend the city. Your army will be here, and we will fight until the last drop of our blood."

I felt weak at the knees as images of the city burning flashed through my mind. *Was this the end?*

Bedwyr followed me as I limped to the hall and sat down at the table. *Could I still run away and hide somewhere?* I heard the guards changing at the gate. Under the dark cloudy sky outside, the city was waking up. *Was this the end of Chadrack?*

"May I give the order for your army to return to the capital?" asked Bedwyr, interrupting my hectic daydreaming.

"No!" I slammed my hand down on the table. I had made up my mind. "We will not fight her."

Our plan to kidnap the redhead had acquired even greater importance. Not only my own life, but the survival of Chadrack might depend on it. I couldn't explain this to Bedwyr, who reacted to my sudden decision with an astonished look.

I couldn't risk the lives of my people.

"But if she is attacking," Bedwyr started to protest, "we have to fight back! Chadrack has never been a country of cowards."

"Would you rather Chadrack be a country of fools?" I stopped him.

His eyes flashed angrily, but his mouth remained tightly shut.

"I share your rage, Bedwyr," I said, maintaining the eye

contact. "But we cannot win this battle."

"Please, let us fight, my Lord," he said. "If you do, songs will be chanted about you and the bravery of your soldiers. We will not fail you!"

"I am sure about that. I have no doubts about your bravery and determination of our soldiers," I said quietly. "But this battle is different. All your songs and legends will not raise Chadrack from the dead if we let this happen."

"Do you count on your sister's mercy?" Bedwyr asked, anger still flaming in his eyes, but his voice cold as steel.

We needed a miracle, not mercy from my sister.

"No," I said firmly. "We will abandon the capital instead. I guess my sister will not have too much use for the empty walls."

I watched the veins in Bedwyr's temples filling with blood. He squeezed the handle of his sword, clearly struggling to accept the decision, but a few moments later, the sword was still in the sheath, and he let its handle go.

"We will do as you command, my Lord," he said finally.

"I was counting on that," I told him, my voice firm and commanding, but my heart still fluttering with fear. "Do you know where we could move all the people in the shortest possible time?"

"There are a few caves high in the mountain – they are large enough but hard to access, nearly impossible for the elderly, women, and small children. The young adults could go there, and we could distribute the remaining people along the bank of the Braaid; in case of any imminent danger we could place them on ships – the river is too wide even for Priestess Hel."

"That's good," I sighed. "Begin the evacuation. I want the army to supervise everything since we don't have much time. Everything must be handled quickly and in the right order. We won't get a second chance. Only leave a small group of guards with me. We will go to the caves at the very last moment, if necessary. Everybody else must go."

"I will start immediately with your permission, my Lord," Bedwyr nodded and left.

I could only guess what kind of turmoil was going on in his head, but he was a good soldier; I was sure that my order for evacuation would be carried out. I only hoped we still had enough time for it.

Turmoil and shouts started in the corridor and outside the window. It was another grim indication of the mess we were heading. Then I remembered Milo. He was keen to go to the caves. Had he recovered enough for the journey? I couldn't leave him behind.

I dashed out of my chambers. A trip through the maze of corridors, halls and staircases brought me to the healer's rooms. I tapped the door politely and waited. Nobody answered. I pushed the door and stepped inside. The healer was busy gathering his phials, dried plants and crushed bones into big leather bags, preparing to leave. The instant I entered the room, he stopped.

"Do you want me to stay, my Lord?" He was pale, nervously turning over the dark brown phial in his fingers.

"No," I told him. "You may leave with the others."

"Thank you, my Lord," he sighed, placing the phial in his bag. "I am bad at fighting..."

"We are not going to fight," I shrugged. "Your skills will not be required here. Where is Milo?"

"The boy from the temple?"

"Yes."

"He left as soon as was able to stand on his feet," said the healer, continuing to pack. "That was a few days ago. I didn't want to bother you..."

"Had he recovered completely?"

"No, but he will be fine," he said, wiping perspiration from his forehead. "Young ones heal fast."

"Glad to know," I sighed, and genuinely meant it. "Where was he going?"

"I don't know," said healer. "As far from here as possible, he said..."

"I can't blame him for that," I sighed.

Milo was frightened, I knew, by the ruthless priest and by my inability to protect him. I only hoped that the boy was smart enough not to go to the south, where my sister and her smoking army were marching. Had he gone to the caves?

I wished the healer a safe journey and left him packing, then retraced my route back to my chambers. Dark fear slowly crawled into my heart and took root there.

How would I be able to withstand Hel, her army, her Ring? I felt completely useless.

I was glad that at least the people of Chadrack had a chance to save themselves and to start a new life somewhere. *Maybe even return home, when the imminent danger dissipates. Who knows?*

I turned my Ring on my finger as I stared into the dark blue depths of the precious stone in the hope of seeing just a hint of what was waiting for us. But the stone was cold and silent.

I lowered myself onto the bed, letting my dark thoughts and sour mood engulf me. I knew I might end up dying here... But I was unable to run away with the others. The Keeper said that protection of the Well was the most important. I couldn't just leave it to Hel.

Later, Carwyn showed up with a food basket. I accepted it gratefully; I was starving. I ordered to pack more food reserves, enough for two dozen men for a few weeks. Then I told him to take his belongings and leave the castle along with everybody else.

"Be safe, my Lord," said the old butler, and I noticed traces of moisture in his eyes.

A rising turmoil – shouts and the sound of women wailing could be heard from outside as the entire capital was set in motion.

"One more thing before you go," I added as an afterthought. "Make sure that all the hearths in the castle are filled with wood, including the one in my room. We will light them up when we leave. My sister needs a warm welcome!"

"I will do that, my Lord!"

I spent the rest of the day on the balcony, watching people running around the castle; it looked like a disturbed anthill. Death approaching was sufficiently grave news to stimulate everybody into action.

Later in the evening, the yard grew silent. I had no idea how Bedwyr did that, but the capital was deserted.

One of the few people remaining was Dahryl, who was in charge of a small band of nine jaegers, left behind for my protection.

Later in the evening, I visited Rhys. He was in the back yard with the gryphon, and Gwyn was the first to greet me.

"You must consider retreating as well," I told him. "Hel can be very dangerous."

"I know," Rhys smiled sadly. "But we need to solve this little thing with the redhead first. Do you think we still have time?"

"We might have two or three days... maybe five, if we are lucky."

"We'd better start first thing in the morning," he sighed.

"And we must be prepared to continue that interrogation overnight if we manage to capture the kidnapper," I told him. "The redhead must be a Sleeper. Keeping him awake might be as difficult for him as it is for us, although this depends on his circumstances in Rehen."

"It's a good idea. But it might be difficult for me to sleep in the castle during the daytime." Rhys said, indicating the gryphon. "Those two are always fooling around."

"Maybe one of the jaegers could have a look at them?" I suggested. "I'll ask Dahryl..."

"I think I have a better idea." Rhys tossed a ball to Gwyn and stood up. "Do you remember Neve, the girl from Ikent? She helped me several times with Gwyn, so I think she might be confident enough to handle him for a day or so. I am sure she would be all right with Bysh as well."

"Hasn't she left with the others?" I raised my eyebrows.

Rhys shook head.

"You asked her to take care of your horse," he said. "Your Knight is here, and so is she. She refused to leave."

"Poor child. But I guess she likes animals. Let's try this..."

Rhys left, and I stayed to keep an eye on Gwyn. The creature happily fooled around with a ball, paying little attention to me.

Several minutes later, Rhys returned with Neve. The girl looked frightened, and I had to stop her attempt to kneel before me.

"We are friends, remember?" I smiled at her. "And I'm glad to see you, Neve. Thank you for taking good care of my Knight. This time, could you take care of Gwyn and Bysh for a day or two while Rhys is away with me?"

"I am fine with Gwyn, sir; we are friends," she said. "But who is Bysh?"

I whistled, and our enormous black dog appeared, seemingly from nowhere. Probably, he was stalking rabbits on the far side of the yard. Neve retreated several steps, her eyes wide.

"Don't be afraid; he is a sweet boy." I placed my hand on Bysh's head. "You only have to make friends with him."

"I have never seen such a big dog..." whispered Neve, but she bravely forced herself to take a step forward and extended her arm for Bysh to sniff.

Rhys stood close to her, ready to intervene at any moment. Bysh growled at first but then started to slowly wag his tail. Seconds later, the dog was licking her face.

Neve glanced at me with a victorious smile.

"Now you need to feed him," I smiled back. "And you will be

friends forever. This is the way how dogs make friends."

"But I have nothing he would eat," the girl shrugged.

"Go and get some meat from the kitchen. It may be deserted, but look around..." I told her and tossed the ball, watching both Bysh and Gwyn running after it.

Neve hurried out.

"Where we could sleep undisturbed?" Rhys asked. "It will be difficult to do so at the castle even after the evacuation."

"I have an idea. We will leave in the afternoon," I said. "Collect whatever you need and let's meet in my chambers. Time is pressing..."

He nodded silently, and I left to gather my things too. It might be a long sleep, and I had to make myself as comfortable as I could.

Rhys was ready to go and in my room well before I had finished packing my pillow and blankets. We also took a small basket of food with us. We didn't want to waste time eating in the castle.

We left through the front door, crossed the yard and went through the castle gate, which was now guarded by only one man. Rhys didn't ask where we were going, and I didn't bother to provide an explanation.

We crossed the bridge and started ascending the steep stairs carved into the black rock next to the waterfall. Before long, it was impossible to talk – the sound of falling streams was deafening.

We climbed at a steady pace without stopping. The evening was spreading its wings already, and it was almost dark when we reached the top of the staircase and stopped to catch our breath. Rhys looked at me, questioningly. I put on my Sapphire Ring and instantly located the secret pattern. It took me a few moments of concentration before the entrance opened, revealing a faintly lit passage inside.

I stepped in; Rhys followed. A few steps later, the opening behind us closed soundlessly, muffling the noise of the waterfall. I went forward until this noise was barely audible and then I stopped.

"It's here," I said, putting my sack on the ground.

"What is this place?" asked Rhys.

"It's a little family trick," I said, not wishing to go into further explanations. "I guess we'll be safe here. Let's try to get some sleep."

We spread out our sheets on the floor, then ate our supper.

I used my Ring to dim the lights above, and we went to sleep.

Nightmares followed.

It was a lovely morning in London, bright and peaceful, but the sense of imminent danger followed me from Chadrack like a dark shadow.

I tossed my blanket away and suddenly froze – the gryphon Ring with the enormous Sapphire was peacefully shining on my finger. *How had it managed to cross the planes of reality when only the minds of Sleepers could travel freely?*

My heart fluttered as I looked into the depths of the blue gem and tried to reach it with my will. I gasped as the sparkling blue sphere appeared in front of me. *The Master of Destiny could perform its magic even here!* I couldn't decide if this was an advantage or disadvantage. I broke the connection, wondering how deep Rehen had got into my everyday life, and I took the Ring off. I had no time for investigations.

My morning coffee tasted like shit – the milk was nearly off, but I added it to the brew anyway, and a snowstorm of tiny flecks of curd was raging in my cup. I still sipped it, preparing for the distasteful job we had to do. I clearly recalled my hopeless situation in the hands of kidnappers, my overwhelming fear and total dependence on hostile people. The thought that I must do this terrible thing to somebody weighed heavily on my heart. I no longer had a taste for revenge. But it wasn't about revenge any longer – I had been cornered and forced to fight, and it was about survival. Our only hope was that we might somehow be able to use the redhead and persuade Hel to leave Chadrack in peace. We had to do this – otherwise, we were doomed.

I called Rick and agreed to meet.

The mirror told that me I needed a shave, but I chose to ignore it. I combed my hair while brushing my teeth, then quickly got dressed. After some hesitation, I put the Ring in my breast pocket and carefully buttoned it. My tiny flat didn't seem safe any longer.

I put on my baseball cap and sunglasses to hide my face and then rushed out to meet the sunshine. The street was busy, but nobody paid attention to my lonely figure hurrying down the street. There were plenty of strange faces in London, and I was just another one.

I spotted Rick waiting for me as soon as I reached Bromley Road. I expected him to be fully equipped, with knives and pistols sticking out of every pocket, but he wasn't carrying anything and was dressed in his everyday blue flannel shirt and jeans. He hadn't attempted to cover his face either.

"Are you ready?" I asked cautiously.

"Yes." He was serious. "Let's do it."

We got in the car and slowly drove down the road where I had seen the redhead unlocking the front door of a family house. The traffic was light here, and soon we found ourselves peeking at the petunia baskets across the street and waiting.

"Have you any plan for how to do this?" I asked Rick.

"The redhead doesn't know me," he said, "so I could get pretty close without him getting suspicious. I might have a few surprises up my sleeve."

That didn't sound encouraging.

"What do you want me to do?" I asked, my voice sounded like we had failed already.

"Just drive." He kept his eyes on the petunias.

"Where?"

He handed me a folded piece of paper. It was a printed out map with our destination circled and the coordinates carefully written at the edge.

"I'll set up the satnav..." I mumbled, studying the map.

"Who is that man?" asked Rick. "He doesn't seem to have ginger hair."

I lifted my eyes from the paper and gasped silently. Our risky venture had just become impossible: one of the Asian men was ringing the doorbell of the house with petunias outside.

"Damn…"

The door opened, and the Asian man slipped inside. I only got a quick glimpse of the redhead as he closed the door.

"He is one of his accomplices," I grunted. "They must be planning something new. It's too late for us to do anything!"

"Let's wait and see…" said Rick calmly.

"They might be planning to get me again," I said, doing my best not to sound hysterical. "Hel is at the gates of Chadrack, and my death would be very handy to her."

"If they are," observed Rick, "the plan apparently hasn't reached the phase of implementation. You are still alive and sitting next to me. We know that something is going on and so we still might have a chance."

The fear was growing inside me, faster than I could deal with.

"What will we do?" I asked, desperation clear in my voice.

Rick was calm. "Let's stick to the plan. We must bring the redhead to that house for interrogation."

"But how?"

"Let's wait and see," he said. "We might have an opportunity."

An hour passed in nervous waiting. Nothing happened. The

petunias waved lazily in the sunshine on the other side of the quiet road; all the plotting was hidden behind the tightly shut doors.

I nearly jumped when the doorknob finally turned, and the door opened. Two men stepped outside, laughing. The redhead fished the key out of his pocket, then locked the door, and they both strolled unhurriedly down the street.

"We are doomed," I hissed through my teeth, shaking my head. "You'll never be able to handle two of them."

Rick didn't answer. His body grew stiff as his eyes drilled into the retreating target. He looked like a pointer dog stalking his prey.

"I'll try to get nearer," he said, opening the door. "Let's keep in touch over the phone."

He crossed the street in front of me and went after the two men. I locked the doors and clutched the wheel, looking at them and seeing nothing else around.

The duo walked down the street, talking and laughing, while Rick followed, several hundred feet behind. I waited, my heart racing. *Was this the end? Had Hel somehow cracked our conspiracy?*

The redhead reached the bus stop, still laughing at something the Asian man was telling him. They checked the timetable and continued their conversation. Rick stopped a few feet behind them, pretending to study his watch. Then he took out his phone and tapped out a message.

"Follow the bus" flashed my phone.

The redhead raised his hand and stopped an approaching red double-decker. All three boarded the bus, and I started the engine.

We headed south. I closely followed the bus down the narrow streets, dutifully waiting at every stop. I kept my eye on the phone, but it was silent.

We reached Bromley, and a few stops later, I spotted the Asian man back on the pavement. Rick and the redhead remained on board. My heart was racing, and I covered my face with a slightly trembling hand as I drove past the Asian man. He was studying the timetable and paid no attention to the cars on the road.

We turned off the High Street on the left, and a few stops later the redhead got off the bus, heading towards the railway station. Rick followed him several paces behind.

I turned left into the car park of a supermarket. There was no need to follow the bus any longer. The next fifteen minutes were the longest of my life.

"We have boarded the train," the next message from Rick read. "Meet us at Swanley station."

I spent a few minutes trying to persuade the satnav to guide me to the required location. A barely legal race against time through the streets of London followed. It was stupid to let Rick risk his life and follow the much bigger and stronger man, I decided. The entire idea now seemed insane. I loudly cursed wobbling in the traffic. *Fool! Fool! Idiot!* I should have retreated with everybody else instead of pursuing this stupid confrontation with Hel's hitman. I was almost sure that Rick would be dead or dying before I reached Swanley.

I was surprised. Rick was waiting for me outside the rail station. The redhead was standing alongside him, looking somehow deflated and crushed. *What was going on?*

Rick calmly took the redhead's elbow. He made no protest, just unhappily walked to the car, then opened the door and slipped inside. Rick closely followed him.

I drove off as soon as Rick closed the door. The redhead sat in the back, growing pale but making no sound.

"Now, give me all the weapons you have and your mobile phone," ordered Rick.

The big man obediently went through his pockets, passing a few army knives and his mobile to Rick. The phone was immediately dismantled and tossed on the front seat along with the weapons.

I wound through the narrow streets, trying to keep heading in a southerly direction, towards where Rick had spotted that abandoned house, suitable for our business. Rick produced a dark cloth bag from his pocket and handed it to our prisoner.

"Put that on," he ordered.

The man put the bag over his head without a single sound, clearly understanding what was going on. Rick produced a rope from his pocket.

"Now your hands..." he ordered.

Soon the redhead had been peacefully tied up and was slumped against the door.

I silently followed the satnav. It was always easy to get lost in the tangled streets of south London, and I wondered how many of the directions from the monotonous female voice the blindfolded red-haired man would be able to remember. Several times I took the wrong exits from roundabouts just to make him more confused. Rick made no comment about that.

Several crossroads later, we emerged onto the motorway. There was a lot of traffic speeding in both directions, and no one paid any attention to our strange passenger with the bag on his head.

I was wholly immersed in driving on the busy high-speed road when suddenly the humming engine was outroared by loud snoring behind me.

"Damn! Don't let him slip away," I screamed. "He might warn Hel!"

Rick punched the redhead's side, and the snoring stopped.

"Start counting aloud!" he ordered. "As soon as you stop, I

will punch you again."

I tried to ignore the monotonous numerals, but the sound of the redhead's voice stirred the creepy recollections in my brain. It was the same voice from that scary night, and that realisation sent chills down my spine. I wasn't ready for that but clenched my teeth and silently drove on.

Several miles later, I turned onto the road for Worthing, towards the forest that was our intended destination.

Rick tapped my shoulder, silently indicating that I should slow down. I spotted the dirt road ahead and turned off the satnav. We had almost arrived.

A mile later, the road ended in front of the abandoned redbrick house with empty attic windows. I stopped the car and turned off the engine.

Rick dragged the blindfolded redhead out of the car and steered him along the narrow corridor to the basement.

It was a large, nearly empty room with a metal bed without any mattress at the centre. I shivered at the very unpleasant memories that this stirred up. Rick removed the bag from our prisoner's head, and he looked at us, blinking. His eyes then turned at the bed, and he understood immediately.

"No need to tag me," he said. "I am not that important. You are wasting your time."

"We will see," said Rick, expressionlessly. "You know what

to do..."

The redhead nodded and went over to the bed.

"It's a pleasure to deal with a professional," observed Rick, quickly tying his wrists, elbows, ankles, thighs and neck to the bed.

The red-haired man made no protest.

"Maybe you could tell us your name now? It will save some time..." were my first words.

"Do I know you?" The redhead frowned, trying to get a better look. "You seem somehow familiar..."

"No, you don't," I cut him off.

"Do you want my name in this world or the other?" the redhead asked casually.

"I would prefer both," I said.

"John here, and Gurney there, if it makes any difference to you..."

"I don't know anybody called Gurney," said Rick.

"I told you already. I am useless. I am not famous or important. I am just another hunter like you."

"Who gives you your targets? Whose orders are you carrying out?" I demanded.

"I am not that stupid," the redhead grunted. "You must be new to this business if you are asking such a silly question."

"Maybe you can tell me who ordered to tag me?" I lost my

patience. I removed the baseball cap and showed him my scar.

"I was sure you looked familiar," he grinned. "I can't answer your question. But the funniest thing is that you were the wrong person – not our target and all that tagging business was a complete mistake. I do apologise for that. Are we done?"

"I think it's too late for apologies," I remarked. "Who was the original target? And who ordered this?"

"You can torture me, but I will not tell you."

"Pity," I told him. "I was hoping to avoid that. You could save some time and effort by just giving us two names."

The red-haired man shook his head.

"What are we going to do now?" asked Rick.

John burst into hysteric laughter. "Amateurs! You don't even have a plan!"

"We have a plan," I told him. "We will wait."

"Aren't you going to tag me?" he suggested. "It is useless; I told you already."

"We'll do that later, if necessary." I turned around and went out.

I was unable to stand it any longer. My hands were shaking, and I had to take a few deep breaths to calm down.

The situation seemed bizarre, but I had a plan. We had no way to verify if any of Hel's accomplices would start bleeding on tagging, but we certainly would attract the attention of someone close to Gurney if he failed to wake up and suddenly began to bleed in broad daylight. All we needed was to wait until dusk.

"Is he tied up securely?" I asked in the yard.

"Yes," Rick nodded. "I double-checked that. But I think we need to keep a constant eye on him."

"All right," I said. "We will take turns. We must keep him from falling asleep. He mustn't be able to cross into the other world and warn anybody. By the way, how have you managed to make him so cooperative?"

He grinned, producing a plastic toy gun from his pocket.

"The fear is always bigger than the real threat..." he whispered, winking.

The rest of the day went slowly, annoyingly and uneventfully. We ate our sandwiches and drank our coffee from the thermos flask Rick had prepared in advance.

John remained stubbornly silent. Dusk was falling, and Rick fitted two LED torches above his bed. The light was strong enough to keep him awake and hurt his eyes.

"Could you put that cloth on my face, at least?" asked the redhead blinking.

"What makes you think we care what you want?" Rick grunted.

"It hurts!"

"So, maybe now you could think of some useful information?

Who was issuing the orders, and who was your primary target?" I tried my best to sound calm.

He moaned and shook his head.

We had waited for another hour when I suddenly noticed a strange jerking movement in John's face – it looked as if he had been hit by an invisible blow. A series of barely perceptible seizures followed.

"I think it's about time," I whispered to Rick. "Let's hurry!"

I loosened John's belt and lifted up his shirt, exposing his hairy chest and belly.

"What are you doing?" John moaned again.

I didn't bother to explain, only took the knife and carefully carved the word "WHO" on his chest. I didn't cut deep – no more than just superficial scratches, but a few tiny droplets of blood appeared along the lines.

We waited, but nothing happened. Maybe we needed to spill more blood to attract attention?

I added a question mark to the end of the word, puncturing the skin a little deeper. John screamed, and his face went into seizures again.

We waited a bit longer. Then letters on his chest started to appear out of nowhere below the word I had carved – not too deep though.

"RELEASE HIM" the message stated.

I smiled. My plan worked! We only had to find out how important Gurney was to my sister Hel. I took the knife and began carving again, paying no attention to John's protests.

"WHO'S ASKING?" said my new message.

I realised I was trembling as I tried to suppress my anxiety while we waited for my sister's name to appear.

A few more minutes passed before John's skin displayed the answer.

"KEELY" the message read.

That was so unexpected that I dropped the knife. My attempt to influence Hel had failed terribly. I meant no harm to my sister Keely, but it was John's turn to confirm the story.

"I will ask you only once, and your life depends on your answer," I told John. "How are you related to Princess Keely?"

John became silent and still for a moment.

"She is my beloved wife," he said, at last, his voice cracking. "You may kill me, I don't care. But, please, don't harm her!"

I lowered his shirt. Our venture was a complete failure. I had been expecting to save Chadrack from my sister Hel by offering to spare John's life in return, but Keely couldn't help me with this. Our mission was over well before the sunrise.

"Release him," I told Rick. "I got everything I could."

"Will it help us somehow?"

"No, I'm afraid not..."

Rick took a knife out of his pocket and cut John's bonds. There was no point in continuing the interrogation.

"No hard feelings," said John, sitting up. "I guess we are even now."

I nodded silently.

"Since this is all sorted out, could I ask *your* name?" John fitted his shirt back into his pants, but his eyes stayed focused on me.

"I'm Kyleb, the brother of your wife, Keely." I introduced myself using my name in Rehen. "This is my close friend, Rhys."

"It's a pleasure, despite the circumstances," John nodded. "And what was this all about?"

"It's no longer a secret," I shrugged. "Priestess Hel is attacking Chadrack. I was hoping you were related to her."

"Maybe Keely could help us somehow?" suggested Rick.

"It might be a deadly venture, and I am not sure if I would go to help Keely if Hel headed southwards," I admitted.

"I will ask her," volunteered John. "Can we return to London now?"

"Yes, we can."

Rick collected our belongings, and we left. The sky was pale blue, already touched by the first light of dawn. We started along the road in silence.

"If you don't mind, I will take a nap," said John. "I need to reassure Keely. She will be worried."

There was no harm in that, I decided. Soon his deep-pitched snoring was filling the car. Rick glanced at me, question in his eyes. I shrugged.

An hour later, we reached John's house. His loud snoring was making the windows shake, but when we stopped outside, he instantly opened his eyes.

"She will think how to help you," he told me. "This situation is difficult without an obvious solution. She needs some time."

It was understandable.

"Maybe we could exchange phone numbers?" I asked. "With your help, Keely and I could communicate in case of emergencies."

John liked the idea.

It was late morning when I dropped Rick at his place. We separated without goodbyes, and I drove home.

I had one more mug of coffee to last me until the evening and ate a light breakfast. Later I returned the rented car and spent my day watching TV. My brain was useless, crushed with fear and empty. Death was approaching, and I had no further ideas on how to persuade Hel to leave Chadrack in peace.

That evening, I ate some cheese for supper, put on my Ring and slipped into bed. Darkness fell over me almost instantly.

I was floating in darkness when I heard a whisper. "Wake up, wake up, sleepy boy!"

The voice was somehow familiar.

"What? Where?!" I sat up.

Hawa's purple eyes were glowing just in front of my face.

"Those are the same questions I was about to ask," chuckled the Keeper. "What are you doing here, Kyleb?"

"Hiding," I admitted.

Hawa was persistent. "Who is after you?"

"My sister Hel – I've told you that already."

"Silly thing, she will certainly find you here. Any Ring can open the entrance. And who is that young man?" he asked, pointing to Rhys. "Is he a prince?"

"No."

"Great! You are spoiling me, Kyleb. I didn't expect you to

bring me a human," Hawa turned to Rhys. "I will feast on him!"

"No! He is my closest, most loyal servant. Have mercy on him, please. I still need his services."

"He looks quite young and tender..." the Keeper pressed, getting closer and inspecting Rhys. "Not too fat..."

"Please... next time I will bring you a lamb! Just leave him..." I sprang to my feet and squeezed between Rhys and Hawa, shielding Rhys with my body.

I wasn't sure if my Ring would be able to protect me from the Keeper if he chose to attack, and I had no other weapons.

"Lamb?" Hawa stopped. "Well, well... You got me – I have never tasted a lamb before. Are you sure you can get me one?"

"Yes, I am sure." I could promise him almost anything.

The Keeper stepped away from Rhys, while I reached into my Ring and added some light to the glowing crystals.

"What do you plan to do next?" he asked.

"I don't know," I shrugged. "I ran out of ideas."

"May I remind you, dear Prince, that there is no place where you could hide from Death." A familiar chuckle followed. "Just prepare for the inevitable. Maybe she will change her mind?"

"You don't sound like you are afraid," I observed.

"You are right," Hawa agreed. "I am not scared. She can't take my life; I don't have one. So, dear Prince, this headache is still all yours."

He chuckled again. I suddenly felt lonely and abandoned, with a mountain-sized responsibility on my shoulders. At least, most of the people of Chadrack had left the capital and moved to safety if there was such a place under the circumstances, and I was glad for that.

"Well, well..." whispered the Keeper. "I must leave you now. I have spared your servant, and I hope you will not forget your promise if you live long enough. I'll be waiting for that lamb..."

"Don't worry," I said. "My memory is damaged, but it's not that bad. You will get your lamb next time I visit you!"

"See you then..." the dark shadow said, already retreating down the steps.

Moments later, Hawa was gone. I turned to Rhys whipping moisture from my forehead.

"Who – or what – was that?" whispered Rhys.

"A friend," I responded. "A monster friend."

"I was so scared, I could hardly move," Rhys sighed. "And I don't get scared easily. I was sure he was going to kill me. Luckily, you intervened..."

"Let's go," I said quietly. "Our mission has failed."

We collected our belongings, and I opened the passage. It was a cloudy outside, around mid-morning.

"How will we fight her now?" asked Rhys, looking down at the valley below.

"We will not fight," I said, watching the passage closing behind us. "There is not a single route to victory this time. We will desert the capital and leave it to her."

"Where will you go?" asked Rhys.

"I have been told that the caves are difficult to access and suitable for hiding," I said. "I will take the remaining jaegers and go there."

"I could show you the way," Rhys offered.

"No," I said. "I want you to leave immediately, and take Gwyn, Bysh and Neve with you. Hel's raven attacked the gryphon before. I don't know why, but he must be important to her. Make sure she can't reach him again."

"As you wish," said Rhys. "What about you?"

"I still have a few days, I suppose," I shrugged. "I'll leave with the last men."

We took the steps back to the castle. Rhys was grimly silent all the way down. I was in no mood to talk either.

We separated at the castle gate.

"Call me first thing in the morning," I told him.

"I will, my Lord," Rhys promised.

I watched as he crossed the yard and then returned to my chambers. I was unable to think of any other strategy. The silence was ripping my skull apart. I paced the hall or studied the map, flinching at every squeak and every footstep outside my window.

The city was empty, and the few men who remained were for my protection only. I still had no plan for how to fight Hel. I had a nasty feeling that simple runaway won't solve my problems. Fear was in the air, paralysing my thoughts. I sneaked into the balcony to have a look at the deserted capital. Several times I saw Dahryl directing guards and bringing food to the watchman at the front gate. The rest of the place was lifeless – the same as my brain, clouded by primordial fear.

Streaks of black mist seemed to be creeping towards me out of every corner – it was only my imagination, of course, but the effect of this was a complete inability to think, to act, or to plan.

When the harsh cry of a bird ripped unexpectedly through silence, my heart nearly jumped out of my chest. I hadn't noticed when a big black raven landed on the balcony railing a few feet away from me. The bird looked at me with its onyx-black eyes and repeated its heart-stopping cry. Was it a sign from Hel?

Another bird landed on the balcony, and I rushed inside, cursing myself for having left the Master of Destiny in my bedroom.

A shadow passed me, but I was the first to grab the Sapphire Ring from the table. A few more cries pierced silence again. Was this the beginning of a battle?

I turned around as more shadows began to fill the hall. I grabbed my sword, ready to fight for my life, and carefully peeked out of the bedroom.

Thousands of ravens were sitting everywhere in the hall, looking at me with their anthracite eyes. Bysh was with Rhys, and I had no one to defend me this time.

"Show up, you coward!" I roared.

The birds looked at me silently. I didn't sense any dark presence this time. *What kind of games are you playing, Hel?*

I raised my sword *en garde*. My sight blurred, and I wasn't sure anymore if the birds were real, or were they no more than just shadows? *Was my imagination playing tricks on me?* Nobody attacked me. I slowly moved among the countless ravens, my sword was drawn, and the Master of Destiny shining on my finger. I didn't risk trying to set light to the birds as before the fire could easily have spread through the empty capital.

My every step was closely watched by thousands of black, unblinking eyes. I carefully glanced around, but the birds remained still.

I made my way out. My Sapphire flashed a warning when I placed my hand on the doorknob, but I opened the door without thinking.

It was silent outside, but I was met by thousands of black eyes there as well. Birds were everywhere, flooding the corridor through the windows. A few ravens shrieked in the balcony as I closed the door and started my slow progression down the hallway.

"What do you want?" I roared again, but only echoes answered my question.

The nearest raven pecked at my boot and the same instant I slashed it in half with my sword. A few moments later, the air shivered as thousands of black wings swirled around me. I ran downstairs, shielding my eyes from the attacking beaks. The birds didn't follow.

What games Hel was playing?

I ran through the empty throne chambers, leaving the loud shrieks behind. Then I stopped. The fire was softly crackling in both of the hearths behind the throne. *Who had lighted it?* The black raven was sitting on the white fur of my throne and looking at me as I approached.

"What do you want?" I stopped in front of the throne and repeated my question.

The bird didn't answer. I summoned the blue sphere in front of me, preparing to strike, but the bird spread its black wings and lifted up in the air with a harsh cry. I flinched, waiting for an attack and losing the suitable moment for my strike, but the bird only circled around the hall a few times and then left through the open window.

I rushed outside, just in time to catch a glimpse of the ravens escaping the castle, lifting up in a dark cloud and moving east.

Then a sudden thought struck me with the force of thunder. The entrance to the Well next to the waterfall still remained exposed! I had to seal it somehow, or Hel would be able to take the Well and enter the capital through the back door.

I rushed to the gate, my sword unsheathed.

"We'll leave as soon as I return," I told the guard. "Be ready!"

He opened the gate without making any remarks.

It was a cloudy but peaceful day outside the black walls. I hastily crossed the bridge and started to ascend the stairs. The way was a long and lonely, upwards the face of the mountain. I wasn't sure this time that I still had a few days to spare.

I could hear the waterfall rumbling to my right. Minutes later, I stopped to catch my breath, leaning on the steep black rock. I looked back, but the castle was already hidden behind the white spray of the streams of falling water.

I still had no idea how to cover up the entrance. The only sound solution was to make it completely inaccessible – a pack of dynamite would be quite handy, but I had to rely on my Ring.

As I neared the waterfall, its rumble became almost deafening. I took a short rest to gather my strength for the final climb.

Once on the top, I placed my sword on the ground, inspecting the entrance at the same time. In simple daylight, it was almost impossible to detect it without prior knowledge, but when I reached into my Ring, the entry became clearly evident. Hawa had told me to defend the Well by all means possible. *Maybe the avalanche would do the job?* I extended my view within the blue sphere, now including the rocks hanging at the edge of the waterfall, just above the entrance. I found a natural crack here and pushed on it with all the force of the Ring. The rock shuddered as water poured into the crack, causing it to expand even more. I hoped that the powerful current would push the rock down to the front of the cliff, sealing the entrance completely.

All I needed was a little time.

"Hello, dear brother!" Despite the raging waterfall, the soft voice reached my ears, sending a wave of chill down my spine.

I turned around, realising that time had run out. Tall young woman on the black stallion was unhurriedly approaching me from the forest. I instantly recognised her from my vision.

"Hello, Hel..." I responded, hairs rising on the back of my neck.

"What a warm welcome," she smiled, and her smile even appeared sincere. "It was unnecessary to go to so much bother and meet me halfway!"

Her creepy dark knights emerged from the forest in the distance.

She dismounted and approached me, still smiling, then hugged and kissed me on both cheeks. The touch of her lips felt like a melting snowflake. I was petrified and didn't have any idea of how to respond. I hadn't expected to see her so soon.

She took the reins of her stallion, still smiling me.

Then the mighty current of the river finished my work at last and pushed the boulder over the edge with a loud bang. The rock hit the ground just a few feet away from us, then rolled all the way to the right and splashed down into the rapids, somewhere below, destroying the steps on its way.

The stallion reared up, whining, and I grabbed the reins, helping Hel to control him. We were instantly wet from head to toe under the cold stream.

It wasn't exactly what I had planned, but it suited my needs perfectly. I could have noticed that sequence of events in my blue sphere if I had thought of expanding the view a little further in time.

The riverbed above the waterfall shifted, and its dark waters poured down through the gap onto the rocky plain in front of us. Muddy streams completely blocked the entrance to the Well, creating a raging, swirling pool, which spilt over the staircase and cascaded with mighty force down on what had been the stairs before. The way to the castle was blocked as well.

"This is what I feared would happen!" I roared through the deafening noise of the falling water, trying to help Hel to handle her frightened stallion.

She pushed me aside with incredible force, and I rolled down on the ground, barely missing a cloud of black fumes from her Ring, which covered the horse. The animal calmed down instantly, and she dropped the reins, then turned back to me.

"Sorry, for this, dear brother," she apologised. "I had no intention to harm you."

"I understand…" I mumbled, getting up.

I had a very clear idea of what those fumes could do to me.

Hel waved to the stallion, and the beautiful animal humbly followed her like a dog paying no attention to the spray of the falling water. I followed them, several yards behind.

My worst nightmare was materialising in front of my eyes: her dark knights had fully emerged from the forest, their smoking spears pointing the sky. All means of the retreat were cut off, and I was entirely at the mercy of my sister.

I reached into my Ring and raised the invisible shield, preventing Onyx fumes from touching me, but this didn't help to lift my mood. I was scared to death. I had no idea how long I could last using this defence, and I wasn't ready to stand against Hel if she would choose to strike first.

She ordered her knights to bring some dry branches from the woods.

"I never thought the way to Chadrack would be this dangerous," she said, turning back to me.

"It is," I shrugged. "My jaegers told me about that loose rock, and I came to have a look at it."

"You are lucky you weren't hit while climbing up those stairs," she smiled.

"You're lucky you weren't hit while coming down them," I added drily.

Hel covered herself with strands of dark mist and started combing her long blonde hair.

"Aren't you going to use your Ring to get dry?" she asked.

"I'd rather wait for the fire," I said.

"I could get you dry with my Ring," she offered.

"No, thanks," I said firmly.

She shrugged. Her dress was dry long before her knights appeared from the woods carrying the branches. They piled them in the centre of the clearing, and Hel lighted the fire using a strand of smoke from her Ring.

I was visibly shivering when she invited me closer, but I didn't drop my Ring protection.

"It seems you'd benefit from a cup of hot tea." Hel smiled and waved her hand, dropping a strand of mist on the ground, where two gracious white chairs and a table appeared out of nowhere.

Two cups of hot brew were on the table, along with several plates of cakes and cookies. I was still petrified and was scared to accept the food, but I didn't want to risk angering her by entirely rejecting the offer.

"What an unfortunate event with that rock," she observed, handing the drink to me. "Is there any other way down to your castle?"

"No, sorry," I said, hesitantly turning the cup round in my hands. "That was the only way down at this side of the plateau. It's a pity, indeed."

My Ring didn't warn me of any dangers, and I carefully tried the tea. It was peppermint with a hint of honey.

"Then it looks like I have the pleasure of hosting you, dear brother, rather than opposite," Hel smiled. "But in that case, we will need a bigger table."

She waved her hand, and the table morphed into a larger version, covered with delicious-looking meats, fish, bread and cheese, as well as fruit desserts.

"Please, Kyleb, help yourself," she said, picking up her plate.

My stomach went into spasms after a single glance at her Onyx, which was leaking faint strands of dark mist. The smoke didn't seem to bother Hel. She placed a large piece of a roasted pheasant on her plate, along with some steamed vegetables and mashed potato, and began to eat.

"I think I will stick with the tea," I said. "I am not hungry."

Her eerie dark knights formed a broad circle around us, standing there like smoking statues in the early evening dusk.

Even the grass around us had grown brown and crumbled to dust. *Was I now a prisoner?*

I sat unhappily on a chair, my wet garments giving me a chill, and watched Death in front of me eating her pheasant. My heart was barely beating, afraid to attract her attention, as I held the delicate china cup with peppermint tea in front of me like a shield.

"I was hoping to have a short stay in your castle, Kyleb," said Hel, putting some fried fish on her plate. "But after that natural disaster, I'll have to change my plans, I'm afraid."

My Sapphire was barely glowing.

"I am glad to see you, sister. It's a pity I can't accept you in my castle," I risked reminding her that I was her family. "But would you share your plans with me? What kind of business brings you to Chadrack?"

"It's nice to visit family sometimes, don't you think?" she said after a short pause.

I found the statement creepy. I managed a nervous smile, still hiding behind the teacup.

"Is that the only reason?" I asked.

Hel stopped eating.

"I would like to postpone all unpleasant conversations if you please," she said. "That spoils the appetite."

She picked the fork again and carefully placed a piece of steamed broccoli in her mouth. I flinched when she started chewing.

The dusk was slowly thickening around, leaving us in a strange circle of light and warmth from the fire, surrounded by the frozen figures of her knights, barely visible in the darkness.

"Would you like a cake with your tea?" she asked, waving the meat and fish out of existence.

I silently shook my head, moving the chair slightly closer to the burning logs. The chill was spreading down the slope of the mountain from the invisible snow and glaciers somewhere high above us. My robes were still damp, and I hated the thought that I would be forced to spend the night here, with only the sky for a cover.

Hel made several more attempts to ease the tension, but I couldn't convince myself to trust her. Every time she smiled at me, I saw the face of Death in her lovely features.

"How are you going to get back to your castle, brother?" she asked, tasting the wine from a large crystal goblet. "Are there any other paths around that obstacle?"

I was concerned by her repeated inquiries. Was she aware of the passage? Had she been there before? The waterfall was rumbling in the darkness, and I wondered if the entrance was still well hidden behind the falling streams of water.

"No, I've told you already," I shrugged, studying her reaction. "Sorry to point this out, but the only way down the plateau is to the south, next to the border with Porlok. You'll have to travel back."

"I think we are both in the same boat now, Kyleb." She tasted her wine. "But I am delighted to have your company. Are you sure you don't want anything to eat?"

I quickly shook my head, placing the china back on the table.

"It's getting late," Hel stiffed a yawn. "I hate to travel at night."

"I feel the same," I nodded. "Are we sleeping here, next to the fireplace?"

"I have a better idea." She placed the goblet on the table and stood up.

A splash of the black fumes from her Ring consumed the table in a blink of an eye. Hel looked around searching for a piece of even ground, and when she found some, another splash of the fumes from her Onyx shaped into a large tent there.

I stood and silently watched since I wasn't sure if her idea included me. I hated the thought of sleeping next to her. Sleeping outside might provide me with an opportunity to sneak away at a favourable moment. But I guessed I wouldn't be allowed to choose. *Still, was I a prisoner here?*

Hel went inside and began to adjust the interior with her magic while I waited. Her knights remained motionless like a ring of stone pillars, sinking into the darkness of the approaching cloudy night.

"Be my guest, Kyleb." Hel appeared in the tent opening again. "It's not a palace, but I have got used to frugal conditions. I hope you will not judge me harshly."

I hobbled after her on my stiff legs, like a lamb entering the slaughterhouse. The tent was quite spacious inside – there was a bed on either side of the entrance. At the far end of the tent was a little table with drinks, cookies and a lit oil lamp.

"You haven't eaten anything," she said. "You could try these if you get hungry. Which bed would you like?"

"It doesn't matter to me as long as I am undisturbed," I mumbled.

"You won't be troubled," she chuckled. "Don't worry."

I didn't undress and slipped under the covers with all my still slightly damp clothes. Hel smiled but chose not to comment. She dimmed the lights with her Ring and got into her bed too.

Several minutes passed, and I heard her breathing calmly, asleep. I still was wide awake, trying to find some way out of this situation. I had the tempting idea of slipping my Ring onto her finger. If the Keeper was right, it might kill her. But if Hawa was wrong? I was sure her Onyx was protecting her, and I would be dead the instant I took my Ring and its protection off. I hated the idea of being dead.

The wind wailed outside the tent, and I felt the silent

presence of her dark knights. I was sure that even if I somehow succeeded in killing her, they would never let me out of the tent alive.

Despite the tension, still thick in the air, I drifted into sleep.

I was woken up by blasts of wind and rain hammering against my window. The weather was horrible, and I was glad I had no need to go outside. Dark clouds were floating low above the city, so low they almost touched the London rooftops with their bellies. They emptied enormous amounts of water on the deserted streets, washing the dusty pavements and carrying garbage away.

My mood was grim, as well. Even now, wide awake in my London flat, I clearly recalled that my body in Rehen was guarded by the dark knights, and Death herself was sleeping in a nearby bed. This chilled my nerves and gave me goosebumps. I had no idea what was going on in Hel's mind.

I must find some way to escape from that tent. With all her knights surrounding it, that wouldn't be easy. I was sure they weren't permitted to snooze a bit while guarding her.

Hel had been as hostile to me as I expected, and I would have enjoyed her company under other circumstances. But her Onyx was a dark and dreadful menace, infusing everything with cold.

I made a cup of my usual morning coffee, but this time it appeared utterly tasteless. I added more sugar to bring out the flavour, but the result was equally bland.

Later I called Rick – no answer. I hung up and tried several more times, with the same result. *Maybe he had left his phone at home?*

I got some eggs from my fridge and hard-boiled them. Strangely, the eggs appeared as tasteless as the coffee. I poured on enormous amounts of salt and pepper, but they still tasted like a wet carton. My eyes were watering from the excessive pepper, but my tongue still refused to respond! I tried some mature cheddar and strawberries I had in my fridge. The result was equally disappointing! It must be some side-effect of the proximity of Hel's Ring to my body – I had no other explanation.

The nasty weather continued to press against my windows with occasional tiny hails scratching the glass, like a lost mouse. I found myself in front of the TV, killing time.

My ability to think was completely paralysed. My mind was dumb and frozen with fear. I had no idea what had brought Hel to Chadrack. She wasn't claiming me as her prisoner, but I had an unpleasant feeling that her dark knights would not let me go if I chose to try. The waterfall was blocking the tunnel to the Well, and the way to the castle – all routes of the retreat I could think of had obstacles, even if I somehow could manage to escape Hel's clutches. My only option was to go to the South-West, along the arboreous plateau, which was squeezed between the steep wall of a mountain range on one side and an abyss on the other. This was Hel's only option as well.

As far as I could remember from the map of Rehen, the earliest moment I could make an escape was just before the border with Porlok, where the plateau ended with a narrow path through the canyon. I could hide in the forest at the foot of the mountain as soon as I got there. Until then, I would be an unwilling guest – or a prisoner – of Death.

The weather kept on raging, and I ordered pizza for lunch, unable even to think about going shopping. The poor driver delivered my order half an hour later and received a generous tip for keeping me dry.

I filled my stomach with another portion of carton-tasting food and made another mug of coffee. The taste was still awful.

Later, I tried to phone Rick again without any success.

The TV kept me company through the afternoon, but I was unable to concentrate on the recent atrocities in the Middle East and famines in sub-Saharan Africa. I felt like a hypnotised rabbit in front of a huge hungry snake. In theory, I could run away at any moment, but in reality, I couldn't escape her gaze.

Later I had a cup of watery tea and a cotton-tasting cake.

As I lay under the covers, I did my best to prepare for my meeting with Death, who was also my sister. Then the darkness took me.

Hel was still asleep. I quietly sneaked out of the tent, trying not to wake up her.

The morning in Rehen was gloomy – low clouds and no rain.

The dark knights were standing around and facing the tent in the same positions as the day before, grim and silent, unmoving – only barely visible strands of dark smoke were rising from their spears. I greeted one of them, but not a single muscle moved in his pale face. I could touch his ginger beard, but his blue eyes didn't focus on me, and I was unsure if he was sleeping or in some trance. *Were they watching me?*

I washed my face in a nearby stream. The forest around me was silent.

I cautiously glanced at the waterfall from a distance. The muddy waters were still falling with mighty power, but I wasn't sure if the splattering current hid the entrance well enough. I summoned the blue sphere from my Ring and looked again at the surroundings, searching for any natural flaws which I could use to build a stronger defence – but I found none. The rest of the plateau around was solid rock.

I dropped the sphere. All I could do now was to trick Hel as far as possible from here without getting her suspicious.

I slowly paced back and forth along the creek, waiting for Hel to wake up. The wind was chilly, but I had no desire to return to the eerie circle of her knights.

I waited, but nothing changed. The tranquillity of the motionless figures and the silent tent lulled me into a sense of false security, and I jumped across the creek sneaking to the dark wall of the forest. Air hissed in front of me as the black spear flashed past, just a few inches in front of my nose and plunged into a tree trunk. I froze. It was a clear reminder of my boundaries. *So I was a prisoner…*

The circle of knights seemed unchanged, but I didn't dare take any more risks. I jumped back across the creek and sat down on a flat boulder.

The spear was still smoking, and the leaves on the damaged tree were starting to brown and fall as though it was early autumn. Half an hour later, the branches were bare, and the bark began to peel away in large patches. The grass, ferns and moss around the tree turned brown and started to wither, leaving only black rocks and dirt.

I waited patiently. Another half an hour passed before the retinue of Death began to stir. The dark knights regrouped and moved to the flanks of the tent as Hel emerged, dressed in black leather. She looked around and waved at me, smiling.

"Lovely morning!" she greeted me.

"Maybe lovely for you," I started to complain indicating the smoking spear just a few yards in front of me. "But your guards nearly killed me…"

"If they had intended to kill you, they would have done so," she said seriously. "But you are right. I will make sure this does not happen again. Don't get angry; they were just confused. And I do apologise."

"Apology accepted," I said coldly.

Hel splashed some water on her face and stood up, watching the smoking spear.

"It's a pity," she said finally, a sudden sadness in her voice. "The tree was lovely."

She plucked the spear out of the tree trunk with surprising ease and returned to her knights. The dark figures silently parted, clearing the way for her. One unarmed man was standing next to the tent – the weapon was his, of course. Hel stopped in front of him and without a trace of hesitation plunged the spear into his throat. The man fell, disintegrating into the dust.

"Will you breakfast with me, dear brother?" asked Death, turning her serene eyes back to me as if nothing had happened.

"Yes." I was afraid to refuse – the demonstration had been very vivid.

I followed her to the tent where the feast was already waiting for us. She poured some wine into crystal goblets and passed one to me.

"I am sorry for that incident," she apologised again. "I hadn't left them any clear instructions. It was my fault, in part, of course."

"Apologies already accepted, dear sister." I forced a smile. "The experience was scary, but now everything's over. Let's forget this."

She tasted the wine then invited me to do the same. I probed it with my Ring first, then sipped a little – it was gorgeous.

"Help yourself, Kyleb," she invited me to join her.

"It's a real feast, Hel," I replied, putting a few pieces of meat and vegetables on my plate and testing it with my Ring as I did so.

She smiled. Most likely, she had noticed my efforts but said nothing. We ate silently, enjoying the delicate meat, fish, and cheese. These were followed by cakes and desserts.

When we finished eating, Hel poured more wine into crystal goblets.

"Maybe, we should start moving," I proposed, cautiously accepting the goblet and trying to hide my impatience to get her as far away from Chadrack as possible. "It's a long journey."

Hel sipped a little and placed her goblet back on the table.

"Yes, Kyleb, you are right. But I don't know how to proceed politely. I have only one horse, and your horses, of course, are unavailable." She shrugged. "It might take a few days to raise a decent tamed horse from the shadows. Maybe you would consider using your Ring to attract some wild stallion if there are any nearby?"

"I have tried already. There are none," I lied. "Don't worry. I can walk like your knights."

"Are you sure?"

"Do I have any other choice?"

She shrugged and sighed.

"Let's move then."

She waved her hand, and the black mist from her Ring consumed the table and everything that was left on it. I went out of the tent to wait outside.

The dark knights were making a reverse-V-shaped formation, preparing to repel any possible attack – but who would dare to confront Death?

Hel stepped outside in her lengthy, black leather gown. The mist from her Ring consumed the tent in a few short blinks of an eye, leaving only the dark circle of bare earth where we slept.

I helped her to mount. Then she took the reins, and the stallion started to trot down the road, away from the waterfall. The dark knights disappeared in the woods long before we reached the shade, but I was sure they had a good rapport with my sister.

The path was familiar, winding between scattered dark boulders and fallen tree trunks, and crossing several shallow streams. We had still hardly exchanged a word since we left. Hel appeared to be in a grim mood, and was not paying much attention to anything.

We moved like dark shadows, silencing every single little sign of life around. Even the occasional grasshoppers stopped their melodies, and I wasn't sure if they were just silenced or dead. The Onyx took the joy of life from everybody and everything. I only hoped that it wasn't permanent.

Several hundred yards later, I lost patience.

"What is bothering you so much, sister?" I demanded. "You look troubled."

"Appearances may be misleading, Kyleb. I am not troubled. I only was remembering," Hel shrugged and then added, after a short pause. "Our father is missing for a long time. Don't you think it's about time to take things back to our family?"

I noted that she didn't say "dead" – that was strange. Hawa

and Keely were more straightforward.

So, it was the throne of the realm that was on her mind! I decided to keep quiet about my alliance with Keely. I was pretty sure that I wasn't fit for the job, and I had no idea of what Hel's intentions were. *Was she going to claim the throne for herself?* Then I was the first in line for accidental death to clear the path for her.

"You are right, sister," I said, cautiously studying her reaction. "What do you think about that?"

Hel frowned before answering.

"You are the eldest brother, Kyleb," she said. "Why are you asking this question? You don't need my blessing to claim your right."

"I still don't feel ready for this," I said, this time – honestly.

"You never will be if you think like this," Hel flashed a quick glance at me. "I don't believe that prophecy indicate anyone other than you: *rivers of gold and blood will come to the realm with the new King...*"

"Oh, *that* prophecy!" I made a surprised face. "That can't be about me. I am not that bloodthirsty, and gold will not be gold anymore if it floods the realm like a river."

"I agree that some parts of that prophesy should be regarded only figuratively. But what happened to your famous nickname – the Bloody, brother?" she asked, laughing. "News is spreading fast. No one has ever fought two victorious battles against two different armies in a single day before, Kyleb. The Oracle is never mistaken."

I was shocked by her implication, but not entirely surprised, knowing the dark secrets of my predecessor. The conversation was slowly slipping onto dangerous ground. *Had I told her too much? If I had been known for cruelty, would she notice the difference in my personality now?* Fear squeezed my heart even tighter.

"I'm far from bloodthirsty." I attempted a nervous laugh, trying to hide my embarrassment. "I have always had a few enemies, but the situation is far from a bloodbath. People survive my displeasure, even in Chadrack. I think the nickname is merely an exaggeration of the real state of affairs."

Hel chuckled, and I suddenly found myself deep in quicksand due to my lack of memories. She knew a lot more than I did about my previous self, and I had to bit my tongue before it spat out too much. Nicknames like that must be earned.

"Don't be so shy, brother." She tapped the neck of her stallion before turning her smiling face to me. "I clearly remember the last time I visited you, I saw a couple of dozens of heads on spikes in front of your window and dead man's skin on the balustrade of your balcony. I can agree – that was only a mere extravaganza – far from a bloodbath. I was always sure that the prophecy is about you, Kyleb. No one else in our family is capable of such things. I've never had any doubts about you."

"That was long ago..." I said, trying to hide my pale face among the shadows of the forest. "Nothing stays in one place. I don't like to remember that..."

"Why?"

I dared to ignore her question and change the subject: "Have you been bored by constant death around you, sister?" I courageously met her astonished gaze. "Have you?"

"It is a natural circle of things," she shrugged. "There is no life without death, and no death without life, Kyleb."

"I know," I said. "This is the theory. But have you ever been bored by what is going on around you?"

Hel urged her stallion onwards, and I was forced to speed up my steps. She didn't answer my question.

Her knights flashed ahead like shadows, barely visible among the tree trunks but still adapting to our pace. My shields held, but I had no idea for how long the Master of Destiny was able to protect me. I felt like a trophy or a prisoner, but I had to lure Hel as far from the Well as possible, away from Chadrak. And I needed to place a few obstacles behind us – to bare the way in case if she might change her mind.

I used her moment of silence to study my immediate surroundings with my Ring. *What should I drag onto the stage next – an earthquake? Maybe a forest fire or a small avalanche?* I saw possibilities in the blue sphere – they were waiting for my will and power of the Ring to be applied.

I hushed away the urge to immediately strike with an avalanche at Hel's knights and sweep them down to the abyss. That would solve only a part of my problem and may leave me stranded in the mountains with her – still too close to the Well. I was sure my sister was far more dangerous than her small army. Forest fires or earthquakes would put me at considerable danger, and I wasn't willing to risk my precious life for any reason.

I considered the avalanche again. I sensed the snow high above, on the top of the mountain, hanging at the edge of the cliff, waiting. I couldn't waste such an easy opportunity. I clearly saw the path the avalanche would follow. It might block the only way back to Chadrack with an impenetrable wall of snow, leaving Hel with no other option as to go forward.

I carefully counted paces until we passed the point where the strike would hit and gain a safe distance. Then I applied the power of my Ring to the cracks in the glacier high above us, increasing the tension and getting ice and snow lose. The earth trembled.

Hel looked around, frightened, and covered herself with even thicker mist from her Onyx.

The earth trembled again as the sound of breaking trees and thunder slowly approached us. I knew we were in no real danger, but still, it was scary to stand on the ground that was visibly shaking, and wait for the approaching force of nature.

Hel rushed her stallion ahead. I fell flat on the ground and covered my head as the enormous wall of snow, spiky with broken trees, appeared and stopped just a few yards from me, blocking the way to Chadrack. The avalanche went further down, leaving the path of destruction behind. Minutes later, it reached the edge of the plateau and dropped down into the abyss, and everything calmed again. The ground stopped trembling.

I took a few deep breaths before I was able to get up. Hel was still on her horse, shaking and crying.

Suddenly I felt guilty.

"Are you hurt?" I asked.

Hel slipped off her horse, and I rushed over to support her. My Ring flashed blue in warning, but she embraced me and, crying, buried her face in my shoulder. I felt her enormous power lurking next to me. It was a strange sensation, like touching the tip of a dagger which is about to pierce your skin. I closed my eyes, silently saying my final goodbyes to this world and cursing myself for having the stupidity to frighten her, but nothing happened. I still was breathing, and she still cried. It took some time before she finally regained control of her emotions.

"Sorry for this, Kyleb," she whispered, her voice still trembling. "I had never imagined how dangerous your mountains could be."

"It's over," I tried to reassure her. "Things like that just happen."

"Not in Patna," she shook head. "Even life on an erupting volcano could be more peaceful than it is here."

"It was unexpected," I admitted, gently rubbing her shoulders. "But it's over. Nobody was hurt."

It sounded like an apology. She managed a weak smile.

"Do you think you will be able to proceed?"

Hel nodded.

"Let's keep on going. I want to get out of here as fast as possible," she said seriously.

I helped her back on her stallion, and we stepped back on the path, leaving the wall of snow behind us. The forest around was dark and silent, but a narrow ribbon of the sky above us started to clear of clouds, letting through occasional sunshine.

Hel was silent, still visibly shaken, and I felt guilty for my overreaction. She produced a crystal goblet with a dark, ruby-red wine from her Ring and gulped it down in a single shot without slowing her horse. Then she cast the goblet away, and it disintegrated before touching the ground.

"That's better," she said, a trace of a smile back on her lips.

For a few miles, we went on in silence. Then we stopped by a creek to let her stallion drink his fill.

"What has brought you so far away from your Patna,

anyway?" I asked, making a clumsy attempt to draw her attention away from the unfortunate avalanche. "And I'd like the real reason, please."

"Vanishing beauty," she said, watching her horse drinking. "I heard that the Hammer had been released. I wasn't sure where it was aiming, and only wanted a last glimpse at everything."

I was shocked by her words. "Who could dare to threaten you?"

"It is not me this time, I am sure," said Hel. "And it is not a threat. Has the Order contacted you?"

I shook my head. I was surprised by the awe with which she referred to that mysterious Order. I had thought it was just another cult, but was I mistaken? Was the Order the real ruler in Rehen? Who could be more powerful than Death?

"Have they contacted you?" I asked, hoping for another bit of information.

"No," she said. "It seems that only Devona was lucky enough to get the warning. But it is not surprising, given her proximity to the Cradle and Rhey. She has always been Rhey's favourite."

"I have heard that the Nightcrawlers have come out of caves," I said, studying her reaction.

"I know." Hel patted her horse on the neck. "That's the reason why the Hammer should be employed this time, I guess. I am just worried about collateral damage."

My heart started its slow journey towards my ankles. *Was Hel implying that this world is about to be destroyed? What would happen to me if it was?*

"That's why you are saying that everything is vanishing?" I did my best to sound calm, but the voice was trembling in my throat.

"Everything is constantly ending and vanishing," she said, avoiding a direct answer. "It's the natural order of things. Could we start moving?"

I helped her to mount her stallion. The already brightening day turned back to grim murkiness, and I could barely see my way as we continued our journey. I had no idea what the Hammer was, but it sounded like a powerful weapon. If it were directed against the Nightcrawlers, most likely the impact would bring down the House of Porlok. Or, maybe, even Chadrack – I recalled Kyaal mentioning the Nightcrawlers, but he wasn't specific on the location. It was suddenly clear why Keely had been so desperate to get to Wagorn, the capital of the realm, as soon as possible. *Was this the reason she was pushing me to claim the throne? Was a civil war with the Regent considered a lesser evil than the Hammer?*

I realised that we were heading towards Porlok, and my heart started racing like a frightened bunny. I looked at my sister. She was calm, despite realising far better than I did what dangers might lie ahead of us. *Maybe the threat wasn't serious enough? Maybe*

I had to turn off my swollen imagination and direct the troubled boat of my soul back to the calm waters? But how could I do that? I had the desperate urge to run as far away from Porlok as possible, but my way was bared. And I had no ideas on how to separate from my sister.

We travelled in silence, paying little attention to the woods, meadows and creeks around us. I was afraid to ask any of the myriad questions humming in my head, and she volunteered no more information.

We stopped at about lunchtime. Hel produced a table with food and a pair of comfortable chairs. Her knights waited at a distance, barely visible.

The food was excellent, but I still probed it with my Ring before putting anything into my mouth. Hel didn't object. She paid no attention to me, seeming immersed in her thoughts.

We ate in silence, and the whole forest seemed to be waiting for us to finish and move on. It was dead calm around; no birds or insects could be heard.

We finished, and fumes from the Onyx consumed all leftovers, plates, cutlery, chairs and the table. Hel didn't say a word. Then we moved on, leaving the only bare ground behind us.

I was trying to walk as fast as I could since I was on foot and slowing everybody down. I had a feeling that the dark knights would keep pace with us even if Hel's stallion had been galloping at top speed. Each time I looked at them, they seemed less physical.

We passed several more boulders and streams on our way along the plateau. Nobody and nothing troubled us. I saw a few more opportunities to create landslides using my Ring but didn't want to slow us down or frighten Hel again. We were too far away from the castle already.

Later in the evening, we stopped in a large clearing, next to a crystal creek, and Hel put up the tent again. I washed my face in the cold stream while Hel performed magic with her Ring and made us a fancy supper. This time, the food was more exotic, bursting with flavours and smells I had never had before. I didn't let my defences down and dutifully probed everything with my Sapphire before letting it approach my mouth. It unexpectedly flashed when I was about to taste some fish, warning me. I stopped immediately and looked at Hel.

She shrugged and put some of that fish on her plate.

"It's *torafugu*," she explained. "The fish is poisonous, but it is a famous delicacy and safe if well-prepared."

"I think I will skip it," I shrugged.

"As you wish..." she replied, eating the fish.

I tucked into meat and cheese, and then later ate some fruit desserts.

"Do you want anything else, brother?" asked Hel.

"No, I'm full. Thank you!"

She smiled and poured some wine into a crystal goblet for me.

Since my Sapphire didn't warn me about it, I accepted and tried it. The wine was exceptional – sweet and floral, with a divine mint aftertaste.

"I would like you to teach me those tricks with the Ring so that I can get hold of such excellent wine like this…" I told her.

"I am not sure if your Ring is capable of that," she said casually. "It is easy with my Onyx, which controls death – nearly all the food we are consuming is dead, and it only requires minimal manipulation to reproduce it. In theory, your control of destiny could bring you some live food, I suppose. You might eat a live carrot or apple, but I doubt if you would try a live rabbit. You would have to carry out the preparation of your food in the usual way. Sorry, but I doubt you can obtain wine by manipulating destiny; it just doesn't work that way."

"Never thought that my food is dead," I gasped. "That sounds weird."

"Indeed," Hel took the biscuit from her plate and inspected it before taking a bite. "Good food is always dead – until life spoils it."

I sipped the wine, feeling a pleasant warmth running through my veins.

"It's a strange and quite confusing theory," I remarked. "I doubt if I fully understand it."

"Yes, it's a theory," agreed Hel, laughing. "And we both know that you have always been an excellent swordsman but a poor sorcerer, brother."

I felt a great sense of relief at this revelation. Naturally, my knowledge of this area was scarce, but I was glad to know that my predecessor hadn't been very keen on it either. That would make my clumsiness less noticeable.

"Yes, sometimes I am bored by having death around me," she answered my question finally, picking up the goblet of wine, bringing it to her lips and taking a small sip. "Not just bored irritated. Sometimes I can't stand it anymore."

"And what you do then?" I asked, puzzled by the sudden revelation.

"I return home," Hel sipped more wine. "There is no life on a volcano. Therefore, there is no death, either. I return home to Patna when I am tired of death."

"Oh…" I looked into her eyes just in time to notice something fragile and vulnerable flashing for a very brief moment and then retreating into the depths of her dark gaze.

"What about your knights?" I asked. "How can they survive on the volcano?"

"They aren't alive," she began to explain, as though it was a well-known fact. "Therefore, they can't die. They are like ghosts, trapped between life and death. But you don't need to worry. My Ring completely controls them."

"Not so completely," I replied, adding a faint smile to the bitter statement. "One of them almost killed me while you were sleeping!"

"That will not happen again. Forgive me, Kyleb," she apologised. "And I have killed the one who did that. Could we forget that incident?"

"Yes, sister," I agreed. "I am sorry for bringing up the subject again."

"Would you like one more piece of cake?" she asked.

I only nodded, extending my plate and watching, while she carefully placed the piece on it, adding some chocolate sprinkles on top.

It was appetising, but, of course, I had to check it with my Ring.

"It's getting late," I said when I finished the cake. "I'm feeling a little tired."

"Let's get some sleep," said my sister called Death.

It was raining. The wind calmed, leaving a monotonous shower to soak the garden outside my window. My bed was warm, soft and inviting, and I had trouble to leave the embrace of my blanket. The long walk with Hel was still making my leg muscles tingle.

I made myself a mug of morning coffee – strong and black, no milk and no sugar – a dynamite edition to shake me up. But it was still tasteless.

Blurred images of cars moved down the wet street as I sipped my dark brew and watched them out of the window. Then I remembered to call Rick.

"You have reached the voicemail of..." an indifferent female voice informed at the other end, and I hung up.

I checked the number and tried again, but got the same result. Maybe he was in a training session already. This wasn't like

Rick/Rhys, as far as I knew him. He was very punctual and conscientious, and this silence was making me increasingly restless.

I called the club, but the receptionist lady had no idea of Rick's whereabouts – he hadn't shown up at work or called, and the customers were getting angry and impatient. I assured her that I was not about to complain. I thanked her and hung up, feeling genuinely alarmed.

I quickly gulped my small breakfast, then washed and got dressed. I had to find out what was wrong. Luckily, the rain had stopped by the time I left the house.

I rushed downhill and took the first bus towards Bromley. Several stops later, I got out and turned down one of the side streets. The rows of terraced buildings looked average, but the street was nice, clean and quiet. I glanced around before approaching Rick's front door.

Nobody answered the doorbell, although I rang several times. Then I tried the door, and, strangely, it was unlocked. I slipped inside and closed the door behind me.

"Hello?"

No answer.

I passed the short corridor and opened another door. It was the living room, and it looked like a dump – everything had been turned upside-down. Clothes, shoes, and small household items were littering the floor. It was unmistakably the aftermath of a disaster!

I reached for my phone to call the police, but then stopped as I realised I would lose the only possibility to have a look into other rooms – I wanted to explore everything first, maybe Rick was lying somewhere unconscious...

The bedroom and kitchen looked the same – an area of complete devastation. Some of the furniture was broken, indicating there had been a fight.

It was clear that Rick was in trouble, but I couldn't find any clues or hints as to his current whereabouts.

The fact that I was stuck with Hel on a plateau and was unable to contact Rhys in Rehen only doubled my worries.

I wandered through all the rooms, again and again, searching for the smallest hint of where he had gone, but there was nothing. Rick was simply missing, apparently having to fight for his freedom on the way.

I closed the front door and left without calling the police.

Light rain was falling again, and I went to the nearest bus stop. I reached home quickly, and soon I found myself sitting in the corner, overwhelmed by the strangest thoughts and suppositions, still with no idea of what to do next.

I picked my phone and called John. With Rick gone, he was the only other Sleeper I knew. He might not be willing to help after that awful night with us. But I had to try.

John answered almost instantly. After a short apology, I briefly described the situation with Rick. He listened without interrupting me.

"And you think it is my doing?" he asked when I had finished.

"No," I replied. "I believe that we have solved the issues between us. But maybe you have some knowledge who else still might be in business? This may put you in danger as well..."

"That's a good question..." responded John after some moments of silence. "I can't think of anyone right now, but I will let you know if I have any ideas. Why don't you ask him in Rehen?"

"Well..." I didn't know how to explain it. "Right now, I am not in Chadrack, and I sent Rhys out of the castle as well, just in the opposite direction from where I am now. I don't know where he is, or if he is still alive..."

"You two had an argument?"

"No," I said. "I am with the sister of your wife, and we are travelling together."

"Which sister?"

"Hel."

He was silent for far too long this time.

"Are you a prisoner?" asked John finally.

"I am not, I guess," I responded.

"But you're not sure?"

"I haven't tried to escape. Under the circumstances, we both have only one route we can follow, so we are doing that together."

"Okay. Keep me informed, please. All these proceedings may be related to my wife as well, remember?"

"I will," I promised, and then hung up.

I knew nothing about the possible enemy and had no idea of how to proceed. Rick was in danger, but I had no way to help him while I was wandering around the mountains with Hel. On the other hand, Rick might have some dark secrets of his own. He seemed loyal, but I knew nothing of his life before he started to teach me the martial arts – on either plane of reality, nor I was too nosy after that. He never mentioned anything about his family or his previous occupations – there might be some clues for his disappearing as well. *But where should I start?*

I was sitting in the corner, full of frustration, staring at a single point, my eyes unfocused, as the rain started again, accompanied by rumbles of thunder and flashes of lightning. The wind was raging, pouring out its anger on trees, tearing off leaves and breaking branches.

But my thoughts were far away, in another reality. I was thinking of my sister Hel and wondering if she would be willing to help me with Rhys. But how could I explain this Sleeper thing to her? I had a nasty feeling that this would not be accepted and might place me in great danger. Or would I better off seeking advice from Keely? She had a Sleeper husband and would understand me better. Or maybe I needed to find the solution myself?

Later in the afternoon, I started silently chewing some cold, tasteless pizza. I spent the evening in front of the TV and fell asleep a little later.

Hel's bed was empty when I woke up. I sprang to my feet and quickly ran fingers through my hair before I went outside.

She was standing among her dark knights, covered with strands of dark fumes from her Ring. She dismissed them as soon as I appeared at the tent entrance and then turned to me, smiling.

"Lovely morning, Kyleb!"

"Yes, sister..."

"Have you slept well?"

"Average..." I shrugged. "My muscles are still aching from yesterday..."

"Maybe you would like to ride with me?" She sounded extremely casual. "I don't want to insult you by offering this, but my Shaitan is strong enough to carry two of us..."

"I think we could give it a try..."

She gracefully waved her hand, and in the middle of the field, a table with two comfortable chairs appeared out of nowhere. Another smooth shake of her fingers and a hot breakfast was served.

We ate quickly and silently. Then Hel signalled her knights to start moving while wiping the table out of existence with her Ring.

Shaitan knew me already, and I had no trouble in getting on him. Hel mounted in front of me, and we rushed down the road. I felt huge muscles twitched and moved under his shiny black skin as the stallion started to gallop. The dark knights in front of us seemed floating through the air like a line of grey ghosts, keeping a steady pace and a constant gap with us.

It was much faster to travel like this. The wind was in our hair, and the sunshine was above us.

Later in the afternoon, we had lunch near another creek.

The rest of the journey was just as silent and uneventful as the first part had been. We stopped just before dusk, having covered a significant portion of the way.

"How do you feel?" asked Hel, sipping some dark ruby-coloured wine.

"Significantly better," I responded.

"You still look troubled," she observed.

"I'm not," I managed a wry smile. "I feel better."

I gathered up all my courage to ask. "Dear sister, was it your magic with those crows at my castle several days ago?"

Her eyes widened with concern.

"Crows? No, you can be sure of that," she shook head seriously. "I have never cast any spell in your direction. You must look somewhere else."

"Do you have any idea where?" I asked, trying to sound as polite as possible.

"Bedelia may sometimes act strangely, but I don't know if that was her... Tell me more! What happened?"

I briefly described both incidents with the crows in my hall, intentionally leaving out the raven attack on Rhys.

"It doesn't sound like her," Hel shook head without trying to conceal her disappointment. A shadow of concern crossed her face as she frowned. "It must be a new player on the scene – and a mighty one..."

Hel let her voice trail, and I could only guess what was going on her mind.

"Do you think it's dangerous?" I demanded.

Hel flashed an angry glance at me. "Of course, it is. We might get wiped out with a single blow. You are the first target, brother, can't you see? Be careful! It was only a warning, but the next strike might be real."

She rose to her feet, streams of black fumes pouring out of her Onyx. I jumped back, spilling my wine.

"I must return to Patna," Hel murmured, destroying the chairs and the table. She raised her eyes to the sky as if seeking for some sign. Her knights quietly surrounded us, and my heart dropped to the ankles.

"Let's get some rest while we can," she said, her eyes still fixed at the sky.

Streams of fumes weaved into a tent around us, less spacious this time. I raised my shield, spilling the wine again, but Hel said nothing. She turned around, adjusting the weave, then created two beds out of the mist. Only then she glanced at me.

"Step aside, brother. Please," she gestured. "I can't risk leaving any life inside."

I moved, and the small patch of grass where I was standing crumbled to dust upon the touch of Onyx.

"Let's sleep," my sister said approaching her bed. She got under the covers without even bothering to remove her boots.

I finished my wine and placed the goblet on the ground, before doing the same. The light blanked out the same instant my head touched the pillow.

Sleep didn't come easy. I could hear Hel stirring in the darkness as well. Then my mind left my body for the journey to London.

In the morning, I got up with, my head still throbbing – Hel's reaction to my story troubled me a lot, and I still had no idea what happened with Rick. All I knew was that he was missing and that he had gone with a fight. I sipped my morning coffee and turned the images of Rick's devastated flat over in my mind. *Maybe I was overlooking something?*

I called John.

"I asked questions, but nobody has any thoughts of what might have happened with your friend," he said after a few short hellos. "I am very sorry, but I have no suggestions."

"Thanks for taking the trouble to do that," I said gratefully. "Could you help me to check Rick's flat again? I have a terrible feeling that I have overlooked some clues. Maybe your fresh eye could help?"

"Well… I am not very busy at the moment."

I gave him the address, and we agreed to meet outside Rick's flat.

I got dressed and ran outside. The weather was beautiful, the sky was almost cloudless, but my heart was heavy with the unknown. I put my hands in my pockets and headed for the nearest bus station. Several women were waiting there already.

The bus arrived, and we boarded. I took a seat at the front and looked through the side window. A few seconds later, I felt an intense gaze on my back. I brushed it off like an annoying fly, but the feeling was powerful, stronger than any I have ever experienced before. I looked back, and my eyes met a set of dark blue eyes looking directly at me. They belonged to a young woman I had never seen before. I smiled, trying to ease the tension, but she didn't return the smile – not a muscle moved on her face; her gaze was still fixed on me, hypnotising.

I tried to ignore her and looked out of the window again, but the tension didn't go away. The hair on my head was standing up on end – it could easily have lifted up my hat if I had been wearing one. I looked back again. The woman's face was expressionless as if in a trance, her gaze still fixed on me. *Maybe I was just in the wrong seat?*

On the next stop, I transferred to another row, but her gaze followed me, as powerful as a floodlight. I distinctly remembered that feeling from my kidnapping. *Who was after me this time?*

I was certain; it wasn't John. *Were that women related to Rick's disappearance?* But it was too late to find out – my bus stop was approaching.

I got out, feeling weak at my knees. She kept on looking at me as the bus gained speed and carried her away.

I waited for the bus with that eerie woman disappear behind the corner. Several more minutes passed before my breathing returned to normal.

The side street where Rick used to live was nearby. I saw John from a distance, waiting for me already. He greeted me as I approached. I decided not to mention the bus incident to him until I was sure what was going on. It was still strange to see the redhead kidnapper peacefully strolling down the street and chatting with me. But life is full of surprises.

A police car was parked outside of Rick's flat and an officer stared indifferently at us as we came nearer. Rick's doors were wrapped in yellow plastic tape: "STOP POLICE". I strolled a few paces ahead, almost managing to give a convincing impression of just being an ordinary wanderer, but John stopped.

"What happened, officer?" he asked.

"Nothing to be concerned about," said the policeman, shrugging.

"That flat looks sealed," said John, pointing at Rick's door. "We live on this street. Can we be of any assistance?"

"It was just a fight between some drunks," officer waved his hand. "The house is a wreck, and there is blood in the basement. Most likely, he went out to stitch his wounds. I am waiting for the guy to return. He needs to explain something."

"Is he alright?" I asked, genuinely concerned.

"I have no idea," said the officer. "We haven't had any information from any hospital yet. Have you seen or heard anything suspicious?"

I hastily shook my head.

"Well..." said John, apparently bluffing, "I am not sure, but I think there was a dark car parked outside that house just a few days ago."

"Did you notice the make of the car?" asked the police officer. "Or the number plate?"

"No, sorry," said John slowly shaking his head. "I wasn't that attentive..."

"Thank you," said the officer. "You've helped us a lot."

"It's my duty," said John and we moved forward.

We slowly went on, trying not to look back.

"Why did you make up that story about a car?" I asked when we turned at the corner.

"It won't help Rick if they keep on thinking that it was only a fight and that he will return after stitching his wounds," he explained. "Now, they will start to investigate."

"But you might end up misleading the investigation," I objected.

"There will be no investigation unless they don't expect him to return. You didn't mention the blood in his flat. It's a bad sign."

"I didn't look in the basement," I said, regret in my voice. "Why is it bad?"

"We still have no idea who was after him," said John. "If it was hunters, Rick most likely is dead by now. I'm sorry about that."

"Maybe they just wanted him for tagging?" I asked with fading hope.

"If it were for tagging, they would have captured him without injuring him. That's crucial," John said, crushing my hopes. "Blood means death in the hunter's world. Sorry."

We walked the next block in silence. I could barely see where I was going: grief was squeezing my throat and tears were pooling in my eyes. I couldn't believe Rick was gone. *Why?*

After a few minutes, John casually broke the silence. "Did you touch anything while you were searching within the flat?"

I shook head. "I don't remember," I said uncertainly. "Maybe... I touched the doorknob for sure, but I am not certain about inside – I don't think so..."

"If you have no criminal background, they may never connect those fingerprints to you," said John. "Anyway, prepare some story. You may be questioned even if you are innocent."

"Thanks, I will think about that."

"Be careful," he warned me. "If Rick was your close friend, those people who killed him might come after you as well."

Did John's warning explain that eerie woman on the bus? I still didn't trust him enough to ask.

We parted at the corner of the next street. There was no point in returning after the police had begun their investigation and no way to get inside without being stopped by that officer.

John, the dreadful redhead, smiled at me and waved his hand, leaving. I stood for a few minutes, still stunned by the news of Rick's death, and then turned into another street, hoping to navigate back to Bromley Road. I had the firm intention of walking the whole way back and avoid buses. I felt safer on the street among people. Nothing major happened on the way.

The rest of the day was dumb and empty. I grieved for Rick, barely looking at the TV at all and fell asleep in the middle of some crazy movie.

I woke up in the tent, and for several minutes, I remained silent, my eyes closed.

I heard Hel getting up and messing around, but I chose to pretend asleep. I needed a plan on how to separate from her. I was sure I could find my way back to Chadrack along the foot of the mountain range. I only couldn't think of any possible way to escape unnoticed.

The pleasant smell of hot food reached my nostrils from the breakfast Hel was preparing.

I stirred and yawned. The time for private meditation was over.

"How are you today?" smiled Hel.

"Better!" I shrugged. "Did you sleep well?"

"Like the dead," responded my sister.

I smiled at the pun but didn't say a word. We ate our

breakfast in silence.

"Ready to go?" she asked when I had eaten my fill.

I only nodded.

The dark knights were getting into their formation when we left the tent, and they started to move without waiting for us.

The morning was lovely. We mounted the black stallion the same way – Hel in front of me – and began our journey down the slope. Shaitan trotted as fast as he could, passing among the trees like black lightning and the dark knights kept up the pace ahead.

The journey was swift and sickening. I mostly kept my eyes closed or semi-closed. Sunlight was flashing through the leaves and branches at tremendous speed like a stroboscope, and that made me dizzy. This had no effect on my sister. She was looking straight ahead, firmly holding reins in her hands.

Later in the afternoon, we finally left the forest behind and reached the narrow rocky road descending from the plateau in large serpentines. The path was narrow, squeezed between cascading cliffs, and we had to dismount. Shaitan was stepping on to loose rocks and neighing angrily, and Hel had to use the magic of her Ring to calm him down.

The way was strenuous. We went a few miles seeing nothing but steep walls and a narrow band of sky above us. I was tired and immensely glad when the walls of rock stepped aside, giving way to the grassy field, unevenly divided by the crystal-clear stream. A dark forest stood on the right side of the creek, while piles of large boulders ran up the steep hill on the other side.

"Let's rest a little," said Hel, stopping Shaitan.

Her dark knights remained higher up the slope, guarding us.

Hel left her stallion by the creek and turned to set up a feast. I watched from a distance as the nicely carved table with a pair of comfortable chairs appeared out of nowhere. The second movement of her hand placed a roasted duck, a large ham, legs of lamb and nicely browned pieces of delicious venison on it. Smoked fish and round cheese followed. Ice cream, cakes, cookies, two bottles of blood-red wine and crystal goblets rounded off the meal.

She invited me to the table.

I felt ravenous and helped myself, putting bits of everything on my plate, but still, despite Hel's reassuring behaviour, sticking to my old habit of testing the food with my Ring. I clearly remembered the incident with *torafugu* and didn't want to put anything even remotely poisonous into my mouth.

Hel poured herself some wine, and we started to eat.

I was halfway through my plate when a strange movement in the forest sneaked into my consciousness. There was no sound, only the barely perceptible motion of shadows. A bite froze in my throat as a human shape emerged from the woods and stopped on the other side of the shallow stream, facing me. The silhouette was dark, dressed in rags, and had a massive bludgeon on the shoulder. More dark shadows were now visible amongst the trees. They looked too familiar. I placed the fork as a slow realisation surfaced my consciousness – ghouls!

"What?" asked Hel, noticing my frightened gaze.

I silently pointed.

She turned around and, for a few seconds, simply stared at the hordes of ghouls emerging from the forest, before she screamed a command. It felt like a blast of wind as the dark knights attacked. Before long, the crystal water of the creek turned red as dead bodies piled up on the other bank, but more ghouls continued to emerge from the forest. It seemed like an army was marching through the woods and just a handful of knights were fighting them.

Hel turned back to me.

"You can't fight them without a sword. Hide!" she screamed. "And shield yourself!"

The flesh on her lovely face was now melting like wax, the bones protruding through the skin and exposing the face of Death! Her eyes flashed black as she raised her bony hand, stood up and turned to confront the hordes of dark creatures swarming from the forest. I sprinted off, looping behind piles of boulders and hopping over shallow creeks as I ran. My Ring was flashing blue as I desperately searched for a place to hide. A few spears hissed past me, barely missing.

I fell to the ground, next to the gaping hole between two large rocks and squeezed inside. Beyond the narrow neck, the dark cave widened, leading somewhere deep into the innards of the mountain. I stopped only for a moment, hastily probing the walls with my Ring until I found a crack and forced my will on it, then rushed away from the opening of the cave. The earth shuddered as the ceiling of the entrance fell in.

I dropped to the ground, breathing heavily and only then realised I was sitting in complete darkness. The only thing visible was my Ring, faintly glowing blue.

"Fool! Fool! Fool! Damn!" I cursed. How was I going to get out of this?

I summoned the blue sphere from my Ring, but it only flashed and flickered away. Several days of constant shielding from Hel and causing a few natural disasters had depleted the Master of Destiny – the blue eye of the Sapphire was barely glowing. It couldn't help me to map the cave or find the exit.

Helpless tears flooded my eyes as I looked around, feeling as blind as a mole. The darkness was absolute, overflowing my imagination with ghosts and monsters.

I felt the ground around me: it was solid, dusty rock. Then I remembered the green shining crystals in the cave of the Well. *Maybe there was a chance of finding them here?* I tried to search for them using the remaining power of my exhausted Ring. I looked around until my eyes began hurting. Then I saw a few greenish sparkles flashing at the far end of the cave. I sprang to my feet and rushed forward. A few steps later, I stumbled in the dark and fell. I caught my breath, cursing, and started to crawl slowly onwards, feeling my way with my hands before I made any move.

Long minutes passed until I reached a bunch of crystals on the floor. I selected the largest one and applied my will to it. The light in other crystals faded, but the one I was holding in my hand started to cast a faint glow like that of a candle. I stood up and looked around.

Rocks were scattered across the floor as far as my improvised light could reach. I went back to the entrance and cursed again. It was completely blocked by large boulders, certainly much bigger than I could lift. I spent five or ten minutes more inspecting the rocks, but the results were equally disappointing. The earth was still trembling after my improvised earthquake, and I couldn't take a risk for further collapses by remaining there.

I must find another way... The bubble of greenish fluorescence from the crystal was too weak to light anything further away than a few yards. I had no idea how big the cave was or if there was any other way out. My flickering crystal was the only source of light, as far as I could see.

I started to search the perimeter of the cave, desperate to find another exit. Minutes passed, seeming like hours, but there were no results. Several times, I stumbled on the uneven ground; a few times I fell, bumping myself on the rocks; and once I dropped the crystal in a cranny and had to spent almost half an hour trying to fish it out. I almost wept when the gaping hole appeared out of the darkness as I approached it with my faint light. It might just be another dead end, of course, but it also might be a mouth of some tunnel leading out. It didn't matter, I had to try it.

The tunnel descended steeply. I slowly went forwards, cautiously probing for any loose rocks or gaping holes ahead, since the light from the crystal was far from sufficient to light my way. The path was clear. Only once did I have to crawl around a deep trench, which I nearly missed in the flickering light. I regretted leaving the other crystals behind – all together, they would have cast more light.

Hours passed until I lost track of time entirely and was deadly tired. Then the walls of the tunnel stepped away and opened out into a large grotto. I took a few steps forward and stopped. The light from the crystal no longer reached any walls. I could just about see tips of several titanic stalactites hanging high above, in the middle of nearly complete darkness.

It was just another cave, deep underground. I was doomed. I could wander around for another day or two, but the grand finale would be the same: my mummified body eaten by worms. Tears of desperation burst from my eyes as I loudly cursed my destiny. I did not have many choices left – I could restlessly wander in darkness and end up breaking my neck in some deep trench, or I could just lie down and wait for the slow death from starvation and dehydration.

I was a mere office rat in London, and I was Prince of Chadrack, but neither of my identities could help me to survive. The Ring on my finger, which was capable of creating earthquakes and avalanches, thunderstorms and tornadoes, was almost entirely exhausted, close to becoming just a piece of jewellery on my corpse.

I dropped on the ground, crying in desperation, clutching the glowing crystal in my fingers. It was unfair. The dust was burning my dry throat, and I nearly choked on a sickening bout of a cough.

I have failed, and I'm going to die – those two thoughts were circling in my head, frying my brain. And nobody could help me. Rhys was dead. I could phone John tomorrow, but I did not even have a remote idea how he would be able to find the hole I slipped into – I was sure that there were plenty of similar holes along both sides of the serpentine that led down from the plateau. I had even more doubts regarding whether he would be willing to risk his life to meet all those ghouls and my raging sister Hel.

I cried until my sadness ran out down my cheeks. Then I sat in the darkness, feeling empty. My eyes were painting monsters around me, and my ears were hallucinating footsteps, rattling and the sound of running water.

It took me some time to realise that the sound of running water was real – I could clearly hear drops splashing into the invisible pool and a quiet stream trickling along its rocky bed. My thirst was killing me. I stood up and looked around as far as my scarce light could reach – all I could see was dust, rocks and darkness. But the sound was clear now. Water was flowing somewhere ahead.

I rushed forward into the dark unknown, stumbling, falling, cursing, then rising and rushing forward again. Sometimes I stopped in the darkness, completely lost among the piles of stones. Those seconds of silence seemed to last an eternity until a drop would detach from the ceiling high above and fell into the dark pool, rippling the surface and providing me with a sense of direction again.

It took my last bits of strength to locate the underground stream. Then I drank my fill of lukewarm water and sat down, leaning on a massive stalagmite. I felt completely exhausted.

Outside the cave, it was most likely well into the night by now. I had to get some sleep.

I carefully placed the glowing crystal next to me and stretched out my aching body on the rocky floor. It felt uncomfortable, but I was too tired to search for anything better.

I switched off the crystal, disconnecting it from the Ring and laying my head on a smooth boulder. My only thought, circling in the darkness, was: *I will die here...*

Then my mind drifted to meet that darkness.

Afterword

You have just read a story from the Sleeper Chronicles series and may wonder which book will take you deeper into the world of Sleepers. It's a difficult question, and the advice is not as straightforward as it may seem. The Sleeper Chronicles is a non-linear series, where the story in book B doesn't necessarily follow the book A, and book C doesn't precede the story in book D. Each main character tells his own story as a piece of a jigsaw puzzle. That piece may be as short as a short story or may grow into several books. Still, not a single piece can reveal the picture of the whole universe, but more details emerge when those pieces are added together.

The stories are listed on the webpage sleeperchronicles.com – in no particular order. It's up to you to decide which piece of the puzzle to pick next.

Ray Zdan

Printed in Great Britain
by Amazon